Take a Chance on Me

Susan Donovan

D0008951

St. Martin's Paperbacks

TAKE A CHANCE ON ME

Copyright © 2003 by Susan Donovan.
Excerpt from *Public Displays of Affection* copyright © 2003 by Susan Donovan.

For information address St. Martin's Press, 175 Fifth Avenue, New York, NY 10010.

ISBN: 0-312-98375-1
EAN: 80312-98375-8

Printed in the United States of America

St. Martin's Paperbacks edition / August 2003

St. Martin's Paperbacks are published by St. Martin's Press, 175 Fifth Avenue, New York, NY 10010.

10 9 8 7 6 5

Emma laughed, relieved to let go of some of her nervousness, some of her pent-up agitation. Then she watched as very slowly—very deliberately—Thomas smiled at her.

It was a deadly weapon, that smile of his, and she wondered if he was aware of its firepower. The smile hovered there, bracketed by deep masculine dimples, sexy and sweet, and it silently laid to waste her well-thought-out campaign of avoidance. Every objection she'd had, every perfectly logical reason she had given herself for forgetting that she'd ever met this man now lay bleeding at her feet.

A smile like that could not possibly lie. Could it?

"God, Thomas. I can't believe you came to my house. Why did you come to my house?"

He gave his brawny shoulders a shrug and looked up from under a thick fringe of dark honey lashes. "I figured my best shot was to surprise you. You know, just kind of show up on your doorstep."

. . . if the right man ever showed up on her doorstep, her heart would know him in an instant . . .

"No way in hell," Emma whispered.

This book is dedicated to Cecilia Beverly Jewelte Cathryn Flick Lewis, aka Gran, a woman who has enthusiastically backed each and every one of my hare-brained schemes. I've always known you were a Jewel—or a Jewell or even a Jewelette, for that matter—regardless of the typo on your birth certificate.

Acknowledgments

The author would like to thank the following people for their expertise and assistance in writing this book:

Marsha Reich, DVM, Behavioral Medicine; Lieutenant Larry Grasso of the Maryland State Police; Sharon Curtis Granskog and the staff of the American Veterinary Medical Association; toy breed aficionado Darlene Arden; Patie Ventre and members of the World Canine Freestyle Organization; Terry and Ollie Corkran of TLC Cresteds; Julian Reading and Jeff "Stax" Carrington of the Frederick Rugby Football team; Kevin C. Hackett, MD, FACS, Adult and Pediatric Urology; Kim Coskey Winkelman; Ellen Miller, Darlene Gardner, Irene Williams, and Marilyn K. Swisher for reading early drafts; and to disco lovers everywhere.

The author takes responsibility for any factual errors or liberties taken.

A special thanks to the FBI agent I interviewed in July 2001 before everything changed.

Chapter 1

It Only Takes a Minute

Emma gasped when she entered the exam room, though she couldn't say which of the two creatures there alarmed her more.

Was it the tiny, shivering collection of skin and bone, skittering around the linoleum on long toenails, eyeballs bulging and urine squirting?

Or was it the six-foot-forever package of man in a power suit, pivoting his blond head, one steel-gray eye narrowed as if to take aim directly at her hormone-secreting glands?

"Good morning, gentlemen. I'm Dr. Emma Jenkins." She pulled a portable exam table from the wall and took a steadying breath before she faced them again. "I understand we're having a few problems?"

"That's correct." The man's voice was as stiff as his posture. "Potentially serious problems, I'm afraid."

Nodding, Emma looked from Mr. Dudley Do-Right to the dog—yes, she'd graduated first in her class and was almost certain the animal on the floor *was* a dog—and back again.

This had to be the *most* mismatched human-canine pair she'd ever seen—and she'd seem some doozies.

These two were Butch Cassidy and the St. Vitus' Dance Kid. Hairless and Mod. Batman and Rodent.

"I'm glad you came to see me." Emma turned to wash her hands, and felt Studly Dudley's eyes boring holes into the back of her neck. He continued to stare as she bent down for the dog, placed him on the stainless steel table, and peered into the little, frightened face.

"So what's happening, Hairy?"

She already had a fairly good idea. The new-patient questionnaire said "Hairy" was an adult male Chinese Crested of unknown age, six pounds, six ounces, of quivering anxiety and incontinence. His owner—a business consultant named Thomas Tobin according to the form— was referred by a Baltimore colleague to her Wit's End Animal Behavior Clinic.

"Let's have a look, okay, little man?" She bent closer and scratched the dog behind one fuzzy, Yoda-like ear. With a sigh, Emma removed the collar of sharp metal prongs from around the dog's neck, and watched relief flood Hairy's dark eyes.

And she wondered what kind of *complete moron* would put a pinch collar on a puny, terrified creature like this.

She straightened to her full height, bringing her eye-level with the moron's red power tie.

"Mr. Moro—Tobin." She let her gaze travel over the clean-shaven chin and the pale, stern mouth. She studied the slight bend in his nose that hinted of familiarity with flying fists and blood, then met his piercing silver eyes. There was a tiny scar above his right eyebrow shaped just like a semicolon.

It certainly gave her pause.

Lordy! Why had this seriously big, seriously bad boy stuffed himself into a suit? With another quick survey, Emma decided he'd be more at home in a black leather jacket and threadbare jeans. The image gave her heart palpitations.

She needed to hold her ground. So she held up the offending piece of metal.

"This pinch collar might be a bit severe for a toy breed, Mr. Tobin." She flung it into the waste can with a resounding *ka-ching!* "And inflicting pain really isn't the way to get a dog to walk alongside you—even the biggest, most aggressive animals. Besides—" She scanned Semicolon Man from his wingtips to the tips of his golden eyelashes and grinned. "You look like you might be able to handle a bruiser like Hairy without the aid of metal spikes."

Thomas Tobin stood ramrod straight near the examination table, aware that he himself was being examined. Clearly, this pet psychiatrist chick had been giving him hell since the second she walked in here, and he didn't much like it.

How in God's name was he supposed to know what kind of dog collar to buy? He spent his life plotting bloody murder with adulterers and psychopaths—he didn't exactly have time to serve as equipment manager for the Butt-Ugly Dog Club!

"Thank you for that update," he said flatly.

Then for some odd reason, Thomas found himself seized with the need to prove to this woman that he wasn't entirely insensitive. So he reached over to pat Hairy's head the way he figured any pet owner would.

The dog cringed with each pummeling.

"Mr. Tobin!" Emma grabbed his wrist, which turned out to be a rock-solid twist of heat, bone, and muscle. "Could you be a little gentler, do you think?"

He stared at her.

She stared at him.

The drum of his pulse hammered against the pad of her thumb and vibrated all the way down into the pit of her belly. And as they remained linked and the seconds ticked by, everything inside her—every cell, every chromosome, every piece of mitochondria—went on alert.

Sexual alert.

"How—" She blinked. The man's skin was on fire. She swallowed and tried again. "How long have you had this dog? Is this the first dog you've ever owned?"

"Ten days," he said. "And yes. This is definitely a first for me."

Emma decided his eyes weren't cruel; they were solemn and powerful and seemed to pin her down and dissect her without her permission. They didn't frighten her, exactly, but they certainly made her feel a bit off balance.

He pulled his wrist from her grasp. "Hairy is mine by chance, Dr. Jenkins."

"That's a difficult way to begin a relationship, Mr. Tobin."

"You don't say?" He tilted his head and locked his gaze on hers. "The question is what are we going to do about it?"

For an instant, Emma was not entirely sure what they were discussing. *The dog,* she reminded herself. *We were discussing the dog.*

With a sigh of relief, she moved her attention from the two-legged enigma to the four-legged one, and bundled Hairy in her arms. She brushed her fingers behind his ears and along his spindly neck.

These itty-bitty exotic hairless breeds had never been her favorite—too prone to rashes, respiratory problems, dental malformations, and any number of behavioral disorders the blame for which she'd like to place squarely in the lap of greedy breeders. And Chinese Cresteds were an acquired taste, most definitely.

But as she looked into Hairy's big, sad bug eyes, she felt a rush of warmth for the tiny dog. He was a living creature. He was scared and anxious and cold and so boldly, unabashedly homely that he was very nearly cute.

She ran her fingers down his back, studying the baby-smooth hide of pink blobs and black spots that looked like bloated raisins floating in puddles of watered-down Pepto-Bismol.

This motif was accented with a scraggly poof of black hair at the tip of his bony tail and a troll-like shock of white fur at the peak of his skull and around his ears. His snout was pointy, like a ferret's.

"Well, now. Have you got it goin' on or what, you little devil?" she murmured into the side of his neck.

Emma felt the heat of Mr. Sexy's gaze, looked up to find him studying her in bewilderment, and wondered again how the hottest man to ever set foot in her clinic had ended up with the world's most unattractive dog.

Then she felt a hot trickle spread down her shirt.

"Piss happens." She smiled and shrugged, reaching for the paper towel dispenser above the sink. Studly beat her to it, and suddenly, one of his big hands was roaming over her damp shirt, rubbing and squishing her breasts with a clump of brown paper towel.

Hell-o! Emma felt her nipples zap to life under his clumsy assault. She was so aroused that she feared flames could be shooting out of her underpants. She'd never been so mortified in her life.

She grabbed his hand. "I've got it."

"Yes, you certainly do," he muttered, stepping back, looking at the floor. "Sorry."

The sound of paper towel brushing over cotton roared like an oncoming freight train in Thomas's ears. He stared at his shoes.

Okay—he'd just felt up the veterinarian. Maybe Rollo was right—he'd gone way too long without a woman, no matter how legitimate his reasons.

Thomas watched, embarrassed, as the molestee tossed

the paper towel in the trash and regained her professional composure. Then she began a physical examination of his . . . his . . . dog. After ten days of cohabiting with Hairy while trying—and failing—to find a real home for him, maybe he should just see the picture for what it was.

It was the picture of a chump and his dog.

Thomas shifted his weight, rubbed a hand over his face, and groaned internally, the only place he allowed himself to groan or shout or laugh these days, it seemed.

He watched the way the vet stroked the dog with the gentlest touch, and noticed that Hairy's trembling eased with each moment he spent in her hands.

He could see how that might happen.

The vet was extremely pretty, in a farm-girl kind of way. The creamy skin of her face, neck, and hands looked warm and silky. Those guileless eyes were the exact shade of her blue jeans. Her smile was genuine and sweet and pushed her whole lovely face into an expression of welcome.

It was pointless, of course, but Thomas couldn't help but wonder what it would feel like to grab hold of that thick braid and yank her up against him. He couldn't help but wonder what all that gorgeous hair would feel like once he'd unraveled it—would it be straight and glossy like polished wood? Would it be wavy and fall in heavy sections in his hand?

As the woman bent over his dog, he let his eyes peruse the rest of her—subtly of course. He was highly trained in the art of covert observation, after all.

She filled out those battered jeans quite thoroughly, from where the denim stretched over her round hips and curvy thighs all the way down to where the straight legs ended in a pair of scuffed-up leather clogs. A nice, full, and hospitable package of feminine flesh she was, not all bony and pointy like some women. And under that long-sleeved T-shirt, he could make out the soft but sturdy shoulders, the ripe swell of her breasts, the inward curve of her waist.

It was painfully obvious that those weren't buttons he'd felt poking up beneath the paper towels. This Emma Jenkins, DVM, was easy on the eyes—and the hands. Maybe the DVM stood for "Damn Voluptuous Mama."

Then he stopped himself, as he always did, and wondered what the doctor's dark side looked like. Sure, the woman was pretty, but he knew all too well that even pretty people had ugly sides, and they could be mighty ugly indeed.

Which one of the four great appetites had ensnared the lovely Emma Jenkins? he wondered. Guns, drugs, money, or sex?

She didn't look like a gang-banger, but after running the Murder-For-Hire Task Force for seven years, he wasn't surprised by anything anymore.

She didn't look like an addict or an alcoholic, but he'd known plenty who managed their masquerades just fine— scout leaders, teachers, ministers—you name it.

No, in his experience it was usually money that motivated women to make stupid choices. Less often it was sex. So the question was which of those two evils did Emma Jenkins serve, and how low did she go?

If it was money, maybe she had a habit of bouncing checks. Maybe she shoplifted steaks from the Super Fresh butcher case. Or maybe, desperate for prestige and a comfortable lifestyle, she'd cheated on her vet school admission tests.

Or it might be more complicated for her, Thomas thought, like a combination of material greed and the desire for sexual control. Maybe the lovely Dr. Jenkins had lied to some rich loser about being pregnant, then trapped him into a marriage he didn't want!

He nodded silently, watching the vet bend toward Hairy's shivering body and listen with the stethoscope. That had to be it—the poor bastard! But she didn't wear a ring, so maybe he'd discovered her deception in time to make a clean break. Good for him.

Thomas sighed, bemused by the truth of it: A man couldn't afford to turn his back for one damn minute.

Which brought him right back to sex—perhaps the greatest weakness of all. How many men had he seen sit across a table from him babbling, crying, driven to acts of sheer idiocy simply because of a *woman*? Too many to count.

He'd seen sex turn brilliant businessmen into cretins. Powerful men into milquetoasts. Moral men into felons.

He'd seen it turn decent lives to shit.

Thomas checked his watch, then crossed his arms over his chest. How much longer could this possibly take? Wasn't this where she handed him some puppy uppers, collected her outrageous fee, and sent them out the door?

But the vet was now peering into Hairy's eyes, nose, ears, and throat. Then she closed her own eyes in concentration and felt along the dog's ribs and into its soft belly.

Resigned to waiting a bit longer, Thomas leaned back against the cabinets and allowed himself to watch her work, watch how her slim, sure fingers moved, how she breathed quietly, how the little frown line puckered between her pretty eyebrows. Thomas felt himself go still inside.

Strangely quiet.

And he wondered how good it would feel to have her stroke *his* belly, maybe while he rubbed his cheek against hers, breathing in the faint flowery scent that seemed to pulse from her skin and hair.

He wondered how glorious it would be to settle in for a nap with his face buried in those stupendous breasts, so comforting, so welcoming, so female—so damn erotic . . .

"So is he eating well?"

"What?" Thomas yelped.

"Eating. Food. Does Hairy do it?"

He straightened. He shoved his hands into his trouser pockets. Why the hell was he fantasizing about the breasts of a lying, cheating, sirloin-stealing man-hater?

"Uh, not much eating, actually. He doesn't seem hungry."

"And what are you feeding him?" Emma noticed that Thomas Tobin had taken a step toward her, and that he was frowning.

Thomas could barely remember her question. "Uh, dog food?"

She winced, then continued the examination. "Could you be a little more specific, please?"

"Sure. Those hard crunchy things. The forty-pound bag."

Emma straightened and put her hands on her hips. "Thrifty is fine, Mr. Tobin—and forty pounds ought to take care of Hairy for a good portion of his natural life—but how big are the individual pieces of food? Did you purchase kibble designed for the smallest breeds? What brand? And do you soak the food in warm water before serving it?"

He tried not to gape at how the stethoscope hung straight down from her neck, separating the two luscious, all-natural spheres straining under wet fabric. They looked like two fresh-baked cupcakes, topped with cherries, covered in a tight film of cellophane.

His blank stare was all the answer Emma needed, and she sighed. Who in God's name would hire this guy as a consultant? He might be eye candy, but he was about as sharp as a bucket of mud.

"Have you ever tried to chew a baseball, Mr. Tobin? Have you ever, say, while drunk at a fraternity party, tried to shove a baseball in your mouth and chew on it?"

He blinked. "Not that I recall."

"Well." Emma pursed her lips. "Hairy needs teeny-weeny pieces of food for his teeny-weeny mouth. A lot of Cresteds aren't even blessed with a full set of choppers. Here. Have a look-see."

She pulled back a pink speckled lip to expose a random display of teeny-weeny teeth.

"Got it," he said.

She sincerely doubted that.

"I could use a hand here. Please hold him—gently—while I clip his nails. How long has it been since you trimmed his nails?"

"I never have," he said.

She reached behind her for a small set of clippers, then bent her head to the task, coming so close to Mr. Buy-in-Bulk that she caught the whiff of smooth, woodsy aftershave mellowed on warm male skin.

"I really didn't know I had to trim them." His voice was almost apologetic and nearly a whisper, and she felt it brush hot over the tiny hairs at the nape of her neck. She continued to clip, trying to keep her hands steady.

One paw down. Three to go.

"Some Cresteds need to have their nails trimmed each week, Mr. Tobin. The nails are fragile and can break off too close to the artery and cause bleeding. See how this—" She turned her head and found him waiting for her, his face so close, his lips slightly parted, his right eye closing lazily as if he were ready to pull the trigger.

Then he moved in even closer and he dropped his gaze to her mouth. And for the briefest, wildest, most implausible second of her life, Emma thought for sure this very strange, very sexy man was going to kiss her.

Oh, *daddy*!

She turned back to the clippers. "Uh . . . and you really need to bathe Hairy once a week in a medicated soap to keep his skin free of pustules. I'll write down the name of the brand I prefer, if you like."

Her pulse was thumping like the tail of a Labrador Retriever. Was it her imagination, or were there really great arcs of heat lightning shooting from this guy right into her ovaries? Did she really just say the word *pustule*?

This was bizarre. *He* was bizarre. And *she* was a wreck!

"I would like that very much," he said, his voice thick and raspy and still so close. "I think I would appreciate your recommendations on just about anything, really."

Three paws down. Heart still pounding.

"And Cresteds are always cold, Mr. Tobin. Did you notice the shaking?"

"Of course."

"When you, uh, acquired the dog, was he wearing any kind of sweater or coat?" She finished the last paw and stood, sighing in relief.

"A sailor suit, actually." He gazed up at her, one eyebrow arched in what Emma thought might be the beginnings of actual playfulness. "Navy blue with white trim. And a matching cap."

He was on the verge of a real smile, and in that instant, Emma realized that this somewhat slow guy was not only gorgeous, he was downright adorable! Did she see the beginnings of dimples? She felt light-headed!

"A sailor suit?"

"Yes."

But then he stood up, and any humor or warmth drained from his face, which made her inexplicably sad.

"Seems the previous owner was a complete flame . . . er . . . a flamboyant type of person. He had lots of different clothes for Hairy. Jogging suits. A leprechaun outfit. Evening wear."

Emma stared at the man in amazement. The things he said were hilarious, but he wasn't even smiling. How could a normal person not be laughing? And why did she have the strangest feeling that he was pulling her close while pushing her away at the same time? What was going on here?

As a rule, she tried her best not to alienate the owners of her patients, because she had yet to meet a dog that could sign a check. But she couldn't hold it in anymore with Thomas Tobin. She let her mouth fall open and she laughed. Loudly. It was one of her snorting laughs, too, the kind that made people look sideways at her in restaurants.

Mr. Tobin gazed at her blankly.

Emma wiped her eyes. "Okay, the thing is, Hairy needs to wear *something* because he's got no hair, right?"

"Oh." Thomas rubbed a hand along his jaw. "I didn't know the outfits were for heat retention. I thought they were, well, you know, fashion statements." He didn't bother mentioning that Hairy's owner was wearing an identical sailor suit at the time of his death.

Emma picked up the chart and began scribbling notes to herself, still chuckling. "Let's see what we can do to make Tom and Hairy get along a little better, shall we?"

"Thomas."

She raised her eyes to him.

"My name is Thomas. Not Tom."

"I see. And I'm Emma." She held the pen in mid-air as they stared at each other awkwardly. It soon became apparent that Mr. Personality had nothing to add.

"All righty then, Thomas. Let's go over the specific behavior problems you've encountered. On your form you say that Hairy isn't quite cutting it in the house-training department, is that correct?"

Thomas nodded.

"Unfortunately, that's rather common with male Cresteds. I'll order a urine analysis and an ultrasound to rule out any medical conditions, such as bladder stones. And when was the dog neutered, Mr. Tobin?"

"Neutered?"

"Yes. The dog has been neutered—his testes were surgically removed. Do you know how old he was at the time?"

Thomas stared at the dog in horror. "I have no fu—uh—idea," he mumbled.

She suppressed a smile while glancing at the form. "I've heard some Crested owners find it helpful to secure a maxi pad over the dog's penis while working on house-training. I'm told it cuts down on cleaning projects."

When Mr. Tobin made no comment, she raised her eyes to him. His face had gone white. His eyes were huge.

"Do *what*?" he whispered.

Emma tried not to laugh. "Tying a sweat sock around the hips with the pad slipped inside seems to do the trick. Be sure to get a brand with adhesive backing so it stays in place."

He continued to stare.

Emma reviewed the rest of the list. "He shakes and howls whenever you run the hair dryer, the vacuum, or the coffee grinder?"

Thomas nodded, his gaze moving absently out the window to the parking lot.

"And he keeps you awake at night with pacing and whining. He chewed the molding around your front door, clawed holes in a wall and a carpet. Your neighbors left you notes that he cries and barks all day when you're gone. Anything else?"

Thomas shoved his hands deep in his trouser pockets. "Isn't that enough?"

Emma hugged the chart to her chest and smiled at him, then glanced down at the frightened dog. Clearly, the first order of business was to convince Hairy that he was safe with Thomas—and that was going to be a tough sell.

She'd already observed that the man hadn't managed to form any kind of bond with the animal in ten days. He hardly looked at the dog. The dog shied away from the man. And every time Thomas's voice contained the least bit of agitation or disapproval, Hairy's trembling escalated.

On the bright side, Thomas seemed to have an open mind about all this, which was more than she could say about some of the owners she encountered. Many people waltzed in here with their minds already made up about how to keep their pets in line, already well on their way to a tragedy.

At least Thomas Tobin was listening.

His eyes remained locked on hers, and she thought she noticed the briefest flash of something deeply human in his expression. Then he looked away.

Had it been loneliness? Longing? Whatever it was, it looked so out of place on that he-man face that she'd probably just imagined it.

"Has Hairy exhibited these behaviors in the past, Mr. Tobin?"

"I have no earthly idea."

She nodded. "Okay. First and foremost, the dog is having trouble adjusting to his new home. I believe Hairy is experiencing severe separation anxiety and panic attacks."

Thomas pictured the scene again. He'd found Scott Slick on his kitchen floor, dead for days, the ugly dog keeping guard at his owner's side, shaking, hungry, and scared. It was the most pitiful thing he'd ever seen.

Yeah, separation anxiety and panic attacks sounded right on the mark.

"Dogs always do things for a reason," Emma continued. "In Hairy's mind, these behaviors make perfect sense—

they accomplish something for him. Will his former owner be taking him back anytime soon?"

"I sure doubt it."

Emma offered him a reassuring smile. "I realize Hairy is a challenge right now, but with relaxation exercises, a consistent house-training regimen, medicine, and a little time, I think everything's going to be fine."

Thomas looked down on the shivering dog and winced. What had he done? Why had he taken this damn dog home with him? How long would he be stuck with him? Would the dog really have to wear a Kotex?

He started to feel queasy.

"Do you have any questions at this point?"

"No."

"Are you all right?"

"Perfect, thanks."

Emma spent the next forty minutes demonstrating the relaxation exercises and working with Thomas and Hairy until they got it right. She was pleasantly surprised to see that Thomas caught on rather quickly.

After making sure the urine test results were normal, she walked Thomas and Hairy to checkout, where she gave them their discharge instructions, shopping list, follow-up schedule, and prescriptions.

Then she slipped into the back hallway, leaned against the wall, and closed her eyes tight.

She felt like she'd been hit by a truck.

What had just happened in there? A grouchy dullard with some sort of personality disorder had just made her hormones throb, her skin tingle, and her panties smolder. It was as if her body had been on autopilot, responding to pheromones and electrical charges that had nothing to do with polite behavior or even common sense.

Could it be that a man too cool to smile had made her hot, hot, hot for the first time in she didn't know how long?

Could it be that she'd felt a jolt of connection with that man? An instant affection, even? How was that possible?

"Woo, Emma! That was one fine specimen!" Velvet Miki leaned her petite body up against the wall next to Emma and giggled.

"He's a nut job," Emma said, slowly opening her eyes.

"Hon, I wasn't talking about the little d-o-g—I was talking about the big hunk of m-a-n." Her assistant then shoved the next patient's chart toward her, and Emma read that Harpo the self-mutilating parrot was preening himself bloody again.

"So was I, Velvet," Emma said, staring ahead blankly. "So was I."

"Damn you, Slick, you sneaky dead fembot!"

Thomas sat in the Wit's End parking lot and thumped his forehead against the car steering wheel, feeling a pair of soulful eyes follow his every move. He glared toward the passenger seat.

"Is there some other way in which I might be of service to you?" he asked the dog. "Speak up, pal. I'm all ears."

Uh-oh.

You don't like me much, do you, Big Alpha? I'd like it better if you took me back in there to the lady with the soft hands.

"You know what I'd like, Hairy? I'd like you to get a grip on yourself. Move on with your life."

Move on? If you'd only heard that bad man's voice, smelled all the anger in him, saw how he banged Slick's head with the blender!

And the noise! The blender kept screeching and whizzing! It hurt my ears! My brain! I hate the blender! I hate the blender! I miss my master! I miss my home!

Uh-oh.

I just peed again.

"Jesus, Hairy!"

I'm such a bad dog.

Thomas swiped the leather seat with the towel he'd learned to provide for car trips, then he rolled his forehead back and forth on the steering wheel and sighed. The horn blared, and Thomas shot up with a start. He turned toward the dog again.

"Look, ace. I'm sorry Slick's dead and you ended up with me."

Tell me about it.

"But it was either me or the business end of a gas pipe, so how about you take your happy pills so I can convince some idiot to give you a home. Sound like a plan?"

Hairy shook some more, then stared at the door latch.

"I'm not cut out for dog ownership. Nothing personal. I work odd hours. I've got too much stress in my life. And I'm not a very nice man, so I'm only thinking of your welfare. Besides, I don't like animals. Hell, I don't even like human beings."

The car phone rang.

"Tobin. What?"

"Good afternoon, Miss Manners—how'd the lobotomy go?" Rollo laughed uproariously into the phone.

"The dog's or mine?" Thomas pulled out into Columbia traffic and headed toward Baltimore. With luck, he could deposit Hairy at his townhouse and get back to court by two for the rest of the Leo Vasilich suppression hearing.

Poor Leo. Talk about women troubles! That guy was the poster boy for what can happen when a man lets his guard down with a female—he ends up facing three to five of hard time.

"I can't believe you actually took that hairless rat to a psychiatrist, Thomas. How much did it set you back, anyway?"

"Two-fifty."

"No way! The guy should be arrested for extortion."

"Yeah, well, the guy is an actual veterinarian and he's a she with a great set of . . . a great setup out here. Anyway, that's just for the office visit and the drugs. It doesn't even count the ultrasound or the supplies I've got to get."

"You mean Hairy's going on doggie downers?"

Thomas riffled through the brochures and workbooks strewn across the seat until he found the little white prescription bag. "Uppers. Downers. Hell if I know." He read the instructions. "Amitriptyline, one-quarter of a ten-milligram tablet twice daily for depression and anxiety. Xanax as needed for panic."

"No freakin' way."

"Better dog living through chemistry, Rollo. Plus, I have to do some kind of retraining program and spring for a crate, a few little sweater outfits, some kind of special food and medicated shampoo and skin lotion shit, plus a pair of clippers, maxi pads, a baby toothbrush, and God knows what else. I better win at poker Friday night, that's all I got to say."

"This is nuts, man! Isn't there some kind of shelter or rescue place you can take him?"

Thomas said nothing, and glanced over at Hairy. The dog had edged toward the passenger door in an effort to get as far away from Thomas as possible, and now stared down at the black tufted seat of the Audi, bony shoulders quivering.

A big lump of guilt lodged in Thomas's throat.

"Hey, Rollo? We had some pretty wild parties at the Theta Chi house, didn't we?"

"Absolutely. But what's that got to do with—"

"Did I ever get drunk and try to eat a baseball?"

The line went silent for a moment before his brother-in-law cleared his throat. "Uh, are you all right, man?"

Thomas knew he was a lot of things—beaten down with guilt over Slick's death, sporting a hard-on for a pet shrink with a fascinating braid, warm smile, and exceptional breasts, and completely baffled by how his life had turned into a never-ending episode of *The Jerry Springer Show*—but "all right" he was not.

"I'm fabulous," he said. "See you Friday. Don't forget my Cohibas."

"Wait! Don't hang up!"

Thomas sighed in annoyance because that's precisely what he was trying to do. "I gotta go, man."

Rollo's voice lowered to a whisper. "Did you just say *maxi pads*?"

Emma stood over the lunchroom sink and wolfed down a piece of cold pizza, trying to ignore Velvet's commentary.

"Oh, come on, Em!" The veterinary assistant licked at her yogurt spoon with quick, feline strokes of her tongue. "He's a guaranteed good time. Marcus said you two have a lot in common. He's legally separated. He was cleared of that insider-trading thingy. And he'll be getting his license back soon, so this will probably be the only time you'll have to drive."

Emma nearly gagged on a piece of crust and stared at Velvet in disbelief.

"He sounds like a real prince, but no. Seriously. I've come to the conclusion that Marcus and I just aren't looking for the same thing in a man."

"Uugghhh!" Velvet bounced up from her chair and tee-tered on her clunky sling-backs until she reached the trash can. She washed off her spoon and leaned against the cabinets, arms crossed over her chest. "Not 'normal' enough for you, I take it?"

Emma stopped chewing and stared at Velvet for a moment. She tossed the rest of her pizza in the trash and wiped her mouth with a paper napkin. "You got it, Velvet—not normal enough. Any man who can't keep a driver's license has issues, and as we've discussed, I'd rather be alone than be with a man who has issues."

"But—"

"I'm living in an issue-free zone from here on out."

Velvet rolled her eyes. "And as a former social worker, I can tell you there is no such thing as an 'issue-free' man, so you might as well give it up."

Emma smiled, replacing a two-liter soda jug in the refrigerator. "I believe you've shared that insight with me on more than one occasion."

"Fine," Velvet huffed. "So what are your options?"

Emma looked at her watch. She had five minutes until her next patient and fantasized about spending three of those minutes in the privacy of the women's bathroom. So that left two minutes for Velvet's daily Cosmo Girl chat. She supposed she could survive two minutes.

"I have lots of options."

"Uh-huh. So let's hear what you've got planned for the weekend." Velvet's dark, crescent-shaped eyes widened a bit and her little lipsticked mouth knotted up into a smirk. Emma could tell she expected to hear the usual list of boring activities.

So she gave it to her.

"I thought we'd all go to the tractor pull Friday night. Leelee has a geography bee competition at the community college Saturday. I'll go riding Sunday."

"Wow," Velvet said, nodding in mock approval. "You're really gettin' jiggy with it."

Emma laughed. "Honestly. I'd much rather spend my weekend with my goofy father, a brainiac preteen, and a traumatized horse than with Mr. Traffic Court, thanks."

She turned to leave but Velvet touched her arm. "Em."

She shrugged her off. "We'll talk about my wild love life later, okay? I've got Mrs. Kline's psycho killer Springer Spaniel waiting for me."

"I just want you to have some fun. That's all."

Emma sighed. "I *do* have fun, Velvet!"

"I mean with a man."

Emma stared at her in defeat. She knew Velvet meant well. She'd been her assistant since the practice opened four years ago, and a dear friend and a hard worker from day one. And since Emma showed Aaron the door last year, Velvet had tried to find a social life for her, often enlisting the help of her boyfriend, Marcus.

The results had been . . . peculiar.

There was the beverage wholesaler who recommended total-body piercing as the path to sexual nirvana. There was the glass blower who slept under a pyramid-shaped canopy to harvest cosmic energy. There was the financial planner who suggested Emma join the Howard County Conservative Council.

A girl had to draw the line somewhere.

Not that her own choices had been stellar. Since she filed for divorce, she'd dated a few men she believed shared similar interests. The veterinary pharmaceutical sales rep lasted a month, until he got transferred and got married. The fact that he'd been engaged had apparently slipped his mind.

She started seeing a vet she and Aaron knew from the University of Pennsylvania. But he lived in Salisbury, and she decided it was a long way to drive for a date, especially after the night she arrived at the appointed time only to find him getting a full-body massage from his summer intern. The intern was clad only in a thong, and Emma guessed it had nothing to do with the office casual-Friday policy.

After that, she'd just said to hell with it and went out on a few dates with the carpenter she'd hired to do some work around the farm. He was funny and cute and looked superb in a tool belt, but apparently forgot to pay the child support he owed to three different women and was currently enjoying a sabbatical at the Maryland Correctional Training Center in Hagerstown.

At least he wrote.

"You're thirty-four years old, Em! You're approaching your sexual peak! You need a man!" Velvet lowered her voice. "It's just not natural to be without one at your age."

Emma patted Velvet's mostly bare shoulder. "Tell Marcus thanks but no thanks." She turned to go.

"At least Thomas Tobin has his follow-up in two weeks!" Velvet offered brightly. "That's something to look forward to, right?"

Emma spun on her heels and gawked at Velvet. "Don't even *think* about trying to set me up with an owner! Besides, that guy is way beyond 'not normal'—he's just plain strange! He's like some kind of robot. I'm not interested."

"But . . ."

"Let's not talk about Thomas Tobin anymore, all right? I don't think I like him." She headed out the door.

"Yeah, but if you put a mustache on him he'd look like a blond version of Tom Selleck back in his heyday!" Velvet nearly shouted out the lunchroom door. "I wouldn't care if he were an axe murderer!"

"A studly robot axe murderer," Emma mumbled to herself, reaching for the ladies' room door. "Sounds like the plot of a good movie."

"It is!" Velvet shouted back. "Haven't you ever seen *The Terminator*?"

Chapter 2

I Love the Nightlife

"Time to get happy, Hairy."

Not this again.

Hey! Don't drop me, Big Alpha! Uh-oh. Here comes that hard little pebble thing shoved into a tiny piece of cheese ... do you think I'm stupid? That I really believe this is some sort of treat? Ack! And who told you that squishing my throat is going to help it go down any easier?

Fine. I swallowed it. Hope you're satisfied.

"Nice going, pal."

Thomas studied the dog for a moment and frowned. They'd just finished another five-minute round of relaxation exercises, but damned if he could tell if the little mutant was relaxing any. All he knew was that his knees hurt like hell and it was Emma Jenkins's fault—she said he had to kneel while working with Hairy because the dog was intimidated by his size.

Thomas sighed and studied the ugly thing. Sure, dogs were basically stupid, but he had to admit that Hairy seemed to get the general drift of the exercises. He'd held the tiny piece of Beggin' Strip behind his back, said, "Hairy, sit!" and, "Hairy, look!" then moved the treat next to his eye and Hairy made eye contact and sat still just like he was supposed to. Then he got the treat. And this was supposed to relax him.

What are you staring at, Big Alpha? It makes me yawn. That's what I do when I'm unsure about things. That and pee. But I'm trying. I really am.

Wait. This is new. Your hands—which are twice the size of Slick's, by the way—are petting me. Softly. It feels good on my skin. Warm and smooth and nice and my tail's wagging because that's what I do when I'm happy.

"All right, Hairy. We've got to have a little man-to-man chat."

Your eyes are a little nicer, too, but I wish you'd smile. I'd feel better about hanging out here in thin air if you'd just smile.

"I got a bunch of guys coming over to play cards tonight and I don't think you're exactly their kind of dog, know what I'm saying?"

I guess it's back to the cave.

"You'll be safe in your crate. We might get a little loud, but we won't hurt you. I'll take you out for a walk when they leave. Okay, buddy?"

Yeah, okay. I don't mind the cave. At least you put a fluffy blanket in here. I guess you're trying to be nice. I guess you're not like the bad man who hurt Slick. I try not to think about my owner much, because it makes me lonely and scared and I start shaking more, which makes me pee.

Thomas closed the door to the crate, draped an old pillowcase over the top, and headed to the entertainment center.

Here comes that strange, sad music again—nothing like the real music Slick and I love so much, the kind that makes us feel like dancing!

I miss him. I miss my sparkling red suit with the matching collar. I miss dancing. I wonder when I'll get to see Soft Hands again.

She felt so nice to snuggle up with.

"Just don't ever get married or we won't have anywhere to play cards. Any microbrews left in the fridge?"

Thomas peered through the gray-blue cigar fog that hung over the dining room table and narrowed his eyes at Vince Stephano. "I'm never getting married and I'll never run out of good beer on poker night," he said impatiently. "You gonna ante up or just sit there and bitch like you do at the office . . . sir?"

Stephano grunted, ignoring the subdued snickers from around the table. The Maryland State Police captain clenched his Robusto in his teeth and said, "I'll see you and raise you ten. Prepare to suffer horribly, my friend."

Thomas let the remark slide, dropping his gaze nonchalantly to the three queens burning a hole through his palm.

Rollo folded. Chick called, but didn't look happy about it. Then Manny went out quietly, and Paulie called it quits with his usual drama, slapping his cards down on the bare wood surface with a flourish of obscenities and sighs.

"Let's see it, pretty boy," Stephano said, jutting out his cigar in challenge as he glared at Thomas.

"You might want to use protective eyewear, boss." Thomas laid down the three lovely ladies with agonizing slowness, the queen of hearts on top.

"You suck, Tobin." Stephano threw down three sevens.

"Shit." Chick offered up a pair of fives.

As he reached out for the mound of poker chips with both hands, Thomas reveled in the feel of the tinkling, clicking bounty. Short of puffing a fine Cuban or holding a beautiful naked woman, this had to be life's finest physical sensation. It was a piece of pure triumph—a moment of unadulterated whoop-ass.

And by God, he'd had few enough of those lately.

"Your music selection is giving me a migraine, Tobin."

Chick's announcement came in his customary West Virginia twang. "Haven't you got any normal music—like Garth or Shania or something?"

"My house, my tunes," Thomas said, stacking his chips in neat, color-coded piles. "Besides, Coltrane is food for the soul. You want to listen to hillbilly drivel, then hold poker night at your place."

Chick shook his head. "Right. That would be a ripsnortin' good time, I'm sure." He took a swig of beer. "I'm lucky just to escape the spouse and spawn one night a month to come here."

"I hear you, man," Rollo said, chuckling. "If we did this at my place, we'd be listening to Barney's Greatest Hits."

"Thomas's music taste is eclectic," Manny offered.

"It sucks," Paulie said.

"What do you expect from four cops, a lawyer, and a urologist? We never agree on jackshit," Rollo said.

Thomas shuffled the deck and called for five-card stud. "You know, gentlemen, there's really only two kinds of music in the world."

"Christ, here we go," Stephano muttered, rolling his eyes.

"Good music and bad music," Thomas continued, taking a slow, sensual puff of his cigar and placing it in an ashtray to his left. He began to deal. "The majority of popular music today is total crap—the fast food of song—no nourishment, no soul, no meaning, no art. It's just a way to funnel more money to the one or two remaining international media conglomerates and pay for the Backstreet Boys to go to rehab."

Stephano groaned and got up from the table. "Beer run. Anybody want anything?"

"I'll help," Chick offered.

Paulie stood up and stretched. "I'm going to hit the john."

"Me, too," Manny said, following him.

Rollo shook his head slowly and chuckled, watching his best friend and brother-in-law deal the cards to empty chairs. "You sure know how to clear a room lately, man."

Rollo studied Thomas. He watched him finish the deal and take another puff, squinting in concentration as he spun the cigar between long fingers.

Rollo wouldn't come right out and say anything, but the truth was, Thomas worried the hell out of him.

Thomas had been through so much this last year, and he'd made it through in one piece. But he'd changed. Shut down. And he and Pam were really starting to wonder if he'd ever snap out of it.

"How are the boys?" Thomas asked.

"Great. They miss you."

Thomas nodded silently.

True, Thomas had never been the world's most outgoing guy. Even in college he'd been kind of quiet, but still managed to crack everyone up with his dead-on, dry observations. The girls didn't seem to mind that he was reserved. It must have added to his mystique, because females were always hanging around the fraternity house or the rugby pitch just to get a peek at him.

The guys at Theta Chi soon decided Thomas was like the house bug light, luring girls in droves, and started calling him "Zapper." Thomas thought it was funny back then. Not anymore. He didn't think anything was funny anymore.

"Pam still working part-time?" Thomas asked.

"Yep. Three half-days a week."

Just look at him—he'd basically gone into hiding. If it weren't for poker night, rugby, and his medical checkups, Rollo would never even see him. No matter how many times Pam invited him over to the house he always said he had to work.

That was a big part of what put him in such a rotten

state of mind—Thomas's work. The sick mothers he met every day just gave him an excuse to keep his distance from people. Thomas used to talk about getting out of law enforcement and teaching and coaching rugby instead, but the last time Rollo tried to bring it up, Thomas changed the subject.

And God—the day he finally got the guts to suggest Thomas look into treatment for depression, he'd nearly been beheaded.

Rollo didn't know how to talk to him anymore. It was as if that day in his office six months ago had changed everything between the two men. The wall Thomas had erected since then made Rollo feel like a stranger.

Rollo saw Thomas giving him the eye through a puff of cigar smoke and tried to smile. "Want another beer, T?"

"No. I'm good."

Thomas had taken the news about his injury very hard, but what man wouldn't? Rollo would never forget sitting at his desk across from Thomas and Nina, seeing the hopeful look on their faces, just before he dropped the bomb on them.

Sure, other couples had broken up in his office before, but this was the worst he'd ever witnessed. He explained the test results and waited for someone to say something, but they just sat there, marinating in the tension for several long moments. Then it happened—Nina let it rip right there in front of him—the list of everything Thomas had done wrong in the last four years. She told him it was over, and headed for the door.

For as long as he'd known Nina, Rollo had always thought of her as private and aloof. Apparently, she'd been saving up for one humdinger of a public display.

Thomas sat perfectly still through the whole thing. His face was cold and expressionless but his knuckles were white around the chair arms. He flinched when Nina slammed the door behind her.

Thomas was Rollo's patient, but he was also the best friend he'd ever had, and the only thing he could think to say was, "I'm so sorry, man."

But really, what else *could* he have said?

And since then, it seemed Thomas only wanted to work harder or stay home and listen to John Coltrane and Charlie Parker and get himself even more depressed. He hadn't had a date in six months. He didn't want to go out drinking with the rest of the ruggers after a match. He didn't want to talk about any of it. Not even to Pam.

Rollo let his eyes travel to the darkened living room, to the little cage he knew was hidden behind a big potted plant. At least Thomas now had that little ugly dog to keep him company. He and Pam thought that was a real positive sign.

Thomas was still giving him the eye.

Rollo smiled brightly.

"You can report to Pam that I'm fine—eating my vegetables, sleeping well, bathing daily, taking my vitamins."

Rollo shrugged, as if that wasn't exactly what he planned to do. He decided to change the subject. "So does the shipment meet with your approval?"

Thomas stared at the cigar balanced between his fingers and grinned.

The Cohiba Corona Especiale was more than a cigar— it was a work of art, a silken extravagance, a thing of beauty. He took a puff, savoring the delicate notes of honeyed tobacco, warm cocoa, and roasted nuts on the back of his tongue, tasting the heat with his brain, his eyeballs, his very soul, glorying in the pleasure of his one and only illicit vice.

Yes, it met with his approval, unlike most everything else in his life, and Thomas closed his eyes, thanking God once more that Rollo had a patient who was an official in the U.S. Customs Agency.

"It's mighty fine, Rollo. Stupendous. Send along my heartfelt thanks."

Rollo took a puff of his own. "Always do."

The men smiled at each other in conspiracy and Thomas took comfort in that brief exchange. Sure, things could be better, but he still had an occasional cigar. He had Rollo and Pam and his nephews. He had work and rugby. He supposed it was enough.

It would have to be.

"Hey, what the hell is that horrible sound?" Chick frowned and cocked his head as he returned to his seat. "Hear it? It's like a cat puking up a hair ball."

"It's called jazz," Stephano muttered.

"No. Seriously. There it is again—"

Thomas jumped up, spun around, and peered into the dimly lit living room. Oh, great. He thought he could get away with keeping Hairy under wraps, but it looked like the jig was up. He jogged to the small pet crate in the corner. He yanked away the ficus tree, creating a shower of small, crisp leaves, then whipped off the old pillowcase.

Hairy was hacking his brains out. He was wheezing, shaking, staring up at him through the metal bars with bulging, frightened eyes. When he sucked in air, Thomas could see his throat collapse with the battle for oxygen.

"Jesus!" He yanked open the latch and reached for him.

"What the hell is *that*?" Stephano's mouth fell open in disbelief.

"It's a dog," Rollo whispered to the men now gathered in closely. "Thomas's dog."

Thomas wheeled around. "He is *not* my damn dog, all right, Rollo? How many times do I have to tell you I'm just keeping him until I can find a home for him?"

"A dog? Are you sure?" Manny seemed genuinely perplexed.

"Is he wearing a sweater?" Chick's words came out in a shocked whisper.

Everyone leaned in closer and felt free to comment.

"That's the ugliest thing I've ever seen."

"It looks like a fetal pig."

"A sewer rat."

"An alien."

"Whatever it is, it's choking to death."

"Damn! It's the cigar smoke!" Thomas ran to the foyer and threw open the front door, taking Hairy into the September night air. He sat on the front stoop, his long legs nearly folded under his chin as he examined the dog.

Hairy continued to cough. His breathing steadied but the wheezing remained.

"Should we call the vet?" Rollo asked.

"Try Terminix," Stephano said, which cleared the way for guffaws all around.

"Shut up so I can listen to him breathe, would you?" Thomas swung his head around and he glared up at his friends.

"Maybe we should call it a night," Manny said. "We've got that early meeting tomorrow and I'm wiped. Let's go in and settle up."

Rollo patted Thomas on the shoulder. "I'll turn off the air conditioning and open the windows. I'll collect for you."

Thomas nodded. "Turn on the exhaust fan in the kitchen, too, would you, man? Thanks."

When the front door shut behind him, Thomas sighed and peered down into Hairy's pointy face. For a moment it seemed as if a look of gratitude passed through the animal's eyes. Then, in the darkness, Thomas thought for sure that Hairy smiled at him. He'd obviously had a few too many beers.

At least the little mutant was still alive, which was a good thing because he'd just spent close to six hundred dollars on medical care and supplies.

"You are one freakin' high-maintenance dog," Thomas muttered.

Then Hairy began squirming in a way that signaled the onset of urination. Thomas unfolded his body from the stoop and released Hairy in the small patch of grass in front of his townhouse. The mutant squatted like a girl the way he always did and took care of business, sniffed around the rhododendrons, then toddled over to Thomas's feet and sat, staring up in adoration to his new master's face.

He was still wheezing.

The tree frogs and crickets were especially loud that night. Emma listened to the soft creak of the front porch rocker as it kept time with the twirling, buzzing, beeping melody that washed over her damp skin.

She couldn't sleep, though she knew she needed the rest. She wondered if she sometimes did this on purpose, just to have an excuse to come downstairs in her nightgown and bare feet and sit on the porch in the dark—alone. It was peaceful here. The hay fields of southern Carroll County smelled so ripe and clean, just the way they had when she was a girl. The stars blinked off and on behind wispy night clouds.

This was her private world. At night, she could think. She could make her wishes. She could convince herself that there was still a chance they'd come true.

Ray's hard head nudged insistently at Emma's knee, and she scratched the soft spot behind the old guy's ear. She listened to his low growl of pleasure and it made her smile. She wished she could be more like Ray—he always seemed so glad for what he had instead of worrying about what he *didn't* have. Maybe that was the difference between dogs and human beings right there, in a nutshell.

Emma plopped her bare feet up on the wide, smooth porch railing and leaned back in the rocker. With her free hand, she twisted her long hair up into a knot. A hot whisper of humid air brushed up the back of her neck and under the backs of her thighs. It tickled. It teased.

She thought of Thomas Tobin again and laughed at herself.

Velvet was so right—it wasn't natural for a woman her age to be alone. She needed a man. Soon. And if she was fantasizing about Robot Boy again, she knew she'd reached a whole new level of desperation.

As she did nearly every night, Emma wondered why it was that a decent-looking, educated, fun-loving, and kind woman couldn't find a normal man.

Was it her imagination, or were they in short supply here in the Baltimore-Washington metropolitan area?

Was it her imagination, or was it really true that with each passing month the odds got less good and the goods got more odd?

She didn't hate bars—she liked going out every once in a while with a group of women friends to hoot it up.

What she hated was the desperate trolling, the scoping, the hunt associated with the human mating ritual. She felt hollow. She felt on display. And no matter where they went, she was always sure she had the biggest butt on the dance floor.

As a scientist, Emma knew what it was really all about— a search for quality chromosomes to perpetuate her genetic line.

As a woman, she knew it was so much more than that. She was looking for spark. Passion. She was looking for love. It was slightly embarrassing to admit, but Emma wanted to be swept off her feet, just once before she died.

She wanted to know what it felt like to be pursued, treasured, spoiled! Was that so outrageous?

Just once before she died, that's all.

It sure hadn't happened that way with Aaron. Emma had come to see her thirteen-year relationship with Aaron for what it was: a pact based on intellectual compatibility and physical familiarity—with a healthy dose of dysfunction thrown in for excitement. They'd been lovers, husband and wife, and business partners.

Then one day, it finally dawned on her. She finally got it through her head that she might have the skills to fix some things for some animals and humans, but she would never be able to fix Aaron Kramer.

It wasn't even her job to try.

"Emma?"

She turned to see Leelee at the screen door of the old brick house. The diffuse yellow lamplight glowed around the girl's blond head, making her look like an angel in a halo of golden curls. Emma's heart melted with tenderness.

"Hey, sweetie. Want me to tuck you in again? Is Pops asleep?"

"Beckett nodded off in front of the TV, as usual," Leelee said, her voice groggy. "Monty Python probably."

Emma walked Leelee up the stairs, letting her arm slip around the girl's thin shoulders, feeling the brush of curls against her wrist.

Leelee looked so much like her mother—lean, long, and lovely. She had Becca's soft brown eyes, too. She also had her mother's biting intelligence and husky laugh.

They reached the top landing and Emma hugged Leelee tight against her, thinking that it was now her job to make sure the daughter didn't make the same mistakes the mother was famous for. Her best friend had certainly left her with a big challenge when she'd left her this twelve-year-old girl.

Emma led Leelee to her room, tucked the lightweight blanket under her chin, and smoothed back a pale curl from her brow. Under Leelee's watchful gaze, Emma leaned down and pressed her lips softly to her forehead.

"Sleep tight."

"I'll try."

"Are you nervous about tomorrow? Is that what's keeping you up?"

Leelee rolled her eyes. "Not hardly. It's all kind of anticlimactic, really."

Emma crossed her arms over her chest and looked down on Leelee's face. "You don't have to compete in the geography bee, you know."

"I said I would. So I will." The girl shrugged. "It's no big deal. I'll be the star of their geek and freak show if they want me to."

Emma sat on the edge of the bed and reached for one of Leelee's narrow hands. The girl was the oddest combination of innocent child and world-weary adult, and Emma knew she had Becca to thank for that. What she didn't know were the details—Leelee didn't want to talk about her life in Los Angeles, leaving Emma to wonder if it was not as bad as she feared or worse than she ever imagined.

"Is there something else on your mind, then?"

Leelee shook her head on the pillow.

"I'm proud of you, sweetie. And I love you. I've loved you since the day you were born—the minute you were born."

Leelee studied Emma from half-closed eyes. "Was it gross—being Mom's coach?"

Emma chuckled. "No, it was beautiful. It was magic. Not gross at all."

"That's because you're used to blood and guts." Leelee's nose scrunched up. "I bet my mom screamed like a maniac—total NC-17 kind of stuff."

"True. But it was still the most wonderful thing I'd ever seen." Emma patted her hand and stood up, stretching.

"Hey, Em?"

"Mmm?"

"I . . . nothing."

Emma felt the corner of her mouth hitch up. "Sounds like something to me."

"Just good night."

"Good night, Elizabeth Weaverton, girl wonder."

After one more touch of her hand to Leelee's head, Emma closed the heavy oak door and stood a moment alone in the upstairs hallway. To her left she could see her father sprawled across his bed, snoring happily, his body lit by the flickering blue light of the TV screen.

At the other end of the hall was her bedroom. She could see in through the open door to the big double bed of her girlhood and the familiar wallpaper of tiny yellow flowers. Emma remembered the summer she and her mother picked out the wallpaper pattern. She'd been thirteen, just a little older than Leelee was now.

Emma's mother had been dead by the spring.

She gripped her elbows and hugged herself tight, thinking that life had a habit of sneaking up on you. Here she was, back in that old bed surrounded by that old wallpaper, a divorced thirty-something raising her friend's child in her dad's house.

Never in a million years could she have predicted this.

She felt Ray nudge the back of her knee.

"All right, old boy."

Emma turned off her father's television, kissed his cheek, then headed down the back stairway to the kitchen. She poured herself a glass of iced tea before returning to the porch rocker.

Ray bumped her leg again, looking for attention, and

she laughed. For a woman without a love life, she certainly felt needed in this world.

Emma let her gaze travel about two hundred yards over to the Weaverton place—now the residence of a nice young couple and their little boy—a small white clapboard farmhouse partially hidden by a line of windblown pines. How many nights just like this one had she and Becca met in those trees to plot out their lives?

They hadn't been too good at predicting the future.

Emma pushed against the railing with her big toe and started the rocker moving again, and Ray let his three-legged, blind carcass fold onto the pine-board floor with a heavy sigh. He had the right idea—it was late.

The groan of the rocker sounded like breathing. In accompaniment, she filled her lungs with warm, wet air and let it out slowly. She put down her iced tea and let her hands stroke the soft skin of her upper arms. She let her fingers brush up her neck and across her shoulders and down the front of her loose, thin cotton gown.

She had a perfectly normal body. A strong body. A bit on the ample side—just like her mother and exactly the opposite of Becca—but what else was new? Emma had never been sleek enough or tall enough or thin enough to be considered chic, as Aaron often pointed out.

Her fingers roamed down her softly rounded belly to her thighs and back up along her sides.

Many women her age had already had a kid or two, their bodies stretched by babies that had grown inside them. What did she have? No stretch marks and a career she loved.

Her touch moved to her breasts.

Many women her age had nursed a baby. They knew what it was like to bring life into the world and sustain it with the magic of their own flesh. What was her contribution? Emma had thought about this often enough, and she always came back to this truth: When a pet became a behavior problem, it was often a death sentence, and she used her heart and mind to give living creatures another chance.

That was her gift to the world.

She laid her head against the rocker and sighed, as her hair swept down around her shoulders and brushed against bare skin. She felt the tips of her breasts rise to hard little peaks beneath her light touch, just as nature intended, the flesh blissfully unaware that it was her own lonely hand that strayed there and not the soft, seeking mouth of an infant.

Or the hot, demanding mouth of a lover.

She moved her hands to the softness of her thighs and pushed the nightgown up and away, letting her thoughts stray to the way Aaron once touched her—but a lethal stab of sorrow and anger came with the remembered pleasure.

So as she allowed her left hand to roam up her thigh, she let her imagination veer off toward Thomas Tobin. She remembered the heat of his skin under the cuff of his dress shirt, the flash of longing in his eyes, the way he almost smiled at her, maybe even almost kissed her . . .

God, how she'd lied to Velvet! Of course she was attracted to him—what woman with a pulse wouldn't be? His eyes were electric. His mouth was stern but sensuous and bracketed by impossibly sexy dimples. He was built out of solid rock.

In Emma's rational mind, she knew Thomas Tobin was too perfect a physical specimen for a woman like her, but this was her fantasy, and by God she was allowed to go ahead and remember how he'd intrigued her, revved her up, how he'd given her goosebumps.

She wondered what made him so damn grumpy. She wondered what he looked like naked.

The thought startled her, but she forged ahead, giggling quietly, trying to imagine what all that hot muscle would feel like under the flat of her palms, what it would feel like to have a man his size press his hard weight into her, wrap his arms around her waist, take her.

She breathed deep, then exhaled slowly.

Her reaction to Thomas Tobin was perfectly understandable—he was just different, that was all. Aaron was slim and wiry and dark and for most of her adult life that's what Emma equated with sex—Aaron's whipcord body, his efficient, medium-sized package of maleness, his quick, light movements and charming smile.

Of course that's why Thomas Tobin fascinated her so. He was everything Aaron was not. He was golden and broad and brooding and looked like he could pick her up, toss her over one shoulder, and carry her away to his cave, where he'd ignore her feeble protests, pin her against the nearest flat surface and . . .

Whoa! Emma shot up out of the rocking chair like she'd been launched from a catapult, the cotton gown falling below her knees.

What time was it? Who in God's name would be calling her at this hour? What the hell was she doing nearly grooming the poodle on the front porch?

What if Leelee had seen her? What kind of example was she setting? Hadn't the poor kid seen enough?

Emma grabbed the portable phone in the hallway and took it back outside where she wouldn't wake anyone.

"Hello?" She was aware she sounded out of breath and somewhat annoyed.

"Dr. Jenkins. I'm very sorry to disturb you so late, but—"

And before she could stop herself, she heard the words slide out of her mouth: "Well, hello there, Thomas Tobin."

Emma winced, aware that she'd just committed a major error. Was there any logical, work-related reason why she'd remember the sound of his voice?

No.

Was there any reason for her to say his name like that, in a sigh and a whisper, unless she'd just been rubbing her hand along the inside of her left thigh while picturing him in a Conan the Barbarian loincloth?

No. And he'd know that immediately. And she could just see him on the other end of the line, one eye narrowed, his mouth drawn in a severe line of displeasure.

So when she heard him laugh—granted it was just a short spurt—she was shocked.

"You got ESP or something?"

Emma forced herself to take advantage of the opening. "As a matter of fact, Mr. Tobin, in a way, I do. It just so happens that I was dreaming about your dog . . . uh . . ."

"You were dreaming about Hairy?"

"That's right. Hairy."

After a pause, Thomas said, "Do you dream about weird little dogs a lot, Dr. Jenkins?"

Only when they're owned by stud puppies like you . . .

"It's very common for vets to have work-related dreams," she said, trying hard to sound authoritative. "It's an outlet for stress. Is there something I can do for you, Mr. Tobin? Is there something wrong with Hairy?"

It suddenly occurred to her that he couldn't possibly know her home number. It was unlisted and she only gave patients her answering service number—for precisely this reason.

"And how in the world did you get my home number?"

"Oh. Under the circumstances, I didn't think you'd mind that I . . . uh . . . had a friend find your number."

What kind of friend had access to unpublished numbers in the middle of the night? What were the circumstances? Emma was waiting.

"It's Hairy. He's been having trouble breathing for a couple hours now and I'm not exactly sure how serious it is or what I should do, but it seems to be getting worse."

Emma straightened to attention. It was possible the dog was having a reaction to the medications she'd prescribed—not likely, but always possible. "Describe his breathing right now, Mr. Tobin, and tell me exactly when and how it started."

Emma listened to Thomas's description of a night of cards and cigars and she found herself relaxing. "Who is your primary veterinarian again?"

"I don't have one."

"What? Well, I'm a behaviorist, Mr. Tobin, and I'm not usually on call for this kind of thing, but I agree that the dog is probably having a reaction to the smoke and it could be serious. Where do you live?"

"Federal Hill. Baltimore."

That was a good half-hour away. "There's a twenty-four-hour emergency clinic in Catonsville called VetMed. You should go right away, and be sure to keep an eye on him during the drive."

"Thank you."

"Take his medications along to show the vet, all right? I'll call ahead and meet you there."

Silence.

"Mr. Tobin?"

Thomas cleared his throat. "You're meeting us there? Why would you do that?"

That was a good question. How many times had she gone out to see a patient in the middle of the night since she and Aaron opened the practice? Exactly once: when Adolph the St. Bernard attacked his owner while she made herself a midnight snack of ham on rye.

"Hairy is my patient," she said.

More silence. "Please call me Thomas, and that's very nice of you, Dr. Jenkins."

"It's Emma, remember?"

When he finally responded, it sounded like he was in severe pain.

"All right—*Emma*."

Aaron Kramer sipped his whiskey and peered into the darkness of the hick bar. Even without the small changes he'd made to his appearance he would be nobody out here. Nothing. He was blissfully invisible—more than a hundred miles from home and a million miles away from his life.

Could he risk thinking that he was safe? Could he really believe that he'd gotten away with it? Could it really be that for once in his fucking life he'd gotten lucky?

It had been twelve days now since he'd killed that weasel, and the police had yet to come smashing in his door. Of all the times in his life when he'd needed luck to be on his side, this was it.

He'd take it.

The truth was, Aaron wasn't comfortable thinking of himself as a killer. It went against everything he thought he was. Sure, he had a few bad habits, but he'd never killed anyone. Scott Slick changed all that. The little faggot had gone too far.

Aaron looked around him—this place would be perfect for his purposes, if the time came. He didn't want to have to do it—and he hoped to God he wouldn't have to—but he was ready just in case.

He wasn't a stupid man, but when he lost big, he could get so angry that he couldn't think straight. If Slick had only been willing to listen to him, it wouldn't have happened. But Slick had laughed at him, told him it was out of his hands now, and Aaron got so pissed off that he reached around, grabbed the first thing he could get his hands on, and hit that little pecker in the head with it—

blood everywhere, all over his new Reeboks and down the front of his shirt.

He'd had to drive out to the boonies and start a fire at the edge of a farm field, where he burned everything to a crisp.

And he'd just paid a hundred bucks for those shoes!

He drained the drink and thought about leaving. He had a long drive and he'd had a lot to drink.

But the woman at the bar was still looking at him, still grinning at him, still sticking her boobs in his direction.

Why the hell not?

He got up and walked toward her. It's not like he was married anymore. Not that that had ever stopped him.

Chapter 3

Heart of Glass

If Emma had been alarmed at the sight of Thomas Tobin in a suit, then how could she describe what she was feeling now, seeing him sprawled out in a waiting room chair with disheveled hair, unshaven face, and worried eyes, his powerful legs sticking out of a pair of loose shorts, his broad shoulders and chest draped in a washed-out rugby shirt ripped at the elbows and splayed open at the collar?

Stunned was a good word. Like a doe in the high beams. Like a dieter looking into The Cheesecake Factory display case. Like the love-starved woman she was, looking at the most delectable serving of man she'd ever seen.

Thomas raised his eyes to the door. He scrambled to his feet, tucked Hairy into the crook of his arm like a football, and waited for her to reach him.

The journey across the waiting room played havoc with Emma's sympathetic nervous system. Her mouth went so dry she was afraid she'd dehydrate while her hands were so wet she had to wipe them on her sweatshirt.

She came to a stop and slowly raised her chin. Thomas hovered over her, his blond head lowered, his eyes wary and waiting. "Hey, Emma," he said in a husky whisper.

A bolt of hot lust spiked Emma to the floor through the cork soles of her Birkenstocks. Just a simple two-word greeting in that raspy male voice and she was toast. A goner.

Hairy began to squirm.

"He's got to pee." Thomas began to walk away but suddenly turned and peered at Emma, like a man double-checking the door lock before leaving on vacation. He narrowed one eye. "I'll be back."

Emma wheeled around to watch the Terminator stride out the door, noticing how long his legs were, how much taller he was than her, how much bigger, and how if she wanted to she could reach her arms straight out and they'd be the perfect height to grab on to his tight butt.

She blinked hard and shuddered. What was she— *insane*? Why the hell did she drive out here—to torture herself? She must be ovulating.

"Your boyfriend's been real worried about his little dog."

Emma spun back the other way. She hadn't noticed there was anyone else in this room, in the world! But an older couple sat on a pair of yellow vinyl chairs just a few feet away, and the woman smiled sadly at her.

"My boyfriend?" Emma was trying to force the haze from her brain. It was one in the morning. She was tired. She was crazy. She was ovulating—how was she supposed to carry on a conversation?

"I'm sorry. Your husband, then?" The woman produced a brave smile and Emma could see she'd been crying. The man had been crying, too.

Emma sank down into the chair next to her. "Actually, I'm the little dog's vet. I'm here to—" She stopped, unsure how to finish and aware it wasn't important anyway. She reached for the older woman's hand, thin and dry in her own. "Why are you here tonight?"

The woman's chin began to crumple and her lower lip

trembled. "Leonora—she's our Shih Tzu—didn't come in from the backyard after Letterman."

"I knew right then . . ." The man lowered his eyes and shook his head. "She always comes in after Letterman."

"She got out under the fence again," the woman said. "We called and called, then went out searching and found her by Frederick Road. There's so much traffic there."

"Do they have her in surgery now?"

She nodded. "The vet already told us not to keep our hopes up. There was a lot of . . ." The woman's voice broke and she began sobbing. Her husband's arm went around her and he completed her sentence.

"Internal injuries, you know."

Emma knew all too well what happened when a Shih Tzu met a Subaru. She gripped the woman's hand while she cried.

She'd seen countless people grieve for their pets over the years, from macaws to Mastiffs. When a pet died, the sense of loss was profound, pure, and uncomplicated. The intensity of the bond between animal and human would forever awe her.

"I know the vets here will do whatever they can to save Leonora." Emma made eye contact with both the woman and her husband. "But when an animal's injuries are so severe that there's no chance for any quality of life—I'm afraid the most humane thing to do is to stop the suffering."

The man nodded grimly.

"She must be a very special dog," Emma said.

The woman's back straightened and she smiled. "Oh, yes! Leonora's the most wonderful dog we've ever had! She's our third Shih Tzu—only two years old."

The husband reached for his wallet and flipped it open. "Here she is."

He placed a worn brown wallet in Emma's palm, open

to a professional studio portrait of a happy little ball of gray fluff. She couldn't help but smile.

"She's a cutie—and I bet feisty, too. Shih Tzus can be a real handful."

The couple began to laugh in agreement, just as Thomas returned.

Emma watched him pass silently through the door and stop, posing like a Viking god in Nikes with no socks, his trusty wheezing sidekick tucked against his side.

Thomas scanned Emma's face, dragged his eyes to where her hand grasped the old woman's, then locked his eyes on hers.

And it happened.

Emma inhaled sharply. Time slammed to a halt. Tectonic plates shifted. Because Thomas Tobin just grinned at her.

He obviously tried to suppress it, but the smile lasted long enough to make his eyes glitter like Christmas tree tinsel and create two deep, heart-stopping dimples at either side of his mouth.

No, this was not exactly the way she'd always imagined it would be—and she'd certainly pictured herself better dressed for the occasion—but who was she to complain?

Emma Jenkins had just officially been swept off her feet.

There was something way too intimate about this, he decided. It felt foolhardy. Dangerous.

It must be because it was the middle of the night, and as he'd seen often enough, the night could conjure up a false sense of intimacy between complete strangers.

Why else would he be sitting in an empty diner drinking coffee and eating blueberry pancakes with a woman he hardly knew, listening to her share details about her life? Why else would he be lulled into telling her anything about his own life? He'd never do that sort of thing in the daylight.

Day or night, in fact, Thomas couldn't remember ever having a conversation like this with a woman he'd just met. He and Emma had been all over the map in the last two hours—college, family, hobbies, work (he'd managed to be sufficiently vague about his job so far), and now she was laughing nervously and explaining that just when she'd decided to separate from her husband, her best friend out in California died and left her kid to Emma to raise.

She tucked a shiny section of hair behind an ear, wiped a drop of coffee off her upper lip with the tip of her finger, and he couldn't take his eyes off her even if he wanted to—even if she had a kid and was on the rebound from a divorce. He simply couldn't stop looking at her.

He'd decided she was more than pretty—she was beautiful. Her hair was thick and straight and fell loose over the top of her shoulders and gleamed under the light fixture above their booth, browns and golds and reds moving in waves, almost as if her hair was alive, breathing when she breathed.

Her eyes were the most delicate blue he'd ever seen. It struck him as ridiculous, but her eyes reminded him of the fuzzy zip-up baby thing he bought for Jack when he was born. Pam put Petey in it when he came along two years later, and the color kept getting softer with all the washing. He remembered how his nephews had felt solid but fragile tucked into his arms, how sweet they smelled after a bath, how new.

Thomas tore his gaze away and stared out the dark window, his heart beating too fast, his chest hollowed out with a sudden sense of emptiness. He looked at Emma again, because he had to.

Her lashes and brows were an almost-black brown, a strange and striking contrast with her light, sleepy eyes. Her nose and cheeks were splattered with faint freckles. As she talked, he studied her mouth, the slight crooked overlap of her two front teeth that struck him as intensely sexy, the way her dark red bottom lip was plumper than the top, the little dip at the center of her upper lip that disappeared when she smiled—which seemed to be all the damn time.

He knew she wasn't wearing lipstick—there wasn't a trace of it on the rim of her white coffee cup. She wasn't wearing any makeup at all, in fact. No fingernail polish. No jewelry. No perfume, just a baseline floral scent that probably came from her shampoo.

She was all natural. All real. And he'd like to rub his hands all over her.

"So, financially, it was a total mess. We invested in the practice as a couple and I guess he deserved his piece, but now I'm in debt up to my armpits and carrying a good portion of the patient load we used to share. Some of the patients did follow Aaron to Annapolis, though."

Her voice was rich with occasional low tones that sounded soothing to Thomas.

"Do you see him often?" he asked.

Emma shrugged. "I saw him Monday—at the lawyer's office. We signed the divorce papers." She waved a hand as if to clear the air. "And occasionally we talk on the phone about cases because we're the only two behaviorists in the region right now. It's kind of a new field—only thirty board-certified practitioners in the country."

"Do you miss him?"

She grimaced, then nodded. "Sure. Sometimes a lot, but there were things that I . . ." she looked away, not finishing her thought.

Thomas waited. He knew exactly what was coming next.

Emma turned back and smiled. "It was for the best. Let's just leave it at that."

Now *that* was a surprise. It was clear that this Aaron

guy was a real dick-head, but Emma hadn't said one bad thing about him. Nothing. He'd assumed the name-calling was about to start. He'd prepared himself to hear Emma's particular take on the standard male offenses: *he was a player; he was unable to communicate; he was a lying, cheating idiot; he did nothing but watch televised sports; he used me as a sex object.*

But all Emma had done so far was smile and recite the essentials: they met in an undergraduate zoology course, dated through college, lived together all through vet school, got married in residency, and planned to build a practice and a life together.

Then it fell apart.

The fact that she'd spared him the gory details was so grown-up—and showed such a sense of basic decency—that it was damn near startling.

"What's your little girl's name?" he asked.

Emma's face blossomed with the most perfect smile Thomas had ever seen. "Her name is Elizabeth—we call her Leelee. She's twelve, and she's the smartest and bravest kid on the planet."

The intensity of her response—of her love—startled him. It embarrassed him. He looked away.

That's when he noticed the flutter of a pointy pink ear under Emma's elbow, the only indication that Hairy had accompanied them. The dog had been perfectly silent, tucked down into the well of Emma's baggy sweatshirt, nestled up just below her breasts, sleeping against her belly.

He swallowed hard. Damn dog—how'd he get there first?

"And what about you, Thomas?" Emma tilted her head and grinned, her heavy hair swirling with the movement. "You haven't said much about your job, but right now I've got to tell you, I'm not buying the consultant story. I'm thinking Secret Service, maybe. I can just see you skulking around the White House Rose Garden whispering into your lapel."

"My lapel?"

"Yeah, you know, 'Sector Four Clear, sir!' " She tossed back her head and laughed, her eyes closing in enjoyment.

Thomas took another swig of his coffee and stared at her, amused, then suddenly annoyed. What was he doing here with this woman? He should say goodbye right now, before he spent any more time with her, before he started thinking crazy thoughts. Before he started liking her.

Besides, he was going to be dragging if he didn't get at least a couple hours of sleep. In just five hours he had one of those Saturday-morning "bagel bashings" at the office. Shit. And he had a match later in the afternoon. Shit. He was thirty-seven years old—way too old to stay up all night and then try to play rugby. It was a sure way to get himself killed.

Those were real good reasons to call it a night. But he couldn't. He wanted to look at Emma's smile, hear her laugh, fantasize that maybe she was as decent as she seemed. He needed to live the lie just a little longer. Maybe just a few more minutes.

"And what makes you say that, Emma?" He watched her hand go unconsciously to Hairy's head, where she caressed the dog's little Don King clump of hair.

She had the sweetest hands, tapered and smooth and sure. He remembered the sight of her with the old couple in the waiting room, so kind when the vet broke the news that their dog had died. Her voice had been comforting and soft. She'd held the old woman's hand.

"I'm an animal behaviorist, Thomas, and human beings are animals just like Hairy, here. So I've gotten pretty good at reading people."

You and me both, babe, he thought. "Like you're reading me now?"

She gave him a Mona Lisa smile and tilted her head. "A lot of times I have to start with the pet owner before I can help the pet, so yes, I've been observing you."

"And how do you do that?"

Emma grinned at him again. He wished she'd stop doing that because her grin had a hypnotic effect on him, making him feel like he was falling down some kind of spinning vortex.

"Mmm." Emma leaned back in her booth, still cradling Hairy against her. "Have you ever read any Agatha Christie? Do you know the character Miss Marple?"

"I think so."

"Well, when I was a kid, I couldn't read those books fast enough—I just inhaled them one after another. And the thing that intrigued me the most was how Miss Marple could peg a person just by watching their mannerisms."

Thomas was starting to sweat a little. They had more in common than she could possibly know. "Really?"

"Facial expressions. Body postures. Tone of voice—all the indirect ways people communicate with each other. Sometimes the words being said and the posturing taking place are at opposite extremes—but it's the indirect communication that always tells the truth." She shrugged softly, still stroking Hairy. "As it turned out, I ended up being the Miss Marple of the dog and cat world—an expert in animal communication—which never relies on words."

As she spoke, Thomas analyzed how he was sitting. He tried to relax his shoulders and listen attentively but not too enthusiastically. He mentally calculated the position of his hands, eyebrows, chin.

She laughed again, her powder-blue eyes glittering. "But don't let me scare you, Thomas."

Vortex time again. Thomas lowered his eyes to Emma's baggy Penn sweatshirt in an effort to avoid her gaze. That turned out to be a mistake, because her body nearly screamed out that she was soft and round and female and within arm's reach. The arch of her throat was graceful. Her wrists were small and elegant. He could see her substantial, firm breasts move with each breath. If she was trying to hide, she'd failed. Maybe it was impossible to hide something so lovely.

Just then, Emma reached under the shiny fall of hair to rub the back of her neck and roll her head around. Thomas peeked up to watch, and began to imagine what it would be like to cup her head in his hands when she did that, maybe while she writhed beneath him, moaning his name.

He needed to regain control of this conversation, which should not be a problem, since it was his forte.

"I'm sorry to disappoint you, but I'm not a Secret Service agent or a spy or anything even remotely glamorous. I'm just a lawyer who specializes in human resources—your basic paper pusher."

Emma narrowed her eyes and Thomas could see the doubt behind the pretty blue irises—she wasn't falling for it. This woman was beautiful, sweet, funny, and smart as hell. Thomas was afraid he might be hyperventilating.

"Uh-huh. Just like it says on your new-patient questionnaire." She took a sip of coffee. "So, do you like your work?"

Thomas shrugged casually, trying not to picture the last few times he'd posed as a killer for hire. He tried not to see the pimply seventeen-year-old who gave him six dollars in change and a PlayStation II game to kill his chess team nemesis. Or the guy who needed his wife's fifty-thousand-dollar life insurance policy to buy a Camaro with a sunroof and drive his new girlfriend to Disney World. Or the housewife who got down on her knees in front of his chair and began to unzip his pants, saying she didn't have the money for a hired killer but knew another way she could pay him for his services.

Emma's question echoed in his ears—*do I like my job?* Sure he did—what's not to like? He prevented the loss of human life. He got scum off the street and behind bars. And the dozen or so people in the world who knew how he made a living told him he was at the top of his game.

"I absolutely love my job."

"And what do you like best about it?"

"The people," Thomas said. "I get to meet fascinating people."

"Of course." Emma took another sip and peered at Thomas over the rim of her cup, clearly amused. "So do you have your own company or do you work with a group?"

Thomas remembered that she was wearing shorts with that sweatshirt and that she had nice legs—not particularly long, but strong and smooth and shapely. No chicken legs on this woman. She said she rode horses—he could picture it. He could picture her riding a lot of things, like the front of his hips.

"A group. We all have our specialties."

"And what's your specialty, Thomas?" Her mouth quirked up provocatively.

He felt a warm tingle shoot through his extremities, hitch a ride along his spine, and settle with a thud in his groin. He had to struggle to recall the details of his standard cover story. "Uh, whatever the situation calls for, really. But mostly I deal with downsizing decisions."

"You axe people." It wasn't a question.

"So to speak."

Emma's eyebrows went up. "You're the guy they call in to do the boss's dirty work. A hired gun."

At that pronouncement, Thomas laughed outright, a sound that shocked him as much as it did Emma. He couldn't remember the last time he'd laughed like that. It was so loud it woke up Hairy, and the dog's pointy little face popped up over the edge of the table and he yawned.

"That's exactly right, Emma. I'm a hired gun."

She frowned at him. "God, that sounds perfectly awful. No wonder you're so grumpy. I'd be in a bad mood too if I had to do that for a living."

Thomas rubbed a hand over his mouth to wipe away his smile. "Yeah, I guess I'm a little rusty at being the life of the party. My best friend tells me that I've been about as much fun as nail fungus lately."

She laughed, reaching across the table to touch Thomas's fingers where they clasped his coffee cup. She stroked him.

Thomas stopped breathing. He stared down at his fingers under hers, his flesh changed yet unchanged, jumping from the contact yet perfectly still. He hadn't wanted her to do that, had he? He hadn't somehow asked her to touch him using some kind of damned indirect communication, had he?

Emma probably touched everyone—the old woman in the waiting room for instance—and it didn't mean anything special. He raised his eyes from their fingers to her face, and he nearly groaned at the tenderness in her expression. She couldn't possibly know how long he'd gone without this. She couldn't possibly know how much he wanted her.

Dear God—he wanted her.

Emma pulled her hand away and leaned back again, meeting his steady gaze. Her face was the loveliest thing he'd ever seen. He really needed to get the hell out of this restaurant.

"Nail fungus?" Her smile was full of mischief. "You do know there's a cure for that, don't you?"

Oh, God. Hell, yeah. He knew exactly what would cure him.

"So what's the whole story of how you ended up with Hairy?" she asked. "I'm just dying to know about the 'flamboyant' guy and why he gave you his dog."

Thomas cringed and finished off his coffee with one big gulp, looking around for the waitress. She was perched on a red vinyl stool at the empty lunch counter, her nose in a romance novel. "He was a friend," he answered, willing the waitress to look his way. She didn't. "He died and I took Hairy."

"And do you plan to keep him?"

When Thomas turned back to her, Emma was waiting for him. Her gaze was direct—no judgment, no criticism, just curiosity.

"I can help you find a home for him if that's what you want to do," she said.

Thomas stared at the top half of Hairy's face, now visible over the edge of the tabletop. The dog's perfectly round eyeballs looked as if they could pop from his bony skull at any moment. But at least he wasn't wheezing anymore. Emma had been right about that—it was the cigar smoke. Back at VetMed, Hairy got a steroid shot and Thomas got a lecture about smoking cigars around the dog and a hundred and twenty-five bucks later they were merrily on their way.

". . . because I know a nice woman in Richmond who might be willing to . . ."

Thomas was halfway listening to Emma, halfway looking at her breasts under the sweatshirt, halfway noticing how he was more than halfway hard just sitting across the table from her, wondering what the hell he was going to do with Hairy.

The dog was a train wreck. A disaster. And he didn't even like dogs, let alone ugly, shrimpy, psychologically challenged ones. And now he couldn't even smoke his Cohibas in his own damn house because the dog had respiratory problems?

What was happening to him? What was happening to his life? Why the hell was he even *thinking* about getting this woman into his bed when there was probably an eighty percent chance that she had some fatal personality flaw and about a hundred percent chance that she'd leave him as soon as she learned about what Nina so lovingly called his "defect"?

Your basic guaranteed catastrophe, right there.

And it was all Hairy's fault. If it weren't for Hairy, he wouldn't be sitting there in the middle of the night with Emma Jenkins, trying not to like her.

He wouldn't be looking at her sensual, soft body parts, trying to figure out how he could touch them.

He wouldn't have to be the heartless bastard who forces an orphaned puppy to live with strangers!

Damn the little mutant.

"I suppose it wouldn't hurt to see if there's someone interested," Thomas said with a shrug. "They'd be nice people, though, right? People who'd take good care of him?"

Emma smiled at him again. "Sure, Thomas," she said.

First off, Emma had never seen a paper-pusher built like Thomas Tobin. He might be pushing stuff around, but she was certain it was heavy stuff like punching bags and barbells and bad guys, not departmental memos.

The man had "law and order" written all over him.

And the story about the way he acquired Hairy? She knew he was leaving out a few crucial details—like how exactly the guy died and why Thomas felt obligated to take the dog home. Emma knew a massive load of guilt when she saw it.

And now Thomas was talking about his rugby team, and she used the excuse just to admire the loose curls of his short hair, the dark blond scruff along his jawline and up his cheeks, the smooth, golden skin below his eyes.

She'd grown accustomed to his appearance in the last

three hours or so, enough that her blood wasn't beating against the back of her eyes like it did at first. Enough that she could breathe normally.

Biological imperatives aside, she was actually beginning to like the man—despite his best efforts. She liked that he was kind to a frightened little dog. She liked his rusty sense of humor.

And she was intrigued by how he tried to hide his smiles, as if joy was something he didn't want to succumb to in public.

She kept thinking about the other day in the exam room, when it felt like he was pulling her toward him and pushing her away at the same time. He was doing it again tonight. She could see him struggle with it when she held his gaze, and especially when she'd touched him.

No, Thomas Tobin wasn't a dullard, despite her first impression. But he was indecisive, conflicted—hardly an ideal psychological profile for whatever kind of cop he might be.

Emma wondered if it was just women who made him nervous. That seemed unlikely—a man as good-looking as Thomas surely had to develop razor-sharp instincts around the opposite sex simply to survive.

Maybe something had happened recently that made him question those instincts.

Emma sat back to ponder these questions and enjoy the view.

"I'm getting kind of old for the game, really. Rollo and I are the senior citizens of our team." Thomas shook his head. "It used to be I was sore for the first half of every Sunday—now it takes me until Wednesday to recover, just in time to show up for practice."

"So why do you still play?"

The corner of Thomas's mouth twitched and he rolled the empty coffee cup between his palms. "I spend a lot of hours behind a desk, so I crave the physicality of the sport. I love hitting and getting hit, how it makes me feel alive. The game takes everything out of me, makes everything else disappear. It always has."

"Have you been hurt a lot?"

His eyes sparkled. "I've been beaten to a pulp more times than a redheaded stepchild, so after nineteen years there's nothing left to lose—believe me. I plan to play until they drag me off the pitch in a body bag."

Emma felt her eyes go wide.

"See this?" Thomas pointed to the semicolon above his right eyebrow. "Stitches here twice—damaged some nerves—you might see me squint every once in a while. My nose has been broken twice. I've had knee surgery, dislocated shoulders, other things. See my hands?" He spread his fingers out on the tabletop.

"The only time I can lay them flat or make a tight fist is in the off season. The rest of the time they're too busted up."

Emma saw a few swollen knuckles and two digits that veered off in strange angles. He actually seemed proud of all this.

"It sounds like a lovely hobby."

He cocked a golden eyebrow in amusement. "Flower arranging is a hobby. Rugby is one of the top four reasons to live."

Emma didn't miss the gleam in his eye. "I'd love to hear about the other three," she said.

Thomas abruptly looked away, and Emma watched him struggle with his response just as the waitress came by to offer more coffee. They both declined.

"I should probably get going," Thomas said, reaching for the check.

"This was nice. Thank you." Emma tried to hide her disappointment that their get-together was over. "It's been a while since I've been out all night." She noticed that Thomas didn't respond to that. "I'm kind of a night owl anyway. Insomnia sometimes."

"Really?" Thomas raised his eyes as he counted out bills. "What do you do when you can't sleep?"

Emma chuckled, recalling her lurid behavior earlier that night. "I mostly sit on the front porch with Ray and listen to the crickets and tree frogs."

Thomas's hands froze and a frown marred his smooth forehead. He kept his eyes away from hers. "So Ray is the guy you're seeing these days?"

Emma nearly snorted with laughter, but stopped herself out of respect for the pained look on Thomas's face. He really *did* like her! It *wasn't* just her imagination!

"Ray's an old, blind, three-legged Shepherd cross with a flatulence problem."

He did it again, Emma saw—he rubbed his mouth with one of his big hands to hide his smile.

"You know, I won't be offended if you let your guard down every once in a while, Thomas. You've got a killer smile."

He shot up from the booth and threw down a tip, then crossed his arms over his chest and looked around nervously. It seemed to Emma that it took everything the man had not to bolt through the door without her.

Once in the parking lot, Thomas jerked toward her, his face stern. He stuck out his hands. "I should probably take Hairy now."

"Oh! Sure." Emma unrolled the sweatshirt from around the sleeping dog and leaned closer to Thomas for the transfer. He reached in, accidentally pressing his hands on top of hers, his skin hot and rough.

"Would you go out on a real date with me, Thomas?"

The question spilled from Emma without the tiniest bit of forethought, and she closed her eyes in embarrassment.

She felt him reach under her hands to find Hairy, then pull away.

When she opened her eyes, he was staring at her, absolutely stricken.

Her heart fell to her feet. "Thomas?"

He was suddenly on her, cupping her face in one of his hands, rubbing his scratchy cheek against her smooth one. He ran his fingers through her hair and down the side of her neck, and pressed his body close to hers, Hairy squished between them.

Emma's heart pounded. She had to lock her knees to remain standing. What was happening?

Then Thomas put his lips against her ear and . . . *oh, God!* He flicked his tongue into the tender hollow underneath, then bit down sharply on her earlobe just before he whispered, "I can't, Emma. I'm not the man for the job. I'm so sorry."

Thomas stepped back, tucked Hairy into the crook of his arm, and jogged off toward his shiny, yuppie car, leaving her blinking in disbelief.

Her body buzzed with shame and surprise and the sizzling rush left behind by his touch, his tongue, his teeth, his voice. It suddenly dawned on her that Thomas Tobin's rejection was hotter than all the actual dates she'd had in the last year—combined!

Tears stung her eyes. She didn't understand! She could have sworn . . . but he seemed . . . he said . . .

Talk about words and actions being in direct conflict! Talk about abnormal men!

As the car pulled away, Emma watched Hairy jump up and press his little face to the glass as if to say goodbye. As the car turned, she got a look at the bumper sticker on the rear fender, illuminated by the first light of dawn: *Life Sucks. Then You Die.*

• • •

Uh-oh.

I'm no expert, but I'm pretty sure you're an idiot when it comes to females. Why did you leave Soft Hands? Why did you rub up against her like that and then make her cry?

Turn around, Big Alpha! Turn around and go back! She's wonderful! She likes you! What's wrong with you?

Humans can be such fools.

Oh, quit your complaining. Yeah, I just pushed aside the towel and peed all over your precious car seat—and I did it on purpose.

Serves you right.

Chapter 4

The Love I Lost

The Volga. The Volga. The Russian river that empties into the Caspian Sea is the Volga, you total flat-liner.

"The Danube?"

Augh!

"I'm sorry. That answer is incorrect. The question now goes to number forty-seven for the grand prize. Would you like me to repeat the—"

Leelee jumped from her folding chair and headed toward the microphone before the man had to waste any more of everyone's time. "The answer is the Volga River," she said softly, then returned to her seat.

As the last remaining geography bee contestant on stage, Leelee gazed out into the audience and tried to look ecstatic. Beckett was on his feet whistling like he did for all her correct answers, unfortunately. Emma clapped and smiled that great big smile of hers.

Leelee sighed. Maybe she should have intentionally missed that no-brainer question just to add a little excitement to this godforsaken stretch of nothingness they called Carroll County, Maryland, where the most thrilling thing she'd seen in a year was the girl fight at the tractor pull last night. Those lovely ladies had more tattoos per square inch of flesh than teeth in their heads. Plus, she'd enjoyed the interesting colloquialisms, like when the skinny one called the big one an "ass-faced heifer."

God, she missed L.A.! God, she missed her friends and the smog and the noise and the variety of people and the energy that made her feel connected to something special.

God, she missed her mom. Craziness and all.

Leelee caught Emma's eyes and couldn't help but smile as her maternal figure gave a little wave and winked at her. Emma was cool—maybe the coolest woman Leelee had ever known. She was smart and pretty and responsible and had her own business and it was so awesome that she'd finally gotten rid of lame-o Aaron!

But why did Emma have to live *here*? Why couldn't they move somewhere halfway decent like Baltimore or D.C., even? For some reason, Emma had it in her head that this was where Leelee belonged, because it was where her mother was raised.

Like growing up here made Rebecca Weaverton a great person or something? Like *that* happened?

She looked down at Emma and Beckett and the most bizarre thing occurred to her: She was looking at her family. Well, her family in the way that Velveeta was cheese and AstroTurf was grass, but the only family she had now. The truth of that made her throat close up and her stomach flip.

"Number forty-seven, that is the correct answer! Congratulations!" Leelee heard the judge's voice get all excited and she knew she was going to have to stand. "This year's Carroll County Middle School Geography Bee Challenge Cup goes to Elizabeth Weaverton, a twelve-year-old from South Carroll Middle! Congratulations, Elizabeth!"

She rose to a sputtering of applause—hey, she knew the parents in the audience weren't exactly thrilled that she'd made their offspring look like total retards. She accepted the lovely plastic marbleized trophy topped with a fake brass globe and thought about what a joke she was. She was too skinny and too smart and had seen way too much of the real world for any of the hayseeds around here to like her. They thought she was a mutant.

God, she hated it here.

Leelee plastered a smile on her face and waved stiffly as a yellow polyester sash came down over her head and a grocery-store bouquet of flowers appeared in her free hand. She stood patiently while a few pictures were taken, noticing how through it all Emma and Beckett never took their eyes from her.

"Thata girl, Lee!" Beckett hollered as she descended the stage steps.

"Congratulations, sweetie!" Emma threw her arms around Leelee and squeezed, and Leelee closed her eyes and let herself float in Emma's embrace. She always smelled wholesome, down-to-earth, like baby powder and sunflowers—something too simple and too real to be found in any Rodeo Drive boutique.

"Not much of a challenge for you, eh, kid?"

"I guess not." Leelee shrugged and looked up into Emma's pretty blue eyes. Her mother had had brown eyes, but lately that was about the only thing Leelee could still remember about her. She couldn't feel the exact pressure of her mom's touch, or recall the smell of her hair. It had only been a year and it was fading away. How long would it be before she'd remember nothing at all?

It was Beckett's turn to hug her. "We were thinking of heading over to the Waffle House to get us some lunch. Wha'dya say?"

"That totally rocks, Beck."

Leelee never cried—God knows Becca had always produced enough melodrama for several households, so why bother? She didn't cry the time they got evicted from the best apartment they ever managed to get. Not when she had to transfer schools three times in fifth grade. Not when her mom got herself killed riding in some second-rate TV actor's car.

Leelee didn't even cry the day she got her butt dragged cross-country to live here in Soybean World.

What would crying accomplish? What had it ever accomplished for her mom? Nothing, that's what.

So it was a total shock to realize that she'd apparently picked right then to start. What was so overwhelming about walking out of the community college auditorium between Emma and Beckett, holding her trophy, heading out to the Waffle House?

The food there wasn't *that* bad.

So why cry now?

It felt weird the way the water trickled hot down her cheeks. She could taste her own tears as they pooled in the corner of her mouth—saltier than she imagined, like the Pacific Ocean off Malibu.

The real bad part was now that it had started, she was pretty sure it was never going to stop. Her knees felt shaky and her stomach felt heavy, like it had fallen too low in her belly. She thought she might choke. Or hurl. All she knew was she had to get away. Get away from everyone, everything . . .

The next thing she knew she was in the middle of the parking lot, on her hands and knees, feeling the burn and sting of gravel under her palms and the skin of her knees. She was shaking. She couldn't stop sobbing. She'd dropped the trophy and it lay broken a few feet in front of her. The ugly flowers were spilled in an arc around her.

Then she heard a high-pitched scream—several long seconds of piercing sound coming out of her that she hadn't even known she could produce. Somewhere in the back of her head she knew it was the sound of not being able to stuff it down anymore.

"Oh, sweetie . . ." Leelee felt Emma's arms go around her and lift her to her feet. She gave in. She let Emma protect her, hide her, stroke her hair and mumble soft words that she couldn't really hear because of the buzzing in her own ears. Then Leelee sensed that Emma was leading her to the Montero, getting her buckled in the back seat and sitting next to her.

Leelee sobbed and sobbed as Beckett drove them home.

After what seemed like forever, she looked up into Emma's face and was greeted with a handful of Kleenex and a smile she couldn't quite read.

"I'm sorry for acting like a complete diva." She wiped off her face and blew her nose.

"Oh, honey, there's nothing to be sorry about."

"I don't know what happened."

"I do."

Leelee took a quick gulp of air and shook her head.

"You're bleeding, Lee."

She brushed off her knees with annoyance. Her stomach hurt something fierce but she tried not to cry anymore. "It's okay. It's nothing. Just a scrape."

She felt Emma's fingers come under her chin and lift up her face. "Not there, sweetheart." Emma's voice was low enough that Beckett wouldn't hear. "You've just started your period."

Thomas could feel the caffeine kicking his brain into overdrive, yet it wasn't quite enough to burn off the fog of the all-nighter. And no amount of coffee would ever mask the truth that he'd behaved like a complete jerk.

He'd been such a jerk to Emma Jenkins.

And she didn't deserve it. That was the hell of it—she didn't deserve to be hurt. In fact, she may have been the first legitimately decent, nice—even special—person Thomas had met in a very long time.

And he'd been an idiot. A jerk. An ass.

Thomas sat at the conference table and watched the rest of the team straggle in. He could hear Stephano out in the hallway, his machine-gun laugh ricocheting down the uncarpeted hallways of the second floor of the Maryland State Police Headquarters. Paulie Fletcher was already at the other end of the table, clutching a cell phone to his cheek, apologizing profusely to his wife.

Thomas knew these Saturday morning get-togethers interfered with ballet recitals, peewee football games, and lawn mowing duties. He grinned to himself with smug satisfaction—as the only unmarried member of the team, he never had to worry about someone else crimping his style, making demands on his time. Not him.

Besides, they only had to suffer through these meetings a few times a year—before quarterly report deadlines and whenever there was a sudden spurt of new cases. September was often one of those times. It made sense, in a sick sort of way. The summer was officially over. People weren't distracted by barbecues, vacations, and weekends down at the ocean. It was a good time to start taking care of those bothersome loose ends they'd been putting off—like murdering friends and family.

Thomas looked up as Regina Massey strolled in, the homicide detective assigned to the Scott Slick case. Regina was a fifty-something grandmother who didn't look—or act—her age. What she looked and acted like was the movie star Pam Grier—all sexy, street-smart, black alpha female. Reg didn't take shit from *any*body. That's how she'd made it in a predominantly white-male line of work.

That's why Thomas liked her.

She winked at him. "Hey, hot stuff. Wild date last night? Looks like you need a nap."

Thomas rolled his eyes. She'd been giving him a hard time for more than a decade, first when he was with the Baltimore County State's Attorney's office and then with the task force. It was part of their routine.

He took a steaming sip from his Styrofoam coffee cup and watched Regina get settled in the chair next to him, smoothing down her silk trousers and adjusting the belt at her trim waist. She sent him a flirty smile, her dark eyes flashing.

Thomas shook his head. "I'm putting the finishing touches on my sexual harassment complaint against you, Reg. I should have it filed this week."

She hooted with laughter. "Oooh, Tommy honey, you know I get all tingly when you use my name and the word *sexual* in the same sentence."

He glared at her—if anyone else had called him that, they'd be in pain now.

"Watch it, Reg." Chick Abels dropped his stack of files on the table with a thud. "He's got nothing against hitting women—remember the Amelia Pilcher case?"

"Sure do." She was still grinning. "Three years for trying to make sure her church choir director never sang again."

"I elbowed her in self-defense," Thomas growled. "She was going for my eyes with a paper clip."

Regina sighed dreamily. "You've always had a way with the ladies, Tommy."

Within minutes, all members of the Maryland Murder for Hire Task Force were gathered around the conference table, Captain Vince Stephano at the far end. The head of the Maryland State Police special operations division unceremoniously tossed a white bakery bag into the center of the table.

"Help yourself to some bagels," he said, and the grins spread around the table like a contagion. Thomas long ago learned this was how the captain apologized for bringing everyone in on a weekend—by providing a selection of the world's worst bagels—dense, inflexible O-shaped objects not fit for human consumption.

As Paulie often pointed out behind Stephano's back, it wasn't really the captain's fault—God never meant for Italians to shop for bagels.

"All right, people, we've got a lot of territory to cover and it's a beautiful Indian summer day and I know we all want out of here so let's get to it."

"You mean a Native American summer day," Manny Chaudury said.

"My apologies to your motherland," Stephano said. "And as you can see we have the pleasure of Lieutenant Regina Massey's company this morning. The lieutenant will be updating us on the Slick homicide." Stephano abruptly swung his gaze toward Thomas and smiled. "But first I gotta know—how's your special friend this morning, Tobin?"

Regina's head snapped around. Everyone else began to chuckle.

"Did she recover?" Stephano asked way too nicely. "She sure was a pretty little bald thing."

"The thing is a he and he's fine." Thomas saw Regina's eyes fly wide in shock. "It's a dog," he muttered.

Regina's mouth fell open. "You got yourself a bald dog, honey?"

"No. Yes. Sort of." It suddenly occurred to Thomas that this could be the break he was looking for—Regina was good with living things. She'd given birth to two kids and they were still alive, as far as he knew. So maybe she'd take Hairy. "You want it?"

She frowned. "What kind is it?"

"The real ugly kind," Paulie whispered, and the whole table cracked up.

"It's a hairless toy breed," Thomas muttered, dropping

his gaze to the fascinating scarred wood of the table. "Scott Slick's dog."

The room went utterly silent. Stephano cleared his throat. "You didn't tell me you took Slick's dog to your place. Why didn't you tell me that thing was Slick's dog?"

"You never asked," Thomas said. "I waited for somebody to claim him, but as we found out, Slick didn't have anybody."

"So how did you end up with it?" Stephano asked, staring at Thomas in disbelief.

Thomas shrugged and nodded to Regina. "Once you guys showed up and the evidence techs got there, you said you wanted him out of the apartment."

Regina nodded. "I sure did—he'd already contaminated the crime scene something fierce."

"He wouldn't leave Slick's side and I kind of felt bad for him. So I took him home with me."

The silence was deafening. All eyes were on Thomas, and he felt like the featured attraction in a circus freak show. He looked from face to face. "What? What's the big deal?"

Stephano cleared his throat. "It's just . . . well . . . that was kinda nice of you, Tobin, that's all. It was a nice thing to do."

Regina's hand brushed his. "I didn't know you kept him, Thomas. That's very sweet."

"Whatever," Thomas muttered, horrified by the compliments.

"Maybe we wouldn't have given you so much shit last night if we'd known the thing was Slick's," Chick said. "I mean, who would have thought Slick would have a dog like that?"

"Who would have thought Slick was gay?" Paulie chimed in.

"True enough," Stephano said. "So, Lieutenant, care to bring us up to speed?"

"My pleasure." She opened up the manila folder in front of her. "At this point, we're thinking Slick had another residence somewhere. We're operating under the assumption that he had an alias we don't yet know about."

Her eyes met Thomas's, giving him a chance to chime in. He did.

"Slick was actively running a bookmaking operation and we all knew it. There—it's on the table." Thomas looked at Stephano, and the captain nodded for him to continue. "As supervisor for this task force, I made the decision to keep working with him even with that knowledge. His information was just too good, and I wanted to keep it coming. I take responsibility for sidestepping regulations on that."

Nobody said anything.

"But it looks like Slick was doing a few other things I *didn't* know about. The apartment I'd been to a couple times and I thought was his home was . . . well, it probably wasn't his primary residence. It was like a hotel room. It didn't look very lived in."

"Some *gentle*men like to keep a clean house," Paulie offered.

"You ought to know," Manny said.

Regina shook her head, disgusted. "You boys are the biggest bunch of homophobes I've ever seen in my life. If you all weren't so insecure about your own sexual orientation you wouldn't have to—"

"Bite me, Reg," Paulie said.

"Enough!" Stephano smacked his palm on the table. "God, people! I want to get out of here, so let them finish. What else have you got, Reg?"

Thomas sighed, rubbed both hands over his tired face, and let his thoughts wander back to Slick. He'd met him about twelve years before, his rookie year with the state's attorney's office. Slick got busted for bookmaking but worked off charges by becoming an informant for a variety of cases. One of them was the first murder-for-hire Thomas ever handled.

A few months later, Slick came to Thomas on his own with another possible murder solicitation. Then another. And pretty soon, Thomas realized that Slick was the best informant he'd ever worked with, and pretended not to notice that his informant—who was supposed to stay on the good side of the law—had turned a little sideline into a thriving business.

He'd seen Slick in action many times over the years. He treated each of his customers like royalty, listened to their lame excuses and blatant lies like it was the most fascinating shit he'd ever heard, and gave people every opportunity to set things right with him. The result was that Slick had customers throwing money at him year-round, even desperation bets in baseball season, and made more tax-free income than he knew what to do with.

As Slick often explained with a smile on his face, guys who bet money on sports lost that money. Not with every bet, but at the end of the season or the year, they'd lost a ton of money. And it became his.

Like taking candy from a baby, he used to say.

They developed an understanding. Thomas would do what he could to keep the cops off Slick's back—no promises—and in exchange, Slick would tell Thomas what he heard in the course of doing business, and for some reason, people tended to confide in Scott Slick when life got ugly.

He had a nice, open face. He listened. He smiled. Then he ratted on them.

One of his customers asked Slick to find someone to whack his law partner. A waitress asked him to find someone to pull the plug on her comatose husband. A junior high school basketball coach up to his eyebrows in gambling debt wanted to collect on his own teenage daughter's life insurance policy. It seemed people believed Slick had connections.

He did—connections to Thomas and the Maryland State Police.

In the years of their partnership, Slick's tips were consistently on the mark—almost all had resulted in felony murder solicitation charges that ended in guilty pleas or trial. And Thomas liked the guy.

But when Slick came to him in July and said he planned to close up shop and wanted out of their arrangement, Thomas wouldn't let him do it. He listened to Slick tell him his customers were getting more unreliable and collection was becoming a real pain in the ass. He told Thomas he had enough cash now to last him three lifetimes, and it was time to cut his losses and relax.

But Thomas talked to him—okay, maybe threatened him a little, with Stephano's blessing—until Slick agreed to keep the operation going through the college football season. Then bam—a week later Slick was lying on his kitchen floor with his head bashed in, little doggie footprints of blood all around his body.

As Thomas had stood there looking down at what used to be Slick, he wondered if his informant had known he was in danger, and that's why he wanted out. If that was the case, then it was Thomas's fault Slick was dead.

And now that he was gone, Thomas realized Slick hadn't just bullshitted his clients or the poor SOBs who came to him for help—he'd been lying to Thomas, too.

Thomas never once suspected Slick was gay. He never doubted that the apartment he'd visited was his home. He never knew he had a weird little dog.

Did everybody have to be a liar? Did everybody have to pretend to be something they weren't?

Thomas was only half listening to Reg review the case. He'd been unofficially helping out with the investigation all along. It was the least Thomas could do for Slick, who, thanks to him, was now the main entrée at the worm buffet.

"Cause of death was blunt trauma to the head, inflicted by impact with the left front corner of the base of a KitchenAid blender," Regina read from the file. "The blender was found next to the victim's body on the kitchen floor, still plugged in, its engine burned out. The victim's skull was crushed above the left temple, under the rim of a cap. Bone fragments in the brain tissue. Massive hemorrhaging, lots of external bleeding."

"I wonder whether the blender was set on chop or liquefy?" Chick asked.

Thomas threw him a severe look but Reg continued unfazed. "Frappé," she said. "And the apartment showed no signs of forced entry. The lock wasn't picked. So it may be that Slick knew his attacker and let him in."

"Usually do," Manny muttered.

"Prints were found all over the blender and the countertop but they came up unknown. Traces of skin and hair found under Slick's fingernails, signs of struggle. DNA analysis is pending. There was a variety of shoeprints found in the plush carpet in the living room, some Thomas's—he was first on the scene—some matching the shoes on Slick's feet at the time of death, others not. They pulled one intact print of a male Reebok running shoe, size ten, a model stocked at nearly every mall in America this year. The rest were a jumble."

"What's the backlog for DNA testing these days?" Stephano asked, taking a few notes.

"At least six weeks for a case without a suspect." And before anyone could say anything Reg shook her head. "I know. It's the worst it's ever been, but there's nothing I can do. Believe me, I'm in limbo on a bunch of cases just waiting for the lab to come through for me."

"So what's this about another residence?" Stephano asked.

Thomas looked up. "There were only three changes of clothes in Slick's closet, right, Reg?"

"Mmm-mmm." Regina skimmed the file. "An overnight toiletry bag in the bathroom along with a few dog care supplies. A bare minimum of food in the cabinets and refrigerator. No magazine subs, no newspaper delivery, junk mail only, no phone or Internet service. Utilities were under his name. But—" She looked up with a grin. "There was an unopened economy pack of condoms in the bedside table, a lovely assortment of gay erotica, and a state-of-the-art entertainment center. Lots of CDs, too."

"All of them disco," Thomas said under his breath. "What a waste of perfectly good technology."

"So we're thinking it was his love shack," Regina said.

"So if his murder wasn't related to his work with you guys, it may have been a lovers' spat."

"Where's that taking you?" Stephano asked.

"We've been digging around the Baltimore and Washington gay communities, trying to figure out how Slick fit into the scene, what kind of relationships he had."

"And what have you got?"

"Not much at this point, but we're still looking. If Slick went to the clubs, nobody's saying. If he had any significant others, they're being real discreet."

"My God," Chick said. "Can you imagine how many customers he would have lost if it got out that he was light in the loafers?"

"He'd have lost 'em all," Thomas said, watching Regina close the file. And then he wondered to himself if that's why Slick had really wanted out—so that he could finally stop pretending.

Regina left the meeting at that point and Thomas took

over. He reviewed the cases coming to trial, the pending indictments, and the list of possible new cases.

Stephano turned to Thomas. "And where do we stand with our man Leo Vasilich?"

The men around the table gave a collective sigh.

"The judge is supposed to have her decision tomorrow on the motion to suppress, but Manny and I went by the book and there's no way they're going to get that surveillance tape thrown out. I'm afraid our friend Leo is fucked."

"The man was just not using his head," Manny said.

"Sure he was—the smaller one," Chick said.

"There but for the grace of God go I," Paulie sighed.

Thomas laughed at that. "Oh, yeah? You're a self-made multimillionaire immigrant who married a beauty pageant queen turned con artist, too?"

Paulie blew out air. "You know what I mean, man. You just never know with women—none of us ever really know."

"My wife wouldn't embezzle from me and give it to her lover. I trust her completely," Manny said.

"You have nothing to embezzle, my friend," Chick pointed out.

"Still, I trust her."

"Leo trusted his wife and she cleaned him out," Chick said. "I don't blame him for wanting to kill her."

Thomas shook his head. "See, Chick, it's all right to be so angry that you *want* to kill someone. The crime is when you decide to go ahead and do it—or in Leo's case, hire someone to do it. That's kind of the whole gist of our line of work."

Chick smiled. "Oh. Now you tell me."

At Stephano's urging, Thomas wrapped up the meeting by making assignments for the weeks to come. He divided up the background research, assigned undercover backup positions, and reviewed electronic surveillance equipment needs for each new campaign. It was going to be a busy couple of weeks.

Driving home, Thomas realized he had a deposition on Monday and needed to stop at the dry cleaners to pick up his suits. It sometimes amused him that he had to plan his wardrobe ahead of time. There were days he'd appear in court in the morning and have to show up at a biker bar to meet a guy for a beer after work—and that required black leather. Other nights called for his cheap sports jacket and polyester slacks, and still others called for jeans, a flannel shirt, and a Jeff Gordon ball cap.

He never went overboard with his undercover wardrobe, but he was aware that a man his size needed to do whatever he could to blend in.

Thomas sighed as he pulled out of the dry cleaners. He couldn't put it off any longer. What choice did he have, seeing that Hairy had peed all over his car that morning?

He took a stabilizing breath and grabbed a parking spot in front of the CVS drugstore. He told himself he could do this. He was an adult, an officer of the court who worked with violent criminals on a daily basis. He could certainly summon the courage to purchase maxi pads.

He entered the front door like any normal customer and began scanning the aisles. He saw the sign hanging there as big as anything—Feminine Hygiene and Family Planning. Bingo. He'd hit the motherlode. Two, three minutes tops and he'd have those pups in a plastic bag and be outa there.

Thomas strode down the aisle—and stopped. He stood before the shelves in a state of awe. Just how many different types of pads and tampons did the female race require? Dear God. Then his eye strayed toward the array of products apparently necessary for the proper functioning of the female reproductive system—douches, yeast infection creams, anti-itching ointments, personal lubricants, pregnancy tests, spermicides. His heart began to race. He struggled to keep his focus.

Thomas scanned row after row. What should he buy? Wings or no wings? Heavy flow or light days? Curved edges or straight? He tried to imagine which of these pads would work best inside a tube sock tied around the tiny waist of a six-pound neutered male mutant dog, but was drawing a blank.

He felt like he might need a hit off the oxygen canister he'd spied in the front window.

"Is there something I can help you find, dude?"

Thomas turned around to see a teenage stock boy staring at him with a smirk. He was leaning one elbow on a dolly full of even more feminine hygiene products—cartons and cartons of them!

"Your girlfriend send you on an errand?"

Thomas gave the kid a smile that positively dripped with courtesy, then said, "At least I got a girlfriend, punk ass." He turned back to the wall of paper products and removed the first thing he saw. At the cash register, he realized he'd selected a forty-eight-count box of extra long pads for nighttime flow.

They'd be perfect. They'd have to be. Because he was never going to do that again.

Ever.

Chapter 5

Macho Man

She would come through for him one last time, he just knew it. Emma wasn't the kind of woman to let a piece of paper stand in the way of basic decency. When she brought up divorce for the first time, she said she would always love him. He remembered how her statement made him laugh at the time, considering the context.

Well, he wasn't laughing today. It better be true, because this was the end of the road for him—and maybe for Emma. The truth was, he was running out of options.

Aaron pushed up on the bridge of his Ralph Lauren shades and checked his gas gauge. He hoped to God she had some cash on her because he needed to fill the tank before heading back to Annapolis, and as they both knew, his credit cards—the ones that hadn't already been confiscated—weren't worth shit these days.

He sighed and cranked up the volume on his CD player. How long had it been since he'd been out to Beckett's farm? God—he couldn't remember, but he didn't think there were this many houses around the last time. The new developments were sprouting out of the ground like fields of giant McMansion mushrooms.

Aaron wondered how long it would be before some developer approached the old guy with a big wad of cash for his land. He wondered how he might be able to get his hands on a piece of that wad.

It would be nice to see Beck today if he was around. He could be a pretty amusing geezer—when he wasn't jumping on Aaron's ass about how he treated Emma.

Aaron caught a glimpse of the farmhouse down the hill off to the left. True, it was a pretty place, surrounded by green and gold waves of farmland, but he'd almost fallen off his chair when Emma informed him she was leaving their Columbia townhouse to live out here with her dad.

He supposed she could live wherever she wanted, but damn—this place was in the middle of nowhere and a good half-hour from the clinic.

So what? It was her life now—hers and Leelee's. Aaron smiled and shook his head. He couldn't get over how that crazy Becca just went and got herself killed and dumped her kid in Emma's lap. Unbelievable.

But there were a lot of unbelievable things about Becca, if he recalled correctly. Emma would croak if she ever found out what had happened the first summer they went out to visit Becca in L.A. But it would always stay his and Becca's dirty little secret, wouldn't it?

Aaron smiled to himself. Oh, yes, he knew firsthand that Becca never put much stock in the whole concept of "safe sex," so it came as no surprise that she'd died giving some sitcom actor such a great blow-job that he infarcted and drove his Jaguar into a canyon. He'd noted the poetic justice of that to Emma at the time, but she didn't laugh.

He turned into the lane and immediately winced. The loose gravel was pinging off the sides of the car, which he'd spent six hundred to repaint and detail only four months ago. Shit!

It hardly mattered, he supposed. If Emma didn't come through for him today, he wouldn't need the car where he was headed. He didn't think you were allowed to bring personal belongings to hell, anyway.

Damn. Why did everybody assume that because he had that "doctor" label in front of his name that he had money, but just didn't want to part with it?

Nothing could be further from the truth.

Gretchen left him last week. She said she'd expected more from him—more attention, more gifts, more, more, more. What was he supposed to do? He was in a stranglehold of debt from setting up his solo practice. He was behind on his business insurance payments, his mortgage on the building, his student loans, even the goddamn utility bills! The sad truth was that Gretchen had been keeping them afloat for many months. It must have just dawned on her a week ago. The way it had once dawned on Emma.

It was probably better for Gretchen that she left when she did. It wouldn't have been much longer before those bastards would've tried to use her as a bargaining chip.

It made him nauseous to think of the night the ugly one lay in wait for him outside the office. That piece of scum popped him in the eye, then thrust some kind of knife under his chin and told him to pay up or die.

He'd heard it all before. But the guy had been so convincing that night that Aaron pissed himself.

He reached the end of the long driveway and could see into the open barn door to Emma. She was moving in a golden spill of sunlight, stacking hay bales up against the aisle, dust and hay swirling around her, and she looked like some kind of heavenly apparition.

Aaron grinned—there were a few pieces of hay in her hair. She looked flushed and pretty the way she always did, an uncomplicated, undemanding kind of pretty. Not like Gretchen—good God, that woman was one wild female. Hot and sleek and always dressed to bring a man to his knees.

He kind of missed her. Emma, not Gretchen. Watching her stand there frowning at him made him laugh. In fact, he missed Emma so much that sometimes he would lie in bed at night and try to conjure up that certain way she smelled—like a breeze through a field of wildflowers. He'd never been able to get it quite right in his imagination.

He felt bad for what had happened, he really did.

But it was good to be free.

Now if he could just catch a break—just one—he was sure he could turn this whole fucking mess around.

Emma tossed the last hay bale on the pile as she heard the rumble of a car engine and the crackle of gravel beneath tires. She'd recognize the sound of that car anytime, anywhere. How many nights had she lain awake waiting to hear it?

Aaron was here. And she bet she knew why.

Emma stepped from the cool shade of the barn into the early evening sun, placing a gloved hand over her brow to shield her eyes.

"How's it going, Em?"

He leaned against his precious Datsun 280 Z, his ankles crossed casually, his thumbs hooked in his jeans pockets, that lazy smile spreading across his handsome face. Emma's heart did a leap off the high dive at the sight of him, then she felt it sink to the bottom with a thud.

Like always.

"What's the problem, Aaron?"

"Can't I just come see you every once in a while?" Aaron pushed off from the antique black sports car and took a few steps toward her, his dark eyes shimmering, his head cocked to the side seductively.

Yes, Aaron was handsome. And no, she wasn't going to succumb to his charm today, or any other day.

"The answer to whatever you're going to ask me is no way in hell." She turned and went back inside the barn, hoping he wouldn't follow her.

Emma needed a moment to deal with the cruel mix of desire, anger, and gut-wrenching sadness that came with seeing Aaron. She took note that there was more anger than anything else this time, and hoped it was a sign of progress.

She removed Vesta's nylon halter and lead from a peg, then pushed back the door to the last stall on the left.

"Come on, girl, let's get some evening air. Bud needs some company." Emma tried to touch the horse but Vesta snorted and tossed her head with uneasiness, keeping a wary eye on Aaron's progress down the center aisle of the barn.

"He's not going to hurt you, baby," Emma whispered, watching Aaron lean back against the rough wooden wall and grin at her. Emma wondered who she was trying to reassure—the horse or herself.

His black eyes locked on hers. He seemed to be measuring the situation, planning his attack.

"You're looking good, Em. Have you lost weight?"

Emma's entire body jerked with the loaded words and she turned away. Aaron knew just how to get to her—he always had. She tried to ignore how much the remark hurt, but her heart was beating hard and fast and it was obvious he'd hit his mark.

"Not that you really needed to. I swear you get more beautiful with each year."

She said nothing, and clipped the lead to the halter.

"It looks like Vesta is really coming along." He flashed her a white-toothed, movie-star smile. "You never give up, do you, Em? The eternal optimist."

Emma hissed with disgust. "Oh, that's me, all right." She brought the skittish horse out into the aisle, nearly trampling Aaron's toes in the process.

"Is she doing any better with her phobias? What have you got her on? Cyproheptadine? Have you taken her off grain?"

Emma ignored the shoptalk and led the Thoroughbred out the barn door and toward the east pasture gate. Aaron was by her side in an instant.

"Looks like you've worked miracles with her, actually. Most abused track horses don't bounce back this good." He shrugged. "But then, you know that."

Emma looked out on the gently rolling land to avoid searching Aaron's expression for signs of sincerity. She didn't care whether he was sincere, she reminded herself. It was obvious what he was really after.

"I don't have any money to give you." Emma tried to sound matter-of-fact, not letting on how much he could still hurt her. "And that box of your stuff is still at the office. If you don't come get it in the next couple of days, I'm throwing it out."

"I'll come get it."

"That's what you've been saying for a year."

She unclasped the chain on the green metal gate and led the horse to the field. Vesta began to fidget at the prospect of freedom, and she pawed at the ground and excitedly tossed her head, making Emma dance around in her effort to unsnap the lead. The instant she was free, the horse bolted, her dark, shiny form racing down the fence line, her head lowered, her mane and tail flying.

"That is one fine animal," Aaron said with a hushed voice. "She really lets you ride her? God, I'd like to see that."

Aaron nodded toward the Quarter Horse in the adjoining field. "And how's the Bud Man doing?"

Emma yanked the chain closed, then looped the lead around her wrist as she headed back to the barn, ignoring him.

"I only need about eight hundred," he said, falling in step with her. "And I can pay you back next week, I swear to God."

They'd reached the barn door and Emma walked ahead of him into the dimness, pretending she hadn't heard him. But she had, and her blood was hammering against her skin and she wanted to scream at the top of her lungs. She wanted to hit him. She wanted to *kill* him!

In all their time together—through the other women and the debt—she'd never been more disgusted with Aaron than she was at that very instant. Maybe signing the divorce papers earlier that week had given her permission to feel everything she'd ever wanted to feel, in a way she never dared when she carried the title of "wife."

There was nothing to salvage anymore. No reason to pretend it could still be all right.

Aaron's hand went to her shoulder.

"Don't you dare touch me!" She spun around.

Aaron took a step back. "Hey, wait a—"

"I wouldn't give you a dime if I were the richest woman on earth! God, Aaron, thanks to you, I'm barely keeping the clinic doors open! I can't believe you've got the gonads to come out here and ask me to bail you out again!"

"Hey, c'mon, Em, settle down. We can talk about—"

"We're not going to talk about anything!" Emma stomped her foot and looked around the barn in desperation, trying not to completely lose it. She took a big breath. "We're divorced. Does this ring a bell? I am your *ex*-wife, Aaron. You are no longer my problem and I don't give a damn what unbelievably stupid thing you've done this time because it has nothing to do with me. Are we clear on this?"

Aaron shoved his hands in his pockets and looked contrite. "It was a parlay and it was one of those fluke things. It wasn't my fault."

Emma threw up her hands, the lead line snapping in the

air. "My God! It's never your fault, is it? It's always somebody else's fault, somebody else's screwup—never your responsibility for making such dumb-ass decisions in the first place!" She felt the tears building and fought hard against them. She would not let him see her cry.

She turned away and hung the rope on its peg, then took several calming breaths before she had the courage to look him in the face.

Aaron Kramer had been a good vet. He could be sweet and witty and fun. Emma had loved him so much, for so long, that she could hardly remember a time when he wasn't at the center of her life.

They'd had their minor differences in opinion through the years, but Emma and Aaron had always shared the same basic philosophy about life and work. But that day about a year ago, the day Aaron lost his cool with a patient, was the end for them.

He'd screamed at an owner—told her right to her face that she was more fucked up than her crazy dog—and suggested she be the one euthanized instead of the animal. The owner ran crying from the practice. The dog was destroyed later that day over Emma's protests.

And Emma suddenly knew that Aaron was a lost cause. That he was beyond her help. That her love no longer made enough difference. It was then that she saw him as two entirely different people. One Aaron was kind and brilliant and loving. The other was so twisted up in his addictions that he no longer even pretended to carry out his duty to care for people and their pets, let alone his duty to her. All that mattered was the rush, the thrill, the sickness.

That day, she knew that Aaron was going down—and she refused to go down with him.

Emma studied him now, in need of a shave and obviously tired, and did the only thing she knew would ever help. "You have an illness, Aaron," she said.

He shut his eyes and groaned.

"You're a brilliant, caring man in so many ways and you've worked so hard to get where you are—I know because I was right there at your side the whole way, remember? But you're going to lose everything." She sighed heavily. "God, Aaron, you need help again, another inpatient program. Please get some help."

His eyes flew open and he laughed bitterly. "What I *need* is a thousand dollars, not another fucking lecture from you."

Emma let go with a sharp laugh of her own. "It was eight hundred just a minute ago—is the interest accruing that fast?"

Aaron rubbed his eyes. "I meant to say a thousand."

"Get out of here. Leave."

"Emma, listen. It's bad this time. Believe me. I'm in trouble." He grabbed her hard around the upper arms. "Please. You've got to help me."

"I said don't touch me!" She shoved her hands flat against his chest until he let go. "I've had an unbelievably shitty day—a shitty week, in fact, that happened to include finalizing our divorce—and I refuse to let you do this to me! Get out of here!"

Right then Emma felt a nudging against the outside of her leg. Ray was there at her side, probably drawn by the raised voices. She watched Aaron's deep brown eyes flicker toward the dog, then return to her face. His expression was now flat, an indication that he'd decided to drop the charm routine.

"You owe it to me," he said.

"I don't owe you a freaking thing!" Her mouth opened in astonishment. "You are something else, Kramer."

"Just one last time."

Emma felt a wave of failure and loss wash over her, so black and airless that she nearly drowned in it. It took every bit of strength she had to put an end to the encounter. She squared her shoulders.

"I'll give you one last deal, Aaron. Take it or leave it. I won't call in all your outstanding IOUs if you leave right now and swear you'll never come back. I don't ever want to see you again. That's worth ten thousand to me, easy."

Aaron said nothing, just glared at her a moment before he turned back to his car. He opened the door and began to lower himself inside but stopped. He turned to her, and cocked his head.

"You have no idea what you've just done," he whispered, the corners of his mouth turning down, trembling. "Take good care, Emma."

The big engine rumbled awake and she watched him race down the lane, an angry cloud of gravel and dust spewing into the air behind him.

Emma stood without moving for a long while, feeling the numbness spread to her limbs, her heart. Then she walked toward the east pasture, folded her arms along the fence, and propped a foot on the lower rail.

The warmth of the evening sun hit her back, and for a moment it felt like somebody was stroking the tension out of her shoulders, like someone's gentle caress. But it was her imagination, and it made her feel so alone.

Right then, it all came crashing down on her—the scene with Leelee that morning, the shameful sting of Thomas Tobin's rejection, and now Aaron's latest attempt to use her. It was too much, and it squeezed powerfully at her chest, wrung out her heart, and she started to cry.

Emma turned her head and rested her cheek on her folded arms. She felt the tears run downhill and tickle her wrist.

Here she was trying to show a young girl how to successfully deal with life, when she'd totally screwed up her own! Who in the world said she was fit to be a mother?

Why was it that she had to pass a grueling three-day board examination before she could care for a Schnauzer yet didn't have to demonstrate any aptitude whatsoever to hold the life of a human child in her hands?

Emma swallowed back a sob and shook her head. The look in Leelee's eyes that morning had been such a raw mix of fear and vulnerability that it nearly broke Emma's heart. She knew all too well how it felt to grow up without your mother there to guide you. It was scary as hell. And she didn't have any magic answers for Leelee. In fact, Emma was quite aware she had no idea what she was doing—she was making it up as she went along.

She sniffled and turned over onto the other cheek, blinking back another round of tears.

Then there was Thomas Tobin. How stupid could she have been? It amazed her that she'd actually thought there was something special about that man, that there had been a connection between them. How had she made the mistake of thinking he was interested in her?

The truth was that he was a conflicted jerk and she didn't want anything more to do with him—not that she'd been given much of a choice in the matter.

She knew that at the core of it, the Thomas Tobin two-step was nothing but a typical case of fear-based aggression. In her mind, she pictured him as a big yellow Lab who'd been teased and hurt one time too many, who'd turned mean in an attempt to protect himself.

He had all the classic signs. He answered many of her questions in an indirect manner. He limited his eye contact. He tried not to reveal emotion. He was uncomfortable with physical contact. And he tried to puff himself up with all that stupid macho rugby garbage in an attempt to insulate himself from future hurt. It was his way of saying to the world, "Back off! You really don't want to mess with me!"

Issues? You bet your ass he had issues!

On Monday, she'd have Velvet transfer Hairy's follow-up care to someone else.

She wiped her eyes and thought of that little dog. Poor Hairy. Of all the animal's problems, the biggest was that he was now owned by an emotionally impaired idiot.

Emma straightened up and looked down at herself—a few pieces of hay clung to the old denim shirt straining at her ample chest. Dirt smudged the thighs of her jeans. Horse manure was packed into the thick treads of her barn boots. She laughed out loud at her own foolishness—*why of course Thomas Tobin found you attractive, Miss Horse Offal! How could any man resist such beauty, such panache!*

Such a joke!

The ground rumbled beneath her feet and Emma looked up to see Vesta racing toward her, all glossy muscle, speed, and fire. She stopped at the fence, snorted and tossed her head.

Vesta stayed long enough to let Emma briefly stroke the white blaze between her huge, dark eyes. Then she was off again.

As Emma watched the horse, she took a deep breath and made a promise to herself. From here on out, she wasn't going to waste another minute worrying about why she couldn't find a good man to love. Instead, she was going to be like Vesta, and just appreciate having the pasture all to herself, the wind in her hair, making the trip under her own power.

If the right man never materialized, so be it.

And if—miracle of miracles!—he showed up on her doorstep someday, her heart would know him in an instant. He'd be normal. Honest. Kind. He wouldn't lead her on or try to use her to support his bad habits. He'd be sweet to her. He'd love her just the way she was. He'd respect her.

Emma decided right then that she'd waste no more en-

ergy pining for some man to sweep her off her feet—
because clearly, once the sweeping part was over she'd end
up sprawled on her butt!

She watched Vesta out in the middle of the field, still
cavorting and throwing her head in joy. It made her smile
to think that maybe she *had* worked miracles with that
horse.

Maybe she could do the same with her own life.

Maybe she really *was* an eternal optimist.

Damn, he felt like a senior citizen tonight. He'd done a
number on his left knee in the scrum. His lower back and
neck were killing him. And he'd smashed up his left hand
something fierce. If he wasn't careful they really would be
carrying him off the pitch in a body bag, and soon.

Hairy tugged at the leash as he sniffed eagerly around
the base of a newspaper box. Thomas gave a few nervous
glances around the street. He couldn't believe he was walking down a public sidewalk with a dog in a sweater. Dear
God, there couldn't be a single thing more humiliating in
this entire world.

Unless, of course, Hairy had been out here in his maxi
pad. Thomas sighed. Walking around, the house with that
thing tied around his waist, Hairy had looked like a—well,
he'd looked like an ugly dog in a Kotex. Thomas had
laughed his ass off at first, but soon discovered the crazy
scheme had saved him about three cleanup jobs in one evening alone.

Emma had been right.

Thomas suddenly groaned in discomfort and stopped to
press a hand into the small of his back while he stretched,
giving Hairy just enough time to skitter around in circles
and tangle the leash around his ankle.

"Damn, Hairy. What have you done now?" Thomas

reached down to unravel the mess and a hot streak of pain raced up his back. He was locked up. He couldn't move. Un-fucking-believable.

"Are you all right, young man?"

Thomas raised his eyes to see the familiar face of the elderly lady from three doors down. He had no idea what her name was—he'd never said a word to her. Obviously, that was about to change.

"Fine, ma'am. Just a little stiff."

"Well, I certainly know all about that." She made several "tsk tsk" sounds with her tongue. "Sometimes you just have to jerk up real quick and face the pain." She gave him a friendly slap on the shoulder. "I'll give you the number for my chiropractor, Dr. Feldman. He's wonderful. He—"

"No. Really. I'm fine." Thomas heaved himself to a stand and watched black patches of agony pulsate on the surface of his retinas.

"I'm Mrs. Sylvia Quatrocci, by the way. I'm a widow." The lady scrunched up her mouth and examined Thomas from head to toe, then wagged an eyebrow. "We've never officially met. You've always seemed too busy to talk before, always so serious."

"Uh-huh." The pain was so bad Thomas feared he would faint. Meanwhile, Hairy had managed to nearly hang himself on the leash and was making wretched gagging sounds.

"Here, let me help you with your little friend." Mrs. Quatrocci bent effortlessly and unhooked Hairy's collar from the leash, then yanked the thin cord of nylon out of Thomas's hand.

"It's an unusual-looking little thing. What is it?"

Thomas stood stunned and annoyed. A little old lady had just rescued him. The last time he checked, it was supposed to be the other way around.

"It's a dog," he said.

Mrs. Quatrocci laughed heartily and looked into the animal's face. "Well, no kidding. But what kind?"

"A Chinese Crested—want it?"

Her face widened in horror. "Of course I don't want it! I was just curious. Here." She shoved Hairy into Thomas's arms. "Be a little more careful with that leash. So what's your name again?"

There was no *again* about it. "My name is Thomas Tobin."

"Well, Mr. Tobin, it was a pleasure. I suppose we'll see each other around, the way we've been doing for the last five years. Maybe now we can exchange pleasantries the way real neighbors do."

"Yes, ma'am."

Mrs. Quatrocci was about to continue her evening stroll but suddenly remembered she had another meddling question. "So what's her name?"

Thomas nearly said "Emma," but stopped himself. "Whose name?"

"The dog's."

"Oh. It's a him. Hairy—H-A-I-R-Y."

Mrs. Quatrocci roared with laughter. "That's just adorable!" She patted Thomas's arm and smiled sweetly. "You know, I never took you for a man with a sense of humor. Just goes to show you that you can't judge a book by its cover."

"No, ma'am. I couldn't agree more."

With that, she moved on. Thomas reattached the $10.95 green nylon leash to the matching $7.49 collar and was about to bend over and return Hairy to the sidewalk when he realized that wouldn't be a smart move. Who'd come along to rescue him next—a kid in a wheelchair?

He pondered the physics involved in returning Hairy to the ground, then gingerly leaned to one side at the waist, dangling the dog above the concrete by one hand, getting as close to the sidewalk as possible before letting go.

Hairy's legs splayed out upon impact and he yelped a bit, but nothing seemed to be broken. And they were off again.

Emma had said that Hairy's anxiety would lessen with lots of exercise. She was right about that. Hairy definitely slept better if he'd had a half-hour walk in the evening. And the medicine, lotions, and relaxation exercises seemed to be helping a little. Hairy shook less. He seemed happier. His skin looked healthier.

Emma had been right about so many things—the pustules, the maxi pads, the crate, the fact that they should be dating.

Thomas groaned, and he wasn't sure if it was because his knees hurt or because he'd just remembered what Emma looked like as he'd walked away that morning. Her smile was gone. Her chin began to tremble, like she was going to cry. Those soft blue eyes looked shocked and hurt.

Did she cry after he drove away? Did he make her cry? The thought made him sick.

Oh, God, that little patch of skin right behind her ear had smelled like summer air and warm, delicious woman. And when he'd nipped that earlobe between his teeth, she'd tasted like a dollop of hot salt-water taffy. He wondered what her other dollops might taste like. He wondered if she might ever be willing to give him another chance.

He wondered why he wanted another chance.

He wondered what was wrong with him.

"Should I send her flowers, Hairy? Do you think she's the kind who likes flowers?"

Hairy looked up at him.

"Is she the dozen-roses type, or the tulip type, do you think?"

Oh, God—just that single little taste of her and it had taken every bit of willpower he possessed not to fold her in his arms and touch her everywhere—those gorgeous breasts, that perfect, round butt of hers, the satiny throat. He'd wanted to put his mouth on hers and taste her on the inside. He wanted to cup her between her legs. He wanted to tell her she was—

". . . such a darling little thing!"

Thomas nearly yelped with surprise. He had company again. Where were all these people coming from? Was Federal Hill overpopulated? And why the hell did everyone suddenly get the urge to take a walk?

Thomas's eyes widened as he did a once-over on the man who now stood beside him. The guy was short and skinny with dyed blond hair and a silver hoop harpooned through his eyebrow. He wore a pair of black leather pants so tight that his lips should have been purple from the lack of circulation.

Then Thomas realized the man had some kind of little dog, too. It looked like a wig on four sticks, wearing what could only be described as a purple halter top and matching, crotchless hot pants. What kind of man would put a dog in such an absurd get-up?

Just then, the man made eye contact and broke out into a glorious smile, and extremely loud sirens began to wail inside Thomas's skull.

"I'm Franco," the man said, holding out a manicured hand. "This is Quiche Lorraine. I don't think we've seen you out before. I'm pretty sure we would have remembered." Franco giggled and gave his head a sassy little shake.

"I'm Thomas." He accepted Franco's hand and shook it. Real hard.

"Ooh! Down boy!" Franco laughed uncomfortably, then rubbed his injured fingers. "So. Are you new to the neighborhood?"

Thomas quickly summed up the situation. Could this nut job possibly think he was gay? And if so, why the hell would he assume something like that? Since when did he *look* gay? Since when did he *sound* gay? Was it something he was wearing? No, he was in a real hetero pair of cut-off sweatpants and an old Orioles T-shirt. Then what could it possibly—?

Thomas looked down at the two dogs, their tiny tails wagging as fast as hummingbird wings as they sniffed at each other's ensembles.

Oh, dear God.

"You know, you don't see too many Cresteds in town," Franco was saying. "I knew a guy a few years back with one, but they're few and far between. How long have you had him?" Franco blinked, his mouth pulled into a pert little smile, waiting.

"You've actually seen one of these before?" Suddenly, Thomas's back pain faded in comparison to the headache now eating away at his brain stem.

"Of course."

"Want it?"

Franco giggled. "Uh, not really."

A sharp "yip!" drew the men's attention to the dogs. They looked down to see Hairy humping Lorraine like there was no tomorrow.

"Goddammit, dog!" He pulled at the leash, then looked at Franco in horror. "Uh, sorry about that, man."

Franco laughed as he reached down to retrieve Lorraine. "It's perfectly natural—just the way dogs decide who's going to be the dominant one in the pack." Franco batted his eyelashes at Thomas. "You know, who gets to be on top."

That was it. That was all he could take.

Thomas mumbled goodbye in the most polite way he could muster, then sped down the sidewalk, dragging Hairy behind.

"Hurry up, you horny little neutered—"

Right then, Thomas swore to God above that he would

never, *ever,* take Hairy out in public again. He'd get him a
little doggie treadmill if he had to, but he wasn't taking this
oversexed, sweater- and maxi pad–wearing, flamer-magnet
on a walk again.

Not in this lifetime.

*What a great walk this has been—three new friends in one
night!*

*I think I'll lift my leg right here on this nice tree. Ahh,
fabulous! Now everyone knows I was here. That I'm male.
That I exist.*

*What a lovely evening! My sweater feels so snuggly. The
sound of my nails clicking on the sidewalk makes me happy.
I feel proud to have Big Alpha at my side.*

*Something feels so right about the two of us males out
in the world together, leaving our scent on the neighborhood. I believe we could accomplish anything we set our
minds to!*

I'm reminded of one of Slick's favorite songs.

"Macho macho man . . . I wanna be a macho man!"

Chapter 6

When Will I See You Again?

When Emma entered the clinic Monday morning, she thought she'd strayed into somebody's funeral by mistake.

There were flowers everywhere.

A huge cut-glass vase of roses—at least two dozen flaming red blooms—sat atop the registration counter. On the small table usually reserved for Lyme disease brochures sat a woven basket overflowing with black-eyed Susans. A blue speckled crock of late summer wildflowers sat near the display for engraved dog tags.

Emma stared in amazement. Then fury.

How *dare* he do this to her?

"There's more in your office, Em." Velvet's dark head popped up over the registration counter, and she was smiling ear to ear. "I read all the cards so I have a general idea what's going on, but I'm still dying to hear the gory details." Velvet sighed dreamily. "This is just about the sweetest thing I've ever seen a man do."

Emma felt her shoulders sag and her spirits sink. In silence, she trudged through the door that led to her office and exam rooms.

"Hey!" Velvet called after her. "Don't you want to see what he wrote, Em?"

"Absolutely not."

"Emma?"

She threw her backpack onto an office chair and clicked on her computer, the anger swelling and burning inside her chest. It was then she noticed the porcelain teapot smack in the middle of her desk, overflowing with carnations and baby's breath, and a matching china plate piled with teas and chocolates.

How *dare* he?

"Em?"

"Get this stuff out of here, Velvet. Now. Please. Before I blow a gasket." Emma logged on the computer with loud, pounding strikes on the keyboard. She checked her e-mail with her back toward her assistant.

Velvet stopped and frowned. "Hey. You really are mad." She plopped down in the empty office chair. "I'm sorry. I just assumed you'd be happy about this. Maybe we should just get right to the details."

"There *are* no details, Velvet!" Emma wheeled around in her chair. "The man is sick. An addict. A manipulator. And you'd think, of all the people in the world, you'd be the last person who needed me to spell this out! God! And why he thinks flowers—freaking flowers!—are going to somehow make up for all the shit he's put me through I'll never know! And to think he had the nerve to ask me for money again when this pointless gesture must have cost a fortune! I just want to go on with my life! Is that too much to ask?"

Emma took a big breath. "Is it?"

She let her face drop into her hands and tried to get a grip on herself. She refused to start off the week like this. He had no right to do this to her—no right! The sound of Velvet's laughter caused her to look up.

"Excuse me? Is there something funny about this?"

"Well, yeah." Velvet kept giggling. "It sounds like you

two managed to cover quite a lot of ground on your first date."

At that instant, Emma saw the elaborate gift basket full of dog treats directly in her line of vision—chewies, biscuits, Nylabones, rawhide sticks. It was perched on the bookcase below the display of her diplomas, bundled up in fancy clear plastic wrap and tied with a huge red polka dot bow. Her mind was reeling. Velvet's comments made no sense.

"You've completely lost me." Emma picked up the computer printout of the day's appointments and groaned. Sigmund Goetz and Roscoe the blue point Siamese were her first order of business. She was at the bottom of her bag of tricks for that poor old man and his schizophrenic cat and she knew it.

Velvet reached behind her for the small white envelope taped to the dog bones. "Here, Em. Read this. It'll clear things up for you." She forced the card between Emma's closed fingers. "This is my personal favorite, but honestly, the one with the wildflowers made me cry. He's not only gorgeous—he's extremely romantic."

Emma stared blankly. "Whaa?"

"Just read this. Then tell me everything."

Emma opened her palm and stared at the envelope, her name written in an unfamiliar hand—bold, squarish letters that took up a lot of space. She pulled out the card.

> *Emma,*
> *Even if you throw away all the flowers, I know you'll keep these for your patients. I apologize for my behavior the other night. I'd like to see you again.*
> *Thomas*

Her mouth fell open. She took an awkward gulp of air and nearly choked.

Velvet jumped up to pat her back. "Are you all right?"

Emma shook her head. "Hell, no, I'm not all right! Oh, my God—this is so *awful*!" Emma threw the card on her desk and quickly grabbed the one tucked beneath the china plate.

> *Emma,*
> *I hope you like chocolate. I opted for every kind of tea they had because I didn't know which you preferred.*
> *Thomas*

Emma leaped from her chair and went flying back out into the waiting room, the door thudding in Velvet's face as she stumbled behind her.

"Emma! Wait!"

She went for the wildflowers first because they were closest, and pulled so violently at the dainty white envelope that its plastic prong went flying across the room, sticking in the vinyl window blinds.

> *Emma,*
> *These reminded me of you—simply beautiful.*
> *Thomas*

She lunged for the black-eyed Susans, her heart pounding behind her ribs.

> *Emma,*
> *You are a lovely and interesting woman and I am an idiot. I hope you like the Maryland state flower.*
> *Thomas*

At that point, Emma began to breathe again. The bundle of cards fell from her limp hand to the floor. She turned toward the registration desk and put one foot in front of the other with the zeal of a woman heading for her own execution.

As her fingers reached inside the explosion of red satin petals, she sucked in the sweet, heavy fragrance and briefly closed her eyes. Her mind went blank. Then she read these words:

> *E—*
> *I'd like to start over. Just tell me what to do.*
> *Yours, T.*

Emma looked up to the fluorescent lights on the ceiling and blinked back the tears now gathering in her eyes. Damn that man! Talk about not fair! She'd had Thomas Tobin all figured out and now what had he done? He'd ruined it! Now she was wondering if he might be for real. Now she was wondering if she had completely lost her mind for wondering that.

"Aaugh!" Emma slammed the card to the floor and shouted, "Holy shit on a stick and goddamn it all to *hell*! This sucks!"

A deep voice came from behind her.

"Ach nein. I haven't heard talk like that since the war." Mr. Goetz shook his head in disapproval. "Most ladies love to get flowers! Vat's za fuss?"

Oh, how lovely—her first patient of the day! Emma wheeled around to see that Mr. Goetz wore his usual mothball-smelling suit, bow tie, and threadbare fedora, and his eyes were as bright and intelligent as always. His cane leaned up against the pet carrier that housed a hissing and spitting Siamese.

Velvet came to the rescue, stepping between them. "Hey, handsome, you're a few minutes early. Your appointment's not until nine-thirty."

"Ya, I'm early, und you can be sure I'll be early from now on—I never knew what I vas missing." He smiled at the women. "It appears za doctor having man troubles?"

"I apologize for my language, Mr. Goetz." Emma smoothed back her hair and straightened her shoulders. "I've been under a lot of stress lately."

Mr. Goetz shrugged. "Maybe za stress would go avay if you give this poor man another chance. It looks like he's desperate, yes?"

Emma looked hopelessly to Velvet, who grinned and shrugged.

Mr. Goetz added, "Obviously, he'd do anyzing to get you back."

Now, that made Emma perk to attention. "Really? Have you ever sent a woman"—she quickly counted—"six arrangements at one time?"

He seemed offended, and waved his hand in dismissal. "Mein Gott, no! I have my dignity!"

By lunchtime, Emma had selected yet another treatment option for poor miserable Roscoe, handled a new referral for canine obsessive-compulsive behavior, met with a pharmaceutical rep, and counseled a weepy young woman faced with putting down a Rottweiler that had bitten three neighborhood children.

Through it all, her thoughts kept returning to Thomas and his assault on her peace of mind. She couldn't just ignore the flowers. She couldn't just ignore the way he'd plowed into her life. All this force demanded an answer, and she had every intention of giving him one.

Just as soon as she decided what to say.

As Emma picked through the lovely assortment of teas— English breakfast tea, green tea, spiced chai, chamomile, orange pekoe decaf—she wished she could just hate him and get it over with.

As she headed to the lunchroom, she wished Thomas

would just crash through the clinic door, grab her by the shoulders, and kiss her senseless.

And as she made eye contact with Velvet, seated at the lunch table waiting to pounce, she wished she'd never laid eyes on the man.

What could she possibly tell Velvet? The truth was she didn't know what to think about Thomas Tobin. She didn't know how to take this display of humor, regret—and yes, thoughtfulness. Did he really want another chance with her, or was this just part of the Thomas Tobin two-step—one tug forward and one push back?

There was one thing she knew with certainty: Thomas was not the right man for her. He had issues—more issues than an annual *Newsweek* subscription, in fact. She needed to calm herself. The situation called for a clear head and a clear understanding of the facts.

As she heated water for tea, she put together a silent accounting of Thomas Tobin's most significant shortcomings.

For starters, he was obviously lying about what he did for a living, leading her to believe he was engaged in something dangerous, illegal, or top secret—bad news for the woman in his life regardless. And the lying itself was a huge red flag.

Plus, he was too serious. He was afraid to laugh. In fact, Emma doubted the man would recognize joy if it jumped up and took a chunk out of his left butt cheek.

But the ultimate danger sign was that he led her on. He convinced her that he liked her, touched her in a way that turned her patellas to pudding, then turned his back on her.

A man like that was truth in advertising—he'd only bring her more pain. A man like that could not be trusted.

She had no business with a man like that.

She'd just gotten rid of a man like that.

Emma sighed. It was a shame that all these flaws were

part of the most divine package of maleness she'd ever seen. A damn shame.

At least the memory of him would stir up her imagination on many a future front-porch night.

But if she were smart—which of course she was—then her imagination would be the only place she'd ever see him again.

The microwave beeped. Her tea water was done. She pulled her chicken salad sandwich from the refrigerator—and waited for Velvet to say something. But her assistant remained uncharacteristically silent, flipping through a magazine, not even looking Emma's way. It was driving her nuts.

Emma began dunking her tea bag—she'd selected the Earl Grey—and counted the seconds until she could bear it no longer.

"Nothing much happened, okay?"

Velvet didn't look up.

"Is this some kind of reverse psychology trash they taught you in graduate school?" Emma picked up her sandwich and mug and went to the table. "Am I supposed to be tortured by your lack of interest and spill my guts to you? Because, really, Velvet, there's not a whole lot to tell." Emma unzipped the sandwich baggy. "He bit me, then told me he wasn't interested in dating me. That's it. That's the whole story."

Velvet slowly raised her eyes, her yogurt spoon poised in mid-air, her dark eyebrows crooked in interest. "Thomas Tobin *bit* you?"

"Yep."

Velvet blinked. "Biting as in chomping down on your flesh with his teeth? Biting as in the referrals we get?"

Emma chewed her sandwich and nodded pleasantly. "My left earlobe."

"Wow. No kissing first? Just straight to the biting?"

Emma pondered that question as she swallowed. What he'd done prior to the bite couldn't really be classified as a kiss. There was no puckering involved.

"Actually, I think he might have licked me first. Then bit."

Velvet's eyes grew wide. "Specify the body part, please."

"The same general area—right under the earlobe. First the lick. Then the bite. Then the part where he says 'No, thanks—I don't want to date you' and runs to his car. Now *that's* romance for you, girl."

"Holy shit."

"My sentiment exactly, as you might recall. I know Mr. Goetz always will."

Velvet shoved her chair from the table and walked over to throw her yogurt cup in the trash. Emma sensed Velvet's shock and had to laugh.

When it came to the complexities of the human mating dance, Velvet wasn't often surprised. From what Emma knew about her relationship with Marcus—which was far too much, really—there was no such thing as proper form.

"Let me get this straight, Em." Velvet began pacing in front of the sink. "You asked him out. He licks your throat, bites your ear, and says 'no'?"

"That's correct."

"How many seconds of bodily contact are we talking about here?"

Emma took a sip of tea. "Well, let's see. He stroked my face, sniffed my hair, then he kind of pressed up against me and my knees nearly gave out."

"Go on." Velvet was back in her chair.

"Then the licking and the biting."

"How hard?"

"Hard enough to sting."

"So we're looking at what—fifteen seconds of body contact?"

"About that—but it felt more like an hour."

Velvet looked stunned. "Em, how hot are we talking? I mean, seriously, how hot *is* this guy?"

"Surface of the sun, Velvet."

"Wow," she whispered. "And what were the exact words he used to turn you down?"

"He said, 'I'm not the man for the job. I'm sorry.' "

Velvet sat back in her chair, her mouth agape, no sound coming out of it. Emma wished she had her camera.

"So what do you think? Do I thank him for the flowers and the Pup-Peroni and start picking out my silver pattern?"

Velvet howled with laughter. "Yeah, right! This guy's a total nut job!" She gripped Emma's wrist, her face pulling into a serious scowl. "I think we should send him to someone else for follow-up, okay? I don't know if it's safe for you to be around him again. He sounds sort of . . . I don't know . . . *abnormal*."

Then Velvet pulled out the big guns: "I bet he even calls his girlfriends 'baby doll' or something equally offensive."

Emma smiled sweetly. "When was the last time I told you you're the wisest employee I have?"

"I'm the only one you have."

Emma continued to smile at Velvet. But she was thinking of Thomas, and the words that came to mind were, *What a waste*.

Leelee flew in the Wit's End front door about three-thirty, raring to go. She enjoyed her Monday, Wednesday, and Friday afternoon job at the office and loved the five bucks an hour she made doing brainless office stuff. She usually snagged close to forty dollars a week—tax-free—and that was decent money for a twelve-year-old in Maryland currency. Not that there was anywhere great to spend it close by, but she could always save it up for a weekend trip to Towson Town Center, Tyson's Corner, or The Gallery at Baltimore's Inner Harbor.

"Kon'nichiwa, Miki-san!" Beckett yelled, walking in the door behind Leelee.

"Kon'nichiwa, Beckett-san!"

Leelee watched Beck's face light up as he jabbered in Japanese with Velvet, the way he did every time he dropped her off. It was like language lab at school, except that Japanese was way cooler than French.

Velvet and Beck laughed at the end of their exchange and Beck shut the front door, the little bell tinkling as it swayed from the doorknob. "Thanks for humoring me, Velvet."

Velvet smiled heartily at him. "Anytime. Obaasan gives me grief for not speaking it more than I do."

"How's your grandma doing these days?"

Velvet shrugged. "Better. Living with Mom and Dad, making my mom's life a living hell with her need to be cooking constantly."

Beckett gave her a naughty wink. "That's our job as old people, you know. We go to secret classes to learn how to drive the younger generation crazy. I got an A-plus, right, Leelee?"

Leelee wasn't really paying attention. She was staring at the huge vase of roses.

Velvet caught Leelee's eye. "Hey girlie-girl. You up to helping me reorganize the empty office today? We've got some new shelves to put up."

"Sure." There were flowers everywhere, and Leelee's heart was thudding much faster than normal. Her throat and chest tightened. Her thoughts raced back to the last apartment they had in L.A., the one-bedroom with the broken air-conditioning, and her mom's last guy. The guy who sent her flowers all the time. The guy who killed her when he drove off the road.

She'd had so many flowers at her funeral.

"Who died?" Beckett joked, scanning the floral arrangements.

Velvet glanced toward the exam rooms before she whispered, "Some guy sent these to Emma. He likes her, but she isn't sure if she likes him. He's a little off the wall."

One of Beck's white brows arched over a sharp blue eye and then he winked at Leelee. "That'd be par for the course, now wouldn't it?"

"Hey, Pops. Hey, Leelee." Emma came sailing through the hallway door with a chart in her hand and a smile on her face. A lady clutching a mean-looking Chihuahua followed close behind.

"Mrs. Bellafonte will need to stop back in about two weeks from now, all right?" Emma turned to the owner. "It was good to meet you and Pancho. Please call if you have any questions."

Leelee watched the normal things take place in front of her eyes, but the sick twisting in her chest had only gotten worse. Her vision began to swim. It barely registered that Emma had already gone back in her office, that Velvet had handed her a stack of charts to file, and Beckett was on his way home.

As Leelee replaced the charts according to alphabetical order, she wondered about the flower guy. Did he love Emma? Would he break her heart the way Aaron had? Would Emma love this guy more than she could ever love her?

For about the millionth time since she'd been transported to Maryland like a hog to slaughter, Leelee wondered if Emma would have been happier if she'd never come into her life.

She shook her head. She needed to chill. Emma was not

like her mom, right? Emma wasn't going to go off half-crazed with lust for some guy she'd just met, like her mom always did. Emma wasn't that kind of woman. Emma was cautious. Emma was safe.

Emma really loved her.

The phone rang, and it jarred Leelee into the land of the living. Velvet was on another line with an owner, and she began gesturing wildly for Leelee to answer the phone.

Leelee picked up. "Wit's End Animal Behavioral Clinic, may I help you?"

"Emma?"

He sounded eager, nervous. "I'm sorry, Dr. Jenkins is on another line." Leelee had no idea why she'd just lied, but she didn't like this man's voice one bit. It was too deep. Too he-man.

"I see."

He sounded disappointed.

"Thank you, Leelee," Velvet's voice chimed in the background. "I've got it now."

Leelee put the caller on hold and stepped slowly away from the phone, feeling her heart sink to her knees.

"I'm afraid Dr. Jenkins will no longer be able to care for Hairy," she said. "We can refer you to the only other behaviorist in the area, a Dr. Aaron Kramer in Annapolis, or to a veterinarian of your choosing."

"Isn't he Emma's ex-husband?" Thomas asked.

If Emma's assistant was surprised he knew about Aaron, she didn't let on. "Yes, he is. Shall I call—"

"I'd prefer to see Emma."

"Really? Well the thing is, Mr. Tobin, Dr. Jenkins doesn't want to see *you*. Capisce?"

Thomas could hardly believe he was getting the God-father brush-off from a Japanese-American vet assistant who, from what he recalled, dressed like a Spice Girl.

"Ms. Miki, isn't it?"

"Yes."

"Did Emma get the deliveries this morning?"

She snickered. "Sure did. The dog treats were an original touch. I was impressed."

"Thank you. But I take it Emma didn't feel the same way?"

"Oh, she liked the treats well enough—just not the treatment."

Thomas closed his eyes and sighed. Velvet Miki was apparently Emma's bodyguard as well as employee, and she had the protective instincts of a junkyard pit bull. His chances of getting by her appeared slim.

"Hey, Velvet, do you think you might be able to help me out here? All I want to do is apologize in person. Talk to Emma. I know I screwed up. I . . . I'm not all that smooth with women."

She laughed. "You don't say?"

"Look—"

"Actually, I think I *can* help you, Mr. Tobin." Velvet's voice seemed quite cheerful. "My suggestion would be that with your next victim, try to work up to the Count Dracula thing instead of springing it on a girl right off."

Thomas had a bad feeling about where this conversation was headed, and swallowed hard. "I'm not sure I understand."

"You chomped down on Emma's ear, then hit the road! I think it might have been a bit disconcerting for her. What do you think?"

Thomas winced.

"She's a sweet woman who's had a rough time lately. She deserves better—in fact, she deserves the very best there is—in men and in life."

"Yes, she does."

Thomas knew he must sound like the idiot he was, but everything Velvet said was true. Emma did deserve the best, and he was well aware that he fell short of that mark. "Just tell her I called. Would you do that?"

Velvet was quiet for a moment, then said, "Yeah. I can do that."

Thomas thought he detected a trace of regret in her voice.

He couldn't stand it another nanosecond. Thomas flipped the sheet off his legs, gingerly sat up on the edge of the bed and heaved himself to a stand.

By the time he got downstairs and ripped the pillowcase off the dog crate, the ungodly noise had ceased.

"Listen up, pal. You're disturbing the peace. I'm tired. And if you don't shut the fuck up I won't be held account-able for my actions. Got it?"

I'm so lonely, Big Alpha. So cold and afraid. I need to be close to someone warm, feel their touch. Take me with you! Get me out of here!

Thomas replaced the pillowcase and began to walk away when the racket started up again. It was a high-pitched keening sound, like the screams from miniature demons from hell interspersed with those little "yips!" that felt like knitting needles being rammed into his ear canals.

I'm going to die if I have to be alone one more night! Please!

"God!" Thomas turned on his heels, threw the pillow-case across the room, and opened the latch. He reached in for Hairy and crammed him into the crook of his arm as he staggered back up the stairs to his bedroom.

"Here. Lie down right here and shut your damn yap." He dropped Hairy to the rug next to his bed. "I'll be up here."

Thomas returned to the bliss of lying flat, pulled the sheet over his legs, and closed his eyes.

This was not working out.

Sure, Hairy was getting better, but the weirdness factor was just too damn high for him to take much longer. Thomas had hit the wall earlier that evening, when he'd found Hairy snuggling up with a pair of his boxer shorts.

Apparently, none of the goddamn squeaky toys did a thing for Hairy. None of the fuzzy little beanbag things, either. None of the chewy rings or the bumpy rubber balls seemed to float his boat.

So what *did* Hairy want? He wanted Thomas's boxer shorts—the white pair stamped with purple and black Ravens football team logos. He carried them in his mouth all over the house. He buried them under the couch. He slept on top of them. He wadded them up and pounced on them.

Thomas eventually tricked Hairy into giving up the damn things. He threw them in the bathroom laundry hamper and shut the closet door, thinking that would be the end of that. But Hairy sat down in front of the door and pined for them, whining and pacing and making pitiful noises that Thomas just couldn't take.

Thomas lay on his back now, staring at the dark ceiling, groaning. All right, so he caved—he gave the dog the shorts. But damn! At least he'd washed them first. There were some things that were just too strange to allow to happen in this world.

Thomas felt himself grin in the dark, remembering how the little mutant sat patiently in front of the washer, then the dryer, his tail wagging. He'd given the boxers back to the dog only after he'd tied them in knots. He figured that if anyone happened to see them hanging from Hairy's mouth, they wouldn't immediately see that the dog had an abnormal attachment to a pair of underwear.

Jesus God, the dog was weird.

Thomas rubbed his face with his hands and tried to go back to sleep. But not two blissful minutes had passed before he felt the dainty impact of dog paws on the mattress, then the pinch of little feet going up his shin, to his thigh, to his bare stomach, then to his chest. Thomas kept his fists clenched at his sides, fighting the urge to fling the six-pound pain in the ass across the room.

At that point, the circling began—tight and fast little spins that went on and on until Hairy apparently thought he'd rearranged Thomas's chest hair to perfection.

Hairy plopped down with a sigh, dropping the pair of boxers next to Thomas's head. The dog curled up and managed to bury his pointy snout in the cozy hollow beneath Thomas's chin.

Thomas lay perfectly still. He tried to relax his fists and breathe normally. He felt the dog's warm skin against his own and looked down his nose to watch the dog's shock of white Billy Idol hair rise and fall with each of his own breaths.

This was plenty weird, Thomas realized, but not in a completely bad way. Just odd. Unusual. But not utterly awful. He tried to ignore the fact that he had an ugly dog sleeping on top of him and closed his eyes.

And before he knew it, he was having The Dream again. But this time it was more than a simple rehashing of the most miserable day of his life. This time, it was worse.

As usual, Rollo sat across the desk from them in his white coat with the black embroidery on the pocket—*Rollo Phelps, M.D., Chesapeake Urology Center*. He was using the same words he always did: injury; motility; rupture; antibodies; infertility.

Rollo spewed out the usual numbers. A normal man has twenty-five to fifty million sperm per milliliter—and Thomas had one million. About half of a normal man's sperm are damaged or deformed in some way—for Thomas, it was ninety percent. And about fifty percent of a normal man's sperm have the horsepower to make the long journey toward an egg—but it was only one percent for Thomas.

And then Rollo reviewed all the options available to them—steroid treatments, in-vitro fertilization, some kind of new sperm injection technology.

But at this point in the dream, things veered off into a completely new direction. Thomas turned to watch Nina rise from her chair and give the speech she always gave at this juncture—*"You've never been overly interested in getting married and having a family, and now it appears you couldn't have children if you wanted to. I'm taking this as a sign. It's over."*

But this time it wasn't Nina giving the speech.

It was Emma.

This time, a dark, curly head didn't turn to give him that look of pity and reproach—it came with a flip of a mahogany braid.

The eyes weren't dark brown—they were powder blue.

It wasn't Nina's voice he heard say *"I'm not wasting one more minute of my life with you."* It was Emma's voice.

The door shut behind her with finality. Then Rollo said, as he always did at this point, "God, Thomas. I'm so sorry."

Thomas turned to face his friend. But Rollo wasn't Rollo anymore, and the black embroidered pocket of the doctor's coat now read *Punk-Ass Stock Boy, CVS,* and the kid smirked at him, then busted a gut laughing and said, "Girlfriend? In your dreams, sucker!"

At this point, Thomas began to surface from the bizarre dream world to a waking state, pulled along by the most outrageously delicious physical sensation he'd ever experienced. Emma—sweet, soft, sexy, unbearably female Emma—was nibbling on his unshaven face, giving little fleabites to the tiny hairs growing along his jaw, moving to the stubble on his upper lip, heading toward his mouth for what promised to be a hot, passionate kiss . . .

Thomas woke with a shout, staring into the bug-eyes of the mutant.

Whoa, relax, Big Alpha! We need to get you together with Soft Hands—and soon.

Hairy yawned.

I slept great. How about you?

Aaron hated to admit it, but he had the hands of a killer. In the light from the motel reading lamp, he could see scratches from where Slick had fought him like a wildcat— using his nails and teeth and kicking and spitting, the little son of a bitch!

The wounds were mostly healed, but Aaron could see faint lines of new pink skin, and it spooked him.

The whole business of killing had made him sick. And now he was going to have to do it again.

Aaron sighed and let his gaze travel around Room 4 of the King of Hearts Motor Court. He'd relocated here and closed the clinic indefinitely to avoid another unpleasant encounter with the Ugly One. He'd had to fire the office girl because he had no money to keep her—he certainly couldn't pay her with the credit card of dubious origin he'd used at check-in, could he?

He took a swig of whiskey and shuddered. Aaron had only started drinking this week and thought the stuff tasted like piss. But he sure loved the effect. There was a time when he'd been proud that he'd managed to dodge the alcohol bullet, but it just didn't matter anymore. Nothing did.

Well, hell. He might be backed up against a wall, but he wasn't an idiot. He knew the secret was to keep the blood off his hands, so this time he planned to be far away—Atlantic City maybe—making sure lots of people saw him.

With one last swallow for the road, Aaron left his motel room. He drove a half-hour to some rotten neighborhood, stopped at the first pay phone he saw, and called the number the prostitute had given him. Some guy named Tom.

He got his *voice mail*. Even hit men had voice mail.

Chapter 7

If I Can't Have You

Emma stared into the full-length mirror on the back of her office door and sighed. She looked fine. Just fine. It would all be fine.

Velvet had tried to convince her to wear the infamous blue dress for this little get-together with Mr. Traffic Court. Emma told her she was out of her mind—on many levels. First, it wasn't even a date—it was one after-work drink. Second, she'd never, ever meet a stranger wearing that dress. It was just too *come-hither*.

Emma purchased the thing only because Velvet had browbeaten her, insisting that she looked fabulous in it. Emma wasn't so sure. The sleeveless smoky blue dress had a little ruffle that fell a good two inches above the knee and a deep, wide plunge of a neckline that, in Emma's opinion, showed way too much of everything she had way too much of.

She'd probably never have the courage to wear the dress anywhere. It was the kind of dress worn by a woman with a surplus of self-confidence, the kind of woman who wasn't afraid to demand the attention of a crowd—or one man in particular.

Emma gave herself another appraisal. No way was to-night the night to break out the blue dress. Maybe there would never be a night. Maybe it would forever stay where it had been for three months now—hanging limp in the back of her closet in a dry cleaner's bag, asking for no one's attention, putting nothing on the line.

She'd chosen wisely tonight, opting for a pair of black crop pants, black sandals, and little black print tee with cap sleeves and a scoop neck. She'd let her hair fall straight down her back. The total effect didn't scream anything, but it was stylish and casual and she felt comfortable.

She was as ready as she was ever going to be.

Mr. Traffic Court had a name, as it turned out—Jason DuPont. In the last few days, she'd learned enough about him to decide that his issues index was low enough to warrant a drink. It turned out he was Marcus's boss. He'd lost his license not because of DUIs, but after causing one too many fender benders while dividing his attention between a digital phone and the brakes. So she agreed to meet him on one condition—she could use the worst-case scenario transportation plan. Mr. Digital agreed.

The plan called for her to pick him up at his downtown office and drive them to the bar. They'd have one drink and chat. Then she'd take him back to his office, where he would get a cab home. This would allow for a clean getaway for Emma, with nobody going to anyone's private residence where there would be any awkward moments in front of anyone's door.

It would all be fine.

After one last glance in the mirror, Emma locked up the office, climbed into her battered Montero, and began the drive into the city. She wished she could muster up some enthusiasm about tonight, but all she felt was jittery and uncomfortable.

And all she thought about was Thomas Tobin, dammit!

Go away, she told him, but in her imagination he gave her that smile from the VetMed waiting room and she had to sigh like a teenager. *Go away and leave me alone!*

Emma drove, glad to be going against traffic during the evening rush hour, trying to concentrate on the road and failing, probably as big a safety hazard as Mr. Digital ever was. Emma's thoughts kept circling along the same maddening path: Thomas to Leelee, Leelee to Becca, Becca to herself, herself to Aaron, and back to Thomas again. The crazy cycle was surely due to guilt—several days had passed and she hadn't yet acknowledged Thomas's gifts. For good reason, however—she still didn't know what she should say, or even what she *wanted* to say. She still didn't know what to do about Thomas Tobin.

The talk she'd had with Leelee last night hadn't helped matters.

It was past midnight when Leelee tiptoed into Emma's bedroom, crawled under the covers, and pressed her little body against Emma's back. In the darkness, Emma listened to Leelee's whispered words, knowing she felt more comfortable in the dark, where Emma couldn't see her cry.

"Tell me something more about her." Leelee wrapped a skinny arm around Emma's waist. "Tell me about the time that thing fell out of her dress at the dance."

Emma smiled to herself in the dark, a rush of love and grief accompanying the image of Becca at fifteen—so much like the little girl now cuddled to her back—wickedly smart, shockingly blunt, the jaw-dropping beauty just beginning to emerge.

Rebecca Weaverton had been Emma's best friend since kindergarten, and stayed her best friend no matter how many years went by, how the miles or the dreams separated them, and no matter how each of them stumbled.

Emma had loved Becca with a force that was part hero worship, part jealousy, and all magic. They were two halves of one whole, Becca with her pale blond curls and eyes the color of butterscotch, Emma with her straight dark hair, freckles, and and baby blues. From age five to age eighteen, every weekend, every summer, every day had its beginning and ending with Emma and Becca together. They shared every secret.

Except one: Emma secretly wished that some of her best friend's sparkle would rub off on her, some of her shine and glamour. Emma always felt just a little bit like a dirty penny when standing right next to the too-bright gold of Rebecca Weaverton.

Getting the news that Becca was dead and Leelee was hers had felt to Emma like a punch to the gut followed by a slap across the face. A year had passed since that day, and she'd yet to recover from the blow that had changed her life.

"Mom was just a few years older than me then, right?"

"Yes, she was. It was the Sweetheart Dance and our band was the featured act. Becca was convinced she looked too flat-chested in her dress because one girl in our class— Frankie Seibert—had really come into her own, if you get my drift. I mean big time. She left the rest of us in the dust."

"I can relate," Leelee said with a sigh. "It's Melinda Stockslager in my class."

"Already? Sorry to hear that." Emma gave Leelee's hand a comforting pat and the girl hugged her tighter. "Anyway, we didn't have the high-tech water-filled bras they have now, so we stuffed two of Beck's handkerchiefs with quilt batting and sewed them up on my mom's machine." Emma chuckled. "They weren't pretty but they did the job. Your mom got up there on the stage and looked just like Madonna—from the early days, not the cone-shaped things she had in the nineties."

"Got it. But didn't anybody notice she'd sprouted hooters overnight?"

"Nice language, Leelee," Emma said, still laughing.

"Yes, they most definitely did. It was *the* hot topic at the dance. But she got up there with the microphone and started prancing around and no one dared say anything to her face. She would have denied it, anyway."

"She always did have a special gift for denial," Leelee said dryly. "So tell me the part where one fell out."

Emma started to shake with giggles. "I was back on drums as usual, and she was skipping across the stage, her hair flying—I think we were doing 'Love Is a Battlefield'— and I look up and see that your mother is definitely off kilter. She had a cantaloupe on one side and a Ping-Pong ball on the other."

Leelee laughed. "What did you do?"

"Well, I started winking and yelling at her and waving my drumsticks and she looked at me like I'd lost my mind. I *had* lost the beat, let me tell you."

Leelee was roaring with laughter now. "I can just see it," she said. "You guys must have sucked."

Emma laughed, too. "Oh, honey, we sucked big time."

Leelee kissed the back of Emma's head. "So what happened next, Em?"

She sighed, catching her breath from the tenderness of Leelee's kiss more than the laughter. "Well, she looked down at her feet and there was the falsie—right in the middle of the stage. So with a big dramatic windup, she throws that sucker right out onto the gym floor. Some guy catches it and throws it into the air. Then the next thing I know, she reaches down her dress and whips the other one out into the audience.

"Then. Oh, God, Leelee—after the show she autographed them for a couple guys on the junior varsity football team!"

"Mom was like that, wasn't she? She had balls."

"Nice language, again, but yes. She did."

"Did everyone really think she was going to be famous one day?"

"Oh, sure, sweetheart. She was the local celebrity. And it wasn't just how pretty and talented she was—it was how alive she was, how her mind was on fire all the time. She was something else." Emma paused for a moment. "You are so much like her, Lee."

"But I don't want to be like her."

"She loved you more than anything."

"So she said." Leelee's voice came out a whisper. "She screwed up so bad—wasting that scholarship, falling in love every three days. She never even tried to find out who my father was. Why did she have to be like that, Em?"

Good questions, all of them, Emma knew. Becca was chaos theory in a short skirt, barely making a living as a screenwriter/waitress/actress/singer and anything else she could find. And never making apologies for any of it.

"We all make poor choices sometimes, Lee. We're human. It's the way we learn. And I think maybe for a woman as smart as your mom was, she was a real slow learner in some areas." Emma felt a little sob shudder through Leelee's thin body. "Becca didn't do such a great job at being your mom, but I know she never meant to hurt you. She did the best she could and now I'm lucky enough to get to do the best I can. And I'm bound to make mistakes. I hope you'll forgive me when I do."

Leelee was so quiet for so long that Emma thought she'd fallen asleep. It was a surprise to hear the next question. "Are you ever going to get married again?"

Emma flipped over and rose up on an elbow to see Leelee's face in the moonlight. The young girl's eyes were wide and sad and Emma nearly cried herself.

"Oh, sweetie! I just got rid of the old model. I think I'll take a breather if you don't mind."

Leelee laughed at that and sat up tailor-style, staring at

her hands. "It's just that, well, the man who sent you all the flowers—" Leelee raised her eyes to Emma's. "I heard his voice on the phone. He sounded excited when he thought it was you. He really likes you."

Emma sat up quickly. She cupped Leelee's fragile-looking face in her hands and tried to smile. "That man means nothing to me, Leelee. He's the owner of a patient and he's . . . well . . . I thought at first there might be something special about him, but I think I was wrong."

She stroked Leelee's cheek. "Just between you and me, I'm not all that optimistic about men right now, and I sure don't see myself starting a serious relationship anytime soon, especially with Mr. Gift Basket."

Leelee nodded, her eyes beginning to sparkle with laughter.

"But sweetie, even if I do fall in love somewhere *way* down the road, I'd still love you. You'd still be my girl. I wouldn't go anywhere or leave you behind. Do you understand that?"

Leelee nodded. "Okay."

"I won't do anything without consulting you. We're a team, and we're going to make the big decisions together."

"Thank you for saying that. Nobody's ever said that to me before."

The relief in Leelee's eyes broke Emma's heart, and she hugged her tight and rocked her in her arms, cursing Becca for being such a screwup, cursing herself for being clueless about parenting, cursing the day Thomas Tobin walked into her exam room and invaded her life like a horde of Vikings.

Exceptionally attractive Vikings . . .

Emma made it to Mr. Traffic Court's office building with a few minutes to spare, and pulled to the curb. A handsome, fortyish man in an expensive suit ambled up to her passenger door and leaned into the open window.

Emma noticed right away that he had lovely green eyes and a great smile.

"So," said her first date in nearly two months. "Looking for a good time?"

Several well-meaning people in Thomas's life had mentioned that he harbored an abnormal number of pet peeves, but he stood by the fact that each and every one of them could be easily defended. Stupid people—that was his number one pet peeve, and it was self-explanatory.

That one was followed closely by nosy people because privacy was sacrosanct; top-forty music because it was homogenized pabulum that ruined society's ability to appreciate real music; shopping malls because they proved that all of America had become a vast wasteland of brainwashed consumerism; and people showing up at his home without a fucking invitation—*because he absolutely hated it*!

Thomas opened the door with a snarl, only to be pushed aside by his sister, Pam, his two rowdy nephews, and an apologetic-looking Rollo, squinting in embarrassment over two overflowing grocery bags.

"When Mohammed couldn't move the mountain he decided to hit the road!" Pam called over her shoulder, heading into Thomas's kitchen.

"Or something to that effect," he muttered.

Pam had already returned for the bags clutched in Rollo's arms. She dropped them on the kitchen table, then promptly came back to the living room, where she stood before her brother, hands on hips.

"This music depresses the crap out of me."

"It's supposed to. It's Tom Waits— Hey, do you *mind*?"

Pam had already switched off his CD player and returned to her position in front of him, her feet in a wide don't-mess-with-me older-sister stance.

He might have been six inches taller and a good eighty pounds heavier than Pam, but she was still two years older, still the person who had been there for him when their mother skipped town all those years ago. And that would always matter between them.

Pam lifted her chin up to Thomas, and he glared down at a pair of gray eyes he knew were nearly identical to his own. She sniffed. "We're having chicken Parmesan, linguine, salad, and garlic bread. Hope you haven't already eaten." Then she turned back toward the kitchen.

"Would it matter if I had, General Mussolini?" he called after her. "Besides, it's five-thirty! Who eats at five-thirty?" Then he muttered curse words under his breath as the boys hung on his legs.

Pam busily unpacked the groceries, keeping her back to her brother. "You've been avoiding us like we had the Hanta virus or something, and I won't put up with it anymore." She turned and shook the box of pasta at him. "With Dad gone we're the only family you have, and I won't stand for your 'I vant to be alone' crap." Pam was now going through his kitchen cabinets. "Do you have any oregano?"

Thomas looked at Rollo and growled. His brother-in-law shrugged, then whispered, "The good news is that I scored a couple Robustos."

"Yeah? So what? I can't smoke in the house anymore because of the allergic mutant rat-face—remember?"

"Oh. Right. But we can go out on the back porch, can't we?"

Pam called out from the kitchen. "Where do you keep your food processor?"

"Sorry, don't have one," Thomas said brightly. "But if I'd known you were coming I would've run right out and purchased the finest model available."

She ignored his sarcasm. "Blender then?"

"In the pantry. Bottom left shelf. But I don't know if it still has all its parts. It hasn't been used since—" Thomas caught himself before he said "since Nina left me."

"Ewww, gross!" Jack stood in the middle of the living room bent at the waist, staring under the coffee table with excited blue eyes and pink cheeks. "Uncle T! Uncle T! There's something in here and it's chewing on your underwear! You gotta see this!"

Hairy made a break from his hiding place and ran as fast as his spindly legs could carry him through the living room, the boxer shorts flapping in the wind from between clenched teeth. The dog shot through the dining room and into the kitchen, where he skidded to a halt at Pam's feet, trembling.

The boys were right behind him.

Uh-oh. I'm going to die now.

"Can I touch it? Can I pick it up?" Petey's face was shining with wonder. "Daddy told me you had an ugly dog but this is really super ugly, Uncle T! Where did you find it?"

Pam reached down to save the dog, frowning, then stared at her brother in disbelief. "Thomas?"

Oh, dear God. The maxi pad. Pam would never let him forget that as long as he lived.

"Give him to me." Thomas grabbed Hairy, whipped off the urine defense system, and opened the back door, tossing the dog outside. "Why don't you guys go play with Hairy?"

Thomas watched Jack and Petey chase the dog, screaming and laughing. Hairy suddenly stopped, sat perfectly still, and dropped the boxer shorts on the grass in surrender.

"Do you think they'll kill him?" Pam asked Rollo in an earnest whisper. "I just keep thinking of that stuffed bunny they ripped to shreds."

"They'll do all right. Look! They're playing toss with him!"

While Pam and Rollo were distracted, Thomas slyly shoved the sweat sock and maxi pad under the kitchen sink, hoping Pam would forget what she saw. Then he came up behind them and watched the boys and Hairy romp around the small fenced yard.

But Pam didn't forget, and a moment later she crossed her arms over her chest, leaned back against the counter, and studied her brother.

"What?"

She smiled sweetly. "Your dog wears a menstrual pad and chews on your underwear—these are very unusual things, Thomas."

He rolled his eyes, then an idea occurred to him. "Hey!" he said brightly. "You want it?"

"Ohhh, nooo—I couldn't do that," she said, her smile widening. "It's obvious you two were meant for each other."

The kids and Hairy played while Thomas threw together a salad and put water on to boil, Rollo smeared butter and garlic on the loaf of Italian bread, and Pam did whatever she was doing to the chicken breasts.

His sister had selected Sibelius's Symphony No. 2 in D from his extensive classical collection. And as he hummed along, Thomas had to admit the Phelps Brigade's invasion hadn't turned out all that bad. Had it really been six months since they'd all sat down for a meal together?

Was it true that they'd not done this since Nina was out of the picture? Thomas caught Rollo looking his way, and figured the insightful Dr. Phelps was probably thinking the same damn thing—and was probably worrying about him again.

He wished Pam and Rollo would stop worrying about him. He was fine. Just fine.

The back door flew open then, and the boys and Hairy tromped through the kitchen looking like old pals.

"Hairy's pretty cool, Uncle T," Petey said.

Thomas grunted noncommittally.

Then Pam turned on the blender.

And all hell broke loose.

"Stop it, Thomas! You're torturing the poor thing!"

"I'm not torturing anybody, Pam! I'm simply interview-ing a witness."

"Oh, God help us," she said, throwing down the dish-towel and stomping back to the oven.

The bad man. The bad man.

The blender! Oh, how I hate the sound of the blender! It went on and on and on!

"Okay, little buddy. You did good. We're done."

Thomas grabbed a Beggin' Strip from the pantry and tore it into a dozen small pieces and held it behind his back. He lowered himself to his knees.

Pam, Rollo, and the boys watched in silence.

"We're going to use our relaxation exercises," Thomas explained in a soft voice, looking up at the crowd. "Give us a little room, okay?"

They stepped back.

"Emma says the object is distraction—when Hairy pays attention to me and the dog treat, he momentarily forgets what he was so upset about and he begins to calm down." Thomas took one bit of treat and held it up to his right eye. "Look," he said in a high sing-song. "Come."

Hairy tentatively came out from under the kitchen table, where he'd spent the last ten minutes the victim of Tho-mas's experimentation: Whenever Thomas turned on the blender, Hairy's ears flattened against his head, his tail curled between his legs, and he began shaking, howling, yipping, and peeing.

Then, as soon as Thomas turned it off, Hairy trembled, but unwound his body and became quiet.

"Come on, pal, you can do it. That's a good boy."

Hairy ventured forward and made eye contact with Thomas as he followed the path of the treat.

"Good boy, Hairy."

The dog took the treat and sat quietly in front of his kneeling master.

"Why are you on your knees?" Pam whispered, not wanting to disturb the fragile peace that had fallen over the room.

"Emma said that I'm so big and Hairy is so little that bending over him would be too intimidating. This way I'm closer to his level." Thomas brought another treat beside his eye. "Look. Oh, good boy, Hairy!"

Thomas repeated the exercise until he ran out of treats and enthusiastically called Hairy to him. The dog jumped into his arms and burrowed his snout into the crook of his master's neck. Thomas stroked him.

"It's all right, ace," he cooed. "I'm sorry I had to do that, but you did good work. I think you've helped me figure something out."

Thomas looked back up at the silent group.

"Emma says that dogs always do things for a reason." He stood up, grunting with stiffness, and removed a small vial of pills from the kitchen cabinet. He took a pinch of mozzarella from the counter and stuck the pill inside, then gave it to Hairy to eat.

"Emma prescribed Xanax for when he gets a panic attack—and this was the worst one yet—and he'd been doing so much better." He looked at his sister, Rollo, and the boys and noted they were staring at him with a combination of confusion and wonder.

"It's a long story, but I think Hairy witnessed a homicide and I just realized the dog isn't as stupid as I'd assumed. I think he may be able to help with the case."

Nobody's expression changed. "I know it sounds strange, and I can't go into the details, but I think Emma might be able to help me with this." Thomas felt himself smile. "I can't wait to tell her about it."

He placed Hairy on the kitchen floor and watched him follow Jack and Petey into the living room.

"Emma's going to love this," he mumbled to himself, just as he turned to see Pam and Rollo giving him open-mouthed stares.

"Exactly when did you perfect the Siegfried and Roy routine?" Pam asked, her brows pulled into a deep frown. "And who the *hell* is this Emma person and when *exactly* did you fall in love with her?"

Just then the doorbell rang, and before he could stop it from happening, that Mrs. Quatrocci woman was inside his home, handing Pam some kind of crispy dessert thing and being invited to stay for dinner.

Rollo pulled Thomas into the living room and looked at his friend, perplexed.

"Since when are you friendly with your neighbors?" he asked. "I thought you had a strict 'no human contact' thing going on."

"I do. At least I did."

Thomas's eyes fell hard on Hairy, who looked up from the slate foyer floor, trembling. Then Thomas headed up the stairs, mumbling, "I got to call some vet in Annapolis about Hairy. If anyone else shows up, don't answer the door."

Emma had been nursing her white wine for an hour, trying to look interested. Trying to stay focused. Trying to stay in the present moment.

On the bright side, Emma had to admit she'd been pleasantly surprised by Digital Phone Man—no, Jason, Jason, Jason, she reminded herself.

Jason was charming and gentlemanly. He'd opened the driver's side door for her in the parking lot and then held out the chair for her at the table.

He was smart—he'd started his own software design company, taken it public, and was now a millionaire.

He was interesting—he had just returned from a safari in Kenya and Tanzania and was building his own vacation cabin in the Garrett County mountains.

He was handsome enough and he had a decent sense of humor, even making light of his traffic court experience.

"With my new wireless headset and voice-activated dialing, I'm going to be the Han Solo of I-695."

So, all these things considered, why did Emma find that she was bored out of her skull?

Oh, damn, damn, damn! The only thing wrong with this man sitting across the table from her was that he wasn't Thomas Tobin. Now how completely insane was that?

"So, I was wondering if you'd like to take a romantic walk along a bed of broken glass, or maybe take a swim with me in the groundwater at the Aberdeen Proving Ground?"

Emma snapped out of her fog, thinking for sure she'd just heard something strange from Digital Phone Man, but she didn't know exactly what because she hadn't been listening to a word he'd said—not one single word the whole night.

"Excuse me?"

He smiled tightly at her. "Forget it."

"Oh."

He laughed, set down his wineglass, and gazed at her across the candlelit table. He really was a nice-looking man.

"You know," he said, "I've never been out with a blow-up doll before."

Emma was startled by the hurt in his voice and tensed in her chair. "I'm so sorry," she said, letting out a huge sigh of relief, exasperation, and frustration all tangled up together. "I haven't been good company this evening. I've been distracted and I apologize. I don't know what's wrong with me."

"Oh, really?" Jason broke into a wide grin. "Then maybe I can help you out—you've been thinking about some man the whole night."

He reached for his wallet. "All I want to know is why you agreed to this in the first place if you're in love with some guy? Marcus was right—you're very pretty and sweet and I probably would have enjoyed this if you'd actually brought your brain along. What do you say we call it a night?"

Jason DuPont told Emma to head on home by herself and he'd get a taxi straight from the restaurant. He kissed her cheek at the hostess stand, and she felt like a complete witch.

She apologized again, hearing herself say something about the timing, and thanked him again for the drink. Then she drove home like a bat out of hell.

She was in the door by seven, and Beckett jumped off the couch in surprise. "Hey! What—"

"I'm gonna change and play my drums!" she called, bolting up the stairs to her bedroom.

Beckett stood in the foyer with his fists on his hips, the *TV Guide* dangling from one hand. "That bad, huh? Wait! Where did you put my earplugs? And keep it to a dull pounding, would you? It's a school night and Leelee's got to concentrate on her homework!"

"Like that's possible around here!" a faint voice called out from behind a closed bedroom door.

• • •

It was just after eight when Thomas knocked politely on
the wide, polished oak door of a pretty old house set far
off the road. He hadn't spent much time in Carroll County,
but the red-brick house reminded him of his grandparents'
place on the Eastern Shore—the same kind of early twen-
tieth century no-nonsense construction with lots of wood
trim, wide doorways, and square angles.

A mostly bald older man opened the door and smiled at
him from behind the screen. Emma's father—he could tell
it immediately. The lined face was dominated by a broad,
sincere smile that offered welcome, even to a stranger, and
the eyes were a soft blue.

At the man's feet was a big three-legged dog with
rheumy eyes, sniffing the air in excitement. He probably
smelled Hairy, who was trying to hide behind Thomas's
ankles.

"Yes, son? Are you here to save my soul? If you are, I
should warn you that you're a few decades late, but come
on in and have a seat."

Thomas found himself entering a big open foyer with
oak floors, a gleaming set of wide stairs, and homey wallpaper. "I'm sorry, but do you mind if I bring in my dog?
I can keep him in my arms."

The old man was beginning to gesture him through a
broad set of pocket doors but turned—and stopped dead.
He stared at Hairy, his face showing a range of reactions,
from mirth to disbelief.

"Lord Almighty, son. That little thing looks like it fell
out of the ugly tree and hit every branch on the way down."

Thomas couldn't help but laugh. "Yes, sir. I think that's
exactly what happened."

Beckett shook his head and pointed to a couch facing

the fireplace. "Why not? Bring him in. I don't think Ray's going to eat him."

Thomas sat. The blind dog hobbled over and plopped down by his feet, sniffing and licking at Hairy. The mutant trembled a bit but seemed to take the attention better than Thomas would have expected.

Thomas watched Emma's father ease himself into a comfortable wing chair and look him up and down. "So? Get to the point, son. You don't dress like any Mormon I've ever seen, so what are you selling?"

"Selling? Uh—"

"I'll be real honest with you." Beckett leaned forward conspiratorially and smacked Thomas's knee with the *TV Guide*. "I'm willing to listen, but unless it gives me back all my hair and makes my willy do the rumba, I ain't buying."

Chapter 8

Turn the Beat Around

"I'm not selling anything, sir. My name is Thomas Tobin and I'm a special investigator with the Maryland State Police." He showed the old man his identification and reached across the coffee table to hand him a business card.

"Beckett Jenkins—retired farmer," Emma's father said with a grave nod. "What in the world brings you out here?"

"Well, I'd like to see Emma—uh, Dr. Jenkins. I'm working on a homicide investigation that might benefit from her expertise. Is she home?"

"Emma?" Beckett shook his head and laughed. "How's a vet going to help in a homicide case?"

"It's a long story, sir." Thomas looked around the high-ceilinged room, dominated by a huge fireplace with a wide oak mantel and matching bookcases on either side. The room was warm and beautiful in an unadorned way—kind of like Emma herself.

Just then Thomas realized the floor beneath his feet was vibrating, and he heard some kind of deep thumping sound, which appeared to be coming up through the heating vents. Then he heard what he swore was Emma, yelling.

"Were you ever a military man, Tobin?" Beckett asked. "I served during the occupation of Japan—Okinawa to be exact. Communications. It's something what's happening in our world today, wouldn't you say?"

"Yes, sir, it is." The sofa was quivering under his body. "No military service, sir. I'm an attorney. Is Emma—is she home?"

"Oh, sure, hell, sorry for my manners. Can't you hear her? She's downstairs banging on those damn drums. She had a date tonight, you know. Another man Velvet-san set her up with. She came home early, so she must not have liked him. The last one she cared for at all was that carpenter—did a great job on the barn stalls, but he's in prison now, did you know that?"

Thomas's eyes went wide. "Really?"

Beckett nodded. "I think I should warn you that my girl is probably not in a great mood. She's been down there banging for an hour and she only does that when things are pretty bad."

Beckett sat forward in his chair and leaned an elbow on his knee. "She's a divorcée, you know, used to be married to a real son of a bitch—had an eye for the ladies and couldn't hold on to a dollar bill to save his soul. A book-smart man, but not good enough for my girl. Never was."

Thomas blinked and stared at Beckett, then felt himself smiling. This guy was quite entertaining. He could see where Emma got her no-frills approach to life.

But then—oh, God! The most horrible stench wafted through the room, and it seemed to be coming from Ray, the three-legged dog.

"You like Monty Python, by any chance?" Beckett asked.

"Monty Python?" This kept getting weirder and weirder. Thomas was nearly gagging and his eyes began to water from the odor.

"Yeah, you know—'I fart in your general direction.'" Beckett laughed. "That's old Ray's specialty, and in my opinion, that has got to be the finest film in the history of modern cinema."

Thomas chuckled, trying not to breathe through his nose. "Sure. *Monty Python and the Holy Grail.*" He cleared his throat and in his best fake French accent he said, "Your mother is a hamster and your father smelt of elderberries!"

Beckett's eyes looked like shiny buttons ready to pop from his face. He tipped his head back and roared with laughter. "A Python man, are you? That's wonderful. Are you single? Come on—I'll show you to the basement. You want to leave that . . . that dog up here with us? We'll watch us some *Animal Planet.*"

Thomas left Hairy on the couch and prayed to God above that he wouldn't piss on anything—he was honoring his pledge to never take Hairy in public in the urine defense system. He followed Beckett to a narrow door just outside the kitchen, where the banging got much louder.

"She's got her headphones on, so you'll have to walk all the way down the steps, turn to the right, and wave your hands in the air to get her attention." Beckett opened the door, then yelled over the noise. "Don't think she'd hear you even if you screamed at the top of your lungs!"

Thomas mouthed a *thank you* before he started down the steep stairs. He held on to a flimsy handrail, ducked his head, and tried to get his eyes to adjust to the dim light. The place was more like a dungeon than a basement, with an uneven concrete floor, sweating stone foundation walls, and a few squat old windows open along the grass line for air. Junk furniture was piled against the walls.

He followed Beckett's instructions and turned to the right.

And he saw her.

Emma sat on a high stool near the far wall with her eyes closed in concentration. She glowed under light thrown off from a crooked old floor lamp. A set of red Ludwig drums was arranged in a semicircle around her on a worn square of olive-green carpet. She looked like she was floating on a little green island in the darkness.

Her skin was glistening with sweat. Her hair was piled in a messy knot on top of her head. She was wearing a bright blue sports bra and what looked like a pair of men's pajama bottoms cut off above the knee, and her Birkenstock sandals. A pair of oversized headphones covered her ears and she continued to bang the hell out of a snare, two toms, a bass drum, and four cymbals.

Thomas couldn't move. He could barely breathe.

Emma's eyes remained tightly closed and she was biting down on her lip and the sweat was pouring down her face—possibly mixed with tears, though it could have been a trick of the light—and every few seconds she'd call out a single word or part of a phrase.

Thomas was mesmerized. He had no idea what she was playing, but the beat was fast and relentless and seemed to be in perfect sync with the beat of his heart. The beat reminded him of sex.

She reminded him of sex.

She suddenly shouted, " 'Hello, I've waited here for you—ever long,' " then leaned her head back and rolled her neck around, apparently in ecstasy, alone with the rhythm she was making with her hands and feet and the lyrics and melody only she could hear. After a few moments, Thomas was certain he saw tears.

Dear God.

Then she let it rip with a bang-bang-bang-bang-bang— BOOM! Bang-bang-bang-bang-bang—BOOM! Bam . . . bam . . . bam . . . bam—TSING!

Oh, dear God.

The sweat and tears were rolling down the hollow of her throat into the deep scoop of her athletic bra, a rivulet forming in the tantalizing valley of her cleavage. Her breasts were so round. So full. Her nipples were hard. She was breathing faster and faster and then she really started to cry.

It occurred to Thomas that this was not right. He was intruding. What he was witnessing was private—or maybe way beyond private. What he was watching might be some kind of religious experience.

But his feet were riveted to the sloping floor and his eyes were popping out of his head and he couldn't move, couldn't breathe, because this Emma Jenkins was the most fascinating creature he'd ever seen in his life and this was the most overtly passionate thing he'd ever seen a woman do in his thirty-seven years on the planet—and she wasn't even naked!

She was wild. She was in a trance. Then she was looking right at him.

"Aaauuuggghhh!" Emma jumped off her stool and flattened herself against the back wall, pulling the headphone jack from the boom box in the process. The room pounded with head-banger rock music. She dropped the drumsticks. With wild eyes, she flipped off the sound, grabbed a hand towel, and wiped the sweat and tears from her face.

"What the *hell* are you doing in my basement?"

Emma stared at him, horrified, embarrassed, knowing she had to be beet red from the exertion and the shame. For an instant, she even considered that she might be hallucinating, that her fantasies had taken a worrisome new tack into the arena of plain old psychosis. She closed her eyes, then reopened to test her theory—he was still there.

"Emma. I'm sorry. I tried—"

"What the *hell* are you doing in my house?"

"I came to talk to you. Your dad let me in. I wanted to—"

"How did you even know where I live?" Then she laughed, wiping more tears. Her legs were shaking. Her chest was on fire from the humiliation. She covered her face with the towel for a brief second and turned away from him. Then she spun back around.

"What the *hell* do you want?" She suddenly realized she was gasping for breath and Thomas's eyes were fixed on her heaving chest. She looked down, then hurriedly plastered the hand towel over her sweaty torso. Then she screamed in frustration.

Nobody had *ever* seen her play her drums like that. Not Aaron. Not Velvet. Not Leelee. Not Beckett—no one. And definitely not in a sports bra with great big nipples on parade—while crying!

Emma stared at the man before her and could not remember a time in her life when she had felt more mortified, more violated. Her drums were just for her, her secret escape, her most private way to disappear from the world, from herself, from pain and loneliness.

"I apologize for intruding. I had no idea—"

She returned to the stool and let her face fall into her hands and began to rock herself back and forth. The towel slipped to the floor. "Please leave," she said, her voice muffled behind her hands.

"I'm sorry."

"Leave."

"Emma . . ."

She raised her head then, and Thomas was lanced by the combination of horror and sadness in her eyes. She looked like a trapped wild creature.

"You had no right to watch me," she said evenly, her voice quiet.

"I didn't mean to."

Emma didn't want this man to know this much about her. She didn't want him to know anything about her, right? He'd rejected her—then tried to woo her back of course, but still . . .

"What do you want, Mr. Tobin?"

He shifted his feet, not missing the cold way she'd addressed him. He also didn't miss the fact that he couldn't cut a break when it came to this woman, that since the moment he'd laid eyes on her he couldn't do a damn thing right.

He'd been tongue-tied, awkward, rude, conflicted, and not entirely truthful.

He'd played with her head. He'd invaded her space. He'd dreamed about her. He'd felt her up in the exam room.

He'd bitten her.

Was Pam right? Was he in love? And if so, was this what love did to a man? Is this what had happened to Leo Vasilich?

"I just want to talk to you for a few minutes."

She rested her elbows on her knees and glared at him. "What about?"

Thomas's pulse was hammering under his skin. He felt hot, bewildered. He really didn't want to hurt her or mess with her head again, but what was the best way to go about this? If he just blurted out that he couldn't stop thinking about her, she'd run away.

If he started off with the fact that he'd lied to her about his job, she'd tell him to get lost.

Maybe it would be best to start with what had happened with Hairy tonight. Hairy was neutral territory, right? Hairy seemed like the best option.

"Well, it's Hairy. He—"

"This is about your *dog*?" Emma's mouth fell open and she remained silent for a long moment before she could move, breathe, get her mouth to work. Eventually, she snorted with laughter. "Hoo, boy!"

She jumped up and rooted around on the floor for her pajama top. Her fingers flew angrily down the row of buttons while she cursed under her breath.

Thomas realized that he'd made a serious strategic error. "No. Wait. Emma. Not all of it. I—"

"I've already transferred your case." She shook out a sheet of clear plastic to cover the drum set and turned off the light behind her. She strode past him in the dimness.

"Please, Emma. Wait." Thomas reached for her hand but she jerked away. "Look—I called Aaron Kramer's answering service tonight and they told me I couldn't even talk to him for two weeks and I need help *now*. It's urgent."

Emma turned toward him and her lips parted in astonishment. What a bald-faced lie! Aaron hardly had enough patients to keep the lights on, as she well knew. Thomas could've gotten in to see him with ten minutes' notice!

"I sincerely doubt that," she said, heading up the stairs.

"It's true, Emma. Why would I lie about that?"

She'd reached the fourth step. When she turned to face him, she realized the position allowed her to tower over *him* for a change. It was a refreshing perspective, and it gave her courage. She scowled down at him.

"I don't know why you lie about anything, Thomas. I just know that you do. You seem to be a consistently dishonest person, and I choose not to spend time with dishonest people."

Thomas hissed from between clenched teeth and shook his head. "I don't lie, Emma."

"See, you're doing it again!" Her arms flew up from her sides in a gesture of futility. "It must be pathological. I can ask around about a good—"

"All right, fine. I didn't come here only because of Hairy, but that is part of it. I really do need your help. But I also need . . . well . . ." Thomas raked a hand through his hair and shut his eyes briefly. "Did you like the flowers and stuff?"

Emma lost her breath for an instant—Thomas had just raised big, gray, sad-puppy eyes to her. She scolded herself.

She would not cave to a pair of mournful eyes.

"I probably should've told you sooner, but yes. That was nice of you. Thanks."

"Well, I'm here to kind of follow up that." Thomas's voice was scratchy and hesitant. "I needed to apologize in person for what happened the other night. I needed to see you again."

Emma put her hands on her hips, which reminded her of the unattractive mess she was. She was wearing a pair of Beckett's old seersucker pajamas she'd hacked off with a pair of scissors. Her hair was a disaster, and she was sweating profusely. She must look like the Bride of Chucky.

"Oh, yeah? What exactly was it that happened the other night, Thomas? I haven't quite been able to figure that one out."

He nodded and rubbed a hand over his mouth and that's when Emma noticed the bandage.

"What did you do to yourself, Rugby Boy?" She took a step down and reached out for his hand, which proved to be a huge mistake. The innocent touch sent a jolt through her limbs that sparked and smoldered deep in her pelvis.

And as she cradled his hand, she realized she didn't have the slightest idea what to do with it. She stared at the muscle and bone, the calluses, the short, square nails, as her blood pounded and her vision blurred.

What she *really* wanted to do was kiss his swollen knuckles. Lick his lifeline. Pull each of his fingertips into her mouth and suck on them one by one.

Horrified, she pushed it away, and his hand smacked with a thud against his thigh.

"Ow!" Thomas looked surprised. "You should probably stick to dogs and cats, Doc."

She laughed then, relieved to let go of some of her nervousness, some of her pent-up agitation. Then she watched as very slowly—very deliciously—Thomas smiled at her.

It was a deadly weapon, that smile of his, and she wondered if he was aware of its firepower. The smile hovered there, bracketed by deep masculine dimples, sexy and sweet, and it silently laid to waste her well-thought-out campaign of avoidance. Every objection she'd had, every perfectly logical reason she'd given herself for forgetting she'd ever met this man now lay bleeding at her feet.

A smile like that could not possibly lie, could it?

"God, Thomas. I can't believe you came to my house. Why did you come to my house?"

He gave his brawny shoulders a shrug and looked up from under a thick fringe of dark honey lashes. "I figured my best shot was to surprise you. You know, just kind of show up on your doorstep."

. . . if the right man ever showed up on her doorstep, her heart would know him in an instant . . .

"No way in hell," Emma whispered.

The whole of Thomas's body seemed to sag in defeat. "It was worth a try."

"No!" Emma reached out and grabbed his bare forearm and the touch was once again electric. She let go immediately. "I didn't mean that . . . exactly." Her head was spinning. "Look, I'm going to take a quick shower and we can talk, all right? Have Beck get you something to drink. It'll just take a sec—"

"Emma, I'm not a liar and I'm sorry for leaving you the way I did." Thomas took a step up, bringing him within touching distance again.

Emma backed up one step, holding on to the railing. "Apology accepted . . . I guess."

"I'm sorry for biting you. Velvet told me you were disconcerted."

Emma raised an eyebrow at that. Disconcerted? Okay, sure. That and lambasted by lust . . .

"I don't usually bite women. I don't know what happened. I couldn't stop myself."

She nodded and swallowed. She was tingling, shaking, pulsing. "It happens."

Thomas's eyes flew wide. "It's happened to you before?"

"No. Not exactly. What I mean is . . . well . . . there are a variety of triggers for the biting response. Usually it's fear and insecurity."

He took another step up and she retreated again. She remembered originally thinking that his eyes were cool and calculating—well, baby, something had changed, because now the silver gaze was pure liquid heat, glimmering, alive with determination, desire, and humor.

It scared the living hell out of her.

"My problem is that I'm conflicted, Emma."

She snorted. "No kidding."

"So you've noticed?"

She nodded. "I've even come up with a name for your disorder. Want to hear it?"

His mouth quivered at the corners. "Do I have a choice?"

"It's the Thomas Tobin two-step—pull me close then push me away. Do-si-do. It's a snap to learn but it gets old real quick."

He smiled again and cocked his head. "I like you, Emma."

She swallowed. "Okay."

"A lot."

Her fingers were starting to go numb. "All right."

"That's not a lie."

"Glad to hear it."

"You make me laugh."

"Great."

"And I like your sense of style." He wagged an eyebrow. "But your buttons are crooked."

Emma looked down to confirm that observation. "How attractive," she mumbled, trying to manipulate the thin old buttons with unsteady fingers. She gave up with a groan.

"And I really do need your help. Will you help me, Miss Marple?"

She jerked her head back in sharp surprise and felt a bewildered smile spread across her face. He remembered her little talk about Agatha Christie? Why was that? she wondered.

"Help with what?" she asked, suddenly a bit more inclined to protect herself. She stepped back again.

"A couple things, actually." He took another step up.

"What things?"

"My dog, for one. I think that ugly little fu—uh, fellow—just might be able to identify a murderer."

"So you *are* some kind of cop! I knew it!"

"I'm a lawyer. That part wasn't a lie. But your instincts were right on. I do specialized work within the criminal justice system—for the state police. It's pretty complicated."

"Oh, I just bet it is," she said with a snort. It seemed everything about Thomas Tobin was pretty complicated.

"But I'll tell you all about it."

"I can't wait. So what else?" She took a step back.

"You mean besides Hairy?" Thomas took a step up and pressed close, bringing his body a hairsbreadth from hers. Emma could feel the heat lightning shooting out from him again, but didn't have the wherewithal to move. She'd lost the ability to resist, probably because her bones had turned to overcooked pasta in his heat.

"Well, Emma, I think I'm suffering from a lack of something in my life."

"Really?" Emma's eyes widened. "Iron? B-twelve?" *It damn sure wasn't testosterone.*

One side of Thomas's mouth hitched up, creating a deep

dimple in his cheek again. He cocked an eyebrow. "You're cute, too."

"Oh, gee, thanks."

God. She needed to regain her ability to think. And though it had occurred to her that she could easily clasp her arms around his neck, fling her legs around his waist, and slurp him up right there on the basement steps, the idea wasn't all that practical. Beckett and Leelee were home and the steps were rickety.

"I'll meet you on the front porch in a few minutes." She turned and ran while she still could.

As Thomas watched her voluptuous backside bounce up the steps, the appreciation he felt for Emma Jenkins slammed into him on all possible levels of consciousness.

Physical? Oh, hell, yeah—he wanted her, sweaty and naked right here on the stairs, right now and forever, his hands all over that ass of hers, his mouth all over her farm-girl skin.

Emotional? Yes, unbelievably so. It was nearly as strong as the hunger in his body and he didn't quite know how it had happened. But it seemed final somehow. Predetermined. Like walking into a stranger's house and knowing you were going to live there one day.

Intellectual? His mind had never clicked into place like this with a woman—not even Nina. Nor had he ever enjoyed talking to a woman as much. So, okay—that, too.

Metaphysical? Spiritual? Sure, why the hell not? If he was going down, he might as well go down in a giant ball of flame, so why not admit that he had felt the unseen hand of destiny the day he walked into her clinic? Weirder things had happened.

There was only one thing he wasn't sure of. He'd have to ask sooner or later, wouldn't he? It was for his protection, and, ultimately, hers.

"Hey, Emma?"

She turned around at the top step, her face flushed and beautiful and her chest rising hard and fast beneath the mis-buttoned pajama top. "Yeah?"

"What were you playing just now?" He inclined his head toward the drums.

"Foo Fighters—an offshoot of Nirvana." She saw the blank look on his face and smiled down at him. "Alternative rock."

"Are they a top-forty group?"

She shook her head, a bit bewildered by his question. "I don't think—but I don't listen to top-forty music."

Emma watched as he shoved his hands deep into the front pockets of his jeans, locked his eyes with hers, and let go with the sweetest, most heart-throttling smile she'd ever seen.

"Hurry up in the shower," he said.

Chapter 9

More, More, More

"My customary fee is two hundred dollars an hour."

Thomas felt his right eye twitch—dear God, he'd forgotten about money—and he could just picture Stephano's reaction when he got a load of *that* requisition form.

He gave a businesslike nod. "Of course. I'll arrange for a professional consulting fee."

Emma's face scrunched up and Thomas watched her nervously fluff her still-wet hair. They'd been sitting on the porch railing for half an hour or more, but her thick hair had yet to dry in the humid air, and slick sections gleamed in the light from the citronella candle between them.

"I don't mean to sound like a jerk about this, but I'll need a written consulting agreement with the state police that specifies how and what I'll be paid."

"You drive a hard bargain, Doctor."

He watched her caress the shock of white fur on Hairy's head. The dog was curled up in the space between her legs, snuggled into the folds of her loose skirt—damn mutant always got the best seat in the house.

"It's just that Aaron left me so much debt." She looked up at Thomas, her eyes full of worry and embarrassment. "Our practice—*my* practice—is on rocky footing right now. My time and expertise are my only capital and—"

"No need to explain, Emma. You're a professional. I need your help. We'll do it right—I wouldn't want this any other way."

Emma sighed, then flashed Thomas a smile that was part relief and part just plain gorgeous. *She* was just plain gorgeous.

She'd come out on the porch wearing this gauzy sundress thing with little straps, and Thomas had been unable to stop staring at her elegant neck and the dainty collarbones beneath the flawless skin. She was such an interesting combination of female loveliness and real strength. Her shoulders and upper arms were soft but obviously worked—wailing on drums, cleaning out horse stalls, comforting frightened animals.

The whole time he'd been sitting there telling her the truth about his job, he'd been lying to himself that he hadn't really noticed the graceful line to her jaw, the ladylike tilt to her head, or the pretty shape of her fingers.

But the truth was, he'd noticed all these things about her, and more.

The dress she'd chosen kind of hung on her like a sack, and except for the loose, square neckline, it managed to hide the goods real well. But the buzz Thomas got from looking at the shapeless dress was getting louder and louder in his brain, as if her modesty was pushing some hot button Thomas didn't even know he had.

As if her modesty was the sexiest thing he'd ever seen in his life.

Maybe it was because most of the beautiful women he'd ever known used their bodies as currency—a means to control men, trap them, turn their brains into mush so things happened the way they wanted them to. Always the way the woman wanted.

Yet Emma seemed to downplay her body, hide its power, with the simple tees, the baggy sweatshirts, the loose dress—and that's what drove him crazy. It made him wonder exactly what was under there—what juicy and round and firm sections of flesh lurked beneath the fabric—and whether they were simply too dangerous for public display.

God help him if she should ever wear anything even remotely revealing. He might stroke out on the spot.

"So how in the world did you get started with this, Thomas? You've got to have the strangest job of anyone I know."

He felt his grin spread from ear to ear. "Coming from you that's really saying something."

"Yeah. No kidding." She giggled and continued to pet Hairy. "You promised me the whole story."

He nodded. "It's simple, really. I was with the Baltimore County State's Attorney's Office about three years when I was assigned a murder solicitation case, and it ended up going to trial. I won. Then when the next one came in, I got it. Then the next. And pretty soon I'd prosecuted a dozen cases and become a kind of expert, and when the state put together a task force they asked me to head it up. That was seven years ago."

"What's it like posing as a hit man?"

He shrugged. "It's difficult, but there's a need."

"Have you ever thought of doing something else—something less . . . I don't know . . . depressing?"

He laughed at that and studied her lovely face. Sure, he had. He used to think about teaching, high school history maybe, where he could do some rugby coaching on the side. He used to think that as a teacher he might be able to prevent at least some kids from becoming the kind of adults he now encountered on a daily basis. But he was probably just kidding himself.

"Doesn't it get to you, Thomas?"

He watched her lean back against the wide brick pillar

and tilt her head. He couldn't remember the last time he'd allowed anyone to ask him questions this personal.

"Sure it gets to me. I've seen enough to know that people are capable of anything. And there are days when it seems like there isn't a decent person on the whole planet. But let's get back to Hairy."

"All right." Emma gave him a soft smile. "You were about to tell me how Hairy's owner met his untimely end."

"His name was Scott Slick," he said, relieved to change the subject. "Age forty-one. Ran a very successful sports betting operation in Baltimore. Died from blunt force trauma to the left temple, hit by the edge of a blender. There was a struggle. I think Hairy was hiding somewhere watching the whole thing. He was sitting by the body when I found Slick dead."

Emma's brows knit together. "Really? Sports betting?"

"Yeah—college and pro football and basketball mostly. But also boxing, hockey, even baseball."

"Hairy belonged to a bookie?"

Thomas laughed softly, amused to hear street slang from Emma's sweet mouth. "Yeah. A very rich bookie. And up until tonight, Hairy had been doing so much better. Then Pam turned on the blender . . ."

As Thomas described Hairy's extreme physical reaction to the sound, she realized he could be right—Hairy may have witnessed the crime. And Thomas may have even hit on the method they could use to glean more details from the dog.

"Besides the blender, have you exposed him to any other stimuli associated with the murder? Have you given him something to smell? To hear?"

Thomas shook his head. "I don't have anything."

"You have no physical evidence?"

"Well, a shoe print. Some trace skin and hair that's being analyzed, but nothing like the guy's shirt or something that

Hairy could get a good whiff of." He watched her nod. "What do you think?"

She shrugged. "We can try. We'll use a process of elimination, introduce one stimulus at a time and categorize his response." She saw Thomas give her a little frown. "Let's backtrack a bit. Dogs have basically four ways to deal with something they come across out in the world—we vets call it the four F's—flight, fear, fight, or . . . well . . . sex."

After a two-second beat, Thomas leaned his head back and laughed, then lowered his eyes right on hers. "*Sex* doesn't start with an *f*."

"Vet humor." Emma swallowed. "Anyway, it's going to take a while, and there is absolutely no guarantee that we'll come up with any helpful information."

"I understand."

"And you still want to hire me?"

Thomas nodded. "Hairy is our only witness. We've got to at least try."

Emma let her gaze fall to the creature in her lap. She stroked his warm skin and scratched behind his ear. "I'll have to think about this a little, establish a protocol for the tests. And I'd like to visit the crime scene and see whatever evidence the police have. Is that possible?"

"You got it, Doc."

"Then it's a deal." Emma stretched out her hand to shake on it. The second Thomas's warm palm slipped against hers, she remembered that touching him was hazardous to her peace of mind. She pulled back too quickly.

"A deal," Thomas repeated, kind enough not to let on that he noticed her nervousness.

They remained quiet, and Thomas looked out onto the sloping lawn in front of the farmhouse. He watched the fireflies flash, listened to the crickets talk. It was beautiful here, peaceful and dark and full of the smells of open land. It brought back memories of the summers he spent with his grandparents, memories long buried by the accumulated sensory assault of city life.

"I haven't seen this many lightning bugs since I was a kid." Thomas nodded toward nature's laser show. "It's wild."

"Yeah. And it's late in the season—I'm amazed they're still out here in those numbers." Emma's voice trailed off as she followed his gaze. "It's like the last singles dance of the year."

"Of their lives," he said.

Emma glanced at him, intrigued. Thomas Tobin continued to surprise her with his somewhat skewed take on the world and the combination of sorrow and humor that leaked out of him. His job went a long way toward explaining his pessimism, but there was more to Thomas than he was sharing with her. She could feel it.

He continued to look out on the grass with what Emma thought might be longing, and a touch of irony.

"Do you know anything about fireflies, Emma?"

"Mmm. A little." She took a deep breath of the night air, and got a whiff of Thomas himself—undertones of male musk with lighter notes of soap and—oregano, maybe? It made her shiver.

"I think I remember reading that the males fly up in the air and the females remain near the grass." She watched the dance of light on the lawn. "The flash we see is the result of a chemical reaction inside their bodies, and along with the flight pattern, it works like a kind of signal to attract potential mates. That's what all the commotion is about."

Thomas shot her a bemused smile. "Isn't it always?"

Emma said nothing, just studied him, watching the graceful turn of his head as he went back to scanning the yard. She wasn't certain what was happening here, but she knew it wasn't about fireflies. It was about the two of them—two very different people who had some kind of strange affinity for each other that neither knew what to do with.

She gave Thomas a good once-over, and the nervous fluttering in her belly was back with a vengeance. The man sitting in front of her was beautiful, something she'd known from the first. But tonight, she saw him with greater clarity, and appreciated what she saw—what she sensed. She felt her blood run hot and her breath quicken. She felt the anticipation build.

And she smiled to herself.

Emma knew the accepted theory on the human sexual response: males became aroused primarily from visual stimuli while females responded to an amalgam of more subtle sensory input—ambiance, so to speak. She looked over at Thomas and nearly snorted with laughter—she was a textbook example of the female sexual response tonight, no doubt about it.

And the stimuli she was getting right now were mighty stimulating indeed. Thomas radiated sexual heat. He broadcast his sexuality. His voice vibrated with it. His eyes sparkled with it. He smelled like sex.

She looked down at his body. He was wearing a pair of worn but nice-fitting jeans and a soft gray, short-sleeved Henley unbuttoned at the throat and untucked at the waist. He was in his usual Nikes with no socks.

His long legs were slung over either side of the wide, flat porch railing. He rested his palms on the thick surface of his muscled thighs as he leaned back. She stared at the way his golden hair shimmered in the candlelight, and the way the light played on the curly blond down of his ropy forearms. And yes, she let her eyes travel down his flat stomach to his narrow hips and the vortex of those big legs, and did a little mathematical calculation having to do with

relative size of anatomical parts. She hoped she wasn't
foaming at the mouth.

She jerked when she heard his voice.

"You got to hand it to the little bastards." Thomas
caught her eye. "They're out there in their flashiest outfits,
facing the possibility of rejection, giving it their best shot.
Those little bugs have guts."

Emma had been looking at his crotch—no doubt about
it. This was an excellent development, but Thomas didn't
quite see how he was going to capitalize on it.

Emma was sparking at him. There she was with her face
tilted coyly, flushing prettily with well-deserved embarrassment. Her hair fell loose on her shoulders and her eyes
shone up at him. A faint smile pulled on those kissable lips.
Her hands caressed Hairy gently and rhythmically—where
he sat between her legs.

Thomas bit his tongue and closed his eyes. With indirect
communication like this, who needed words?

He opened his eyes and locked his gaze with hers, knowing with certainty that biology had the upper hand tonight,
over there on the lawn and right here on the porch railing.
In fact, right about now, Thomas could say with confidence
that for him, biology had *become* reason. Biology ruled,
biology spoke, and God yes, he was listening.

He wanted this woman. She was special. She was different. He'd been waiting for her.

Could it possibly be that simple?

"I can't help but see that you're flashing at me," Thomas
whispered.

Emma's eyes went huge and she laughed nervously.
"Only because you've been flashing at me."

"How kind of you to notice."

"Would you like some more iced tea?" She'd abruptly
dumped Hairy into his arms, jumped off the railing, and
swept away their half-full iced tea glasses before he could

even respond. She was already inside the house, and he sat there, stunned.

If Thomas didn't kiss her soon, he would implode—no question about it. He had to fix things so that when she came back, he could nonchalantly get her into a good kissing position.

He placed Hairy on the floorboards of the porch. "Go play with stinky Ray." As if he understood, Hairy toddled over to the much larger animal and circled around by his side, then curled up and plopped down, soliciting only a few curious sniffs from the old, blind dog.

The front screen creaked open, then slammed shut, and Thomas turned to see Emma walking toward him on alluring bare feet. The foyer light shone through her filmy dress and provided a nice outline of her hips and breasts. Her hair lifted off her shoulders in the light breeze. It was like a scene in a wet dream, only better.

Emma gave him a shy smile and bent forward to put the glasses of tea on the table, and *oh, yeah,* Thomas looked down the neckline of her sundress. He tried not to. He really did. But he was too weak. And her breasts were creamy and full and looked like they'd fit perfectly in each of his big hands. They looked perfect. Perfect. Perfect. Perfect.

Implosion was imminent.

As Emma resumed her place across from Thomas, sitting cross-legged and leaning up against the column again, she saw that Thomas had done some rearranging in her absence. He'd moved the citronella candle behind him and left his pillar to scoot much closer to her. There was nothing between them anymore, and it made her a little nervous.

"What are you thinking?" he whispered.

That I want to jump you and howl at the moon, she thought. What she said was, "It's a beautiful night," and nearly rolled her eyes at her pitiful lack of imagination.

"The most beautiful I've seen in a long time, Emma."

Her heart stopped. "Really?"

She noticed that she'd somehow adjusted her position to mimic his. She'd straddled the smooth wooden shelf with bare legs, shoving the sundress down for coverage. When had she moved? Why couldn't she remember moving?

But she was now painfully aware of the exact location of every part of her body, because certain parts of her were starting to hum. Her breasts felt irritated and confined even in the loose dress. She felt her thighs fall open a bit more, relaxing, parting, and that small fine-tuning caused her to swell and moisten under her dress. She caught Thomas's eye and began to strum and tingle all over.

Hoo boy.

Emma needed to regroup. This was not the way it usually worked with her. She was usually slow to build, slow to burn—but there was nothing slow in the way she responded to Thomas. It was hard and fast and hot and like nothing she'd ever felt before in her life. Not with Aaron. Not with anyone.

And the kicker was he hadn't even touched her. She'd been rendered stupid just from looking at him. Being near him. Thinking about what it would be like to press her lips against his, place her palms against that muscled wall of a chest.

Thomas captured her eyes with his, so penetrating, and the corner of his mouth hitched up. Her head began to spin—had she really ever thought him cold and unfeeling? Had she called him "Robot Boy"? Hadn't she seen right from the start that this man was burning, scorching *alive*?

Of course she had. But she'd been protecting herself, staying smart, considerations that were apparently no longer important because the only thing that mattered to Emma was that he touch her. Now.

"Thomas?" she whispered, not sure what she was asking for, just that she was asking for it.

He scooted forward another notch and balanced his weight on his hands as he leaned in. Emma found herself doing the same, the inside of her wrists widening her legs as she leaned closer to him. She was buzzing with awareness and knowledge—of the proximity, the heat of him.

He moved closer, and Emma took in the masculine contours of his face in the low light, the solemn look in his eyes, and bit down on her lower lip in anticipation of his kiss—because kissing was exactly what was going to happen now and she damn well knew it.

Then Thomas narrowed his right eye—taking aim—and slowly dipped his head. His lips parted, showing a hint of his white teeth.

And he fired—his mouth was hot and smooth and as soon as his lips covered Emma's, she was lost.

Thomas shook, his whole body tensing and shuddering from the power of the kiss. For a blissful moment, he slipped his tongue along the seam of her sweet mouth, taking it, taking her, as if he was absolutely certain this was the right thing to do.

But the certainty was soon replaced by a sickening panic. She was a woman! He didn't trust women! And even if he could, she wouldn't want him. How could he have forgotten that little detail?

But then Emma parted her lips to receive him and the response was so earnest and trusting and female that he lost his train of thought. He moved his mouth against hers mindlessly, blindly, trying to remember what it was that he was concerned about, what was at the crux of his hesitation.

Right. This woman deserved the best. She deserved it all. And he'd never be able to give it to her.

He tried to pull away, but Emma's soft hands slipped up the sides of his neck and her fingers eased into his hair and a small gasp of need flowed from her mouth into his.

And that's when it happened—a great surge of confidence came over Thomas, clearing the way to her, disintegrating all his doubts, shouting a resounding "Yes!" to everything that was Emma. He didn't know where it came from, but he thanked God for it and rode the crest of this baffling force, feeling himself grow hotter, stronger, harder, until it took everything he had not to attack her like a platter of buffalo wings at a Super Bowl party.

God, she tasted sweet and smooth. She felt like wet silk, as soft as he knew she would. And somehow, for some reason, he was suddenly sure this would all work out in the end. It would be all right. It would be great. No doubt about it.

Thomas's kiss left Emma dizzy.

His lips were firm but gentle, and they slipped delicately, lovingly, over hers. His tongue was doing all kinds of remarkable things—sliding along her bottom lip, tasting, tempting, pushing, flicking. It was almost as if he was sampling a delicacy he'd never had before, something exotic. Then she heard him breathe her name against her mouth— "Emma"—and it sounded profoundly carnal, so much desperate need packed into two simple syllables. She was going down fast.

He pulled his lips away and hovered just inches from her face.

"I need you closer. I need to get my hands on you or I'm going to die."

His voice was strained, the look on his face pure need, and she found that all she could do was nod and swallow. Instantly, he cupped her bottom in his two big hands and pulled her to him, closing the gap between them with decisiveness. She fell forward, her hands slapping down onto the tops of his thighs. The worn denim did nothing to hide the muscle and heat beneath.

Then—oh, damn. His hands began to move over her bottom, stroking up and around, lifting from underneath with wicked fingers, squeezing, then finally coming to rest on her hips. It was a thoroughly possessive gesture that stunned her, and though somewhere in the back of her mind she realized she should be worrying about the fact that his hands were on the biggest asset she had, it didn't matter.

Her self-consciousness had melted in the heat of his gaze, his touch. His hands and eyes stayed locked where they were for a very long moment, enough time to pass a message to Emma: there was no turning back.

Then he grabbed her thighs and pulled her legs up and over his, scooping her up in his arms. She thudded against the hard, muscled front of his body and her head fell back from the force of it. He arched over her. He took her with his mouth.

Now this was some kiss, and Emma felt her body dissolve and become profoundly alive at the same instant. She held on through the shock wave of wonder and pleasure that came from being clasped in his powerful arms, prodded by his slick tongue. This was nothing but pure sensation, complete sensory overload, and she brought her arms around his rock-solid back and heard herself groan.

God, he was amazing! So big and dense and her hands wouldn't stay put on just one spot—they pushed down his hard biceps to his elbows, across his back and into the nape of his neck, and oh, she needed to feel his skin—skin on skin! Her fingers wiggled underneath his shirt, smoothed up his stomach, and landed on the scorching surface of his chest.

Oh, *daddy*!

Never in her life had she had anything remotely like Thomas Tobin in her hands. She could hardly believe he was real, and a single word throbbed through her brain like a mantra: *More. More. More.*

Then he hoisted her up onto his lap and there was no mistaking what had just jammed between her legs and she nearly screamed with the thrill of it. Thomas was a big man—just as she'd hypothesized—and the knowledge of that caused her brain to short-circuit.

So she pushed her sundress up around her waist.

Then she felt her hips begin a slow rotation, back and forth, up and down, side to side against his fabulous erection, as though—if she wiggled in just the right way, rubbed up against him in just the right spot—she could get through the barriers of silk, denim, and zipper to what she really wanted.

Him.

It slowly dawned on her that she was acting like a crazy woman.

Then she felt his hands travel up under the back of her sundress and toward the front of her body, where his palms spread wide over her bare breasts and he growled—there was no other word for it—he growled into her mouth as he drew big circles over her nipples with the flat of his palms, then pinched, rolled, until they stung with need.

Her lungs began to burn. Her toes began to curl. It was the beginning of the end.

"You want me right here, right now, don't you?" Thomas had freed his mouth from hers long enough to gasp into her ear. "Tell me what you want, Emma. I'll do it."

It occurred to her that unless something seriously huge happened in the next few seconds—on the scale of earthquake, fire, flood, or asteroid impact—she was about to drag Thomas Tobin to the barn, where she'd tell him exactly what she wanted and expect to get it. Big time.

Then she had the oddest sensation that they weren't alone.

She stopped her gyrations. She stilled her hands. "Stop," she whispered to him. "Please. God. No."

Emma eased away from Thomas's body and turned her head.

Leelee stood behind the screen door, framed in the hall light, her face wracked with horror and rage. A small cry escaped her mouth. Then she whipped around, her summer nightgown swinging at her shins, and raced up the stairs.

"Oh, *shit*!" Emma extricated herself from Thomas's grasp and stood on the porch, hugging herself, then hiding her face. After a few gulps of air she looked back at Thomas, still on the railing, somewhat hunched over and gasping for breath.

What had she done?

"I've got to go to her." Emma could feel the heat flying off the surface of her skin into the evening air. She was coming down from her high, away from the edge. She was seeing things the way a mature adult woman responsible for a child should see them, not some sex-crazed maniac.

Thomas was experiencing a slowdown of his own, but he also felt in shock—not just from the sudden loss of her heat and passion—but from the otherworldly power in just that one taste of Emma Jenkins.

He'd been right—this was going to work out. It had to. Because nothing in his life had ever felt that real, and suddenly Thomas felt compelled to claim her, mark her for his own so that no other man in the world could ever touch her.

All from just one kiss.

"Emma, I—"

"I know," she snapped. "You are absolutely right."

Thomas frowned and eased down off the railing. "I didn't even say anything." He took a careful step toward her.

She straight-armed him in the chest. "Yeah, but you were going to say it was a mistake, and I completely agree. I'm glad we're on the same page."

"Dammit, I was not going to say that!" Thomas grabbed her outstretched hand and pulled it to his lips. "Emma. That was *not* a mistake." He kissed her little clenched fist and made eye contact. In a soothing voice he said, "Baby, that was a lot of things—wild, surprising, amazing—but a mistake it wasn't."

"Okay. No. Wait. I can't talk with you about this because I've got to go to Leelee. Do you understand? I have to go to her—now. She's the most important thing in the world to me."

The instant Emma withdrew her hand from his grasp her knees gave out. She started to fall, but Thomas caught her in his arms.

"No!" Emma went rigid and twisted away toward the door. "Oh God—I've screwed up so bad." She looked up at him, her eyes brimming with tears. "Leelee's in there! My dad's in there! And I'm out here behaving like a—" She let out a frustrated groan. "We should forget this ever happened. I'll help you with Hairy, but this—whatever this thing is between us—it's just not the right time for me. Good night."

"Stop right there." Thomas spun her around, and before she could protest, he put his mouth on hers again, calming, stroking, sealing the understanding between them.

"There are no mistakes between us, Emma." He kissed her forehead. "Take care of Leelee. We'll talk tomorrow."

She was already gone. The screen made a sharp crack when it closed, followed by the deep thud of the old oak panel door and the slide of the dead bolt.

Thomas stood on the porch, still erect, still in shock, still trying to get his bearings. He felt a soft brush against his ankle, and saw Hairy gazing up at him.

Thomas let go with a sharp laugh. "That sure sucks, doesn't it, pal?"

No kidding, Big Alpha. What are we going to do now?

"We'll figure something out." As Thomas bent down to retrieve the dog, Hairy leaped into the air to meet him halfway, as if making it easier for him.

Thomas smiled and cocked his head, taking a moment to study the dog. "Huh." Then he tucked Hairy under his arm and headed down the front steps.

Thomas dropped the dog on the passenger seat towel. "When am I gonna catch a break with that woman, Hairy? When monkeys fly out of my butt?"

If Hairy had been physiologically capable, he would have laughed. *Poor Big Alpha.*

"Let's go home, little buddy."

Hairy grinned up at him. *Yeah. Let's go home.*

Aaron woke up gagging.

His arms were imprisoned painfully at his sides. His head was tilted back at an unnatural angle. The metal felt cold and hard in his mouth and he could taste the blood pooling in the soft upper palate.

Dimly, he realized he could choke to death on his own blood in this position.

He felt his eyes fly wide in terror, but he couldn't see much—other than the open-pored, scarred skin of the Ugly One, too close in the light of the motel reading lamp. The Ugly One must be holding the gun. Aaron couldn't see the other man at all, the one who held his arms.

"Time flies when you're having fun, doesn't it?" The Ugly One's breath was sickeningly sweet, like peppermint over rotted flesh. "We get every fucking penny, or you die. We get half of it Friday or we torch your precious little Z. Do you understand?"

Aaron tried to nod but the gun barrel scraped against the tender flesh of his mouth with the slight movement. Another stab of pain ripped through him. All he could think was, *Not the Z! Anything but the Z!*

Aaron felt himself being turned on his side. He heard the cracking thud on the back of his head just as the world went black.

Chapter 10

I Feel for You

"What are you, friggin' nuts?" Stephano's laugh nearly shook the picture frames off his desk. "You want me to authorize the payment of eight thousand dollars to a pet psychic?"

"For God's sake, Vinny—I said *psychiatrist,* not *psychic*!" Thomas looked to his captain, then Lieutenant Regina Massey, then back to his boss. "She's a doctor of veterinary medicine who specializes in animal behavior. It's a new and very specialized field of study."

"Uh-huh." The captain's eyes glazed over. "You know, Tobin, I think I'd have a better chance of justifying eight grand so me and the wife could go to Bermuda and sit around drinking banana daiquiris. The answer would have to be no."

"Then I'll pay her myself."

In truth, it was a possibility Thomas had already considered. He owed Slick everything he could do for him. Besides, he saw it as an investment in his future—his future with Emma.

"So would that be a problem? Kind of like my own private consultant?"

Stephano's two eyebrows bunched together over the bridge of his nose until they formed a unibrow of thick, black consternation. "What? Are you doing her or some-thing?"

Thomas straightened in his chair. "Jesus, Vinny. You're a pig."

Stephano's expression relaxed. "Oh. She's an *ugly* pet psychic."

"No!" Thomas shot up out of his chair, then sat back down, bewildered by his own behavior and painfully aware of Reg's amused expression.

He rubbed a hand over his mouth. "Look. She's a lovely lady and she's damn smart and she thinks there's a chance we can get Slick's dog to tell us what he knows about the murder."

The captain smiled with sudden understanding. "Oh, I think I've got it now—a 'Ruh-roh-Shaggy' Scooby-Doo thing, right?"

Massey and Stephano cracked up.

Thomas knew going in that this wouldn't be easy. He was prepared for this. He took a deep breath.

"The dog was there. He's the only material witness we have." Thomas ignored the ongoing laughter. "The dog probably saw everything, heard everything, smelled every-thing. We just need to find a way to find out what he knows. Dr. Jenkins can do that."

Regina cleared her throat before she spoke in that smooth, hot-chocolate voice of hers. "All right, counselor." She grinned at Thomas. "Let's just say your pretty Dr. Do-little can perform this miracle. But just think for a minute—how in heaven's name can we introduce any of it as evidence? Are we going to put the puppy on the stand? Have him put his paw on the Bible and swear to tell the truth so help him . . ."—she started to snicker—"*dog*?"

"Very funny, Reg." Thomas had to wait a moment for the guffaws to die down. "Work with me here—you got witnesses lining up and begging to talk to you about the Slick homicide?"

"No," she said, giving him the look he knew from experience translated into *smartass*. She sighed. "The three other residents in the building were at work. Nobody in the area saw or heard anything."

"All right." Thomas felt he was getting somewhere. "So, what if the dog can lead us to someone—something—that *is* admissible in a court of law? What if he can narrow it down enough that we get a break in the case?"

"It's still a lot of money out of your pocket." She cocked her head and frowned. "You still think you're responsible for Slick's death, Tommy?"

He hissed. "There's a good chance I am."

Thomas left his chair and retreated to the window. He shoved his hands in his pockets and looked out over the lush green lawn of the state police headquarters.

After a quick glance back at Stephano, he said, "I forced the guy to stay in the game when he wanted out—a few days later, he got himself killed."

"But his murder may have had nothing to do with him being an informant," Regina said. "We're still pursuing the domestic dispute angle."

"But there's a chance it *was* related to his being my informant." Thomas spun on his heels to face Regina. "What if the real reason he wanted out was that he feared for his life? What if someone had found out what he was doing for us and started blackmailing him?"

After a moment, Thomas returned to his chair and sat down heavily. He rested his elbows on his knees and looked up at Regina.

"So, yeah, Reg—it's worth it to me. You know my dad left behind a decent estate and that I'm no slouch when it comes to the market. I won't miss the money. It's the least I can do for Slick. He was a decent guy . . ."—Thomas looked down at his hands—"and the best informant the team ever had."

Regina smiled wistfully. "Must be nice to be able to throw away a wad of cash like that."

"It won't be thrown away."

"Okay. Fine." Stephano waved his hand around impatiently. "I don't see how it would violate departmental policy, but Jesus, Tobin, you don't usually do crazy shit like this."

Thomas smiled. "Tell me about it."

Emma canceled her afternoon appointments and was home by one-thirty. She gulped down a peanut-butter sandwich and a glass of milk, changed into her riding pants, pulled on her boots, and headed out to the barn to tack up the horses. She'd take Vesta, of course, and Leelee would ride good old Bud, a twenty-year-old Quarter Horse so laid-back that he could be ridden safely through a cruise missile attack. Bud usually had a calming effect on Vesta, and Emma was hoping that today he'd mellow out Leelee as well.

The girl had locked herself in her room last night and was still furious in the morning. As Beckett blithely threw waffles into the toaster and hummed to the oldies radio station, Leelee and Emma engaged in a tense standoff over the breakfast table.

Leelee's expression—the few times she even acknowledged Emma's presence—was sharp and accusatory. Emma knew her own face must have broadcast all the guilt she felt.

What had she been thinking, making out with Thomas like a horny teenager? She'd been thinking nothing, obviously. Thinking had nothing to do with what happened last night with Thomas—it was all impulse and instinct and animal lust.

Lust the likes of which she hadn't even known was possible.

So Leelee continued the silent treatment all morning, her mouth pulled in a thin white line of disapproval as she went about her routine. The performance reminded Emma of the way Thomas had looked the day they'd met.

This afternoon's plan to get Leelee to open up wasn't particularly original, but it stood a decent chance of working. She'd wait for Leelee at the bus stop with the horses. She'd take the girl's backpack and give her a leg up on Bud, not allowing her a moment to escape.

Then they'd ride down to the creek. They'd talk. They'd hash it out. And they'd have themselves some damn quality time whether Leelee wanted it or not!

Emma waited at the end of the lane, keeping Vesta calm with gentle murmurs as Bud stood next to them like he didn't have a care in the world—probably because he didn't. Bud had lived a fine life for a horse. He'd been a colt when he arrived at the farm twenty summers ago, Emma's birthday present the year her mother died. From the moment she laid eyes on him, Emma knew the chestnut horse with the soulful eyes was special. And he'd proceeded to ease her sorrow, loosen the knot in her heart, just by being who he was.

Bud had introduced Emma to the magical bond that can grow between companion animal and human being. Bud had been her inspiration for doing what she did for a living. Bud had been her rock.

She glanced over at the horse and he nickered, just as a flash of bright yellow moved through the trees. The diesel brakes whined and hissed as the bus came to a slow stop at the mailbox.

"You're on, Bud," Emma whispered to the horse, watching Leelee descend the steps. "Do your stuff."

Leelee was already scowling as her feet hit the gravel.

She swung her backpack over one shoulder and shook her head, silently saying no to whatever Emma had planned.

Emma waited for the bus to leave before she dismounted from Vesta, flipping the reins over the split-rail fence. She brought Bud forward and held out her free hand for Leelee's backpack. "We'll leave this here." She tossed the bag against the fence.

Leelee put on her utterly bored face and crossed her arms over her chest. "Let me guess—we're going to get in touch with our inner goddesses while communing with nature."

Emma couldn't help but laugh. The fact was, Leelee was a riot—pessimistic and surly, yes—but a riot all the same. She reminded her of Thomas.

"What I'd like is for you to get your little boo-tocks in touch with this saddle, please." Emma locked her fingers together and smiled at Leelee, waiting to give her a leg up. "Come on, Lee. It's just a ride. Besides, I know how much you want to go out and check on Mr. Martin's corn crop."

The jaded pre-teen mask fell away from Leelee's face, and she started to giggle. With a sigh she headed toward Bud, stopping to stroke his thick neck and accept his wet kisses. Then she placed her Dr. Martens boot into Emma's cupped hands and popped into the saddle.

"Okay. So where are we off to?"

It took a moment for Emma to mount Vesta—she was a moving target—but soon they were on their way down the lane, side by side at an easy walk.

"I thought we'd go over through the old Weaverton property and down to the creek, then back up along the Martins' field to the woods. Sound like a plan?"

Leelee remained quiet for a moment. Then she said, "I suppose you're going to talk to me about that man."

Emma risked a glimpse at Leelee. She was sitting rigid in her saddle, her gaze straight ahead, the afternoon sun glinting in the honey-gold twists of her hair.

"His name is Thomas."

"Thomas the Tongue," she said wearily. "I suppose he's the flower guy?"

"Yes."

"Are we going to talk about sex now?" With that question, Leelee swung her face to look at Emma, and her mouth was clenched tight, her eyes were hard and her cheeks pink.

"Would you like to talk about sex?"

"No, I would not. I'd prefer a 'don't ask, don't tell' policy with you, if you don't mind—you know, a nice change of pace from Mom. Besides, it's none of my business."

Emma let that comment sink in for a moment and weighed the possible responses. She wanted to do this right, this whole parental guidance and open communication thing. But what was *right*? This was one of those moments when she wished Leelee had come with an owner's manual.

"In a way, you're correct—it's not your business. But I told you I wouldn't make any decisions without you."

Leelee let loose with a snort of disgust. "Really? Looks like you were making decisions just fine on your own last night."

Emma didn't know what to say.

"And did you check out the guy's dog? It was totally woo-woo—like a midget hyena in a sweater. I'd give anything to have a dog like that—it was the funkiest thing I've ever seen. A little bit of L.A. right here in Mayberry, RFD."

Leelee's words hit Emma with a thud. When had Leelee seen Hairy? How long had she been standing at the door?

"How long were you watching us?"

"Long enough to see you work it, girl."

"That's enough, Leelee." Emma didn't know whether to slap her or pull her close and try to kiss away all the pain—

twelve years of accumulated insecurity and loneliness—and that was the central challenge of Leelee. Yet another human being with a case of fear-based aggression. It reminded her of Thomas.

And then it dawned on her. She looked over at the young woman and nearly laughed out loud at the resemblance. Tall, golden, smart, funny, pessimistic, sad—if it weren't for the fact that Thomas had never met Rebecca Weaverton, Emma would be certain she'd uncovered the secret of Leelee's paternity.

Or maybe he *had* met Becca . . .

Leelee shot her a suspicious glance. "What?"

"I don't know—nothing, I guess."

"What, Emma? You're giving me this totally weird look."

She shook her head and chuckled. "I like him, Lee. That's what I was thinking. I've decided I like Thomas Tobin."

Leelee said nothing for several long minutes, as they headed toward the old Weaverton place. They rode in silence along the line of pine trees.

"Does he like you?"

Emma smiled a little. "Yeah, I think so."

"Well, he's a hottie, that's for sure."

"Really?" Emma was a bit surprised by that assessment.

"Definite babe material—if you're into old guys with woo-woo dogs."

They took a break down by the creek. Leelee sprawled on the grass while Emma secured the horses, pulled out juice boxes and granola bars from her fanny pack, and plopped down beside her.

"Refreshment, ma'am?"

Leelee looked up and smiled. "Why yes, thank you,"

she said primly, piercing the waxed cardboard with the straw. She took a long sip. "A lovely vintage."

Emma grinned at her and leaned back on her hands.

"This is nice, Emma. I'm glad you took me on a ride." Leelee was quiet while she concentrated on removing the granola wrapper. "And I'm sorry I clammed up on you this morning. I acted like a total jerk."

The words flowed over Emma like a warm breeze, and she sighed quietly. With this adjustment in Leelee's mood, it was time to clear the air.

"I'm trying to be a good mom, Leelee."

The girl's head popped up, alert to the serious tone in Emma's voice. "I know you are."

"It's difficult sometimes. I'm learning as I go."

Leelee shrugged and took another sip. "I know."

"So I want you to know that I don't enjoy having to say this."

Leelee frowned and looked around like she'd missed something. "Say what?"

"That I'm angry with you." Emma sat up straight and turned to face Leelee. "That it was inappropriate for you to watch me with Thomas last night—it was an invasion of my privacy and I don't want it to happen again." Emma paused, gulping down enough air to continue. "And I expect you to speak to me with respect—always. I love joking around with you, Lee, but I sure didn't appreciate the comment you made about me 'working it.' Or the name you gave Thomas. You went over the line."

Leelee's mouth fell open. She dropped the granola bar to the ground.

"I meant it when I told you I'd never make any major decisions without consulting you. But the thing is, I'm an adult woman. And I get lonely sometimes. And I may want to start something with someone at some point—maybe

Thomas, I'm not sure—and you'll have to find a way to understand that if it happens."

Leelee said nothing.

"There may even be times when I'll have Thomas or another man over to the house, and I expect you to treat them with respect as well."

Leelee's sob cut through the quiet air. She was on her feet before she realized she was moving, walking away, fast, toward the water.

This isn't happening. This isn't happening.

Emma jumped up to follow her. "Leelee, please look at me."

Her ears were buzzing and the tears made her eyes sting, but it was her chest and throat that hurt the most—a kind of squeezing ache, like a fist clenching around nothing, but still clutching, grabbing, gripping the emptiness inside her until it burned.

"Sweetheart."

"Sometimes, in the mornings, they'd still be wasted, you know?" Leelee was embarrassed to hear her voice come out in such a tiny whine, like she was five years old or something. "Sometimes I'd be getting ready for school and they'd be doing it in the kitchen and I couldn't get any cereal."

Emma thought she would die. Right there.

She raised her hands and pressed them softly to the narrow shoulders in front of her, feeling every bone in Leelee's body shake.

Damn Becca.

"The most psycho part of it was that I hated all those men—really hated them—but that didn't stop me from pretending that they might be my dad. It's so weird to walk around every day and not know who your dad is, Emma."

Leelee felt Emma's hands on her head, stroking, holding, and she leaned into the warm touch.

"I'd see men walking around L.A. and I'd stare at them—construction workers, suits, slackers, every different kind of man imaginable—and I'd look for someone with my color eyes or the same shaped jaw. It was totally lame, I know."

"No, sweetheart. It wasn't."

Leelee laughed bitterly. "And I used to see these dads with their daughters, you know, at places like the mall and the movies and stuff, and I used to get all creeped out by it. It was like I didn't really believe the guys loved those girls just because they were their daughters. I was always looking for proof that there was some other gross reason they wanted to be with them—a sexual reason—because it's all I'd ever seen a man be."

The tears were rolling down Emma's face now.

"The weirdest thing of all is, unless he's dead, there's some man out there right now who might be able to love me just because he's my dad, you know? But I'll never know who he is. I'll never know what it feels like to be loved like that."

Leelee let her face fall into her hands. And in the privacy of her own palms, standing by the creek next to a soybean field, she screamed at the top of her lungs the one thing she'd always longed to say: *"It's not fair and I hate her for it!"*

Emma lost track of time. She'd collapsed to the bank of the creek and let Leelee fall across her lap and cry. And she'd cried and cried—and Emma joined her—until the sun started to set and Vesta was a nervous wreck. Emma knew they had to head back.

They were quiet on the ride home, and Emma let Leelee be in control of what they talked about. Emma never guessed that Becca was that far gone, but Leelee said there'd been at least a couple men each week.

She hadn't known. She hadn't known!

She'd been in Philadelphia in vet school and Becca was in Los Angeles ruining her baby girl's life!

"It's nice to have Beckett, though," Leelee finally said, smiling.

Emma felt drained, her joints loose, and near tears again. But she managed to smile back. "He loves you just for being you—the same way he's always loved me. You know that, don't you?"

She nodded shyly. "Yeah. I think he's pretty cool, too, but . . ."

"But he's not your dad."

Leelee nodded.

They came within sight of the barn, and Vesta began to fidget. Emma was concentrating so hard on calming her that she almost didn't hear Leelee speaking.

". . . so I'd like to get to know him."

Emma looked over and brought the horse to a stop. "What, honey? I didn't hear you."

Leelee rolled her eyes heavenward and groaned. "I *said*, I know you're not like my mom when it comes to guys. I know you haven't had any kind of, you know, *relations* with a man since you sent Aaron packing. And I know Thomas the Tongue—whoops, just Thomas—must be special. So what I *said* was"—Leelee nervously brought her gaze to Emma's face—"that I'd like to meet him. Get to know him. Junk like that."

Chapter 11

Love Don't Live Here Anymore

Emma had never done anything like this in her life, and as she watched Thomas slice through the yellow police tape across the apartment door, her stomach flipped in anticipation and dread.

This was the home of a murder victim. She was going to see where Scott Slick's body was found. And she was going to try to help solve a crime.

At long last, she was going to get to be Miss Marple.

Thomas closed his penknife and stuck it in his pocket as he looked down at her quizzically. Emma cringed. He'd obviously seen her excitement and now must think she was some kind of real sicko to be smiling at a time like this.

"After you, Miss Marple," he said. Then he winked at her.

Chills went up her spine as she stepped inside the living room, and Emma wasn't sure if it was because of where she was or the man she was with. Both scared her a little.

"The evidence techs have been over the place several times, but please try not to touch anything."

"Sure. I underst—" Emma stopped in her tracks. Well, *duh*! Of course there would be blood on the floor. Slick got hit in the temple with a blender and it cracked his skull, and head wounds bleed like the devil. But still. The blood had dried in a sickening spread of brownish red, like red dust.

She tried to picture a person ruined enough inside to take a human life. The shudder rolled up from her feet to the tips of her ears in one quick wave, and it felt like a forewarning to her, cold and mean and close.

Thomas's hand settled between her shoulder blades and, like magic, the trembling stopped. In its place she felt a warmth begin to spread—entirely too much warmth, in fact—and she suddenly felt overheated, overaware of how close he stood to her, how crisp he smelled, how handsome he was in his charcoal-gray power suit.

"You okay, Emma?"

She looked up into his face. This was too weird. Thomas was gazing down at her with his eyes so hot, his mouth so sexual, his body pulsing with life and heat and the unmistakable energy of a creature who needed to mate.

And all the while they stood there in the cold, empty place of death.

She started to sweat.

"I'm fine. It's just a little overwhelming."

Concern creased his dark blond brows. "We can leave."

"No!" Emma shook her head. "I need to be here. Let's get to work."

Thomas let his hand drop away from her back as she stepped forward into the kitchen. It was odd seeing Emma here, and he watched as she moved through the brightly lit room, looking up at the ceiling for some strange reason, examining under the lip of the kitchen cabinets above the tile floor, peering under the modern black glass-and-steel dinette set.

He nearly laughed when he saw her crawl under the table and lie on her back, like Petey and Jack when they played fort.

Emma started to hum to herself, a tune he didn't recognize, and she drummed her fingers along her khakis to keep the beat. All the while she studied everything around her, the walls, the underside of the table, the tile, the chair legs.

"There's some dried urine under here. On the baseboard, the chair legs, the tile. I bet the little guy was hiding under here when it happened."

She turned her eyes to the bloodstain.

"The view is unobstructed from this angle."

She scooted out then, hopped to her feet, and smoothed out her simple cotton tee and chinos. When she turned toward Thomas, her braid slipped over her shoulder.

Thomas felt his loins clench and his body temperature soar.

"But the really interesting question is this: Did Hairy manage to stay quiet enough that the bad guy didn't even know he was here? Or did Hairy lose it like he did at your house, and the murderer just figured the dog wasn't worth worrying about?"

Thomas was unable to follow her reasoning, which was forgivable, because he couldn't stop thinking about how her breasts felt cradled in his hands.

"Uh, I'm not sure I see what you're getting at. Why would anyone worry about a dog being a witness?"

Emma nodded and smiled. "My point exactly. Someone who knew a lot about dogs, had their own dog maybe, or had trained a dog—that person might be uncomfortable with the fact that a dog had just seen them murder someone. That person might have felt compelled to get rid of the dog while they were at it."

Her smile widened, and Thomas thought about running his tongue over that tiny overlap of her two front teeth, sucking that ripe lower lip of hers into his mouth.

"But someone who didn't know anything about dogs wouldn't have cared one way or the other if a dog witnessed the murder. So the question is, was Hairy able to stay quiet?"

Emma pointed under the table. "Did he hide under here, silent as a mouse, watching the whole thing, waiting for the bad guy to leave?"

Thomas watched Emma continue to search through the kitchen, peering close but not touching any of the surfaces already dusted in lime-green fingerprint powder. She leaned into the pantry and came out frowning and pointing.

Thomas looked in. "Sure. You can pick it up."

Emma held out a small bag of dog food and grinned. "Now *this* is good dog food, Rugby Boy. Expensive, but well worth it for the quality protein."

He nodded. "Hand it over, Doc."

"We can take it?"

"Slick doesn't need it where he is, that's for sure."

Thomas tucked the unopened bag under his arm and then reached out as Emma shoved a set of small bowls in his hands, both emblazoned with the name Hairy.

"I wondered how you knew his name," she said, giving him a friendly pat on the shoulder.

He then followed Emma as she walked through the rest of the apartment. She stopped briefly in the living room, pointing out a little dog bed in the corner of the couch, and Thomas grabbed that, too.

She looked briefly in the bathroom and laughed when she found a plastic caddy filled with dog grooming supplies. "Again, nothing but the best." She handed it to him with a smile and Thomas realized he was running out of hands, and that against his better judgment, he was going to be removing things from a crime scene.

Also against his better judgment, he was contemplating a relationship with a woman.

Emma reached the bedroom and stopped dead. She stared at the king-sized bed covered in zebra-stripe satin and piled high with red pillows. Then she examined the floor-to-ceiling black lacquer entertainment center on the opposite wall.

"Holy moley." She bent down to peruse the video and DVD titles. "You weren't kidding that this guy was a bit on the flamboyant side."

She straightened up, put her hands on those lovely hips he'd just been staring at, and Thomas watched her face light up as she surveyed Slick's CD collection. "Wow. All disco. All the time. This guy knew how to get down."

Thomas heard himself chuckle, and it reminded him that Emma was the sweetest, funniest, most interesting woman he'd ever been around. He liked her so much. He enjoyed her company. He wanted to get his hands under her shirt so badly that his knuckles ached.

She went to the closet next. The louvered doors were already opened, also sprinkled with powder. She turned quickly to ask him a question about what she could and could not touch when her braid went flying over her shoulder, and Thomas responded as reliably as one of Pavlov's dogs. Everything below the waist perked up and was raring to go.

"Sure. Go ahead," he heard himself saying, then nearly hyperventilated when she got down on her hands and knees and pulled out two boxes from the back of the closet.

Oh, yeah. Oh, yeah. Oh, yeah, his id chanted, because Emma's ass swayed a little when she reached, and swayed a little more when she scooted backward, and then got all packed nice and tight in her pants when she sat back on her heels.

Dear God, he wanted to clutch her hips and take her from behind. He wanted to open her up like a new Wal-Mart.

"Thomas?"

Emma swiveled at the waist to talk to him, her face alive

with laughter and surprise. "Did you look in these boxes?" She suddenly frowned. "Is something wrong?"

What was wrong was that they hadn't talked about what happened on the porch the other night. What was wrong was that Thomas was going to lose his mind if he didn't resolve all the unanswered questions about Emma Jenkins and what he was doing paying for her consulting work, staring at her spectacular ass, needing to be in her presence.

A lot of things were wrong.

"Not a thing," he said, lowering the dog food bag over the decidedly unpleated front of his trousers. "Find something interesting?"

"Ooh, yeah. Check this out." She pulled a box across the carpet and with dainty fingers held up a tiny blue sequined garment, then a matching headband with a jaunty peacock feather. "Nice, huh?"

Thomas blinked. Oh, *that box.*

Next, Emma held up a silver lamé jumpsuit with a rhinestone collar, then the green leprechaun ensemble. Emma put everything back in the box and cast him a sly glance. "You know, Tobin, unless Hairy had more than one St. Patrick's Day costume, I think you've already seen this stuff. Am I right?"

Thomas cleared his throat. "Yes, I did. I thought it would be fun for you to find."

Emma shook her head and got back on all fours to shove the box into the closet. Thomas gritted his teeth.

"Huh." She stood up, hands on hips, and frowned. "Has Hairy demonstrated any kind of special skills?"

"Skills?" *Like falling in love with my underwear?*

"Yeah, like jumping through hoops or standing up on his hind legs or spinning or flipping or anything? Things a circus dog would do?"

"Hairy? *My* Hairy is a circus dog?"

"I have no idea," Emma said, laughing. "But he sure

does something that requires a festive wardrobe."

"Yeah. So did Slick. Remember the sailor suit I told you about? The one Hairy was wearing when I found him?"

Emma nodded, a cute little divot forming between her eyes.

"Well, I guess I failed to mention that Slick was wearing a matching outfit when he died. Little sailor cap and all."

Emma crossed her arms up under her breasts, stretched one leg out to the side and tapped her toe. "Anything else you need to tell me?"

Several things, actually, he thought. "Nope," he said.

Emma pursed her lips and squinted at him, maintaining her impatient schoolmarm posture. She looked unbearably sweet, he thought.

"You better not be shitting me, Tobin." Her voice was decidedly unsweetened.

"I hear you." *I'm a dead man when she finds out the check I gave her is my money.*

He watched Emma march back to the entertainment center and peer at the CD player. She hit the ON button, then pushed PLAY, and suddenly the whole apartment came alive with the throbbing disco beat of the Village People's "In the Navy."

If it weren't for the sight of Emma's laughing face, her lovely hips rocking back and forth, and her sweet voice singing " 'Where can you find pleasure, search the world for treasure . . . ?' " Thomas would've been certain that he'd died and taken the express elevator to his own personal hell.

Chapter 12

Shake Your Groove Thing

"Oh, for God's sake—disco dancing dogs?"

While Emma laughed, Thomas couldn't help but stare at her over in the passenger seat of his Audi. She looked exceptionally pretty in the sunshine, those streaks of burgundy and gold dancing in the lustrous pleat of her dark braid. The rosy cheeks. The shining blue eyes.

She looked like a freaking Ivory soap commercial.

Not that that was a bad thing. In fact, it conjured up a real pleasant image—Emma all wet and pink in a steamy shower, where he'd volunteer to lather her up—*but good*.

"No joke," she said. "There are a couple groups that hold regional and national dance competitions. Everybody wears elaborate costumes and does difficult routines—and it's not just disco, we're talking country line dancing, hip-hop, *Riverdance* stuff. You name it."

Thomas shook his head and briefly shut his eyes. "How has this been allowed to happen in our country?"

Emma let loose with a loud guffaw, and Thomas glanced over in time to see the way she threw back her head, the feminine line of her jaw, the sweet pale throat, the succulent little earlobe he'd once held between his teeth. He licked his lips.

"Well, Thomas, you're the guy who says people are capable of anything."

She turned toward him and her eyes crinkled up with amusement. "This is just another unusual thing that human beings do in their spare time—they dance with their dogs. You got to admit that it's harmless enough. And I figure if we find the group Scott Slick belonged to, it might give you a lead in what happened to him, right?"

It was possible, so he nodded. "You ever seen one of these dance competitions?"

"Yup, a couple. They're lots of fun."

"I'll take your word for it."

She laughed again. "I'll make a few calls this afternoon, see what I can find. Are you free tonight? Can we try a few things with Hairy this evening?"

"I'm free until about ten-thirty. I've got to work tonight."

"What are you working on?"

As Thomas glanced at those blue eyes brimming with curiosity and intellect, he thought maybe the real attraction of Emma wasn't the physical at all. It was her mind. Her sense of humor. Her innate kindness. All wrapped up in that modest, soft-smelling beauty.

How was a man supposed to defend himself against all that? Why would he even want to?

"The team is starting a new campaign tonight. Some guy in Hancock asked around about getting rid of his ex-wife— a pretty common situation—and we're . . . well, I'm meeting him at midnight for a drink. We're going to talk things over."

Emma bit down on her bottom lip, briefly checking the interstate traffic before she turned to face Thomas. She was frowning.

"What happens during one of these things? What exactly do you do?"

Thomas gave her a gentle smile and shook his head. "Not very many people know the specifics of what I do, so I'm trusting you to keep it to yourself. All right?"

Her nod was so enthusiastic that it made Thomas laugh.

"You're an exceptionally trustworthy person, aren't you, Dr. Jenkins?"

"Absolutely."

"No, I mean it. Look at yourself." He extended a hand toward her and grinned. "You spend your life taking care of needy living things. You've accepted your friend's kid as your own. You keep your dad from getting lonely. You pay your bills. You don't suffer fools and don't lie. You're an exceptional person."

She leaned away and studied him. "I try to be *decent,* if that's what you're getting at—but that doesn't make me exceptional."

"If you say so." Thomas loved the way Emma blushed.

"So what's going to happen tonight?"

Thomas put his eyes on the road. "The guy asked a hooker if she knew anyone who'd do the job. She called the local police, who called us. We've already interviewed her. So when I show up tonight, the guy will think I'm the hit man from Killers 'R' Us."

"Ah, yes. Your consulting firm."

Thomas laughed. "Right."

"Where are you meeting him?"

"Some hole-in-the-wall tavern. The team's never used the place before, so my people have been up there for the last few days doing background—interviewing the employees, checking all the exits, figuring out where everyone will be stationed."

Emma frowned. "Is he dangerous?"

Thomas tipped his head thoughtfully. "You never know. Most people who go looking for someone to do their dirty work don't carry guns. But every once in a while . . ."

Emma drew in a sharp breath.

"We take care of each other, Emma." He smiled at her, pleased that she worried about him. Another excellent development.

"So what will you say to him?"

"I'll get him to give me the name of the target, the specifics of what he wants done, ask for a down payment of some sort, and arrange the next meeting. We always try for two meetings—it shows clear intent. And we'll be recording everything on video and audio."

Emma's eyes widened. "You go in wired? Like on TV?"

"Absolutely. A camera inside my shirt button. A microphone inside my ball cap. Two guys in a communications van outside. At least four backup people inside the tavern— and everybody can hear everything."

"Hmm," Emma said, brushing a finger over her lips. "But how come you do the actual undercover work when you're not a cop?"

He caught her eye and couldn't help but smile at her. Right then he realized he'd smiled more in the last two hours than he had in the last two years.

"It's a team effort, so at the beginning I made a point of knowing firsthand how all the jobs were done—background preparation, remote electronic surveillance, backup, and playing the role of the hit man. It went so well the first time that I did another and another and pretty soon everyone on the team realized that, for some damn reason, people like to chat with me about murder. I'm a good listener, I suppose."

Thomas felt the heat of Emma's eyes all along the length of his body, from his shoes to his hairline. He didn't dare look at her.

"I think it's because you look the part," she said softly. "At first you look kind of dangerous—the bump on your nose, the squint, the scar, the fact that you don't smile too much . . . the fact that you're so . . . uh . . . big."

The air inside the car felt too heavy, too warm, while Thomas waited for her to finish her observation.

"But your eyes can be very expressive when you let them, Thomas—understanding even. I bet you reel people in with your eyes. Like you've done with me."

Oh, yeah, there is a God!

He stole a glance her way, expecting to see her usual smile, but was greeted by eyes sharp with fear.

"What happened on my porch was kind of a fluke, Thomas. It was too much, too fast, and for the time being I can't be anything more than your friend and co-worker. Let's focus on helping Hairy and getting to the bottom of Slick's murder. Okay?"

Shit. It was not okay. Not at all. It was a mess.

Thomas was ready to risk getting involved with her. He wanted her. He wanted to be with her in bed *and* out of it. It amazed him. Thrilled him. Made him feel alive.

"How long is a 'time being,' Emma?" He reached out across the gearshift to find her hand, so warm and silky and petite in his own. With a rush of hot relief, he felt her fingers wrap around his.

"I'm not sure," she whispered. "It depends on a few things—Leelee, mostly. She's been through the wringer, and I can't do anything that would make her feel her place with me is threatened right now. Can you understand that?"

"Sure." Thomas kept his hand on hers as long as he could, but he had to let go as he shifted down at the exit.

"Thank you." She straightened in the seat, folded her hands in her lap, and whispered, "But that doesn't mean I didn't like it, Thomas."

His head spun around faster than Michelle Kwan doing a triple-axle. "Yeah. I noticed how much you liked it."

The flush that raced up her throat to her cheeks was too

adorable to believe. Just then they pulled into the Wit's End parking lot.

The shy smile Emma offered put a vise grip on his insides. "Why don't you and Hairy come over to the house for dinner tonight and we can set up a few tests afterward, maybe shake our booties a bit before you have to work?"

Thomas nodded, completely amenable to a bit of bootie shaking as long as it was Emma doing the shaking. But he'd already figured out the real purpose of the get-together.

"Is this 'meet the potential new boyfriend night' at the Jenkins house?"

When they'd both stopped laughing, Emma touched his hand again and gave it a friendly squeeze. "I should probably warn you that Leelee's not an easy crowd to work. Don't expect much of a welcome."

Thomas nodded, bringing her hand to his lips. He planted a soft kiss on her knuckles. "I'll just be my charming self, then."

Emma got out of the car and leaned in the open window. "It wouldn't hurt if you dress extra sharp tonight, Rugby Boy. Do you own a white polyester bell-bottomed suit by any chance?"

Thomas the Tongue was about five minutes early, Leelee noted from her bedroom window. How completely pathetic. But she had to admit that he drove a truly superior car with a bumper sticker that made her laugh. So maybe she could stand him for one night.

Then he unfolded himself from the front seat, and he looked like he was twelve feet tall.

In his hands was a bouquet of flowers—daisies, maybe—tied with a long yellow ribbon. God. The poor man needed some remedial assistance in the gift idea department. Besides, they looked too little-girly for Emma. Those red roses had been more her speed.

He was dressed nice for a Baltimore guy—a pair of black slacks and a dark eggplant shirt that looked silky and expensive. He looked urban cool, even, though she didn't know why he bothered out here in Tractor World.

She was about to turn from the window when she saw something skitter out of the car onto the gravel—Hairy! Emma had told her all about the dog's disco dancing career and it was the coolest thing she'd ever heard! And he was here!

All right!

Leelee ran down the front stairs just in time to answer the doorbell, mad at herself because she was still second-guessing her overall plan for the evening. There had been so many possible ways to scare him off.

The punk-skank plan had been her first choice. She could've dyed her hair blue, stuck temporary tattoos up and down her arms, and put in a fake nose ring. But Emma and Beckett would have just laughed their butts off, ruining the effect, so she scratched that.

There was the silent-treatment option, where she could've given him surly looks and refused to speak to him while smiling at everyone else. But Emma would've been seriously hacked off if she did that, and she preferred to avoid another lecture about respect.

She even considered the needy-orphan routine, where she'd hang on him and thank him for agreeing to be her daddy. She figured that would get him running out the door the fastest, but it was the one gag she didn't have the cojones to pull off.

That left her with being herself. Totally lame-o, she knew, but it was too late to do anything about it. She was already at the door, wearing her low-rise Mudd jeans, her Dr. Martens, and an Old Navy stretch top with a big purple butterfly appliqué. Her hair was up in a clip. Her hand was on the old brass doorknob. She opened the door.

Wow.

"Leelee?"

He bent a little at the waist and smiled down at her—wow again. He was so big!

"I'm Thomas. It's nice to meet you."

"Yeah. Whatever. Come in if you have to." God—give him a mustache and he looked like that hot old eye doctor dude from the *Friends* reruns.

Then Emma rounded the corner from the kitchen and Leelee tried to make her exit.

"Wait, please."

A big hand came down on her shoulder and she turned to see that Thomas the Tongue was handing her the flowers. What—was she the maid now?

"Okay. I'll put these in a vase for Emma."

"They're for you, Elizabeth," he said, smiling, and Leelee felt her eyeballs basically pop out—and she wasn't sure if it was because no one had ever given her flowers before or because she'd just gotten a load of his dimples.

"Really?" Oh, God, she sounded like a complete loser. "Whatever. Thanks." She nearly ran to the kitchen because she was seriously embarrassed and she didn't want him to know she was smiling like a dweeb—besides, she had no desire to watch the two of them kiss again.

So why was she peeking around the kitchen door, spying on them?

"Hey, Emma," Thomas said. Emma stood there smiling like she wanted to jump into his arms. Leelee was in serious danger of spewing.

"Hi. Ready to disco the night away?" Emma asked.

"I'm a dancin' machine. Watch me get down," Thomas answered.

Leelee rolled her eyes. Definite heaving potential, here.

Then—total shocker—Thomas the Tongue leaned down and gave Emma a dry little smack of a kiss on the cheek, and Emma smiled all nice and sweet, but nothing wet and sloppy happened at all between them—no fluid exchange whatsoever.

Emma hooked her arm in his and walked with him to the living room. "I've got some interesting news for you about Scott Slick—or should I say Simon Slickowski of Smyrna, Delaware, last year's World Canine Dance Association's Team Disco Champion?"

Leelee started giggling. Emma had said Thomas would be left speechless by what she'd found out that afternoon, and she'd been right. Thomas looked down at her and his jaw dropped open.

"What the hell—" he said, as they disappeared through the archway.

Hey, Bright Eyes.

Something brushed against Leelee's ankle and she squealed with excitement. The disco dog jumped into her arms, and he was even uglier in good light! Oooh—his skin felt totally creepy! Bare and silky where a normal dog was supposed to be fuzzy. She started laughing. She couldn't help it. He was *so cool*!

"I'll put your flowers in water for you," Beckett said, now standing behind her, staring at the little dog. "I think we've seen better-looking roadkill on Route 27, wouldn't you say, Lee?"

Hey, TV Man, at least I got all four legs and attempt to keep the offensive smells to a minimum—nothing personal, Ray.

Leelee handed over the flowers and gazed at the creature in her arms. "Oh, Beck. He is by far the best thing I've seen since I left L.A." She scratched behind the dog's fuzzy ears.

You're not so bad, yourself, Bright Eyes. Oh . . . just a

little to the left . . . that's it . . . you got it. Now harder.
Oooh, yeah . . .

It felt like Thomas and Hairy had been around forever.

Hairy made himself at home in Leelee's lap, eyes closed in ecstasy as she stroked his bony head. Leelee's daisies sat in a place of honor on the coffee table in front of her.

Thomas seemed to fit this old house. When he stood, he was in perfect scale with the ten-foot-high ceilings, his arms and shoulders just as strong and basic as the living room's thick crown molding and baseboards. When he sat, as he did now in the chair next to Beckett's, he seemed relaxed, comfortable with his right to be here.

Emma listened with contentment as the two men laughed and talked about everything from women's professional basketball to their favorite Monty Python dialogue. The last of the day's light was slipping through the front windows on a pleasant breeze. The white sheers rippled. The cozy group was bathed in a wash of pure gold.

Then Emma's breath hitched—somehow, the friendly scene before her had just become something more—one of those impossible moments, when time hovered, when the air stilled, when hidden love and magic were revealed.

Thomas chose that instant to turn toward her, laughing at something Beckett had just said, and his gray eyes locked on hers with a flash of awareness. Though his laugh fell away, a faint smile remained, and she could see that he felt it, too. And Emma's heart grew very quiet.

She'd know him in an instant . . .

He nodded at her almost imperceptibly, then turned back to her father, and she realized that not once in all the years she'd been with Aaron had he ever seemed to fit here. He was preoccupied. Antsy. Always checking his watch.

Beckett used to remark that Aaron would rather be anywhere else on the planet than out here at the farm, and Emma knew it was true.

So why did Thomas Tobin—a man she hardly knew— seem so at home in her house, in her life?

And what would she do about it?

Emma knew it all came down to whether she'd trust her instincts. Looking back on her life, she was aware that in every single instance, her gut-level response had been the right one. Whether she chose to pay attention to it was another matter. And the trouble always started when she let her thoughts override her instincts.

So which would she listen to tonight?

Her brain told her to watch for falling rocks and hairpin curves and to remember that bridges freeze before roads.

But in that golden moment—when Thomas looked at her, when he smiled at her, when she saw him sitting be- tween her father and her daughter—her instinct was telling her that something wonderful was right around the next bend. That it was okay to go a little faster than usual. That she'd be safe.

Emma felt Leelee's eyes on her, and turned. She was grinning.

"Hey," Leelee said. "You said we were going to boogie- oogie-oogie till we just can't boogie no more."

Hairy raised his head and yawned.

"You're right." Emma hopped up from her chair and crossed to the armoire that housed the TV and stereo. She looked over her shoulder. "What'll we try first—the Bee Gees or Donna Summer?"

"Ooh, the Bee Gees!" Leelee squealed, jumping off the couch, Hairy tucked under her arm.

Within minutes, Thomas and Beckett had the furniture pushed to the edges of the room, Emma had the music queued up, and Leelee had positioned Hairy in the center of the rug. Then everyone stared down at him. He began to shake.

"Do you think he still remembers how to dance?" Leelee asked.

"Absolutely." Emma smiled at the expectant looks in everyone's faces. "If Hairy is who I think he is, he's a highly trained pro. I think we're in for a big treat."

She squatted down and touched his frightened face. "It's okay, little man. We just want to have some fun. Show us what you got."

Emma rose and hit PLAY, and the room throbbed with what she'd always considered the soundtrack to her childhood—the high-pitched wail of the Brothers Gibb.

" 'Oh, you can tell by the way I use my walk . . .' "

"Oh, my God!" Leelee squeaked.

"Give the man some room," Beckett said, pushing everyone back like a police officer at an accident scene.

Thomas gravitated toward Emma and took her hand in his—warm and big and just right. He was shaking with laughter. "Okay. I've officially seen everything now," he said into her ear.

Several things impressed Emma. First, Hairy was perhaps the most agile little canine she'd ever seen. He'd just executed a flip with a full twist. He could spin on his hind legs. He flawlessly kept the beat as he pranced and swiveled and made sharp cuts on the rug.

The second thing that impressed Emma was that she swore, despite everything she knew to the contrary, that the damn dog was smiling.

His sharp yips and howls brought her out of her trance.

"What does he want? What?" Leelee jumped around worriedly, looking to Emma for help. "Why is he barking at me?"

"I think he wants you to dance with him," Thomas yelled over the disco throb.

"Yeah? Oh, how totally cool!"

Thomas's hand tightened around Emma's, then he brought his arm around her shoulder and held her—really they held each other—because they were laughing so hard they could barely stand.

Whatever Leelee did, Hairy mimicked her. If she turned a sharp left, so did he. If she did a little cha-cha-cha, he did, too. If she leaped, he leaped.

"I'm going to pee my pants," Emma laughed.

"You know, I've heard tying a maxi pad inside a sweat sock works wonders for that," Thomas said in her ear.

"I've gotta get the video camera!" Beckett raced from the room. "They ain't gonna believe this down at the Moose!"

Thomas was pretty sure he'd just gotten his ass kicked by a twelve-year-old.

"Leelee, I'm not sure *vair* is an actual word." Beckett reached for the dictionary that lay on the floor at his feet.

The girl rested her chin in her hands and looked up at Thomas, her eyes crinkling as she grinned at him.

"Whadya say? You gonna challenge me, Mr. Tobin?"

He sighed, leaned back into the chair, and looped his fingers together on his lap. The two of them had gone head-to-head for an hour now, and all he had left were the letters X and Q and there was nowhere on the Scrabble board to put them. "No. My brain hurts, Lee. You win."

"Well, I'm going to look it up anyway, because she can be sly sometimes . . ."

"Beck!" Leelee looked offended.

"Oh, hell's bells, here it is—'the skin of a kind of squirrel with a gray back and white belly.' Now how in God's name did you know that, Lee?"

She shrugged. "I read a lot, I guess."

"Good game, junior." Thomas reached across the letter-dense board to shake her hand. It felt tiny and soft in his palm. "So what kind of things do you like to read?"

"I don't know—biographies. History. Adventure. Science fiction. Romances that Emma approves in advance." Leelee shot Emma a quick glance. "Just about anything, really."

"Do you have any favorite authors?"

"Sure—J.R.R. Tolkien, Barbara Kingsolver, Judy Blume. Emma took away all my Tom Robbins novels when I moved here from L.A., though."

He couldn't help but smile. Who let their twelve-year-old daughter read Tom Robbins? It was probably a good thing Emma arrived on the scene when she did.

"How about music? What kind of music do you like?"

Leelee snuggled back into the couch and Hairy returned to her lap. She stroked his ears. "Have you ever heard of the Backstreet Boys?"

He supposed it was good that Leelee was normal in some way. "Sure have," he said, trying to sound enthusiastic.

"Well, I'm in love with every single one of them, even the married ones." She sighed. "But Mom used to listen to lots of different stuff at home that I like, too—reggae and ska. Alternative. Texas blues. Jazz. You know she and Emma were in a band together when they were teenagers, right?"

Thomas watched a flush spread across Emma's cheeks as she sprang up to clear the drinking glasses.

"I'll get that, honey." Beckett took the glasses from her and suddenly Emma stood in front of Thomas with nothing to do but look embarrassed.

"Really?" he asked.

"Yeah," Leelee said. "They sucked."

Emma shrugged, thick hair shifting over her shoulder. "I'm afraid it's true."

"We've got a few videotapes of their shows if you want to see—"

"Time for bed, Lee!" Emma slid Hairy out from Leelee's arms and hauled her off the couch.

"But I don't have school tomorrow!" Leelee wailed. Emma pushed her toward the stairs.

"Good night, sweetie." Emma kissed her cheek.

"Wait!" Leelee spun around and ran back toward Thomas, looking up into his face with expectation. "I'll make a deal with you—you let me keep Hairy for the weekend and I'll go to bed now." A mischievous smile spread across Leelee's face, and in that instant she reminded him of Pam—except for the color of her eyes, she could be Pam's kid. Or his.

"If it's okay with Emma." His glance landed on Hairy and the strangest pang of jealousy hit him—he was going to miss the little pecker. "But you've got to let him out pretty often or you'll have a big mess to clean up. And he'll want to sleep in bed with you. He gets kind of cold and lonely otherwise."

"Oh, sure! Cool!" Leelee scooped Hairy from Emma's arms and ran out the front door with him. Emma turned to face Thomas with a crooked grin.

"It *is* okay with you, isn't it?"

"Why not?" Emma spread her arms wide in surrender.

"Here." Thomas dug into the front pocket of his slacks. "In case you need to bring him back and I'm gone, here's a key to my place. Just drop him in his crate."

Emma accepted the key just as Beckett came out of the kitchen and excused himself for the night, giving Thomas a friendly slap on the shoulder, and Leelee burst in the front door and started up the stairs. She stopped halfway and leaned over the polished oak banister.

"Thanks, Thomas." Her butterscotch-brown eyes danced in the foyer light. "I was afraid you'd be a complete and total loser, but you're pretty cool. Do you think you could teach me how to drive your car sometime?"

Thomas wasn't sure he'd heard correctly. "You want to drive my *car*? You're twelve."

"Just on the driveway. It's the hottest car I've seen since I moved to Maryland."

He felt the corner of his mouth hitch up. "Maybe someday."

She smiled at him and was gone.

Thomas stood in the hallway with Emma, his hands shoved in his pockets, a strange sense of pleasure spreading through him. Emma was looking up at his face, shaking her head.

"What?"

"Amazing."

"What is?"

She blinked, then laughed. "God, Thomas. Everything—everything's amazing."

"Sit with me a minute?" He reached for her hand and walked with her to the couch, where he pulled her down next to him. He let his arm drape across her shoulders, and sighed.

"I did pretty good tonight, didn't I?"

Emma snorted and shook her head. "You want to hear her nickname for you?"

He crooked his neck to look down at her. "I'm not sure . . ."

"Thomas the Tongue."

"Ouch."

"I told her it was disrespectful."

"Thanks for defending my virtue."

They sat in the quiet for a few moments, Thomas feeling more comfortable and relaxed than he could ever remember. Being with Emma seemed to do that for him. She snuggled closer.

"I passed the test, didn't I?"

Emma pulled away from his side to get a good look at him. "Thomas, you and Leelee are two peas in a pod—oh! Wait—that reminds me!" She was suddenly gone, and his arm fell to the couch cushions.

Emma sat on her heels as she rummaged through the lower bookshelves, and Thomas had to look away. He'd managed to get through the whole night without a single lustful thought about her—okay, that was an exaggeration— but he'd done pretty damn good and he didn't want to blow it now.

She returned to the couch, her finger holding her place in a big photo album. She didn't open it. Instead, she looked up at him with uncertain eyes.

"This is going to be a strange question, and you might get pretty angry. But, well, Becca—"

"Wasn't the world's most conscientious parent?"

Emma shook her head sadly. "There's no polite way to ask you this, Thomas. See, Leelee doesn't know who her dad was and you two look so much alike that I just have to know." She unceremoniously flung open the book and jabbed her finger at the glossy page. "Did you ever sleep with her?"

The album hit his lap with a thud, and he looked down at an eight-by-ten color photo of two beautiful women. One of them was a fresh-faced, joyous Emma, the wind blowing her hair back from her face as she laughed. The other was obviously Becca.

And Becca was drop-dead gorgeous. Like a movie star. Like an angel. And he'd never seen her before.

"How old were you two here?" He realized his finger

was lightly tracing the shape of Emma's face in the photograph.

"Twenty-five. I was in vet school and was visiting her in L.A. when this picture was taken. Leelee would have been about three."

Thomas dragged his eyes from the photo and looked into Emma's face. She was waiting for his answer, holding her breath, that small divot carved between her brows.

"I never slept with Leelee's mother," he said, watching her eyes close in relief.

"I'm so sorry I had to ask you that," she breathed.

"I don't sleep around, Emma. My last relationship lasted four years. I've had one or two brief encounters, but I remember them all and I'm fairly certain I don't have any offspring running around unaccounted for."

"I'm sorry."

"Don't be." He closed the album and handed it back to her. "I've got to get going. I've got to call Reg Massey on my way to Hancock—she's the detective who's handling Slick's case. Where did you put—"

Emma handed him a stack of computer printouts—everything she'd discovered about Simon Slickowski, the dog disco dancing king—and walked him to the door.

"Thank you for a wonderful night, Emma." Thomas felt he was forgetting something, then remembered that Hairy was spending the weekend with Leelee.

"You're angry with me."

He looked down onto Emma's bent head and, without thinking, touched his fingers to her chin and raised her face.

"No I'm not, because you're right, Emma—she looks like me. In fact, she looks just like Pam did at that age. It's kind of spooky and I'd be lying if I said I didn't wonder the same thing for a second. But I'm not her father. I never had sex with Becca Weaverton. I think I would've remembered."

"I imagine you would."

Thomas cupped her face tenderly in his palm. "You two must have made the boys nuts."

Emma snorted. "Becca was the nut-maker. I just went along for the ride."

Thomas smiled down at her. Emma of the baggy sweatshirts really didn't know how beautiful she was. He leaned close.

"Well, you make *me* nuts, Emma Jenkins. But I guess I'll just have to learn to live with that—for the time being."

He kissed her on the cheek and left.

Chapter 13

The Hustle

The guy who'd just walked into the bar had to be Tom—he looked like one seriously cold son of a bitch.

The hooker said to expect a big guy who'd been on the receiving end of a few punches. This man certainly fit the bill. Aaron watched him casually scan the dark room until his eyes stopped right on him. With a slight nod, he walked toward Aaron's table.

No, Tom didn't exactly look like a rocket scientist, but he appeared ruthless enough to do what had to be done—what *he* didn't want to have to do himself.

" 'Evening, Larry." The hit man slid into the booth.

"Tom?"

"That's my name."

The killer sprawled back against the seat like he was bored. His eyes were mean. He obviously was not going to be the one to start this conversation.

"So how long you been in this line of work?" Aaron asked him.

"Long enough," the killer said.

"Ever been caught?"

Tom blinked at him. "No, Larry. If I'd been caught, I'd be in jail."

"Right. So what'll you have?"

"I'll take a Bud."

Aaron jumped up from the booth and ordered a bottle of Budweiser for the hit man. Nothing more for himself; he needed to keep sharp.

When he reached into his pocket for five dollars, he noticed his hands were shaking. God, he was really going through with this—he was going to pay someone to kill Emma.

If she'd only given him the money. If she'd only listened!

"Here you go." Aaron tried to keep his voice steady.

"So what's the story, Larry?" The hit man took a big swig and stifled a belch. "Something I can help you with?"

Aaron stared at the killer. He seemed awful blasé about the whole business, but he supposed it was just another job to him. Yet the man's expression was anything but relaxed. His eyes were intense. Wise.

"It's my ex-wife," Aaron managed. "She's worth a small fortune."

"Yeah? How so?"

"Life insurance."

Tom frowned. "You're still the beneficiary?"

"Yeah. We agreed to stay on each other's policy for two years to make sure one of our uh . . . businesses stayed afloat should anything happen."

The killer leaned forward on his elbows and straightened the bill of his cap. He yawned. "What line of work are you in?"

Aaron flinched. Tom sure was asking a lot of questions. Like a cop.

"My work isn't important."

Tom shrugged. "So what can I do you for?"

"I think that's obvious."

The hit man smiled. "Look, Larry. I'm a busy guy. You need a hand with something? Fine. You changed your mind? Great. But I got better things to do than sit around here and play footsie with you." He stood up to leave.

"Wait."

The hit man hovered over him and looked mean as hell. He was perfect for the job. Aaron couldn't risk trying to find someone else. He was probably just being paranoid. And he'd come this far . . .

"Just wait a minute, okay?"

"You ready to do business?

"Oh, God," Aaron said. "I don't have any choice."

Thomas didn't trust the guy. Not that he trusted any suspected solicitor, but this one set off all his warning bells.

He was half in the bag and covered in a week's worth of scraggly beard, but his bright blue eyes burned with an eerie, sly intelligence. He spoke like someone with a college education. He was a small man, no more than five-nine and one sixty, but he held himself like someone used to a position of authority.

Thomas watched Larry go up to the bar, scanning his clothing for any signs he was carrying concealed. He saw nothing obvious.

When Thomas stretched and said, "Let's party," he knew he'd appear to be talking to himself should anyone be looking. In reality, he was doing another sound check.

Chick was tending bar tonight, and gave Thomas a slow nod to indicate everyone was on board. Thomas reviewed to himself where the others were stationed. Manny and two technicians were in the electronic surveillance van down the street. Paulie was alone in the next booth with his head bowed over a beer, just like every other sorry sack in the place.

Four troopers were pulled from other assignments for tonight's campaign. Two of them—including the only woman on the team tonight—were at a small table near the front door. Another trooper was stationed outside by the kitchen door, and another was in the front parking lot.

All team members were armed and wired for sound. In the van, Manny could hear and see everything. As the one coming face-to-face with the suspect, Thomas was un-armed, as usual—there was nothing the solicitor could grab that way.

By the time the solicitor got back to the booth and started playing games with him, Thomas had already de-cided the guy was not your average Hancock tavern rat. The team's background investigation revealed that he'd only stopped in a few times before and no one at the bar knew his last name, what kind of car he drove, or where he lived. In the four days they'd staked out the establish-ment, Larry had never stopped by.

Thomas didn't like the way this smelled. Not one bit. And he decided to give the guy one more chance to go on record, and if he didn't bite, he was getting his people the hell out of there.

Thomas stood up to leave. It worked.

"I hate her," Larry said as soon as Thomas sat back down. "It was all her fault. The divorce."

Now they were getting somewhere . . .

"She was perfect. Did you ever know someone who was perfect?" He looked up to Thomas, his eyes watering. "Do you know how goddamned annoying it was to be married to someone who's so fucking *good* all the time?"

Now this was a complaint he'd never heard before. "Can't say that I do, Larry."

Larry shook his head. "Such a goody-goody bitch. I couldn't stand it anymore. She was on my back all the time about everything, like I couldn't be trusted. Then she di-vorced me—took fucking *everything*. Ruined my life."

"How much is she worth?"

Larry raised his eyes. "Two hundred fifty thousand if it's an accident." He laughed bitterly, then grimaced. "And how much of that is going to belong to you, Tom?"

"Not a dime, Larry." Thomas smiled. "I get paid up front. In fact, when this is over, I don't care what happens to you or your insurance money. I don't even know you."

Larry returned his smile, and Thomas saw that he had gleaming, professionally straightened teeth framed in that patchy beard.

"That works for me," Larry said. "So how much?"

"Depends on how much you got and what kind of job you want done. Why don't we start with the basics—what's her name, how do I find her, and what do you want done?"

Larry's face fell. He tightly clasped his hands together on the table, but they still shook.

"Don't tell me about it, okay?" Larry's strange blue eyes were swimming in tears when he looked up. "I don't want to have any kind of picture in my head that's going to make me crazy for the rest of my life. I just need the money. That's all. It's only the money . . ."

Then Larry dropped his face into his hands and cried.

Thomas waited, trying to appear disinterested while his chest grew tighter with each passing second. He still hadn't managed to get what he needed—the name of the intended victim, explicit instructions to commit a felony, a payment. The solicitor had even carried the beer to the table in a bar napkin, as if he didn't want to leave prints.

Thomas realized Larry might be too smart—and too cautious—to incriminate himself.

"I gotta go to the john." Larry was up and walking away from the table, headed toward the men's room.

"Solicitor is moving," Thomas said aloud, already seeing the trooper leave the jukebox with Paulie on his heels.

It went wrong fast.

The trooper outside the kitchen left his post and walked into the front room, apparently hoping to put an extra set of eyeballs on the solicitor.

But Larry hadn't gone into the men's room. He'd gone into the ladies' room, squeezed through the window and was gone.

Moments later, Thomas stood in a dark patch of woods behind the garbage Dumpster with Paulie and Chick, picking burrs off his flannel shirt.

"How'd he know?" Chick asked. "How in the hell did he know?"

"Not sure," Thomas said, looking around in the darkness. The guy had escaped on foot, probably to a car parked a good way off. The team was out looking for him, but Thomas wasn't holding his breath.

They'd screwed up—and that was all there was to say.

"Not exactly a textbook operation, gentlemen," Thomas said.

"We didn't get shit, did we?" Paulie asked.

"Nope." In fact, they didn't even know Larry's real name.

Thomas pushed aside the brambles and stalked toward the parking lot. "And I'll tell you—I'm a little worried about the ex–Mrs. Larry, whoever the hell she might be."

"So how's Dr. Dolittle these days?" Regina kept her eyes on the road and her demeanor one of casual interest, but she didn't fool Thomas. She was digging for details.

"She's good." He looked out the passenger window to the industrial flatland north of the Maryland border.

"I see."

They were on their way to take a peek at the life of Simon Slickowski, aka Scott Slick. Since Emma's discovery, Regina had been able to put the pieces together with ease. The bottom line: Slick led a double life. His primary residence was in a trailer park in Delaware. Everything he owned and everything he did—from his car registration to his credit cards—was done under his late mother's name. In Baltimore he was Scott Slick, the bookie. In Delaware, he was Simon Slickowski, Vernelle's boy, a quiet man who worked part-time at a video store and doted on his weird, ugly dancing dog.

In Vernelle Slickowski's savings account was more than three-quarters of a million dollars.

Thomas sighed—just what he needed. Additional proof that no one could be trusted, that no one was who they claimed to be.

Except maybe Emma. Responsible, sweet, funny Emma.

"I'd like to meet her," Regina said. "Just to thank her for helping us out."

"Sure."

Things were moving fast with her, but for some reason, it didn't scare him.

He'd invited Emma, Leelee, and Beckett to his rugby match this coming Saturday, then over to his place for dinner with Pam and Rollo and the boys. He hadn't decided what to serve the horde, but it had to be something that didn't involve turning on the blender.

He'd made reservations for just the two of them next Friday at Bayside Stella's, and he'd called early enough to snag an outdoor table. He hoped the warm weather would hold.

In short, he was doing his damnedest to speed along the "for the time being." He was patient. He was gentlemanly. He could wait until she was ready.

As long as it didn't take too much longer.

"So tell me about her."

Thomas looked over at Regina and frowned. "Who?"

She laughed and smacked her hand on the steering

wheel. "Damn, Tommy. Don't bullshit me. How long have I known you?"

"Far too long, actually."

She snickered. "I know there have been more than a few women in your life. And Nina—Lord, Lord—it took you long enough to figure that one out."

Thomas sighed. "Don't try to spare my feelings or anything, Reg."

"Oh, now, honey, you know Nina wasn't the right kind of woman for you. You need someone fun-loving to balance you out. You need a woman who likes to let loose and smile and laugh—someone who knows how to love you." She crooked her head and smiled at him sweetly. "Damn, Tommy—you and Morticia made just about the most sour-assed couple I ever laid eyes on."

"No, really. Let it all out, Reg. I can take it."

She laughed some more. "So tell me about her. What's this vet like? Is she all those things?"

Thomas stared at Regina for a moment, the electrical wires and chemical holding tanks whizzing behind her head through the window.

"She's the best, Reg." He heard the astonishment in his own voice. "The best thing that's ever happened to me."

About an hour later, Thomas stood in the living room of unit 64 of the Smyrna Spring Trailer Court, realizing why Slick's Baltimore apartment had seemed a bit empty. He'd apparently used this trailer as a life-sized junk drawer.

A huge display case took up most of the paneled living room wall, filled with mementos of Slick's dog-dancing days—trophies, photographs, and framed medals from ceiling to floor. Closets were crammed with every conceivable type of dog collar, lead, or accessory in addition to costumes of both the canine and human variety. In a small file cabinet were Hairy's veterinary records.

A quick look revealed that Hairy was six years old, had been neutered at the age of nine months, and was purchased from a breeder for $2,500.

Un-fucking-believable.

The rest of the place indicated that Slick hadn't been concerned about much else. A red velveteen sofa was spilling its stuffing to the floor. Dirty dishes covered every available surface in the minuscule step-up kitchen. The floor was stacked with magazines, newspapers, and used paper plates.

But their best find was an elaborate computer system in the back bedroom that held the details of his bookie trade, and Regina instantly had about a thousand new leads in Slick's homicide.

"I haven't been in here since Vernelle died two years ago, so's I didn't know Simon let things go like this."

Maxine Barnhardt was the park's rental agent and the Slickowskis' next-door neighbor. In the ten minutes since she'd opened up the trailer for Regina and Thomas, she'd gone through two unfiltered Marlboros and a Diet Coke.

"You say you've got the little dog down in Baltimore with you?" she asked Thomas.

"Yes, ma'am."

"Well, I'll take him off your hands if you wanna."

Thomas couldn't help but laugh. Just two weeks ago, he would have fallen to his knees and kissed this woman's slipper-encased feet in a fit of gratitude. But that was two weeks ago. A lot had happened in two weeks.

"No, ma'am. I think I've already found a home for him. Someplace where he has another dog to play with and lots of land. He seems very happy there."

She took a long suck off her cigarette and shrugged. "Too bad. I always thought Hairy was sorta cute. Especially in his leprechaun outfit."

• • •

Emma was quite proud of herself. She'd been sitting on the sidelines for well over an hour and hadn't yet begun to pant or drool. She was carrying on a nice, friendly conversation with Pam—a lovely person—while Leelee played with Petey, Jack, and Hairy, and Beckett chatted up the coaches and players.

Emma prayed that no one could see that she was in agony sitting there in a folding chair in the sunshine, that she was fighting off a nonstop flow of X-rated thoughts, words, images, and sensations. She prayed that no one could tell that she was so sexually frustrated that her eyes were crossing.

The day hadn't started out that way. At first, the spectacle of the game made her laugh. To her uninitiated eye, rugby looked like nothing but a moving ball of chaos powered by naked male thighs and calves, all put to a soundtrack of grunting and yelling and cussing.

Then it amazed her—the sheer force of it, the grind and slam of bodies, the elegant violence, the raw emotion.

It was like football, only wickedly carnal.

She must have asked Pam a hundred questions: Why had Thomas wrapped black masking tape around his head? *To protect his ears from rubbing into players' hips and thighs in the scrum.* What was the scrum? *A kind of huddle that starts every play.* Aren't you afraid Rollo will get hurt? *He's already been hurt. They all have. It's part of the game.*

And then Thomas exploded down the field, yelling and pointing as he ran, the number five on the back of his black cotton jersey stuck to his sweat-soaked back, his big, muscular body eating up the ground.

"Oh, yeah, Rollo!" Pam stood and screamed when her husband dived over the goal line to score.

The action paused briefly, and Thomas turned toward

the sidelines, taped hands on hips, gulping for air, sweat pouring down his throat. He caught Emma's eyes and smiled.

And that's when the X-rated thoughts began. Starting with the particularly potent idea of licking the sweat from his entire naked body.

A year was an awfully long time to go without a man. Leelee seemed to like him. Right then, she decided to go for it.

Emma wiggled her fingers at him, and he waved back awkwardly, then shook his head as if he'd embarrassed himself.

When the play resumed, she felt Pam staring at her. Emma smiled politely.

"Thomas said you really helped him with his investigation."

"I didn't do much. I just figured out who the victim really was and things started falling into place."

"Have they arrested anyone yet?"

"Not yet, I don't think. But the computer records from his house in Delaware gave the detective lots of new leads."

"That's great."

Pam was a statuesque woman, with smooth tanned skin and the same arresting gray eyes as her brother. Her blond waves were streaked with the barest hint of silver and pulled back from her face with a tortoiseshell headband.

"Hairy seems to be doing better," Pam said.

Emma followed Pam's gaze to the dog running in circles in the grass, the knotted boxers in his mouth, all three kids chasing him.

"I can't tell you how happy I am with his progress." Emma looked back at Pam and nodded. "He's really loosening up, getting less anxious every day. I think it was just a matter of convincing him he's safe and loved. Underneath it all, he's a real special guy."

Pam began to choke, and reached for the can of soda by her feet. She took a sip, then let loose with a huge smile and touched Emma's forearm. "I'm sorry, but we *are* talking about Hairy, right? Not my brother?"

The two women sat in silence for a moment, evaluating each other as the rugby game exploded in grunts and referee whistles in front of them. Emma was the first to start giggling, then Pam joined her, and pretty soon they were laughing so hard Emma thought she'd fall out of the folding chair.

Steaks had seemed the easiest, and Thomas was glad he had extra, because somewhere between the car and the front door, Beckett met Mrs. Quatrocci and invited her to join them for dinner.

Thomas really couldn't say he minded. Since the night Pam hauled the old lady over his threshold, she'd stopped by quite a few times with food. Her tuna casserole tasted like a scoop of ocean bottom, but he had to admit he was getting addicted to her brown, bubbling fruit cobblers. They were delicious with ice cream.

Watching Mrs. Q flirt shamelessly with Beckett tonight, Thomas realized the old lady was probably just lonely. He didn't wish loneliness on anyone. God knew he'd had his share of it.

Thomas flipped the steaks, amazed at the way his house and yard literally thumped with life around him. Leelee had brought along some of Slick's disco CDs, and the kids and Hairy were dancing in the living room. He listened to the roars of adult laughter pouring out the kitchen window and smiled wistfully—damned if his own loneliness hadn't ended the day he'd acquired a six-pound mutant dog.

"Hey, Rugby Boy."

He spun around, the grill tongs snapping in the air in surprise.

"Hey—watch those things!" Emma's entire face lit up when she laughed. And Thomas corrected himself—his loneliness had ended the day he'd met this woman.

"Thanks for having us today—it's been so much fun."

In his mind, the idea of *having* Emma included a bit more than a rugby match and a steak. "You're very welcome," he said. "So what did you think of the match?"

Emma's eyes widened. "Nice hobby. It makes ice hockey look like high tea."

He snapped the tongs close to her nose and she twisted away in playful horror. "Watch it, Thomas. I might bite back this time."

He smiled at her, and in his mind he let it all play out: the hell with waiting. He would grab her around the waist and pull her up against the front of his body and say to her, "No more playing around, baby. You were made for this."

The idea punched the air right out of Thomas's lungs. There was no gravity anymore. There was only the imagined press of her soft, warm body and that wild, roaring vortex of desire.

He stared at her.

She stared back.

Then he imagined that she'd raise her sweet arms around his neck and close her eyes and offer him those plump, parted lips to suck and crush.

Dimly, Thomas heard the barbecue tongs clatter to the cement.

It would be hot, hot, hot, and Thomas would know it was the wrong place at the wrong time in front of just about all of the wrong people he could imagine, but he wouldn't give a flip because he'd be getting what he wanted, what he so desperately needed: Emma—warm, willing, wonderful Emma.

And he'd grab onto that ass of hers, and she'd wriggle and push up against him like she had on the porch—

"Uncle T! Uncle T!" A little hand yanked on his pants pocket and the daydream was over. He looked down into Petey's excited face, then to the breathless woman a few feet beyond his reach, and started to laugh.

No, he didn't want to go back to lonely. But he sure as hell was looking forward to being alone with Emma.

Chapter 14

Ring My Bell

"You're on fire, girl."

Velvet stepped back, tapped a finger on her cheek, and made one last inspection of Emma's ensemble. She wore the short and clingy blue dress with the little ruffle, the strappy sandals, and a pair of funky clip-on earrings Velvet had borrowed from Obaasan. She'd even convinced Emma to wear a bit of lip gloss tonight, a warm rose shade that accentuated her mouth.

The man was toast.

"He's going to slobber all over you."

Emma laughed. "Please. I get slobbered on all day, every day. I'm going for something out of the ordinary, here. Jaw-dropping shock, maybe."

Velvet nodded. "I hope his heart's strong. That's all I got to say."

Emma turned back to the full-length mirror on the inside of her office door. It was really here—the Night of the Blue Dress, the night she never thought would arrive. And with a minor adjustment of her cleavage, she smiled at herself and caught Velvet's eye in the mirror.

"Here goes nothing."

"Another man falls."

"But what if he doesn't?" Emma twirled on her two-

inch heels, feeling elegant and feminine in the split second
before she started to totter. Velvet grabbed her elbow.

"I mean, what if I'm imagining all this? What if he's
really not as interested as I am? He's been so . . . reserved
lately. Polite. He hasn't even tried to kiss me one single
time since that night on the porch. He just stares at me."

"Because you asked him to wait, didn't you?"

"True . . ."

"So the man's respected your wishes. This is a good
thing, Emma, not a bad thing."

"I guess. But what if he's cooled off since then?"

"Then he's about to warm up." Velvet reached over to
fluff Emma's hair. "You're hot tonight. Sexy. Fabulous."

Emma scrunched her nose and peeked at the mirror
again. "You know what? Maybe you're right. If those
words have ever applied to me, it would be tonight."

She giggled at her reflection and turned to examine her
behind. "I think I'm at my peak. Tonight. In this dress. I've
never looked this good in my life and probably never will
again. This is it—the zenith of Emma Jenkins. I hope you
feel honored to witness it."

Velvet groaned.

"No. I'm completely serious." She put her hands on her
hips. "I'm thirty-four. From what I understand, it's all
downhill from here."

She turned—no wobble this time—and grabbed her little
black purse. "I'm off. It's now or never. Wish me luck."

Velvet shook her head. "You don't need it, hon."

The hostess led Emma to the outdoor dining deck and instantly her eyes found Thomas.

He sat at a picnic table near the railing, looking out over
the water, two bottles of beer already centered on the brown
butcher-paper tablecloth in front of him. He wore a white

button-down shirt with the sleeves rolled up to the elbows, a pair of khaki pants, and brown leather loafers with no socks.

His long legs stretched out lazily under the table. His wide shoulders hung relaxed. He leaned on his forearms, the tendons and muscles in his neck exposed. It made him look vulnerable somehow, big and masculine but human all the same. It made her smile.

He turned to her.

A sharp "Bing, bing, bing, bing!" sliced through her brain. And she knew it was the sound of hitting the jackpot—like when the *Price Is Right* Showcase contestant won the car, the trip, *and* the twenty-five grand in one fell swoop.

A flash of surprise seemed to widen Thomas's eyes, but he instantly replaced it with a cool, unruffled gaze. He was quite capable of keeping his face unreadable when he wanted to.

He stood up.

She moved closer, the awareness intensifying with each step. It poured over her, hot and sizzling, leaving the tiniest suggestion of fear in its wake. The friendly little bells had been drowned out by the roar of her own blood.

She couldn't remember the last time she was this nervous, this self-conscious—this revved up—and tried to focus on placing one sandaled foot in front of the other in as ladylike a manner as possible. Thomas's eyes didn't stray from her face, but she was certain that other people were staring at her from head to toe, whispering things like "Did you get a load of that fleshy woman in an obscene blue dress?"

Emma suddenly feared the worst: a side seam was about to split open; her boobs were about to pop from the neckline like champagne corks on New Year's Eve. She couldn't do this.

Oh. But she already was, wasn't she?

Thomas's face remained perfectly inscrutable, though Emma thought he might have flexed his jaw. There was no smile. No mouth opening with shock. No drool. Nothing.

Her heart sank. She must have been overly optimistic. Maybe she looked so bad that he was embarrassed for her, embarrassed to be seen in public with her.

She reached the table, and Thomas cupped her bare elbow with a wide, warm palm.

"Hey, Emma."

He guided her down as she tried to fold and twist her tightly sheathed body onto the bench, which was no small feat. By the time she was seated, she was breathless, rattled, perspiring, and feeling horribly overdressed—or underdressed, depending on how she decided to look at it.

Why hadn't she worn the simple black outfit she'd chosen for her date with Mr. Traffic Court—comfortable, modest, dark enough that she'd simply faded into the background?

She closed her eyes in mortification. *Why in God's name did I wear this dress?*

Why the hell did she wear that dress? Thomas wondered.

Did she want to see him weep like a helpless infant? Did she want to see him die an agonizing death? Was she subjecting him to some strange, convoluted female test that he was predestined to fail?

Or had she changed her mind? Oh man, was she chucking the "time being" crap and hitting on him? Because it was inconceivable that she didn't know what she was doing to him—and every other man in the place—in that dress.

It had taken every ounce of strength to remain standing when she'd walked across the deck to their table, all her good parts on display all at the same time—the slender neck and creamy shoulders, those unbelievable breasts, those juicy hips, thighs, legs . . .

He swallowed—hard. What was he supposed to say? What was he supposed to do?

Thomas felt a trickle of sweat run down the center of his spine.

He tried not to stare at her, but he was weak—always so weak in her presence—no different from any other schlub under the spell of a beautiful woman.

So while Emma got comfortable and glanced around, he stared at her, unable to form words, aware that he must look like one of those old Looney Tunes characters who transforms into a wolf with one peek at a gorgeous dame, his long, red tongue lolling out of the side of his mouth, his eyeballs shooting straight out from their sockets, then snapping back, all to the sound of "AH-OOO-GAH!"

She looked at him.

He was a dead man.

From the grave, in a raspy groan, he asked, "Hungry?"

"Yes, I am. How about you?"

He felt one side of his mouth twitch and knew he couldn't stop himself. "I'm always hungry, Emma," he said in that dead man's voice.

Emma dragged her eyes all over him—that golden-boy face with the broken nose, the big shoulders, the sexy mouth . . .

"Nice place," she said.

"My favorite," he said.

They were surrounded by laughter, the squawk of sea gulls, the clatter of dishes, and the crack of mallets on crab shells. They were festive sounds—summer sounds—nearly ready to be packed away for the winter season. She took a deep breath and savored it.

The deck snuggled up to a little man-made beach along Bayside Landing. At least thirty people were crammed onto picnic tables on the deck and another fifteen sat at dining tables on the narrow strip of sand, under umbrellas, surrounded by transplanted palm trees and tiki torches. The combination of a legitimately pretty setting and tacky décor was pure Baltimore, and it made her smile.

Glancing around, she noticed the word *Tobin* scrawled in pencil at the edge of their paper-covered table. Thomas must have called ahead and reserved this table and now there she was, with him, in public, with his name in big letters for the world to see. And it made her feel special.

Why was that? She was fiercely attached to her own last name and never took Aaron's when they married. In fact, she'd never even considered hyphenating it—Emma Jenkins-Kramer just never sounded right to her.

But Emma Jenkins-Tobin? Now that had a nice cadence to it. Familiar, even. Like she'd heard it all her life.

Emma sucked in a mouthful of air and started to cough.

Thomas offered her a bottle of Corona, a lime wedge perched on the lip of the glass.

"Here. Shall we make a toast?" He tapped her bottle with his own. "To smart consultants."

"To Hairy."

Thomas nodded, raising his bottle again. "To Hairy the Strange Little Dog. If it weren't for him, I'd be sleeping alone every night."

He tipped back his beer, and Emma watched Thomas's lips kiss the glass rim of the bottle, his tongue press into the round opening, his throat muscles ripple as he gulped.

How long had it been since the completely outrageous kiss on her porch? A couple weeks. Or a nanosecond. Or several lifetimes ago. The truth was, she'd forgotten how time worked.

"I called ahead and placed our order. I hope you don't mind."

Emma was relieved to talk—it kept her brain busy. "Let me guess—crabs?"

All around them was the evidence of serious crab consumption—tables heaped with piles of shells, buckets on the deck floor overflowing with shells, bowls of drawn butter, empty beer pitchers or bottles, and only an occasional basket of rolls or bowl of coleslaw or corn. This place was for genuine crab connoisseurs only.

"Yep. Crabs." He quickly looked away.

Emma sighed. It appeared Thomas wasn't going to say anything about the dress. The window of opportunity to mention her appearance had just closed, and he sat there, not saying anything about how she looked, not even able to hold her gaze.

It wouldn't have taken much. A simple "You look pretty tonight," or "That's a nice dress," and she'd have already vaulted over the table and crushed his body in an upper-thigh death grip.

But he didn't say a thing. And that said it all, didn't it?

Their waitress arrived with a huge platter of hard-shell crabs. "Two dozen large," she said, lowering it onto the center of the picnic table. Another waitress followed close behind with butter, coleslaw, and soft, white rolls. "Anything else?"

"Thanks. I think we're all set," Thomas said with a friendly nod.

Emma's eyes flew to the waitress—it was pure female instinct. She was a pretty redhead no more than nineteen, and she was flirting outrageously with Thomas. Apparently, it didn't bother her that Thomas was nearly old enough to be her father—the little Jezebel! Emma watched the girl give Thomas a playful smile. "Let me know if I can do anything else for you."

Emma snorted. *Right*. It was all she could do to keep her next thought to herself. *Over my dead body, cupcake*. But then the waitress turned, swinging her slim hips all the way back to the kitchen.

The jealousy thumped Emma right in the center of her

chest. She froze, surprised by the force of it. But then, of course women would find Thomas attractive—didn't she remember her initial response to him? She nearly had to be hosed down!

And really, so what if women flirted with him? She and Thomas were just friendly colleagues, correct? Nothing more. She had no claim on him. She had no expectations.

So she was wearing the infamous blue dress for him? So she was plotting to scratch out the eyes of a teenager for him?

She was even wearing clip-on earrings for him! She was thinking about hyphenating for him! She was *falling in love* with him!

Emma dropped her head in her hand and rubbed her forehead. "I'm in serious trouble," she said out loud.

Thomas laughed softly. Emma raised her eyes to him, certain that he'd just witnessed her painful journey to self-awareness. But he wasn't even looking at her.

"Yeah, it's a thing of beauty, isn't it?" He stared at the red mountain of steaming crabs, oblivious to all else. Then he peeked over the platter and shot her a grin.

She smiled back. She straightened up. "So how many of those can you eat, Rugby Boy?"

"I could eat 'em all." He wiggled his scarred eyebrow and the semicolon danced. "But I suppose I'll save a few for you."

They spent the next hour eating crabs, telling stories, and laughing. Thomas talked more tonight about himself than he ever had—probably because he no longer had anything to hide from her.

He talked about some of his cases. He talked about his childhood—how his mother had left when he was ten, never to be seen again. "She's been married several times since. She was in Italy last we knew, about ten years ago."

"I'm sorry," Emma said.

"Yeah, well, it was a rough lesson," was his only comment.

Then he talked about how he'd introduced Rollo to Pam one spring break and it was love at first sight. When he talked about Petey and Jack, his eyes sparkled.

Though the conversation was enjoyable, she was shocked by the way Thomas ate—the quick, methodical dismantling of the crustaceans, the well-placed whack of the mallet, rapid-fire sleight-of-hand movements followed by fast transfers to his mouth, then bam! An entire creature had been picked apart, licked clean, and its remains tossed to the heap of shells at the other end of the table—all while talking.

What Thomas told her next explained his skill—his grandfather was an Eastern Shore waterman, and he used to take him out on the crab boat as a kid, when Chesapeake crabs were plentiful.

"I checked with the owner here tonight—half of these pups aren't local—they're flown in from Texas and Louisiana." Thomas dipped a claw into the drawn butter and popped it in his mouth, scraping it clean. "Did you know the price is up to sixty-five dollars a dozen for good-sized hard-shells these days? I remember my granddad used to get half that much for an entire bushel."

Emma's breath caught—he was spending close to one hundred and fifty dollars on crabs tonight?

Thomas noticed her worry and waved it away as he threw another carcass on the pile. "It's worth it to me. This is a special occasion. I can afford it."

"The state police must pay better than I realized."

He hummed thoughtfully as he chewed. "I make enough to get by, but I also got extra help along the way. My dad was a big-shot corporate attorney and he left me and Pam a nice chunk of change when he passed away. Money's not a problem for me."

Emma looked up in surprise, then smiled wistfully. "Now *that's* something I look forward to hearing myself say someday."

Thomas remained quiet for a few moments, letting the guilt wash over him—again. He should have told her that he paid her consulting fee. But she wouldn't have wanted that, right? She wouldn't have agreed to work with him, right? She wouldn't have had any reason to spend time with him.

He couldn't keep putting this off. He had to come clean—about everything.

"Emma, I—"

"Thanks again for snagging the contract for me, Thomas. I'm sure it wasn't easy and you probably got a lot of ribbing about it. I wish . . ." Emma stopped and stared down at the dinner roll in her fingers. "I really needed the money—my practice needed it."

Thomas shook his head and began to say something but Emma jumped in again. "Aaron wasn't the most responsible person in the world. Money was a constant struggle with us and he had some personal problems that got us into trouble. But it was my fault too, for letting him get away with it."

Thomas answered her in a soft voice. "Beckett told me."

Her head snapped up and she blinked. "He did? When? What did he tell you?"

Thomas shrugged. "The first night I came to your house. He told me, and I quote, 'Aaron had an eye for the ladies and couldn't hold on to a dollar to save his soul. He wasn't good enough for my girl. Never was.' "

Emma snorted and took another sip of beer. "That about sums it up, unfortunately."

Thomas waited for a few more details, but they didn't come. He had to smile—the only human being in the world he wouldn't mind opening up to him about a failed relationship wasn't interested in doing so.

"You're a very private person, aren't you, Emma?"

She tipped her head. "Not really. Not with the people I'm close to—the people I love."

That sentence shot him through with pain—she didn't love him. But hold on. Of course she didn't love him! They'd only known each other a couple weeks! And yes, he was extremely attracted to her, but he didn't exactly want her to love him, did he? He didn't want *any* woman to love him!

Did he?

"Thomas, do you remember that night on my porch when we kissed?" Emma stared down at the brown paper tablecloth and her voice was barely more than a whisper.

"Only every other second."

Her breath was coming fast and her pulse was kicking hard and all she could think was that he didn't say anything about her dress. He didn't say *anything*! It was obvious that whatever was happening was a bit one-sided—he might not mind taking her to bed a few times, but he didn't like her enough to notice she'd gone to extreme lengths to look nice tonight. He didn't like her enough to be courteous. Respectful. Appreciative.

She had to remind herself that this was not the type of man she wanted in her life—even for a few nights. She deserved more, and though she'd convinced herself that Thomas *was* more, she had to admit she may have been wrong.

She needed to take charge of this situation, take care of herself. If she didn't, who would?

"When I said this wasn't the right time, I meant that in a couple ways." She bit her bottom lip with nervousness. "It's not just Leelee."

When she brought her soft blue eyes level with his, Thomas nearly moaned with longing.

"I just signed my divorce papers, Thomas. I just got out of an extremely bad situation, and I'm not exactly at my best—I'm kind of exhausted, actually." She let her elbow rest on the edge of the table and cupped her chin in her hand, looking at him. "It took me a long time to realize that I wasn't responsible for Aaron. It took everything I had to get out of that relationship. Do you understand what I'm saying?"

"Sure I do." He cracked another claw. "You're scared."

Emma sighed and shook her head. "I'm saying I need to be very careful. I'm trying to decide if I'm ready to get involved with anyone—with you—beyond being friendly business partners. I'm not convinced that you're the right kind of man for me."

She sat back and said nothing more.

Thomas's movements had slowed considerably. He used a napkin to wipe the streaks of red spices and butter from his fingers and grabbed for his bottle of beer. He took a long, slow drag, and let his eyes wander from that lovely, confused face to that dress again. Damn, he shouldn't have done that!

How ironic. She'd just told him he wasn't her type and he'd picked that particular moment to nearly explode in his chinos just from looking at her. All that thick, gleaming hair, that succulent cleavage, those ripe, red lips slippery with butter.

Never in his life had he known a woman as fun, appealing, smart, delicious—oh, Jesus, as *fuckable*—as Miss Marple over there, and all he wanted was to clear off the tabletop with one violent sweep of his forearm, lay her down on the butcher paper, and let his tongue slip over every goddamn inch of that farm-girl skin. He wanted to stretch his body over hers, feel her wrap around him, hear her scream his name.

He wanted . . . *her*.

Thomas put down the beer bottle and looked her right in the eye. He'd heard her words clear enough. And as he studied her, observed her body language, he heard that, too. And the actions were speaking much louder than the words.

The sexual heat gathered around them as fast as the twilight, and it pushed against his chest, against his cock, and into his brain.

Yes, her words said, "I'm not sure." But the soft pleading in her eyes, the way she'd been jealous of the waitress, the seductive pout of her lips, her quick breathing, *that fucking dress!*—all of it screamed, "Put your hands on me—now!"

Thomas didn't know what to do. He could hardly breathe.

So he started in on another crab.

Emma simply stared at him. Her lips were on fire. She didn't know if it was the beer, the heavy-handed dose of Old Bay spice on the crabs, or just plain sexual greed, but her lips felt unbearably sensitive and swollen and a liquid fire was rushing through her veins.

She watched Thomas as he ate—consumed was more like it. His mouth and chin were smeared slick with butter. He was an eating machine—evenly paced in his movements, denuding one helpless creature after another. It was a kind of lusty, barbaric dance that made her dizzy.

A loud *crack!* pierced the air and she jerked. He'd smashed the mallet down on a crab leg, using far more force than was necessary, not saying a word, his eyes now fierce on hers. He looked exactly like he did that night in the diner parking lot—absolutely tortured.

Then came another loud crack of the mallet, followed by more silence and staring, and the quiet was growing heavier, darker, breath-stealing. Emma felt how the air itself became heavy, rich, and dripping with the promise of sex.

Sex. Sex. Sex.

The two of them couldn't seem to escape it.

Suddenly, Thomas picked up a new victim, held it with both hands, and wrenched apart the crab legs until they formed a wide vee in front of his mouth. His eyes locked on Emma's as he licked a drip of butter off the inside of his wrist.

Emma jumped in her own skin.

Then she watched him ever so slowly suck a plump tidbit of white backfin meat from a tendon. He licked his lips. He made a raspy sound somewhere between a moan and a sigh of pleasure.

"All right. Friendly business it is, Dr. Jenkins." His eyes were hot and mischievous. "Would you say you're satisfied with the progress we're making with Hairy?"

Emma didn't know if the speech and language center of her frontal lobe still functioned. She couldn't take her eyes off him—the man knew what he was doing. Yes, indeedy-doo. He worked to a nice, even rhythm. He knew how to pace himself. Spreading. Pulling. Licking. Grinding. Eating.

"I think I'm getting real close to being satisfied," she said.

Emma let the very tips of her fingers brush against a few of the places she now imagined him putting his mouth—the hollow at the base of her throat, her temples, her lips. She absently dropped her hand to the tops of her breasts and lazily dragged her fingers over her cleavage.

Thomas nearly howled—she'd just left a glittering smear of butter on her breasts! How thoughtful of her to provide the condiments, because he'd long ago decided her breasts would taste like hot bread right out of the oven—and he planned on doing some serious carbo-loading.

"I think we work well together," he mumbled, his eyes glued to her butter-topped flesh.

"Uh-huh," she agreed.

Emma wiggled around on the bench, horribly uncomfortable. Her dress suddenly felt way too tight. Her underwear didn't feel tight enough.

And it was back—Bing! Bing! Bing! Bing!—as his eyes flashed in the tiki torch flame, his skin glowed bronze in contrast to the white shirt and white teeth, and as his pulse throbbed beneath the tender skin of his throat.

She reached for her beer—suddenly parched—and brushed her fingertips up and down the sweating neck of the Corona bottle. "Thank you for keeping things businesslike between us, Thomas," she said.

"Of course." He smacked his lips. "I think we both know it's always going to be serious business with us."

Emma let go with a soft, strangled whimper. And right then, she knew, she was about to behave like a very bad girl.

What is Emma doing? Thomas's heart pounded. His throat constricted. And he watched—oh, yeah, he watched.

She looked up innocently from under those thick, black lashes and raised the beer bottle to her lips. Moisture beaded and dripped down the side of the bottle. Her lips glistened.

Ever so slowly, she inserted the rounded tip of the bottle into her mouth, pulled it out once to let her tongue swirl around the slick ridge of glass, then pushed it between her lips.

Then she swallowed.

Thomas was going down—down into the vortex without any hope of rescue. Which was fine with him.

She let the bottle slip out again with a faint sucking noise, keeping the very tip of her pink tongue inside the opening. Then she repeated the whole excruciating process before she set the bottle down with shaking hands.

"Serious business," she whispered, slipping her little pink tongue along her wet bottom lip.

Thomas was in pain from the chest down. He grabbed the mallet. He grabbed the last crab on the platter. And he began to hammer out a slow, sure rhythm, his eyes fused with hers, hot and penetrating.

Pound.

Pound.

Pound.

Pound.

Until the poor crustacean was mashed to a pulp, and Emma grabbed the edge of the picnic table and pressed her thighs together as she felt the tingle radiate to her scalp, her toes, realizing, as it was happening, that she was spontaneously combusting right there on the outdoor dining deck of Bayside Stella's, while an impatient crowd stood around waiting for a table.

Emma didn't quite know how she came to be standing in the parking lot a few moments later, car keys in hand, Thomas at her side. Perhaps it was for the best.

But there she was, and then Thomas was standing in front of her with that pained look on his face again and he was saying the strangest thing . . .

"I paid your consulting fee, Emma. I couldn't get it authorized, so I used my own money."

"What?" She fell against the Montero as if he'd pushed her.

"If I hadn't, you wouldn't have had any reason to spend time with me. I misled you and I'm sorry. It wasn't right."

Emma couldn't get enough oxygen to her brain. She was still buzzing from that very strange and very extraordinary public orgasm—and he'd lied to her. Again! She'd performed beer-bottle fellatio for a man who could not tell the truth!

The next thing she knew, she was driving away, alone, glad that they'd taken separate cars. Within minutes, she pulled into a 7-Eleven parking lot, cut the engine, and sat there in the dark.

The first two words out of her mouth came in a hoarse whisper.

"*Oh,*" she said.

"*My,*" she said.

Then she took a huge breath, and let it out.

"*Gaaaawd!*"

Then she cried.

In his Audi, Thomas's hands shook even though he gripped the leather steering wheel with all his might. He clicked on a Thelonious Monk CD and tried to calm himself.

He clicked it off immediately and stared at the road ahead in silence.

I am in one very large, big-time, bad-ass, hell of a mess.

He drove faster.

I'm completely in love with Emma Jenkins and she hates me.

He drove faster still.

What a bad time to tell her the truth.

He looked at his watch.

And now I have to go to work.

Chapter 15

Do Ya Think I'm Sexy?

Emma knew that Thomas had been out all night for work and, with any luck, would still be asleep. She tucked Hairy under her arm, inserted the key into his townhouse door, and quietly stepped inside.

Emma intended to put Hairy in his crate and leave. She didn't want to see Thomas. In addition to being ashamed about her public out-of-body experience last night, she was thoroughly pissed off.

Because he'd lied to her. Because as much as she wanted to pay him back every dime he'd given her, it was already gone. The money now belonged to Baltimore Gas & Electric, Allstate Insurance, Charm City Mortgage, and American Veterinary Supply, and she'd have to borrow yet more cash from Beckett to repay Thomas. What a mess.

Emma entered the room and let her eyes adjust. It was dim except for a narrow sliver of light that shot through a gap in the drapes. The low hum of music wrapped around her, and she recognized the sultry groan of Tom Waits—a piano man whose music should be banned everywhere but in seedy bars in the middle of the night, for the listening enjoyment of only the most severely drunk and depressed patrons.

It certainly wasn't suited to a sunny Saturday morning like this one.

Emma cocked her head and listened closely, now hearing more than just raspy lyrics and the tinkling of piano keys. She also heard the saw of deep breathing. Hairy squirmed out of Emma's arms and ran toward the couch—and her gaze followed.

She could just make out what lay on that couch, all stretched out and almost naked. Thomas's face was turned away toward the cushions, one burly arm bent across his bare chest, the fist closed in sleep. The other hand lay open, palm up, along the top of his right thigh.

He wore nothing but a thin pair of athletic shorts that looked gray in the muted light, the drawstring tied loose and low on narrow hips, his long legs stretched across the cushions.

Even in the poor light, Emma saw that he was golden, sculpted, perfect—the most exquisite male animal she'd ever laid eyes on. Too bad she'd never trust him again.

Then she wondered how many seconds it would take her to strip naked and start rubbing her flesh all over his.

"No, Hairy!" she hissed. "Damn!" She wasn't fast enough. Hairy hopped right on top of Thomas. The dog nosed his arm until it flopped over the edge of the couch, and began circling to find the sweet spot on his chest. Emma held her breath, expecting to see the poor thing hurled through the air.

Then she smiled—this ritual was nothing new to Thomas, apparently. He acknowledged the dog's presence with a clumsy pat to the head and a garbled greeting of "Hey, pal." Still asleep, he adjusted his body and turned his face toward Emma.

She stood completely still, unable to move even if she'd wanted to. She simply watched the dog ride the rise and fall of Thomas's chest as the tears rolled down her cheeks.

She was crying? What a lame-o thing to do, as Leelee would say. She wiped the tears away with the back of her hand, amazed and horrified by the tight sensation in her chest, the trembling in her limbs.

She didn't want to feel anything for him! He'd misled her, even if his motive was a nice one. A real nice one. Oh, hell—the man had paid eight thousand dollars just to have her near him!

Emma watched him sleep, trying to hate him and failing, seeing only how sweet he looked, how sexy—how lovable. Thomas Tobin, the surly, sneaky, undercover hit man, was so lovable.

Hairy had just nibbled his master's jawline, little flea-bites that made Thomas chuckle in his sleep and wave his hand to shoo away the dog. Hairy persevered, nipping a cheek and then an upper lip until Thomas began to groan and mumble.

Emma leaned closer and tried not to laugh. It seemed that a real friendship had blossomed between this man and this dog, and she was feeling quite proud of her role in the transformation when Thomas whispered something, and she tensed. Had she heard correctly? Had he just said her *name*?

Emma was studying Thomas's moving lips when a devilish smile spread over his face and he moaned, "Oh, yeah, Emma. Put your mouth on me."

Her hand flew up to stifle a gasp. Hairy skittered down Thomas's body as if to get out of the way, and Emma watched the dog jump down, race across the room, and curl up in a ball in the recliner.

Thomas mumbled something else and Emma turned back—to find that his eyes were halfway open and he was gazing at her behind heavy lids. Before she could escape, he grabbed her, crushed her against the front of his body, gripped the back of her head, and forced her mouth down onto his.

The top of Emma's skull nearly blew off. His lips were hot and impatient, and he was mumbling to her even as his tongue entered her mouth, flicked inside her. His other hand clamped down on her butt, grinding her crotch against his, and there was no escaping the man's outstanding attributes.

"Oh, yeah," he groaned against her lips. He dragged his hands to the back of her thighs and pulled until she was spread wide across him. "Ride me, Emma."

A strangled cry flew from her throat as she tried to end the crush of his embrace, the attack of his mouth, the spreading of her legs. She got a hand loose enough to smack his cheek.

Thomas went completely still beneath her. He released his death hold on her body, relaxed the lip-lock. And Emma pushed herself up from his chest, panting.

"Jesus!" Thomas sprang to life, throwing her off balance and sending her backward to the end of the couch, where she landed with a thud on his insteps. "Ow!" he screamed.

When he yanked his feet out from under her, Emma's rump hit the sofa arm.

"What the hell—" Thomas was fumbling behind his head for the lamp and Emma shielded her eyes from the abrupt glare.

She listened to him mumble swear words for a moment or two, then peeked out from between her fingers. Thomas's short curls were crushed to the side of his head. He was unshaven. His eyes were wild and rimmed with red.

And he was tugging on the drawstring of his shorts, now tented with the Big Daddy of all erections. She let her hands fall from her face so that she could ogle.

Then their eyes met. Thomas blinked at her several times and opened his mouth to speak. "I'm not sure what—"

Emma cut him off. "You!" she screamed, pointing like she was identifying a pickpocket on the street. "You lied to me again!"

"I did. A huge mistake."

She glared at him, catching her breath. "You will never lie to me again, Thomas."

"That's absolutely true."

"And what about . . . well . . . the other thing you did to me last night?" She crossed her arms under her breasts with a loud harrumph.

He blinked some more.

"Would you mind telling me how I had an actual . . ." Emma stopped and shot a glance toward Hairy—who was watching them intently. She continued in a whisper. "Look, Thomas. I had an *orgasm* on a picnic bench last night, surrounded by crab parts, without you even *touching* me. Would you please explain how that happened?"

Thomas waited a beat, not sure if she was through with her question, or even if it *was* a question, or if it might possibly be a redundant one. She seemed to want an answer, but he had no idea what to say—he was still half-asleep. Besides, all the blood that used to be in his brain was now in his shorts.

"I'm . . ."—he fumbled for the correct words—". . . sorry about that, too?"

She snorted and tossed her loose hair from her shoulder. "I'm so angry with you!" Emma was desperately trying to keep her emotions in control, but there were too many to get a handle on—hurt, surprise, lust, and fear were right up there at the top of the list. "You're making me crazy," she said with a shaky voice.

"Emma—"

"How? How the hell did you get to me without laying a finger on me?"

Thomas smiled and the dimples popped to life even as his right eye narrowed. She hated when all those things happened at once—it made him so adorable she couldn't concentrate.

"Indirect communication, Miss Marple."

"Oh." After a sigh, she went right back to being indignant. "And what was *this* all about?" She pointed to his mostly naked body. "Were you dreaming about me just now?"

"Wouldn't be the first time." Thomas straightened up and rubbed his hands through his hair and over his face, nearly slapping himself awake. He stared at her.

She stared back.

Neither moved.

"Um, you're the expert, Emma, but I think we're having one of those 'four F' moments here, wouldn't you agree?"

She laughed at that. Thomas was actually quite funny—for a compulsive liar. With a sigh, she sat farther back on her heels and took a leisurely look at the man stretched out before her. His eyes were sleepy and dangerous. His body was long and brawny and nothing but glowing muscle covered in downy blond curls. The shorts were now tugged lower on his rippled abdomen, pulled by an erection so obvious that it should have been sporting a festive pink bow and a gift tag that read "For Emma."

She cleared her throat. "And which one of the F's are you leaning toward right now, do you suppose?"

"Mmmm." He draped a chiseled arm over the back of the couch and crooked a knee provocatively, shifting his weight. Emma checked out the Big One again and felt her mouth go dry.

"Well, you certainly don't frighten me." His voice was low and thoughtful. "And I don't particularly feel like fighting anymore. So I guess that leaves flight or—"

"Fucking me."

Silence.

Emma could not *believe* she'd said that! She clenched her eyelids shut in a reflex of utter mortification, tight enough, she prayed, to put an end to her very existence.

"Yep—that would be my first choice," he said in a hoarse whisper.

Did she dare look at him? With a wince, Emma opened her eyes. The muscles along Thomas's jaw were clenched tight and the tendons strained in his neck. He swallowed hard, his Adam's apple sliding along the length of his throat. His right eye was now just a slit.

"In fact," he continued, "since it's going to be nothing but the truth from here on out, here's the truth, sweet-cheeks—I've wanted to fuck you since the instant you walked into the exam room and that shiny braid of yours flew over your shoulder. And I've felt like fucking you every damn time I've had the pleasure of being in your company since then—the emergency clinic, the diner, the diner parking lot, your basement, your porch, Slick's apartment, my car, the—"

"Fine. I get your—"

"And right now. Let's go."

"—point."

He was already on his feet and hovering over Emma, his hand outstretched to her, his groin level with her face. She thought she might cry again.

"Move it, Miss Marple. We're going upstairs."

"But what about our working relationship?" Oh—now was a swell time to get all prim and proper, but Emma figured she should at least pretend to be the voice of reason, even if that voice just came out in a pitiful squeak.

"It's Saturday. I try not to work on Saturdays if I can help it."

"That's not what—"

He grabbed her hand and pressed it to the front of his shorts. She knew this was going to be a huge mistake, but Thomas Tobin was proving hard to resist.

Real huge. Real hard.

Emma's lips went numb. All she could do was nod her

head real slow because who was she kidding? This was where they'd been going since the moment they'd met, whether she wanted to admit it or not.

She was simply the product of thousands of years of human evolution—a process that had fine-tuned Homo sapiens into the most sexual primates on earth. And she was just a healthy female of breeding age, one who'd gone more than a year without sex. Which wasn't natural. Not natural at all.

He pulled her to her feet, and before she knew what was happening, Thomas put his shoulder to her belly, tipped her off the ground, and flung her over his shoulder.

The air whooshed from Emma's lungs as they headed for the stairs. Then Thomas slapped a big hand down on her ass like he owned it, and she gasped. His other steely arm clamped around the back of her knees.

How was she supposed to respond to this kind of man-handling? No one had ever picked her up like this—outside of that Conan the Barbarian fantasy, to which this bore a striking resemblance, she realized.

Emma felt helpless, breathless, and a tiny bit petrified. But all she could do was stare at the receding steps and the upside-down view of the bulging muscles along the back of Thomas's thighs and calves, thinking the whole time that she was surely giving the man a herniated disc.

"Thomas, put me down. I'm too heavy."

"You're not too heavy."

"I am. Put me down."

"I plan to—on my bed."

The last thing Emma saw before they turned the corner of the upstairs hallway was Hairy, sitting near the bottom of the steps, his head tipped to the side and his lips pulled back in what she once again swore was a smile.

Are those monkeys I see flying out of your butt, Big Alpha?

• • •

Once inside the bedroom, pure panic hit.

His hand was on her butt—her *butt*!—which she knew he wouldn't find very appealing once they got to the down and dirty. How had she let it get this far? Pretty soon he'd be seeing the whole enchilada, right there in broad daylight, and he was bound to lose his appetite for Mexican.

The derriere in question hit the mattress and Emma bounced a few times, long enough for her to watch Thomas straighten up, put a hand to the small of his back, and stretch.

"Told you I was too heavy."

His eyes swept down to where she sat on the corner of the bed, gripping the mattress like it would keep her from falling off the edge of the earth.

She wasn't too heavy—she was perfect—the juiciest, most delectable collection of womanly parts he'd ever had the pleasure to put his hands on. He wanted to eat her alive. He wanted to make love to her in ways never before attempted in the history of their species.

Emma felt his stare work its way all along her body, from her feet on up. She started to squirm when his eyes returned to her hips and thighs. His expression turned serious, angry even. Emma knew the end was near. She wished he'd just say it!

"Let's get naked," he said.

Her pulse shot through the roof. Why was he doing this to her? He'd just glared at her in disapproval. He hadn't said anything about the blue dress, so he couldn't feel real affection for her. Could he feel sorry for her, was that what this was? A charity bopping?

Emma sucked in air at the sight of Thomas peeling off his shorts. He was nude underneath—completely, gloriously, mouth-droppingly nude.

And if this was the man's charity hard-on, she'd hate to see him in the throes of real lust.

Then, as if magically summoned, all the lovely ladies appeared in Emma's imagination, shoulder to shoulder like a police lineup—every woman Thomas Tobin had ever taken to bed. There they were, glamorous and disgustingly thin, a parade of lingerie models, flight attendants, *Entertainment Tonight* correspondents, and each had perfect hair, perfect teeth, perfect makeup, and perfect little tushies.

She suddenly felt sick with dread.

"Emma?"

She realized she hadn't moved, hadn't even started to remove a single item of clothing. She simply stared at the deluxe model of manhood in front of her, jutting hard, thick, and already decorated with a single, crystalline drop of fluid.

She wanted to decorate him with her lips, her tongue. She wanted to embrace him, pull him inside her body, ride him, let him split her in half.

Drunk with lust—drowning in it—Emma began to unbutton her jeans, still staring, telling herself if she didn't do this, take advantage of this limited-time offer, she'd kick her own ass from here to eternity.

Her own big ass.

It hit Thomas like a metric ton of rock.

She was staring at him, grim-faced and silent.

She could tell!

He hadn't dared get this close to anyone since Nina. On the night he was injured, she'd touched him and told him he seemed swollen. Then, in a voice full of more accusation than concern, she'd told him that something was definitely wrong with him.

Since then, Rollo had assured him that his appearance was normal, but Emma was a scientist—a doctor, for God's sake! A person who knew how to neuter dogs! And she was staring at his package like someone who'd just taken a bite of Mrs. Q's tuna casserole.

His hand froze inside the bedside table drawer.

He must be crazy.

Why had he just dragged this woman up the stairs to his bedroom? He had absolutely no business bringing a woman into his life—his home, his heart—especially this extremely beautiful, kind, good woman.

But it was too late—because she'd taken off her clothes. His throat tightened. His cock jumped. She was nothing but soft, supple woman flesh—rich burgundy nipples that puckered into long peaks, creamy and succulent thighs and hips—and dear God, she deserved so much more than a pessimist with a bum nut and not enough sperm for a pickup basketball game.

Emma Jenkins deserved a whole man. A real man and a real relationship. A few kids someday. She was the world's most natural mother, and all those kids were going to be lucky little bastards.

But it was too late to stop, and with robotlike movements, he tore open the little foil packet that was all for show, slid on the condom and walked toward the bed. She was naked, staring up at him with huge blue eyes filled with . . . what? Disgust? Pity?

He came closer, put his hands on her shoulders and pressed her on her back. He let his eyes sweep down her body—ripe and and willing and opening beneath him—and he knew he couldn't go through with it.

He couldn't do this to her—he would not lie to her or mess with her head—ever again.

And if that *was* pity he'd just seen in her eyes, he sure as hell didn't want it!

Thomas heard Emma sniffle, felt her sob, and he pushed himself off the bed and away from her, his gut in turmoil, his heart ripped to shreds.

"Goddammit," he muttered, turning his back to her, lost to her, to reason, aware of nothing but how defective he was, how damaged and unworthy.

He nearly laughed aloud. The most alluring woman he'd ever laid eyes on was naked on his bed, crying. What a total disaster—a total disaster when all he wanted was total oblivion, total immersion in her, a moment to wallow in the comfort and female softness of her and lose himself in her love.

All he wanted was her love.

It took every bit of strength Emma had to pull herself up to a sitting position. She folded her arms across her chest as if it would stop the shaking, staunch the bleeding.

That sure hadn't taken long. All she had to do was strip and all the fire and magic from downstairs was doused—gone—and nothing was left but a man with issues and a woman looking at rejection. Again.

Rejection.

Issues.

Baggage.

Emma wanted to scream!

Why did sex and love have to be so unbelievably *complicated*?

Thomas started to move. She watched him stalk toward the bathroom, providing her with a nice view of the high, muscular, man-ass that under any other circumstance would have made her punch-drunk with the pure wonder of it. She saw how the muscles rippled in his back as he reached in front of him to rip off the condom. She heard the soft *ping* as latex hit the inside of the wastebasket.

Right then would have been a good time to put her clothes on, but Thomas chose that moment to return to the bedroom, and Emma froze. He was still ferociously aroused, but his eyes were cold, as cold as she'd ever seen them, and his wide, sensual mouth was pulled in a thin line of despair.

"I have something to tell you," he said.

Thomas had reached a decision in the bathroom. The way he figured, he could make some bogus excuse and ask her to leave and lose her forever, which would probably be to her benefit, or he could tell her the truth—all of it—and hope beyond hope that she'd still want him.

What was the worst that could happen? He'd lose what he would have lost anyway, but at least he would have tried. At least he would have been a man about it.

"You deserve the truth," he said.

Emma gathered in her legs and wrapped her arms around her shins, compressing herself into a ball to stop the trembling. She didn't want him to see her shaking—from shame, from need. She didn't want him to see her naked.

"Spare me, Thomas." She looked at the wall. "I know perfectly well what you're going to say, and I can tell you from experience that I don't want to hear it." She took a steadying breath. "Give me a second and I'll get out of here, all right?"

She knew what? he wondered. That he was infertile? That he was dying from wanting her so much? That she looked amazing sitting like that, the lips of her little swollen sex peeking out from behind those tapered ankles?

Did she know he wanted to get down on his knees and worship her with his tongue? Did she know he wanted to pull those soft thighs of hers wide open and push his cock up inside her, disappear in her, die in the heat and relief and bliss of her? Did she know he wanted to give her everything, take away all the bad stuff that had ever happened to her and give her nothing but pleasure in return? Did she know all this?

"What do you think you know, Emma?"

She looked up at him, and the shock slammed through

her entire body. His cold expression had been replaced by
something hungry and desolate. And his erection! It was
huge—more impressive than only a moment ago—and she
simply didn't understand! If he didn't find her attractive,
then why was he so . . . large? Why did she see desire in
his eyes? What was going on?

"I think it's time for some direct communication." Thomas took a step closer. "You tell me what you know,
Emma. Then I'll tell you what I know."

She exhaled sharply and launched off the bed, grabbing
for her clothes. "I don't want to play this game anymore,
Thomas," she snapped.

"This is no game. Tell me what you know."

She grabbed a shoe off the floor. "You want to know
what I know? Well, listen up, Studly—I know I've had
enough! You lie to me, seduce me, and then back off, then
lie again, seduce me again, and back off again! You're
killing me!"

She pointed the toe of a clog in his face. "You're a nut
job, that's what I know! A whacko! And I don't understand
why it's so damn hard to find a decent man in this town!"

Thomas felt his mouth fall open.

Emma tried to jam a foot into the leg opening of her
underwear but missed, and her toe got caught on the crotch
panel. As she hopped on one foot and cussed under her
breath, Thomas watched those fabulous breasts jiggle and
sway, all high and full and tipped with the most exquisitely
formed, seriously suckable nipples he'd ever hoped to see
as long as he lived.

She pulled the little strip of beige lace up over her
mound. The panties clung tight and low on her luscious
hips. And then it hit him.

Oh, fuck everything—he loved this woman and there
was no turning back. He wanted to ravage that body. He
wanted to soothe that spirit. He wanted to hold her, make

her forget everything in the world but the fact that he loved her. He started to tell her that, but he wasn't fast enough.

"And here's what I'd really like to know—why is it that no one has ever fallen madly in love with me? What's wrong with me?" Her face was flushing and her eyes glittered with unshed tears. "Why hasn't someone ever swept me off my feet? Ravaged me? Made me forget everything else in the world but hot, wild passion? Just once, dammit?"

She shook her bra in his face to make her point. "You made me think that it was going to be *you,* damn you, and then you just reject me! That's the meanest thing anybody's ever done to me, and I let you do it twice! Go figure! I must be a complete idiot!"

She was waving the bra around like a semaphore, her eyes and hair wild. "And you . . . you *bastard*! If you didn't think I was sexy enough for you, why didn't you just tell me before I threw myself at you?"

Thomas found his voice long enough to say, "Huh?" Then his tongue nearly hit the floor.

She'd managed to shove her arms through the straps of her bra, but in her fury, forgot to clasp it. Two useless lace cups just hung there, separated in the front, skimming above the jut of her nipples, accentuating the round curve of the underside of each breast. With every ragged breath she took, the lace caressed the pale, creamy mounds of skin.

His whole body began to tremble, like a cat sprung tight before the kill.

"You obviously didn't think I looked good last night or you would have said something! I kept waiting for you to say something! But you didn't, you big jerk!" She gulped in a mouth of air. "I'm so sick of jerks I could scream!"

His eyes locked on hers.

"Stop staring at me!" The tears slipped down her face. "I hate it when you squint like that—it feels like you're looking at me through the cross hairs!"

"Stop, Emma."

"And I'm terribly sorry if you didn't think I looked nice in that dress, because listen up, big guy—that was as good as it's ever going to get with me, so if I didn't do it for you, then we've definitely hit the wall!" She began to wrestle with her jeans.

Thomas felt the rumble of a laugh begin deep in his chest, but knew he'd screw himself *but good* if he let it out. Emma needed tenderness right now, not laughter.

He took a deep breath. Obviously, the dress was the test and he'd failed miserably, just as he knew he would. It was time to beg for a makeup exam.

Thomas dived to his knees before her, his big hands ripping the jeans from her calves, then forcing her hips to the edge of the bed. Once she was seated, he grabbed her face, cradled it in his palms, and watched her eyes go wide with confusion. She began to shake beneath his touch, his gaze.

"What are you—"

His lips captured hers, hot and demanding, and the fire Emma had felt downstairs was back, but burning higher. His kiss was a slam of raw energy, raw need, and okay—so he *did* want her, but what about five minutes from now? Emma tried to wrestle free of his mouth, but he tightened the grip on her hips.

His lips traveled down the side of her neck. Using just his teeth, he dragged a bra strap down one arm and then the other until the bra fell on the bed behind her. His big fingers moved from her hips to brush up along the tender inside of her legs, stroking, coaxing.

Emma heard herself draw in a shuddering breath as she helplessly opened her legs for him. The unmistakable scent of her arousal slammed into her nostrils, and she nearly died from shame.

Oh, God! Why was she letting this happen? How stupid

could one woman be? What was wrong with her? She needed to get him off her somehow—claw him, kick him, bite him if she had to—and run for her life. It was what any woman with a shred of self-respect would do.

But every cell of her body called out in ecstasy at the way he touched her. She was lost—it was too late—and she decided she'd worry about her utter destruction later.

After the pleasure.

When he was finished with her.

Chapter 16

Let's Get It On

When Thomas ended the kiss and pulled back, Emma saw that his eyes were filled with tears. Of all the things she'd never expected to see in this lifetime, Thomas on his knees before her, naked and crying, was right up there.

What right did he have to cry? She was the offended party here! And she reminded herself that he was a jerk, a conflicted jerk!

"Emma, I'm sterile. The woman I was with for four years—Nina—she left me when we found out."

Emma went completely still. He brushed his thumbs over her cheekbones. His hands trembled.

"I want you so much." Thomas laughed at his own confession and shook his head. "So damn much. But I think you deserve more than what I can give you, the best of everything, the best man there is. You deserve a real relationship with real possibilities—and I should have stopped this right at the start."

"Oh, Thomas . . ."

"I tried, but . . ." Thomas lowered his head and his voice. "I couldn't. I'm falling . . ." He raised his eyes to hers again. "I'm crazy about you, Emma."

"Oh."

"I'm sorry for the two-step."

Emma watched a fat tear plop over his bottom eyelid, and her body clutched in on itself. He couldn't have children? He was crazy about her? He wanted a relationship—one serious enough for it to even matter that they couldn't make babies together?

She was overflowing with a confusing swirl of joy and sadness. She thought her heart would crumble.

"How—" She stopped, puzzled. "You really can't have children?"

He gripped her face tight between his hands. "Jesus, Emma—I could come inside you for years nonstop—which sounds pretty good to me right now—and there'd never be any little Thomases or Emmas running around. I got hurt playing rugby seven years ago and thought I was fine. Then I reinjured myself at the end of last season, and it turns out I'm sterile."

He stopped, his eyes filled with uncertainty. Emma managed a nod. "Go on."

"There was a rupture—do you want all the medical details now, or can they wait?"

She brought a hand up to cover one of his, where it cradled her cheek. He was still shaking. "The details can wait."

He nodded, and exhaled in relief. "The bottom line is my sperm count's decimated. I thought maybe you could tell by looking at me. That I can't make life." He gave a small shrug. "I just seem to spend my days with death."

Emma couldn't say anything. She just gazed down into his face, stroked his hand, and felt the sadness roll through her. Good Lord! Here she was worried that she wasn't sexy enough for him and he was thinking he wasn't virile enough for her!

If this weren't so pathetic it would be funny.

"I'll understand if you don't want to see me again."

Emma let loose with a burst of startled laughter and

pulled his hands into her lap, where she held them tight. "I don't mean to laugh—of course I want to see you—but it's just . . . well, I assumed this was about me."

"What about you?"

"The way I look. I mean, oh, God, I'm well aware that—"

"Yeah, what the hell was all that yelling about, Emma?" Thomas frowned at her.

"Me. My body. Aaron always told me that—"

A groan roared from Thomas's chest and his fingers clamped down on Emma's thighs. "What did that son of a bitch do to you, Emma? Tell me right now."

"He didn't *do* anything to me." She leaned away. "I just assumed I wasn't . . . you know . . . glamorous enough for you, because I'm pretty fleshy and I'm kind of basic and—"

"Stop right there." Thomas began rubbing her arms as if he were trying to warm her up. "Let me get this straight: Aaron, that dick-head of an ex-husband of yours, told you that you weren't beautiful? And you actually *believed* him?"

Emma snorted. "Wait a minute. I'm not some meek little housewife, okay? But I have eyes. I know I'm not really beautiful in the conventional sense, and I actually appreciated that Aaron was straight with me and didn't try to flatter me with a bunch of lies."

Thomas closed his eyes. "Oh, Jesus."

"It's not such a big deal. I've known it all my life. I mean, compared to Becca, I . . . oh, who cares now?" She sniffed. "The important thing is I'm smart and capable and . . ." Now it was her turn to cry. "And I just assumed you didn't find me attractive enough, even in the blue dress, to want a relationship with me."

Thomas had been shaking his head back and forth, slowly and deliberately, letting her ramble. But after that last statement, he couldn't listen to any more.

"That's enough." He brushed aside the silky hair stuck to her wet cheek and held her sweet face between his hands again. He wanted to kill that fucking Aaron—eviscerate him for planting such lies in Emma's lovely head.

"Look at me." Thomas brought his face close to hers. "I have eyes, too, baby, and I'm telling you—you are absolutely gorgeous. I didn't say anything about the stupid blue dress because it left me speechless. I was tortured. Insane. I wanted to lay you down right there on the picnic table! But you're the one who said you wanted to keep it all business between us, right?"

She nodded, frowning.

"I didn't know what to do, Emma! Tell me what the hell I was supposed to do! You set me up to fail either way!"

She gulped and her eyes went big and round. "I did, didn't I?" She rubbed her forehead. "I'm sorry, Thomas—what a mess."

"Baby." His voice had dropped a notch and it was rough and unsteady. "Believe me when I tell you that I loved looking at you in that blue dress." He peered up under her lowered lashes. "The only thing I didn't like about it was that all the other men in the place got to see you in it, too."

In a high squeak she said, "Really?"

"I love the way you look. I love your shape."

"Even my butt? Because Aaron—"

"What about your butt? Man, I have *got* to hear this."

Emma squirmed a little. "Forget it. This is the most ridiculous conversation I've ever had in my life."

"I'm kind of enjoying it—"

She glared at him. "I'm a thirty-four-year-old doctor of veterinary medicine and I refuse to waste another second of anyone's time discussing the pros and cons of the bundle of muscle that allows me to walk upright."

Thomas roared with laughter. "But I *want* to talk about

it. That bundle of yours is the only topic I'm interested in right now. So what did he say?"

Emma's mouth fell open, then she slammed it shut in defiance.

"What size do you wear?"

She nearly jumped out of her skin. "What? I'm not going to tell you that!"

Thomas laughed softly and let a finger brush along the curve of her waist, the fullness of her hip. "Well, sweet-cheeks, you're sitting here in front of me and I can see it all, so what does it matter if you tell me the number?"

She flashed him a doubtful look.

"I'm going somewhere with this, Emma. Trust me."

She hissed in surrender and turned her face away. "Twelve."

"And?"

Her head swiveled back. "And what?"

"And what's wrong with that? I spend half my life studying people, taking mental measurements for descriptions, and I know for a fact that the average American woman is a size fourteen. So you're smaller than average."

She frowned at him.

"How much do you weigh?"

"For God's sake!" Emma tried to get up off the bed but Thomas clamped down on her thighs. She looked at him, incredulous. "Really, Thomas—if this is your idea of fore-play, it's not getting me hot, just bothered."

Laughing, Thomas dropped his head and planted little kisses on her kneecaps. "I'm just trying to understand," he said, nuzzling her knee. "If you tell me how much you weigh, then you won't feel like you've got anything to hide, right?"

She groaned.

He waited. "I'll go first: I'm six-three and two twenty."

Emma gulped. Yowzah! And it was nothing but muscle,

power, and grace. In comparison, her stats sounded down-right diminutive.

"Okay." She took a breath. "I'm five-five and about one forty-five. Aaron always said my butt was too big. Happy now?"

Thomas leaned back and reached up to run his fingers through her hair, looking into her blue eyes for a long, quiet moment. Aaron had done a number on her, no question about it, and it was now his job to correct the math.

"People can be exceptionally cruel, Emma," he said softly. "And people can be power-hungry and people can be stupid. Apparently, your ex-husband was cruel, power-hungry, *and* stupid."

Without warning, he rose up on his knees, grabbed a handful of her hair, and tipped her head back, then kissed her thoroughly. He slid his lips over her and his tongue into her, and bit down on that carnal lower lip of hers, sucking it into his mouth, all to illustrate the extent of Aaron's idiocy.

Then he whispered in her ear, "I think you are the sexiest woman I've ever known—especially your butt." His fingers slid down around her bottom, working their way beneath her, cupping her, holding her. He pulled her like that to the very edge of the bed and held her there, tight in his hands. He nibbled on her neck as he continued to murmur in her ear.

"Your butt is like a neon sign that flashes the word *SEX* over and over in my brain. Your butt is like all the perfect forms in nature wrapped up into one little pair of lacy underwear. Your butt is my reason for being."

She snorted again. "Stop it. There's such a thing as over-kill."

"Oh, I disagree." He kissed and suckled at her throat, her collarbone. "I think we're just getting started on our relaxation exercises, Dr. Jenkins." He pulled back enough for her to see his face, and he hitched up his lips mischievously.

"Roll over," he commanded.

Her eyes flew wide. "Pardon me?"

Before she could protest, he'd flipped her over onto her stomach and stretched her legs down and apart, her feet dangling off the bed. She felt completely exposed, the air hitting her bare back and shoulders and the inside of her thighs. She sensed Thomas hovering over her, close, his breath warm on the small of her back. She began to tremble.

"Stay." His command was deep and serious, but his voice shook with laughter.

Emma giggled, but a spark of real fear flared inside her. It seemed there was always a touch of fear in her response to Thomas, because it was too intense, too fast, and all unexplored territory.

What was he going to do to her?

She craned her neck to look over her shoulder. "Is this where you tell me to bark like a dog for you?"

Thomas laughed again, then leaned down and kissed the side of her cheek. "Maybe later. Right now, I'm going to redirect your attention—you're going to get so interested in what I'm doing that you won't remember what upset you in the first place."

Emma started to giggle—realizing she was about to get a taste of her own medicine—but abruptly stopped when Thomas slapped his two big hands down on her rump and ripped off her underwear in one quick swipe. She felt the fabric drag along the back of her legs and fall off the end of her toes.

His hands came back to her bottom, raising her until she was a few inches off the bed and her knees slightly bent. He held her there, his touch firm and unmoving. And hot—so wonderfully hot where he grasped her.

Then he moved his palms in delicious, rhythmic circles, caressing, then pulling apart, pushing together, and Emma could hear his breath coming as fast as her own. She could hear him make little noises in the back of his throat that were part grunt and part murmur, and she tried not to imagine what she must look like in this position. She tried not to worry. She simply tried to *feel*.

"I'm an ass man, Emma." His hands continued to caress her, cup her, grip her.

"That's good to know," she mumbled, half into the sheets. Half out of her mind.

"Well, actually, I'm a breast man, too. And a leg man. But mostly an ass man."

"Okay," she squeaked. "I got all those things."

"Hell yes, you do, Miss Marple." His hands slid up into the dip in her back, thumbs touching, then let his fingers slide down into her waist, around the swell of her hips to her bottom, where he grabbed on and started over.

"And my God, you've got one fine ass." His fingers began to stray down the furrow of her bottom and she felt the bed move as he came up behind her.

His tongue landed hot and wet on her flesh and she nearly screamed at the intensity of the sensation. He licked her, dragged his lips and tongue across her, and flirted with the crease of her. She felt his tongue flick and his teeth nip and then one of his hands was sliding hot and slow up the length of her spine until it grabbed a handful of her hair. At the same time, his other hand moved down, down, until he cupped her sex.

Emma knew instinctively that she'd just been claimed.

"Every inch of you is beautiful," he whispered, his breath hot on her skin and his lips vibrating against her flesh. He was such a big man that he could be every place on her body at once—her hair, her sex, her back—and Emma heard herself make little whimpers of pleasure, soft moans, then a startled cry when his long fingers tickled the opening to her body.

His fingertips separated her, slicked around the swollen tissue, but didn't enter her.

Emma lost it, just like the night on the front porch, and her body seemed to move of its own volition. Her hips began to circle slow and rhythmically, pushing against his touch, pulling away, until she was lost in it, suffocating in the pleasure, rubbing her face into the bed as she moved her hips.

For what seemed like an eternity, Thomas just let his fingertips play along the wet rim of her, spellbound by her greedy wiggle and the sight of his big fingers up against her beautiful little pussy—so puffy and sweet and so ready for him.

Emma was into sex. He'd figured that out by now and said a little prayer of thanks.

And being naked with her, so close to her heat, hearing those little noises she made, getting drunk on her scent— he couldn't remember experiencing this kind of buildup before, this kind of exquisite torture, pressure, agony.

Never in his life had he wanted a woman this much.

"Please," he heard her whimper. Her hips began to circle a bit faster and he smiled, keeping his fingers just on the outside of where she needed them, aware that he was teasing her.

It was time to end at least some of her discomfort.

He adjusted his touch, slowly pushing down into the liquid heat, and let his middle finger make contact with her stiff little clitoris.

Emma groaned low and deep. Thomas brought his lips to her ear as he let his finger flick over her slippery heart-beat. "I've been dying to get close to you, put my hands all over your body, make you come. I think you're going to come a lot for me, aren't you, baby?"

She moaned.

He wanted her to wait. He wanted her to go higher. He wanted it to be exceptional for her. He wanted only truth between them, right now and always.

He pulled his hand away, and with gentleness he picked her up and turned her around so that she sat on the edge of the bed again. He kneeled before her, pleased to see that she looked dazed by desire—sleepy and drugged and trembling with anticipation.

"Now you know how I feel about your little blue dress and what goes in it," he said, trailing a finger down her kneecap. "And you know exactly what I am and what I'm not. So what happens now?"

Emma exhaled, shuddering from his hot touch and his words and the intensity of her desire and sorrow. "I'm so sorry you can't have children."

Thomas looked up into her wet blue eyes, her face and breasts framed by the fall of all that glorious, dark hair. She put her hand on the top of his head, like a benediction, and he let his chin drop to his chest in heavy relief.

"You really thought it would matter—that I wouldn't want you?" she whispered.

He nodded.

"Oh, Thomas." Emma reached for his chin and tipped it up. His eyes were closed and his face was tight with emotion. She leaned down and kissed the little semicolon scar, then his eyelashes, his temples, the golden skin over his cheekbones, his dimples, his lips. "I want you, more than ever, because you trusted me enough to tell me the truth. Thank you for that."

He nodded, his eyes still closed. "Can you forgive me for paying your fee?"

Emma let her hands stroke his soft, short curls. She cupped her hands around the hard curve of his skull and dropped a soft kiss to his forehead. "I forgive you."

"I want you, Emma."

"I want you, too. I want to know everything about you. I want to experience everything with you. I want more than I've ever had."

Thomas jerked as he felt Emma's small hand close around his erection.

"And man, oh man, do I ever want *this* bad boy." She swirled her tongue along his earlobe and then bit him, feeling the shiver course through his body.

"You're a sexy, funny, complicated man, and I've wanted you from the very first moment I saw you. I couldn't help myself."

"Oh yeah, Emma—"

She smiled with pleasure—the pleasure of hearing him say her name in that deep, resonant voice. In Thomas's voice, the two syllables of her ordinary name sounded like desire itself.

She drank in the vision of the man on his knees before her, head thrown back, eyes closed, jaw clenched.

She removed her hands from his erection and caressed his muscled ass, roamed up his back, slid her hands to his shoulders. It was a bittersweet place—a great ledge of muscle and sinew that seemed to be the home of both his strength and his sorrow.

"If she left you, she must not have loved you."

Thomas opened his eyes and looked right up into Emma's face. "I was closed off. Unwilling to commit." He shrugged, his body rippling under her hands. "Finding out I was a spermless wonder made it easy for her to move on, and I don't blame her."

Emma moved her palms to cover the rounded muscles of his chest, lacy with blond wisps and dotted with silky, pink nipples.

"Did you love Nina, Thomas?"

"I realize now that I didn't."

She let her hands flutter down the ridged surface of his abdomen and ran a finger along the edge of the flat, smooth navel.

"Have you ever been in love?"

His stomach quivered and he breathed faster. "Just this once, I think—I'm still trying to figure it out, Emma."

Her heart skipped a beat.

"And you? Did you ever love anyone besides Aaron?"

She moved her hands over the sweet indentations near his hipbones and down into the darker, springy thatch of hair, then clasped him at the root.

"Only you."

He groaned and threw his head back. Emma stared in wonder at her woman fingers on the man flesh made red-purple and hard with blood. Without a doubt, it was the most shockingly beautiful sight the world had to offer.

She wished she were an artist and not a scientist, someone who could capture the graceful lines of him on canvas or in clay—the aching perfection of the physical. But she wasn't an artist. She was just a woman who had the privilege to touch him, see him.

Love him—if he'd let her.

Thomas's erection twitched in her hands, and she smiled. She brushed her fingertips over the plump head and its swollen, velvet edge, then let her fingers slip down to the rigid flesh again. Veined. Hard. Thick.

And it occurred to her that the man's penis was soft on the outside and steel on the inside—the exact opposite of the man himself.

"I'm sad, Thomas. I'm so sad about the babies." She leaned down to rain kisses along his cheeks and beard stubble and under the ledge of his jaw. "But it doesn't affect how I feel about you. It's scary how much I want you. I've never felt anything like it in my life."

She reached beneath to cup his testicles, and his eyes shot open.

"It's all right, Rugby Boy." She smiled at him, gently exploring his heavy sac in one hand while stroking his length with the other. "I know everything now. There's nothing to hide, right?"

Thomas shuddered, and Emma watched him flex his back and bring his hands up to hover before her—then tenderly claim her breasts. It was the first time he'd touched her there since the front porch.

And for a long moment they simply closed their eyes and cradled each other, savored each other.

Until it wasn't enough.

Thomas was the first to move. He dipped his mouth to one of Emma's nipples and swore he heard a sizzle on contact with his wet tongue. Her flesh hardened and elongated in his mouth, begging him to suckle and tease and nip, first one, then the other, until both nipples were rock hard, glistening, and ruby red, and Emma was groaning.

Thomas widened his mouth to feed on as much of each glorious breast as he could. She was heavy with arousal and the flesh seemed to melt in his mouth.

Her breasts were perfect. Perfect for his mouth to suck and lick and bite. Perfect under his hands. Perfect for him. And he never wanted to stop making love to them.

Emma let go of him and leaned back on her hands to support herself. She threw back her head and cried, "I'm so sorry I yelled at you and called you names!"

It was difficult to keep the suction going while laughing, so Thomas moved his kiss to the hot and tender skin of her throat. While he did this, his hands came down on her inner thighs.

Emma rose up to look at him.

"Spread your legs for me, baby," he said.

She whimpered, and let her legs fall open.

"Wider. All the way." He looked from the tender juncture of her thighs back to her eyes, and saw the sweet female vulnerability in both places. "I need to touch everywhere, Emma. I need to see everything. Do everything."

He lowered his head. When his fingers spread her open, Emma sucked hard on her bottom lip to stop from screaming. Then his tongue lapped, slicked around, probed, while he slid the tip of his middle finger inside her. Right about then, she gave up trying to be quiet.

"And you don't have to apologize, sweetcheeks—you're awful cute when you're calling me names." Thomas laughed deep, pushing two fingers in to the last knuckle as he smiled up at her. "But you're even cuter when you're all wet and swollen and ready to be fucked."

"Thomas—"

"You sure you still want me?"

She laughed, then gasped as he whirled his thumb over her exposed clitoris. "Oh, yeah."

"Do you want this, Emma?"

"More," she breathed.

He pushed in a third finger, stretching her impossibly wide, and decided maybe this was the approximate thickness of his cock, although right at that moment it felt as big around as a grain silo.

He pistoned his fingers in and out of her, pressing against her swollen little clit. He felt it pulse with each rock of his hand.

"Now!" Emma yelled out, meeting his invasion with her own greed. "Please! Oh, my God, Thomas! *Now!*"

Just as she began to spasm against his fingers, Thomas pulled his hand away, pushed her on her back and replaced his fingers with all of his cock—one long, slick slide home.

She rippled against him and the sound of her hungry little moans made it nearly impossible to keep from mindlessly ramming into her. But he stayed focused, stayed with her as she shuddered, took her pleasure, and then took more.

Emma came hard and steady while the exquisite cycle went on and on. He entered her, slid all the way out, then pushed slowly way back in—bigger and thicker than anything she'd ever had inside her before. She gasped for breath.

When she could, she opened her eyes to see that exceptional face gazing at her, the skin around his eyes pulled in concentration and pleasure.

"My beautiful Emma." His hands cupped her cheeks and his mouth came down on hers, and his hot, sleek tongue licked into her opened lips, pierced her mouth as he pierced her body.

Good Lord, he was blistering and huge and heavy and all over her and inside her, and she let herself go, let herself feel for the first time in her life the unbearable pleasure of physical domination.

But it was domination wrapped up in the safety of love—and oh, *daddy,* it was everything. It was the secret of life.

When he reached for her wrists and pinned them over her head, she screamed with surprise and pleasure.

Then he moved slightly higher on her belly and started a deeper and faster grind, and in a flash of wonder, Emma knew that there was even more acute physical joy to be had. And as all of his tough, solid weight gnashed directly against her and thrust deep inside her, she started to lose it again.

"Come for me, Emma."

Thomas let go of her wrists and reached under to grab her butt—he seemed to do that a lot—and plunged even deeper inside her. "I knew the minute I saw you. It's you, Emma. Damn, it's you."

In that instant, Emma surrendered her heart to him, along with her body, and the world caught fire.

He slammed into her so hard she nearly fell off the edge of the bed—the edge of consciousness—and she wrapped her legs around his hips in an act of self-preservation. Then she was coming again, gripped by the pulse, riding the wave, relentless, never-ending—and there was nothing but Thomas. Thomas in her, under her, on her, with her. And it was more than she'd ever dreamed.

He cried out her name in rhythm with each frenzied spasm of his climax, and once he'd emptied himself into her he collapsed, panting into the crook of her neck, nuzzling her, kissing her, murmuring unintelligible things in her ear.

Emma lay in awe, her legs still hooked around his narrow hips, dazed by the feel of his hot breath on her throat and his heartbeat slamming against her breasts. How she loved having him this close to her—closer than she'd ever felt to another human being in her life. How right this was.

"Emma . . ."

She brushed her fingers down his spine, and Thomas arched into her touch like a friendly domestic shorthair. He made a primitive noise into the side of her neck that sounded—and felt—just like a purr.

She couldn't stop smiling at the wonder of it all.

This man wasn't a moody robot—he was a battle-scarred tomcat who needed a loving home. And though she'd always been more of a dog person, she had a feeling that was about to change.

She had a feeling a lot of things were about to change.

"How are you, baby?" Thomas's moist kisses below her ear made her tingle all over.

"I'm alive. I think."

He laughed, and the press of his cheek against her throat told her the dimples had returned. She wished she could see them. After a long moment, he pushed up and looked down on her, his face impossibly open, full of humor and warmth—the most endearing face she'd ever seen.

"Do you mind if I call you that—'baby,' I mean?"

She let loose with what she feared was a completely goofy grin. Nobody had ever called her that before. It made her feel small, delicate, and so very feminine. It made her feel treasured.

"I like it, actually. Don't tell Velvet."

Thomas dropped his head and showered her with sweet kisses. "Thank you for making love with me, Emma."

He was thanking *her*? "Anytime, Rugby Boy."

"Oh, yeah?" He raised one hand to brush the hair from her forehead and let his fingers trace over the arch of her brow.

"Mmm . . ." Emma closed her eyes in pleasure.

"Am I squishing you?"

"No! You feel really good right where you are. Do you think you could stay awhile?"

His smile spread slow and he continued to stroke her cheek, her chin, her ear, her bottom lip. "I warned you I'd like to come inside you for years on end, but I'm afraid you're going to suffocate if I don't move."

He rolled onto his side, taking her with him, and she snuggled up against his solid body, lulled into sweet, warm peace with the beat of his heart, the stroke of his hand on her hair, the rhythm of his breathing.

Emma didn't know how long she slept, but she woke with something hard prodding her hip. She opened her eyes to find herself sprawled half on top of Thomas. He smiled down at her.

"Hey, Emma."

She laughed—the guy may be shooting blanks, but his trigger worked fine.

"Hey, big guy."

Thomas folded his arms around her and kissed her gently. "I wasn't exactly prepared for this—for you. I know I didn't do such a smooth job with all of it. Sometimes I just assume the worst, you know?" He kissed her chin, her throat. "But I won't hurt you again. I won't ever let anything hurt you."

Emma smiled against his neck. "Don't make promises, okay? Just hold me, Thomas. Make me forget everything but you."

"I can do that." He nuzzled under her jaw. "But you've got to let me make just one little promise to you."

"Thomas—"

In one movement, he pulled her up on top of him, spread her thighs and pushed inside her. After the initial surprise, Emma felt her body melt around him, pull him in. She wantonly wriggled on him, allowing herself to sink all the way down, skewered. His.

He put his big hands on her hips and lifted her, just a bit.

"I promise not to hurt you."

Then he brought her back down.

"I promise to take care of you."

Back up.

Emma fell forward, her hands on either side of his head, her breasts dangling in front of his mouth.

Back down.

He mouthed a nipple, then the next, tonguing, biting, rubbing his cheeks over them until they were once again raging red, swollen and hard.

Up.

"And I promise to ravage you until you can't take any more."

Down. Hard.

Emma shuddered, overwhelmed by the sensation of his

mouth and teeth on her, his flesh hard inside her, his words seducing her.

Up and down.

She didn't want to cry again, but she couldn't help it—it was simply too much, too wonderful.

Up and down. Faster. Harder. Rougher. She detonated, the heat searing through her, Thomas's quicksilver eyes burning right through to her soul.

When she caught her breath she said, "It really *is* you, isn't it?" Her voice broke as the tears stung her eyes. "You're the man who's going to sweep me off my feet."

Thomas stilled. He let the nipple pop from his mouth, and grinned up at her.

"Consider yourself swept, babe."

Chapter 17

Heaven Must Have Sent You

It took Thomas a few moments to decide why everything seemed out of whack. Then he felt Emma curled up next to him and his eyes moved to the clock and he realized that the glowing green numbers were afternoon numbers, not middle-of-the-night numbers, and that he was starving.

He also realized he needed a shower and a shave.

Then it occurred to him that he was outrageously happy. It felt weird, but it was a good kind of weird—no, a great kind of weird—and he thought maybe he could get used to it.

Emma was dozing again, her eyelashes spread on her cheek like a Spanish dancer's black lace fan. The white sheet only half covered everything she was and everything she'd given him so generously, with so much enthusiasm.

He'd never made love to a woman like her. She was bold and rowdy and juicy and flat-out orgasmic.

When she told him it had been more than a year since she'd had sex, he nearly wept—with sadness for her and a giddy sense of victory for himself.

She was all his! Talk about a moment of unadulterated whoop-ass!

He looked down at her now, round and soft and smiling in her sleep, one delicate hand spread out over his heart, the fingers half-buried in his chest hair.

Thomas smiled at the symbolism of that—after all, the woman held his heart in her hand.

He closed his eyes and breathed deep from her hair. Emma's usual tantalizing floral scent was nearly drowned out by the rich and thick smell of excellent sex.

The best sex of his life—sex that engaged his heart and his spirit as well as his body—bonding sex, loving sex, big-time, bad-ass, let's-get-married sex.

Oh. So *that's* what that felt like.

Thomas sighed, aware that it was a sigh of contentment and surrender. He'd surely done it now. He'd put himself at the mercy of a woman. Thank God he'd had the presence of mind to pick a reliable one. A good one. One who didn't listen to top-forty radio. One who wouldn't lie to him, steal from him, plot his demise, or betray him.

Thank God he'd put himself at the mercy of Emma Jenkins, the world's most trustworthy person.

He nearly hit the ceiling when Hairy jumped on his stomach. Great! He'd forgotten the damn dog had been roaming free through the house the whole day. He was afraid to think about what the downstairs looked like.

Yo, stud puppy. I gotta piss like a racehorse.

"Yeah, yeah, I'm coming, pal."

Thomas removed Emma's warm hand from his chest and her sticky thigh from his hip, and rolled out of bed. He threw on his shorts and staggered down the stairs, Hairy skittering ahead of him like a rat with a hot date.

Thomas let him out the back door and watched as he barely made it to the edge of the patio before lifting his leg on the nearest shrub. When had Hairy stopped peeing like a girl?

And then it occurred to him that the dog hadn't required the urine defense system in many days.

And then he noticed that not a thing was out of place

downstairs—no scratch marks on the door, no holes in the rug, no puddles of urine on the tile.

"Life is good," he mumbled to himself, turning his attention to making a pot of coffee. He decided to whip up some sandwiches and take them upstairs to eat in bed with Emma—he didn't want her getting out of his bed for a long, long time.

Maybe the rest of their lives.

Unless it was to take a shower.

With him.

The phone rang.

"Tobin."

"Dammit, Thomas! Where are you?"

It took a moment, but Thomas eventually understood the significance of this call. It was Rollo, obviously phoning from the sidelines of the pitch. He could hear the whistle of the rugby official in the background and the shouts and grunts of the scrum.

Thomas had forgotten he had a rugby match. It was the first match he'd missed in at least a decade. He blinked.

"Thomas?"

"Yeah. I forgot, I guess."

After a moment of listening to Rollo breathe, he heard Pam's voice in the background, running through a list of questions she wanted relayed to her brother via her husband, and they all had to do with Thomas's physical health and state of mind.

Thomas rolled his eyes. "Tell Pam I'm fine, wouldya? It's just . . . well . . . Emma's here and I'm not going to make it today. In fact, I think I might just pack it in permanently."

Rollo's laughter started low and soft and then Thomas heard it rumble and then eventually explode in his ear, only to be followed by a series of obnoxious hoots and whoops.

Thomas hung up on him.

As he pulled out the lettuce, tomato, and turkey from the fridge, it occurred to him that it was true, he'd found something he craved as much as hitting and being hit, that made him feel profoundly alive, that made everything else disappear.

His real reason for living.

And the bonus was that making love to Emma was somewhat easier on his knees and lower back and, with any luck, it was something he could keep doing until he was a very old man.

He was about to set the sandwich makings on the kitchen table when he saw her. She stood in the doorway, in the white oxford shirt he'd worn last night.

Dear God, he'd always loved the sight of a beautiful woman in a man's shirt. But this was *Emma* in *his* shirt, and the buttons were cock-eyed, and her hair was falling in a messy cascade down one side of her face, and he could see down into her lusty cleavage and up into the sweet vee of her inner thighs. It was almost more than he could handle.

A rosy flush extended from her chest to her cheeks and her eyes were sparkling and her lips were puffy and he adored her.

He absolutely adored the woman.

"Hi," she whispered, leaning up against the archway. "I think the phone woke me up."

Everything Thomas held in his hands crashed to the tabletop. "Hey, Emma."

She blinked and ran a hand through the shiny fall of hair. "Is this going to be awkward, Thomas? Because I was really hoping we could skip that part. I just want it to be . . . oh, hell, I don't know . . ."

"Perfect?" In two strides, he'd eaten up the space between them. He didn't know what he'd do once he got to her—he just knew he had to get there.

He picked her up and carried her to one of the kitchen chairs, where he cradled her in his lap. He smiled when he felt her arms go loose around his neck, her kisses land on top of his head.

"Do you have any plans for the rest of the day?" His question was muffled as he rubbed his face between those breasts, so comforting, so welcoming, so female—so damn erotic . . .

Emma began to laugh, and Thomas closed his eyes and let his face enjoy the ride.

"Actually, I started out the day with a long list of errands to run, but I have a feeling I'm not going to get to any of them."

"You're so right." He couldn't help it. His hands were already up inside the shirttail and all over her bottom and lower back, rubbing, caressing, wanting.

Emma arched into his touch. "I was supposed to take Leelee shopping this afternoon. I better call her."

"I'll call her." Thomas stood up, plopped Emma down on the edge of the table, and reached for the kitchen wall phone. He kept one eye on Emma while he dialed. She looked so lip-smacking good that he knew even a brief conversation would be a challenge.

"Leelee, this is Thomas the Tongue."

"Hah!" she said. "Did you kidnap her or something? We were supposed to go to the mall."

"Yeah. I know. Here's the deal, junior—jewelry, furs, cruises, vacation property, tech stocks, whatever you want, it's yours. And you can drive the Audi in the driveway. But it will have to be tomorrow."

Leelee hissed with impatience, then giggled. "Can I drive it the whole way down the lane?"

Thomas swallowed hard as dual images duked it out in his brain—the imagined sight of his car going into the ditch and the reality of Emma crossing her legs, the shirt falling open across her upper thighs.

"Your wish is my command, Leelee."

"Awesome. Will you take me to Tyson's Corner?"

"Yeah. Sure. Sounds fun." Thomas hated that monstrosity of a shopping mall more than he hated Celine Dion, but Emma was leaning back on her hands and she was smiling like she loved him.

"So I'll see you guys tomorrow?"

Leelee's voice suddenly sounded young and timid, and Thomas jolted at the change. His throat clamped tight. "Hey, Lee? I appreciate this. I really do. I'll make it up to you, kid. I promise."

"Oh, you know you will," she said, laughing. Then after a moment of quiet, she said, "I guess I'm going to have to learn to share, aren't I?"

Thomas smiled at that, and he felt his chest expand with a warm heat and a strange flush of connection, and it dawned on him that in the space of days he'd gone from a man who preferred to be alone to a man who happily had two women to take care of, make promises to—two women to love.

"I'll be learning right along with you," Thomas said.

He hung up the phone and turned to face Emma, who had unbuttoned the shirt and was reclining back upon her elbows. A stream of afternoon sun spilled over the pale silk of her breasts and belly, and put a spotlight on the sweet heaven between her thighs.

"What's for lunch?" she asked, shaking out her hair and smiling wickedly.

"Tongue," he said, closing in on her. "Specialty of the house."

. . .

It was nearly dark and there was a twinge of fall in the air as they walked down the sidewalk, holding hands. Hairy skittered under their feet, sniffing and peeing on everything in his path—mailboxes, wire mesh trash barrels, street-lights, and tree trunks.

Thomas smiled down at Emma and squeezed her hand.

She was awed by how quickly she'd come to love this man, by how much love there was inside her to give him.

Emma gazed out absently at the Federal Hill evening traffic, headlights flickering on, and knew that she'd never once felt this way with Aaron.

Yes, there'd been a wild flare of endorphins at the be-ginning, but even then Emma was aware that something wasn't quite right between them. Aaron made sure Emma knew that she fell short of his ideal woman. He made sure she blamed herself for the lack of zing in their relationship.

And what had she done? She'd disregarded her intuition and married him anyway, because she figured that it might not be perfect, but it was close enough.

And what about this man who now held her hand? She looked up and he smiled down at her again—the private smile of a lover who knew her well—and she felt the truth sink into her bones: she was made for Thomas, and he was made for her. It was that simple.

In her mind she saw Mother Nature in her flowing white robes and her crown of blossoms, scanning her clipboard and arranging things so that Emma Jenkins and Thomas Tobin would be alive on earth at the same time, in the same geographic vicinity, so they could find each other.

She glanced down at the little dog at the end of the leash and had to laugh. Maybe Hairy was Mother Nature's em-issary. Maybe she owed her happiness to Hairy.

"What's so funny?"

Emma shook her head. "I was just thinking that Hairy

is the most unusual dog I've ever known. He's weird even for a Crested."

"You got that right, babe."

"And sometimes, I look at him and I get this feeling he really understands what's going on. He's unusually intelligent. I swear—and I know I sound like one of my crazy clients and should be shot—but I swear he smiles at me sometimes."

Thomas cocked his head. "I've had the same feeling."

"Huh." She studied the dog for a minute. He peed on a bus shelter. "So you're not even tempted to give Hairy to that Maxine woman up in Delaware?"

Thomas laughed. "Hell, no! Hairy's not going to live in a trailer park if I have anything to say about it."

"You're going to keep him?"

"I think I have to, now."

"Why's that?"

Thomas shrugged. "Because he's Leelee's dog now as much as mine. He stays with you guys half the time. Besides, I think I'd miss the little butt-ugly fu—fellow."

Emma leaned closer and wrapped an arm around his waist, laughing. It was nine o'clock—meaning they'd been lovers for about twelve hours. It felt as comfortable as twelve years.

"Besides, some things are just meant to be." Thomas pulled her tight. "Don't you agree?"

"Sure seems that way."

Thomas had driven her to delirium on the kitchen table, then made her a turkey on whole wheat. They made love in the shower, then took a nap, heated up leftover pizza for dinner, and made love again before taking Hairy on his evening constitutional.

And each time and every minute in between, Emma felt linked with Thomas, a kind of body-and-soul melding she'd never once experienced in thirteen years with Aaron.

She thought back to the first time she saw Thomas's face, to that spark of connection she felt. And she wondered if all they'd done was fan the spark until it ignited, and they'd never have to suffer through another cold night as long as they lived.

"I want to marry you, Emma."

"Whaa—?" She nearly tripped before Thomas could pull her into his arms.

"I didn't mean to scare you."

"Too late."

He smiled down at her, chuckling. "It doesn't have to be right now. We don't have to jump on the first plane to Vegas, but I want to marry you. Soon. Would you be my wife?"

He was looking down at her with that tortured expression, and Emma knew he was absolutely serious. He wanted to *marry* her! Her mouth fell open.

Hairy's leash was now tangled in their ankles, and he began to make gagging noises just as Emma heard a friendly voice call out, "Well, hello, stranger!"

She whipped around to see a very blond, very leather-encased man standing near them. He was accompanied by a female Cockapoo in a tennis outfit whom Hairy had already started humping, tangled leash or no.

"Hey, Franco."

"Hi, Thomas."

As Thomas unknotted Hairy's leash, Emma felt the man's eyes scan her from head to toe, and it clearly wasn't interest she saw in his eyes—it was jealousy.

Oh, Lordy!

"This is my fiancée, Emma Jenkins. She's a pet behaviorist. Emma, this is Franco and Quiche Lorraine."

The shock pounded Emma so hard that she couldn't speak. She simply extended her hand and tried to smile while the Franco person oohed and aahed about her job.

Thomas had just asked her to marry him! He'd just proudly announced that she was his fiancée! Didn't she have a say in any of this?

Besides, what in the world would it be like to be his wife?

As she watched Franco chat with Thomas, she wondered if she was strong enough to be married to a Viking love god in Nikes with no socks, a man whose appeal apparently extended to people of both genders.

"Have you set a date?" Franco's eyebrows rose in nicely groomed arches. "As it happens, I'm a wedding planner." He somehow managed to squeeze his fingers into the pocket of his leather pants to extract a small silver case. He handed Emma a business card.

"Intimate gatherings, beer brawls, anything in between. So how long have you been engaged?"

Emma really *did* try to get her lips to move, but it felt as if the nerve endings had been severed.

"About thirty seconds, Franco." Thomas laughed, turning his Christmas-tree-tinsel eyes on Emma. "Hell, she hasn't even had a chance to say yes yet."

Emma's tongue felt like it had been super glued to the roof of her mouth.

"Whoops!" Franco stifled a giggle and swept down to snatch Lorraine. "We're out of here. Sorry to intrude. It was nice to meet you, Emma. See you, Thomas."

After Franco rounded the corner, they stood together in silence for a few moments. Then Emma dared look up at Thomas. His head was cocked to one side, his smile was soft, his expression sheepish.

"So?"

Emma swallowed. "So *what*?" She was relieved that her voice still worked.

"Intimate gathering or beer brawl?"

"Whaa—?"

"Really. What do you think about my question? Are you pissed off, ecstatic, what?"

"I'm . . . I'm dumbfounded."

"Yeah." He chuckled. "Me, too."

Thomas bent down, scooped up Hairy and turned him around to face home. He found Emma's hand and they began to head back.

"I know that wasn't the most romantic proposal in the history of the world, but I've been feeling kind of spontaneous lately." He looked at her sideways and wagged his semicolon. "It's been kind of a mind-blowing day, hasn't it?"

"You could say that."

"It's something to think about, anyway. You. Me. Lee-lee. Assorted domesticated animals. It sounds right."

"Leelee?" At that, Emma stopped in her tracks. "What are you saying, Thomas?"

He raised his eyes up to the sky and shrugged, and Emma stared at his big silhouette in the twilight. When he lowered his gaze, she was jolted by the stark tenderness in his expression.

"I'm a man who can't have kids. She's a kid who needs a man to be her dad. I happen to love her mother more than I ever thought I could love anyone. She happens to love my fruity dog. I'd say it's damn near perfect."

Emma looked around for a place to collapse—she needed to sit before she fell. She staggered over to the marble front steps of someone's tidy red-brick townhouse and tumbled down. Thomas landed right next to her.

"I know this is a lot, baby. You can ask Pam or Rollo or my rugby teammates or the people on the task force—I'm not usually like this. I guess I'm just . . . just afraid that—"

Emma threw her arms around his neck and hugged him as tight as she could. When his big hands spread over her back, she felt the peace slide over her. It was like she'd reached a quiet understanding with the universe, as if Mother Nature herself had just put a big check mark on her clipboard and given Emma a wink.

She started to laugh. "Okay," she whispered in his ear.

His body relaxed against hers. "Damn, that's great."

"But let's go slow." She looked up into his face. "Let's give Leelee a little more time before we tell her. Let's give ourselves a little more time."

He nodded, the dimples deep and sweet beside his smile. "Anything, Emma." He gave her a gentle little kiss and held her face in his hands. "Anything for you."

His car burned.

The 1978 Black Pearl Datsun 280 Z with a V-8 engine, five-speed overdrive, and the below-standard exhaust system—his heart's delight, the one love that never let him down—was going up in flames in the parking lot of the King of Hearts Motor Court.

Aaron watched helplessly as the new paint job peeled away from the steel frame like skin from bone. Black smoke stung his eyes and tasted sour in his throat. The yellow and red flames licked up from under the hood like ugly laughter.

He heard the wail of the fire engines and realized the ugly laughter was coming from him.

Well, why not laugh? Because at this moment, he could honestly say that his life was officially, one hundred percent fucked. There was nothing left of what he had only a year ago. Literally—poof! It had all gone up in smoke.

The funniest part was that his first instinct was to go to Emma, sweet, forgiving Emma, the glue that had kept him from splitting in two, the epicenter of everything that was decent in his life. A year ago, she would have taken him in her arms, held him to her breast, stroked his head. She would've found a way to make him laugh about this. She would have kissed away his pain.

The sirens shrieked inside his head.

Okay, fine. Two years ago, maybe. This time last year, Emma was handing him divorce papers.

But it was all real once, wasn't it? He'd had that woman by his side every day and in his bed every night. He'd had her love. He wasn't making that up, was he?

What the hell had he done?

As he watched the firefighters hook up a limp yellow hose to the hydrant, Aaron saw his mistake with more clarity than ever.

He'd let his compulsion get bigger than his love. He'd taken her for granted. He'd never really admitted how much he loved her. Then he'd let her go.

He'd ruined his marriage. He'd ruined his life.

The hose swelled and burst and he watched two firefighters wrestle to control the violent blast that soaked the Z. In a matter of moments, the car had been reduced to a charcoal briquette, oozing with fire retardant foam and hissing with water.

Aaron closed his door and retreated into the gloom, pausing when he saw his reflection in the rusty mirror.

Too bad the Z hadn't had enough gas in the tank to blow sky high. Too bad he hadn't been blown up with it.

He didn't even recognize the man he saw in the mirror. That man had no center. No heart. No Emma.

That man had who knew how many more days to live? And nothing left to lose.

Chapter 18

Love Hangover

The first splashes of crimson and gold dotted the tree line between farm fields, and the sky was a sharp, cool blue. Emma tilted her face and breathed deep, feeling the sun on her skin and the pleasant rock of her hips in the saddle.

The rush she got from loving Thomas hadn't dissipated in the last few weeks, but it had mellowed, found its own rich and pleasurable rhythm. And lately her happiness seemed to be a physical entity in itself, something that sat deep inside her, weighted and sure, at the core of everything she did. And she could feel it growing every day.

She looked over at her riding companion, and chuckled to herself. Thomas seemed more relaxed on Bud today, less like a man with an iron rod up his spine. And Bud seemed resigned to carrying Thomas, no longer gazing at her with that pitiful, put-upon expression. It did her heart good to see the two of them getting along.

"It's gorgeous out here," Thomas said, the way he always did when she took him riding.

"I'm glad you think so."

He turned to her. "You're gorgeous out here."

"I'm glad you think so."

"Let's get naked."

Emma laughed. The man needed a prong collar. Admittedly, not having to worry about pregnancy or disease sure allowed for things to be spontaneous. And she'd lost track of how often and in how many places they'd been spontaneous.

Not that she was complaining.

"Do you think that thirty years from now you'll still try to seduce me with that particularly charming phrase?"

"If you still want to be seduced."

"I will if you're up for it."

He shot her a smile framed in dimples. "If there's Viagra now, baby, just think what will be around when I'm an old man. They'll have to tape it down when they lower me in the ground."

"You scare me."

Thomas roared with laughter, and she could still hear him snickering as he followed her down the narrow path to the creek. Once they dismounted and flipped the horses' reins over tree limbs, Thomas immediately pressed up against her back and enfolded her in his arms.

"There's a word for your medical condition, Thomas." She snuggled back against him. "It's called priapism, and I hear it's horribly painful."

He kissed the side of her neck. "I'm in pain all right."

His fingers were unbuttoning her denim jacket, brushing over her breasts beneath the T-shirt, fluttering down to the snap of her jeans.

"That house up there belongs to Mr. Martin," she said between shallow breaths. "He's a very nice Mennonite widower."

"Sorry. He can't have you. You're mine."

His hot palms were flat against her belly and the tips of his fingers were sliding down under the elastic band of her underpants. She started to shake. He always did this to her—made her tremble and flush with heat until she was pushing into his hands and squirming against him.

"But he might see us down here," she whispered.

"Nobody's looking, Emma. Nobody but me."

Somehow, her jacket was already in the grass and her shirt was bunched up under her chin and her bra was unsnapped. And somehow, he'd already shoved her jeans and underwear halfway to her knees and she was groaning.

Emma reached back blindly with her hands to find that he'd also managed to remove most of his own clothing, and she was impressed—turned on and impressed.

He twirled her around.

"I love you so much." His kiss was hot and erotic and the sun felt so delicious on her bare skin that she didn't care about Mr. Martin, only Thomas. Just Thomas.

And she found herself dragging her lips down the side of his neck, onto the muscles of his chest, and leaving a trail of kisses and nibbles down the center of his body until she was nearly on her knees.

Thomas bent down and placed his shirt on the grass beneath her.

She peeked up at him. "That was quite chivalrous of you."

"I have a big ulterior motive."

"I can see that," she said, smiling. Then she put her lips around it, and Thomas spread his feet and growled in raw male satisfaction.

"You're so good to me, Emma. Why are you so damn good to me?"

She smiled while she worked, feeling the tremors move through him, inhaling the delicious musk of him. His fingers thrust into her hair, his big hands clasped her head—but he didn't push, just held, touched, rode along as she moved.

"Emma—"

Thomas fell to his knees, his face drawn in wonder, then kissed her again, rougher, lifting her bottom until she was off the ground, suspended by the desperate clasp of his hands and the crush of his lips.

He broke away for breath. "God, I love this."

"Me, too." She pressed up against his erection.

"It's everything, Emma. You're everything."

He'd set her down gently and smiled. He turned her, his hands sliding all over her body, hot in contrast to the cool breeze. He guided her onto her hands and knees as he positioned himself behind her.

Emma whimpered in need. She couldn't wait, couldn't wait for him to get inside her.

She felt the press of his smooth belly against her soft bottom, the prod of his rock-hard cock, poking, teasing, missing the mark so often that she had to reach underneath and touch herself to relieve the distress.

"God, Thomas, don't tease me! I can't stand it!"

Oh! Then he was there, taking her from behind, a big, hot spike that killed her, resurrected her, made her into perfect form and perfect sensation, and it was the best thing she'd ever felt in her life—best in the way it was every time he became a part of her.

She was delirious with it—the feel of one of his hands cupped over her stomach as the other reached up to pinch her breasts, squeeze and roll her nipples until she was calling out for more and begging him to never stop. She was swimming in the rhythm, the rushing need, as he rammed her harder and slid his hand down her belly to her clitoris, so swollen and tender that she knew she was teetering on the edge.

"God, yes!" she hissed.

Thomas lowered himself over her back and laughed into the crook of her neck, still pounding into her. "You're my wild thing, aren't you, baby? Think you could bark like a dog for me now?"

"Let's not go too far with this," she said.

Thomas stopped moving.

His hard chest curved against her back and he brought his lips close to her ear. "We've already gone too far, Emma, but not far enough. Do you understand what I'm saying?"

A hot flash raced through her blood. Yes. She knew exactly what he was saying. His body was sheathed inside her, cupped protectively over her—but it wasn't nearly enough. Why was that? Why did she want so much more of him, so much more *from* him? Why did she want to reach down into his soul, pull it out, and wrap herself up inside of him?

How could she love him that much?

"I can't get enough of you, Thomas." She pushed her hips into him. "It'll never be enough."

He pulled her up to kneel in front of him, encouraged her to lean back against his chest. Thomas stroked her hair, overwhelmed with the combination of lust and love this woman churned up inside him.

He breathed her in, touched the real beauty of her body and her heart that made him want to fuck her deeper, love her endlessly, protect her and belong to her. Forever.

Her head fell back against his chest and she turned her face so that his mouth could find hers.

She tasted like joy, like one of her smiles, and Thomas felt nothing but absolute connection, like he was plugged into the wettest, hottest, most powerful electrical socket in the universe.

"Did you know it could be this way?" he whispered, cupping her breasts, nuzzling her neck as he thrust into her.

She cried out, overwhelmed with the hot rush of emotion and stab of pleasure that left her gasping, lost.

"Because I had no idea, Emma. No idea . . ."

She felt a drop of his sweat—or a tear—fall to her

shoulder. She reached around and pulled his face to hers again. She kissed him. And the circuit was complete.

Emma felt like she was going to die.

"I'm sure it was Mrs. Q's tuna casserole." Thomas kept his voice in a whisper as he patted the cool washcloth on Emma's forehead and kissed her cheek. He winked at Lee-lee. "I think I might have hurled the first time I tasted it, too."

They all laughed.

Beckett shushed them. "She's going to hear you. It wasn't that bad. She's a damn fine woman."

Thomas wagged an eyebrow at Leelee, which sent the girl into hysterics. The burgeoning affection between Sylvia Quatrocci and Beckett had diverted some of Leelee's attention from her own love affair, much to Emma's relief.

"Gag," Leelee had said the other day. "Isn't there some kind of law against old people kissing?"

Not that Leelee seemed particularly opposed to having Thomas around. As Emma watched the two of them now, she was filled with an easy sense of well-being. All the pieces of her life were falling into place. All the pieces of herself seemed just the right shape and size to fit the big picture, for the very first time.

Emma groaned and pushed herself to a sitting position on the couch, and Thomas immediately reached to support her back. "I'm good, really, guys," she said. "Let's finish our game. And Pops, please go tell Mrs. Q to stop cleaning the kitchen."

Beckett looked down at the Scrabble board and sighed. "I quit anyway. I ain't seen a vowel in two turns."

"Vowels?" Leelee grabbed for her imaginary pistols and pointed them at Thomas. "We don't need no stinking vow-els!"

Emma smiled as Thomas accepted Leelee's challenge with a wicked grin and pulled her to the Scrabble board.

Hairy chose that moment to jump up into her lap, the boxer shorts hanging from his mouth.

"Hey, little guy! Did you come to comfort me?"

You're looking mighty green around the gills, Soft Hands. You smell different, too. What's going on with you?

"I'm okay, Hairy. Don't worry."

She kissed the little dog's snout, then scratched behind his ears, smiling as he held her gaze with his bug-eyes. It was nothing short of miraculous how Hairy had improved. He was off his meds. He no longer needed the maxi pad or the crate or the relaxation exercises. He'd settled into a comfortable routine of a life equally divided between the farm and Federal Hill, and he seemed happy, well-adjusted, and calm.

And he was staring at her.

Uh-oh.

"What is it, Hairy?" Emma laughed uneasily. "You can stop staring at me now." Her headache swirled. Her stomach lurched.

"Oh, boy," she mumbled, tossing Hairy aside. She staggered toward the bathroom.

"Are you okay?" Thomas was on his feet and right behind her.

Uh-oh. Uh-oh. Uh-oh.

Three days later, Emma was still sick to her stomach and so tired that her arms and legs felt like they were encased in wet cement. She couldn't remember the last time the flu had hit her this hard, and was reevaluating her decision to come to work the way she always had in the past.

"I must be getting old." Emma accepted the new-patient questionnaire from Velvet, and scanned information about a calico who'd compulsively licked her front paws bare. "This virus is knocking me on my butt."

"Whatever you say."

Emma looked up to find Velvet glaring at her, her hands propped on her hips.

"What's that supposed to mean?"

"Emma . . . is there . . . well . . . ?"

"What?"

"Could you possibly be pregnant?"

Emma's hands fell to her sides and she heard the chart slap against her leg. "Excuse me?"

"Pregnant. With child. Expecting."

"No." Emma quickly resumed reading. "You can tell Mrs. Wilson to come on back."

"Not yet. Just a minute."

Emma was already shaking her head. "Look, Velvet. I've got the flu, okay? I'm not pregnant. There's no way." She started toward the exam room.

"Why not?" Velvet was close on her heels. "We all know you and Thomas are . . . uh . . ."

Emma threw open the exam room door and whirled around to face her friend. "There's no way, okay? Let's get Mrs. Wilson in here so I can go home and die."

Velvet was in her face now, her expression menacing. Emma's heart began to race. This was ridiculous. She couldn't be pregnant! She just *couldn't* be . . .

"I'm running to the CVS for a pregnancy test," Velvet said. "Don't go anywhere."

An hour later, Emma was so freaked out that she couldn't tell if the twin blue lines were real or the result of blurred vision and trembling hands. Velvet was pounding on the door again. How long had she been in the bathroom? How could this have happened?

She looked at herself in the mirror, splashed cold water on her face, and smoothed the hair back from her brow.

She looked pale and tired. She looked shell-shocked. Well, hell. She looked pregnant.

But Thomas was sterile.

Emma flung open the door and held up the test stick like the Statue of Liberty's torch. "Thomas said he was sterile."

Velvet's mouth dropped open. *"What?"*

Emma returned to her perch on the closed toilet lid and rested her head in her hands. "He was injured playing rugby and had all these tests . . ." She looked up and blinked. "I don't understand."

Velvet squatted in front of her and dug her manicured nails into Emma's knees. "What are you saying?"

Emma snorted. "I'm saying I don't know what the hell is going on! I'm pregnant, Velvet! Pregnant when there's no way I should be!"

Velvet got up and began to pace the tiny bathroom. It was making Emma's headache worse.

"And he's . . . ?"

"The only one since Aaron, yes. And I went off the pill after the divorce."

Velvet pursed her lips and stared down at Emma. "Did you see his medical records?"

"What?"

"Is there any chance he was lying to you?"

"Of course not!" As soon as the words escaped Emma's mouth her heart twisted in a cold squeeze of doubt. Yes, he'd lied in the past . . . but that had been different . . . before his heart-wrenching confession at her feet and the way he'd loved her since . . .

"I can't even think that way." She shook her head and stared at the absorbent strip dangling from her fingers.

"Why not?"

"Because I love him too much. It has to be some kind of fluke." Her head fell back in her hands.

"What are you going to do, Em?"

"I'm going to tell him."

"Of course—"

"And we'll figure this out together."

"How far along do you think you are?"

Emma looked up and smiled, a rush of excitement moving through her.

"Three weeks at the most."

"What are you going to do?"

"Do?" Emma got up, pressed past Velvet and headed for her desk chair. She swiveled back and forth, biting her lip.

"What are you going to *do,* Emma?"

She blinked back tears, not sure whether they were tears of joy or distress. "I guess I'm going to have a baby. Is that the weirdest thing, or what?"

"And what do you want *him* to do?"

Emma laughed a little, and Hairy jumped in her lap. He'd been asleep in the dog bed in the corner of the office, where he hung out during the day when Leelee was at school. "He's already done it," she said. "He gave me a baby."

Velvet rolled her eyes. "You know what I'm asking, Em! I'm asking you if you want him to marry you!"

Emma absently stroked Hairy's head and felt a small smile play on her face. "Actually, he asked me to marry him a few weeks ago."

Velvet's mouth hung open. "What was your answer?"

"I said yes."

"Holy shit."

"Exactly."

"Is he stopping by this afternoon?"

"At five-thirty."

Velvet stuck her hands on her narrow hips and tilted her head. "Are you okay, Em? You look completely blown away."

She laughed, somewhat hysterically. "That would be because I *am* blown away. A month ago I was alone. Now I'm in love! I'm going to get married! I'm going to give birth!"

Emma launched herself from the chair and threw Hairy to the floor.

"But right now I'm going to be sick."

Chapter 19

Don't Leave Me This Way

Thomas arrived at Wit's End a few minutes early, anxious to see Emma, worried that she was still feeling under the weather.

The bells jingled as he pushed open the front door and nearly ran over Velvet Miki, who was on her way out. He gave her a big smile.

"Hey, Velvet."

"Asshole."

Thomas whipped around and stared after her. He couldn't quite figure that woman. She was always mad at him for some unknowable offense. Thank God Emma was steady as a rock.

He found her sitting at her desk, Hairy asleep on her lap. She offered him a weak smile and Thomas immediately saw that she seemed sad. Her cheeks lacked their usual pink flush and her eyes some of their sparkle. She looked fragile to him, and his heart lurched.

"Hey, baby. You still feeling bad?"

Emma nodded. Now he could see that her eyes were red, like she'd been crying, and a stab of apprehension went through him.

"Hey, what's wrong?"

He went to her, pulled her up from the chair and into

his arms. She felt thin to him, and the worry escalated. "Are you okay, Emma? What is it? Did you go to the doctor? Tell me."

She started to cry, and threw her arms around his waist and buried her face in his chest. Then it hit him—brain tumor. Of course. He finds the only woman in the world for him and she's dying of a brain tumor.

Emma pulled away from him. "Have a seat, Thomas." She directed him to the chair and leaned on the edge of the desk.

Her eyes were swimming in tears, blue as an in-ground pool, but there was something in her expression he'd never before seen. Fear—real fear. Oh, God, it was going to be bad.

"There's no way to sugar-coat this, so I'll just tell you." She hugged herself tight, an obvious gesture of self-defense. Why in the world would Emma be afraid of him?

She took a huge gulp of air and locked her eyes on his.

"I'm pregnant."

And just like that, the air left his lungs and his brain went black.

Then he felt it—his heart was a a tiny pebble in a giant slingshot and it was pulled back, back, back . . . waiting . . . waiting . . . then flung into the void.

While his heart crashed through the emptiness, the rest of him saw nothing. Heard nothing. Felt even less. And his only thought was, *Un-fucking-believable.*

Then slowly, oh so slowly, the empty buzz of shock became an internal roar of grief, and he allowed the words to form in his mind: Emma had been with another man. Emma had betrayed him. Emma was not his Emma after all.

"Wow," he said.

There were those blue eyes he'd loved only seconds ago, still searching his face, waiting for him to say something more. But there was no response for this, was there? There was nothing to say.

He got up from the chair.

"Thomas?" Emma's voice sounded shaky and small.

When he got to the door, he turned toward her. He could see her chest tremble with each breath and his eyes strayed to her belly, where an impossible baby grew inside her.

He really didn't want to know the answer, but he felt the awful question surge up his throat and spill from his mouth.

"Who's the father?"

Emma left the edge of the desk and took slow, measured steps in his direction. "What the hell kind of question is that, Thomas?"

He knew his laugh sounded cruel, and the remarkable thing was how little he cared. And how much he hurt. "It's the only question there is. Who's the lucky guy?"

"Don't you dare do this to me."

She stepped closer, and Thomas saw that her eyes blazed with anger, with sorrow. For a split second, he wavered. But he regrouped, seeing her suffering for what it was: a fine female performance.

Thomas watched Emma move in slow motion, cupping her hands low on her belly. "I don't understand, either, but that doesn't change the fact that we're having a baby—and you're the father."

The words cut into his heart and gut. They were words he'd convinced himself he'd never hear as long as he lived, yet she'd just said them. And God, how he wished he could believe her.

But there was no way he could believe her.

And the sickening truth was this: he'd been made cretinlike by a woman, his brains liquefied by the lure of sex, connection, *love*. Move over, Leo Vasilich—the new poster boy for male stupidity has come to town!

"I don't . . . sorry . . . I can't even . . ." Thomas wiped his hand across his mouth in an attempt to stop the trembling in his lips and chin. "I can't talk to you right now."

He turned away from Emma and started down the hallway, every muscle in his body aching with loss and shock. In a few days he'd call her to settle things between them. But for now, all he could do was put one foot in front of the other and get himself out of there, away from her.

Away from the pain.

"Thomas! Don't do this!" She was right behind him. "Talk to me!"

He kept walking.

"Thomas!"

He heard Emma's shout even as he closed the car door and started the engine. She was standing in the doorway to the clinic, her eyes wide, tears streaming down her cheeks.

For just an instant, he recalled how she'd looked in his dress shirt, leaning against the archway of his kitchen, sleepy and well loved and ready for more.

It seemed like some other man's memory.

He pulled out of the parking space.

"Don't do this to us!"

He heard her plea just as he put in a John Coltrane CD and cranked up the volume, wondering, briefly, who the *us* was.

Herself and the baby?

Or the two of them—Emma and Thomas?

Uh-oh. This is bad. So very, very bad.

"Where the hell is the Tylenol?"

Emma tossed things out of the drawers and cabinets like a crazy woman—paper clips, rubber bands, files, pencils— making a huge mess. Talking to herself. She threw the stapler across the room and Hairy ducked.

I'll just be hiding over here in the corner . . .

"It's aspirin you shouldn't take if you're pregnant, right? Tylenol's okay, right? Oh . . . ugh . . . not again . . ." Emma stumbled down the hall to the bathroom.

Oh, I wish I could dial the phone. I'd call Bright Eyes or TV Man or that Velvet woman. Because Soft Hands shouldn't be by herself right now, that much is obvious.

Speaking of obvious, you are such a complete idiot, Big Alpha!

Emma staggered out of the bathroom and headed to the spare office, Hairy at her heels, and began throwing things from the new supply closet.

"You stupid, stubborn two-stepper!"

You got that right.

"Shit, Velvet! Where's the damn Tylenol?"

Uh-oh. She's crying so hard now. And there's nothing I can do to help her. Nothing . . .

A large box tumbled down from a shelf, followed by a rain of medicine samples, and Emma slumped down on her knees in the middle of the mess and sobbed.

"Oh, Thomas! No! This can't be happening!"

Oh, Big Alpha. What have you done? She's practically howling now. Okay—maybe I should go to her, lick her, nuzzle her, wait . . . wait just a darn minute . . .

What's that smell? What is it? Who is it?

Uh-oh. It's the bad man.

The bad man has been here! His scent is everywhere . . . everywhere . . .

Emma raised her head to the sound of scratching. Hairy had jumped inside the box and tipped it over, and was now frantically digging with his front paws, sniffing, whining, and shaking.

The dog popped out of the box, one of Aaron's old baseball caps in his mouth. Hairy's tail was flipped up between his legs. His eyes were nearly bursting from their sockets.

Then he peed all over the carpet.

Uh-oh. I'm such a bad dog.

Emma wiped her eyes with her palms. "Good God, little man, what's wrong?"

This is it—I've got to make her pay attention. She has to understand this. Okay. Emma, look!

She watched the dog keep the hat in his mouth, stand on his hind legs and spin. Then he did a little roundabout and a back flip, just like one of his dance routines.

Then he howled, louder and higher and with more desperation than she'd ever heard from such a small animal, and she sat up straight. Slowly, she began to tremble with understanding. "Hairy?"

Soft Hands, listen to me! This hat belongs to the man who killed my master!

"Oh, my God, Hairy. Oh, my God, no."

Leelee didn't expect them back this soon. She put aside the book *Guns, Germs, and Steel,* which Thomas had bought her at the mall, and stood up from the porch rocker. She stretched, waiting to see Emma's old Montero come down the lane first, followed by Thomas's silver-bullet Audi.

Maybe he'd let her drive it again tonight.

Leelee squinted. She didn't recognize the car—some kind of maroon beater Chrysler with a vinyl roof that might have been white at some point in the last century. She couldn't see who was behind the wheel, but the car was making sputtering noises like an old man with a nasty case of bronchitis.

The car skidded to a stop in the gravel and Aaron got out.

Aaron?

"What are *you* doing here?"

"Where'd Beck go?"

Leelee took a few steps down the porch stairs. "What?"

"I just saw Beck turn out of the drive. Where was he headed, Leelee?"

The hair stood up on the back of her neck and along her forearms. There was something wrong with Aaron. He looked weird. "Beck went to the grocery. What's it to you?"

"When's Emma coming home?"

Leelee shrugged, instinctively stepping back up the steps to get away from him. He followed her. "They should be here any minute and I don't think you're welcome here."

"You know everything, don't you, you little brat?"

Okay. She was scared now. Something wasn't right with the way his eyes looked. Like he was drunk or something, but Aaron didn't drink. Did he?

She took a deep sniff of him and smelled liquor, and her stomach flipped. "I want you to leave, please," she said.

"Oh, I don't think so."

"I'm going to call the police."

"No you're not." He grabbed her by the upper arm and pulled her over to the railing, pushing her down until she sat in front of him. He leaned into her, much too close.

"Who's 'they,' Leelee? You just said 'they' are going to be home any minute."

"Emma and Thomas—her boyfriend."

The look on Aaron's face was priceless, and if she hadn't been so scared she would have laughed at him. Aaron had always been the big man, so certain he was the one who called the shots.

"Boyfriend." The word came out in a hateful hiss of liquor breath and she had to turn her face away. "When the fuck did she get a boyfriend?"

"Nice language to use around a child, dipshit." She tried to squirm away from his grip. "Let me go."

"Who is this guy? Answer me." Aaron's fingers tightened on her arm.

"You're hurting me, loser."

"Who is he?"

"What does it matter to you?" Leelee heard her voice go high and loud and she sounded like a frightened little kid. "You don't have any business butting into Emma's life. Now that she finally got smart and got rid of you, she's never been happier—"

Aaron's hand whipped across Leelee's face and her head snapped back from the impact.

"Shut the fuck up."

"Oh, my God—"

"I said *shut up.*"

She couldn't believe it! This was something she'd always pictured happening in L.A.—that she'd be walking down the street and some crackhead would stick a gun in her face and threaten to kill her. But not here. Not someone she knew. Not in Wholesome World. This was too bizarre to be real.

But when Aaron's palm hit her face again, she knew without a doubt it was real. The pain was sharp, and the metal of the gun felt cold against the hot place on her cheek where he'd just hit her. And she started to cry.

"What are you doing, Aaron?" There was nothing she could do to stop the tears, and now her whole body shook. "I don't understand why you're doing this."

"Of course you don't."

"Why are you hurting me?"

"I wish I didn't have to."

She opened her eyes to find him smiling down at her.

"When's your birthday, Leelee?"

"Whaa—?" His fingers dug into her arm and he shoved

the gun into the hollow below her cheekbone. What a strange thing to ask.

He continued to smile at her. "The month and year you were born."

"I, uh—"

"How *old* are you? You're supposed to be some sort of fucking genius, right? So answer the question—when is your fucking birthday?"

She gulped down air, and got another whiff of the liquor on him. He stunk to high heaven. She thought she might hurl. "May fifth, 1989."

Aaron chuckled to himself in a creepy, soft way that made Leelee cringe.

"Well, that answers that." He smiled at her again. "I always wondered if you might be my kid. Wouldn't that be cozy? Close but no cigar, as they say."

Leelee's throat hurt and her chest felt tight and it was the ugliest feeling she'd ever experienced in her life—ugly because she realized she was so desperate that she was actually disappointed that Aaron wasn't her dad. Because then the hole would be filled—even with a complete loser—but it would be *filled at last*.

She was so ashamed and so scared that she started to cry hard. Was he going to kill her now? Was he going to wait for Emma to come home and kill her, too?

But Thomas would be with Emma . . .

She sniffed and raised her head. "You won't get away with this. Thomas will kick your ass."

Aaron scowled at her, then checked his watch. "I said shut up."

"He's a special investigator with the state police and a rugby player and he loves Emma more than you ever did and he'll squash you like the larva you are."

That was the last thing Leelee remembered.

• • •

Oh, God. Oh, God. Oh, God.

With shaking hands, Emma picked up Aaron's old base-ball hat and, as if she needed to know for certain, she brought it to her face and inhaled.

Yes, it absolutely smelled like Aaron to her pitiful human nose, so she could only imagine the intensity of the scent for Hairy.

The dog was a pathetic, trembling mess. His tail was still curled between his legs and his back was hunched and he was telling her . . . telling her that Aaron had killed Scott Slick.

Oh, God.

Emma's hands went flying through the box of junk. She didn't know what she was looking for but she needed proof that she was wrong, that Hairy was wrong, that this could not possibly be true.

She pulled out a half-dead racquetball, a sweatband, a pair of gym socks, the cuff links she gave him on their second anniversary, a birthday card she'd given him a few years ago, old patient files that he should have taken with him, a scratch pad, a few veterinary textbooks . . . Emma's hand went back to the pad, and flipped through the pages.

She'd found something all right, but it didn't ease her mind. Page after page contained Aaron's familiar penciled scrawl, numbers and the names of sports teams that would look like gibberish to anyone unfamiliar with bookmaking.

Unfortunately, she knew just what she was looking at. And on several pages, Aaron had written Scott Slick's name and phone number.

She had to reach Thomas. Despite everything—everything that had just happened here between them, he had to know this. Detective Massey had to know this. Aaron had to be caught.

And then the image popped into her mind: how desperate Aaron had been the last time she'd seen him, lowering himself into the Z and saying, "You have no idea what you've just done."

If he was capable of killing Slick, he was a violent man. Had that been a warning? Some kind of threat?

Emma pushed herself off the floor and punched in the numbers to Thomas's beeper, then called the state police to get a message to Regina Massey. Then she called home. When no one answered, the flesh on her arms prickled into goosebumps and her breath came shallow and quick.

Leelee.

Oh, God. Leelee!

Thomas didn't consciously know where he was headed until he pulled into the parking lot of Chesapeake Urology Associates and cut the engine.

He had no idea whether Rollo was still in his office. He had no idea how late Rollo saw patients on Thursdays. He could be at a meeting. He could already be home. Thomas had no idea.

But he needed him. Now.

Thomas whipped open the glass door and it slapped against the waiting room wall. Until he saw the startled expression on the receptionist's face, Thomas hadn't even considered that he might look like a deranged fiend, a man on the edge.

Which, of course, he was.

"May I help—"

"Where's Rollo?"

"He's with his last patient, but . . . Mr. Tobin?"

Thomas flung open the door that led to the exam rooms and doctors' offices and took wide strides down the white fluorescent-lighted hallway, scanning, listening, until he heard Rollo's voice from behind a closed door. He pounded on it.

"What the—" Rollo's face went from anger to shock in the blink of an eye. "Thomas?"

"I'm sorry. It's an emergency. I'll be in your office."

"Is it Pam? The kids?" Rollo looked like he was going to keel over, and Thomas suddenly felt like a jerk.

"God, no. Nothing like that."

The anger reappeared and Rollo lowered his voice to a harsh whisper. "Goddammit, Thomas, this better be good."

He closed the door in his face.

Oh, now wasn't this pleasant? Thomas looked around the nicely appointed office, remembering clearly that fateful day. He sat right here in this same leather chair as Nina sat beside him and said to Rollo, "Excuse me, but we are not an infertile *couple*. I am perfectly normal. He's the one with the defect."

Women. Why was it that the worst moments of his life—and the best—were in the company of women?

Why had he allowed himself to trust a woman?

Why had he loved one?

Was it worth it—the moments he'd spent in Emma's company, in her arms, inside her body, hearing her laugh, seeing her smile, feeling what he would have sworn to God above was love?

Maybe it was. Maybe that was the real hell in all this— that he wouldn't have done a thing differently if he'd known in advance that it would turn to shit.

Maybe it was worth it just to know what it felt like. Just once in his life. Maybe it had been worth it to his own father, all those years ago.

With a sigh of disgust, Thomas promised himself not to be so hard on the next fool who wandered his way looking for a hit man, lost and desperate because of a woman.

His beeper went off again, making four calls from Emma

in the last half-hour. He'd talk to her when he was good and ready and not a moment sooner.

"What the hell, Tobin? I was with a patient!"

Rollo pushed past him and threw himself into his office chair. He looked as fierce as he did on the rugby pitch, big and nasty and ready to knock heads.

"Emma's pregnant."

Thomas watched the air empty from his best friend's lungs, his face soften.

"Say again?"

Thomas rose from the chair and started to pace. "She's pregnant. I'm about to blow. Punch a wall. Break somebody's arm. I don't know what to do."

"Sit down." Rollo stood up from behind his desk when Thomas continued to pace. "Sit down, dammit!"

Thomas wheeled on him. "She had the nerve to tell me she hadn't been with anyone else! I want to believe her! *God,* how I want to believe her—"

"Sit down, Thomas."

"Fuck!"

"Sit down."

"But I'm sterile! I'm supposed to be sterile!" Thomas glared at him. "Right?"

Rollo reached over his desk and grabbed Thomas by the tie. "I said sit down. Right now."

He collapsed with a thud.

"Can I get you a soda or a cup of coffee?"

"God, no."

Rollo picked up his phone. "Giselle, I've got a situation here. Please bring me Thomas Tobin's chart."

Rollo ran both his hands through his thick brown hair and took off his small wire-framed glasses, rubbing the bridge of his nose. Finally, he looked up.

"How far along is she?"

"Hell if I know."

"How long have you two been sexually active?"

"Three Saturdays ago. And we've been real active."

"Oh, boy."

"What? What the hell is that supposed to mean—*Oh, boy!*—like you're on the Tilt-A-Whirl at the fair or something when I'm telling you that the only woman I've ever loved just lied to me! She—"

After a meek knock, the door opened a crack and the receptionist inserted Thomas's file through the gap.

Rollo was up on his feet. "Thanks," he whispered, looking sheepish.

Thomas watched him open the chart and nod to himself. He threw his glasses across the desk.

"What is it you want to ask me?"

"Huh?"

"Why are you here, T? What is it that you want me to tell you?"

"I don't know—"

"That I made a mistake six months ago and you're not really sterile? Because I can't tell you that. You are sterile by all conceivable medical measurements."

"I know that."

"Do you want me to assure you that there is absolutely no chance whatsoever that you could have fathered that child? Because I can't tell you that, either."

Thomas leaned forward in his chair. *"What did you just say to me?"*

Rollo laughed and threw up his hands.

"I don't have any magic answer for you, T. You took a pounding seven years ago and the swelling and pain eventually went away and it looked like you were in the clear. Then last winter . . ."

Rollo flipped open the chart again. "Complete rupture of the bloody membrane, recurrent scrotal pain and atrophy— you ignored the pain, buddy, and by the time you got in here, your body had already had several months to fight off what it considered a virus invading your body cavity—your own sperm. The damage was done. You'd built up anti-bodies to your own sperm."

"You told me this already."

"What I told you, Thomas, is that your semen analysis showed you were far, far below normal ranges and were considered sterile. But I also told you that you had *a few* healthy sperm left with *some* motility—not many, but some."

Thomas was up and out of the chair and his voice was so loud it bounced off the wallpaper and zinged over the surface of the windows. *"Are you telling me that I could be the actual goddamn father of that baby?"*

"Sit down, Thomas," Rollo said calmly, and Thomas slammed down into the chair again. His head felt like it would explode.

"Maybe—just maybe—that's your baby Emma's carry-ing. She could be telling the truth."

Thomas rubbed his hand across his mouth and stared at the pocket of Rollo's coat—it didn't say anything about the CVS stock boy. This was not another one of his dreams. This was real.

The worst fucking nightmare he'd ever had.

"Oh, dear God."

"Look, T. You are technically, virtually, medically in-fertile. But you still produce sperm—and a couple of them still have some get-up-and-go. Maybe you had one real champ and he made the clutch play for you, man."

"Oh, dear God."

Rollo shrugged. "As your doctor—and as your *friend*—I've got to tell you that this isn't about numbers, it's about trust. You can always get an in vitro DNA workup if you have to, but you need to decide right now—you either trust the woman or you don't. Which is it?"

"Dear God in heaven."

Rollo reached over the desk and gave Thomas's cheek several quick, light slaps. "Are you hearing what I'm saying?"

Thomas looked at Rollo and swallowed. "That's my baby, isn't it?"

"I'm a doctor, not an odds maker, T." Rollo closed the file. "I've seen some strange things in my line of work, and I'll be the first person to tell you that bad shit happens all the time. But I think maybe there's room in the universe for really excellent shit to happen, too."

Rollo put his hand on Thomas's arm.

"Maybe this is one of those times—a time for excellent shit. A miracle even."

"Oh, Emma, baby. Oh, no." Thomas rolled his eyes to the ceiling, then looked down at his pager: six calls from her now.

He jumped up and Rollo followed him to the door. "What're you gonna do, man?"

Thomas wasn't sure what to do with his own face— should he be beaming with pride? Crying because he was such a moron? He ended up turning, throwing his arms around his best friend and squeezing as hard as he could.

Rollo stared at him in shock.

"I'll tell you what I'm gonna do, man." Thomas planted a big, smacking kiss on Rollo's cheek. "I'm going to get married—that is, if Emma can ever forgive me for what I just did to her—if she can still love me. Then I'm going to be a husband and a father."

Thomas reached for the doorknob and turned back to Rollo. "Score a few more Cohibas in the meantime, all right? We're gonna need 'em."

He shut the door, leaving Rollo standing in the middle of his office, laughing, shaking his head, rubbing his cheek.

"There goes poker night."

Chapter 20

Kung Fu Fighting

She raced down the farm lane, aware of nothing but the panic and dread that churned inside her. Everything was falling apart, breaking into pieces, and if anything happened to Leelee she'd never forgive herself.

Never.

The truck cleared the last stand of trees.

And Emma screamed.

Aaron had Leelee. She was as limp as a rag doll. He dragged her, her heels cutting into the gravel as he backed toward the open door of some disgusting old car. Leelee's wrists were tied behind her back.

Emma barely stopped the truck before she jumped out and ran toward them, calling out, begging Aaron to let her go.

"Get back!" Aaron heaved Leelee onto the back seat and pointed a gun at Emma's face. She skidded to a halt.

"Please! Aaron! God! Don't—"

He shoved the gun into her side. "Come on, Em. We're taking a ride."

Emma's brain went numb from the assault of all the impossible things that were suddenly real. Aaron had a gun. He was drunk—*drunk?*—when she'd never seen him take a single drink in the thirteen years she'd known him. And the look in his eye was crazed, wild, empty.

She tried to reason with him.

"Aaron—I'll give you anything—"

He shoved her between the shoulder blades, and as she stumbled toward the front passenger seat, Emma blinked in wonder at what she saw—Hairy had jumped from her truck and was now slinking low in the grass along the drive. She caught the dog's eye just before he skittered between the tires and jumped through the driver's side window of the old car.

Aaron leaned his back against the rusty door and poked the gun into Emma's belly. He sighed.

Emma's eyes darted to his face, and she saw that in addition to being drunk, he was exhausted. Thin. And he hadn't shaved or taken a shower in perhaps weeks.

"Aaron, please—"

"Don't make this any worse than it has to be, Em."

She flinched—Aaron was stroking her cheek with his free hand.

Through the shock and fear, she stared over his shoulder to watch Hairy in action. He snatched Aaron's wallet from the front seat, sailed out the window, and dropped the wallet under a bushy sedum by the porch. Then Hairy hopped back in the car and soared over the front seat and onto Leelee's lap.

What was the dog doing?

"I wish I didn't have to kill you, Emma."

Aaron dragged a finger along her lower lip and she moved her eyes back to him. He came closer. The choking fear and the smell of alcohol and old sweat made her want to vomit.

"You should've given me the money when I asked nice. And now I have no choice . . ." Aaron leaned into her, the gun jutting into her navel, and brought his lips to hers.

Emma's eyes darted back to the car, where Hairy was

now nibbling on Leelee's chin, her upper lip, licking her eyelids. Leelee regained consciousness and stared silently at Emma through the window—clearly terrified. Hairy sailed out the window and hid in the grass.

Aaron ended the kiss, then pulled baling twine out of his pocket and wrapped her wrists tight in front of her, the sharp threads digging into her skin. She hissed with the pain.

"Get in." He pushed her down on the seat. "If you give me any trouble, I swear I'll shoot Becca's sewer-mouthed little bastard kid, and don't think I won't enjoy doing it. She's a pain in the ass." Aaron glanced at Leelee, who pretended to be out cold. "But damn—she's gonna be as hot as her mom. I can already see it."

Emma swallowed hard. She was going to be sick for sure.

As Aaron walked around the front of the car, Emma took a deep breath and told herself to think. Think hard. But all that came to her were the words *Don't get in the car, whatever you do . . .* How many times had she read that? *Never get in the car with the assailant.*

But what choice did she have? If they ran he'd shoot them—she had no doubt that Aaron was psycho enough to do it. If she tried to fight him, she'd put three lives in danger—her own, Leelee's, and the baby inside her.

At that realization, Emma began to tremble from head to toe.

The car moved. She checked the rearview mirror and through her tears saw little Hairy sitting in the lane. He'd witnessed everything—and had Aaron's wallet. Would he try to tell someone what had happened? And who would understand him if he did?

Thomas would.

But where was he?

"Thomas," she whispered, shutting her eyes, blinking back the tears. "I need you."

Aaron must have heard, because he laughed hard and poked her in the ribs with the gun.

"Ain't love a bitch?" he said, pulling out onto the road. "Nobody's there when you really need them."

Thomas put the magnetized blue flashing light on his dashboard and drove like a wild man out to Carroll County.

Emma wasn't answering any of her phones, so Thomas figured she was in the barn, saddling up Vesta for a nice ride. But maybe she shouldn't ride now because of the baby, especially on a horse as feisty as Vesta. Maybe she'd take Bud. But what if she fell? Would she be careful? Would she take Leelee with her just to be on the safe side?

Thomas felt his stomach do another round of somer-saults—Emma was somewhere thinking he'd turned his back on her and their baby. Wherever she was, her heart had to be breaking.

He couldn't drive fast enough. Each second that passed was time she didn't know he trusted her, believed her, loved her more than he'd ever guessed a man could love a woman. Every second cut a deeper wedge between them, ate away at their future.

Oh, Jesus, what had he done?

His car phone rang.

"Emma? Baby, is that you?"

A female snicker wafted through the earpiece. "Sorry, Tommy. It's just me."

Thomas felt his heart slide to his feet. "Ah, hell, Reg. I'm sorry, but I can't talk right now—I'm in the middle of the biggest crisis of my life, my . . . how did you describe me and Nina together?"

"Uh . . . sour-assed?"

"Bingo. This is the biggest moment in my sour-assed life. I gotta go."

"Thomas, wait. I got a voice mail from your Emma. She she said her ex-husband, some guy named Aaron Kramer, killed Slick. Does this make any sense to you?"

"What? No! Absolutely no sense, Reg. When did she call you?"

"About an hour ago. I'm looking through Slick's computer records right now for mention of an Aaron Kramer. And listen, Emma sounded hysterical during the call and now I can't reach her. She's not at either number she left for me, and—"

"Shit," Thomas hissed.

Emma must have called Reg soon after he walked away from her. Emma was pregnant. Under stress. Maybe she'd snapped. But Emma wasn't the kind to snap.

"I don't know what the hell's going on, Reg, but if that's what the lady said, then she had a reason. Bring him in. He's got a vet practice in Annapolis. I'll deal with all this later, okay?"

"Okay. So what's going on with you? Is everything all right?"

Thomas laughed into the phone. "God no, everything's not all right. Everything's messed up. I'm an idiot. Reg, look—how does a man convince a woman that he's more sorry than he could ever say, that his life would be nothing without her?"

Regina sighed. "Lord, Tommy. What have you done now?"

"Either of you move, I start shooting."

Aaron got out of the car. He backed to the motel room door not two feet away from the parking spot, and inserted the key, never taking his eyes from them.

He ushered them quickly inside.

He locked the door and flipped on the overhead light. Then he closed the drapes, making sure there were no gaps in the folds of musty fabric.

Emma's gut tensed as she scanned the evidence of Aaron's dive off the deep end. Empty Jack Daniel's bottles were knocked over on the dresser and floor. The threadbare room was littered with chip bags and scribbled-on bits of paper—sports bets. A pair of dirty underwear was flung over the lampshade.

"Nice crib," Leelee said.

He laughed, then pointed the gun at the floor in front of the dresser and television. "You. Smart-ass. Sit down over there." He put the gun at her temple. "If you move, I kill you."

Leelee nodded, and slid down onto her bottom.

"You." Aaron grabbed a scarred wooden chair from near the window and pointed the gun at it. "Here." He held it for Emma.

"Now listen up, girlies. Here's the game plan." Aaron poured himself a drink with the gun pointed at Leelee and his eyes darting back and forth between the women. He slammed back the whiskey and hissed between his teeth.

"It's going to be your basic murder-suicide. Leelee kills you—" He pointed at Emma. "Then kills herself. And the insurance money is mine."

"Insurance?" Emma's mouth fell open. "This is about our life-insurance policies?"

"Why, yes it is!" Aaron mimicked her surprise. "Thank you again for being kind enough to keep me as your beneficiary."

"Oh, God." Emma closed her eyes. It was the only thing he'd asked for in the divorce settlement, that they'd remain beneficiaries on each other's policies for two years, a guarantee that at least one veterinary practice would thrive if anything were to happen to one of them. Since they'd gone into debt together in residency and later as business partners, she thought it was equitable.

And now he was going to kill her for it.

"You don't have to do this," Emma said calmly. "We can work something out. I won't go to the police. No one has to know—"

"Shut up!" he screamed, waving the gun in her direction.

At that moment, it occurred to Emma that the man in front of her was a stranger. She knew nothing about him. Maybe she never had.

And she'd be damned if she'd let him hurt two innocent children.

"This is not going to work, you know," Leelee said from her place on the floor. "They have insurance investigators and criminalistics people like on *CSI*. It'd be a no-brainer to figure out you did it for the money."

"Shut . . . the . . . fuck . . . up," Aaron whispered. "Do you *want* me to blow your head off? Is that it?"

Emma was trying to get Leelee's attention—because shutting up sounded like a real good idea right about now. But Leelee wasn't looking.

"Besides, your bitchin' new ride is right outside for the world to see."

Aaron stalked toward her. Emma willed the girl to *be quiet*. "And what's my motive?" Leelee continued. "I'm the Carroll County Middle School Geography Bee champion, for crying out loud!"

Aaron clicked off the safety and stuck the gun to Leelee's mouth. "This will shut you up."

"I'm pregnant!" Emma screamed.

Aaron turned his head and stared at Emma. Leelee gasped and sat up straighter.

"What?" they both yelled at the same time.

"I'm going to have a baby, Aaron. Please let us go. Don't kill us. I'll give you everything I have if you just let us go."

Aaron cocked his head, as if considering her offer. "Who's the father?"

Emma swallowed, her eyes darting from Leelee's shocked face to Aaron. Then back to Leelee—the girl had begun to furiously saw her wrists against the little metal drawer pull behind her back.

"The father is Thomas, my fiancé."

"Fiancé?" they both yelled.

"Yes."

Aaron stared at her with narrow, ugly eyes, and Emma checked quickly to see that Leelee almost had her hands free.

"Pops and I will sell the farm and give you all the profit." Emma's voice was soft and steady as she held Aaron's gaze. "It's worth a fortune to developers now—*millions*, Aaron. Think about it. That would be so much better than whatever my insurance might be worth. And you can have it all."

As a sickening smile spread across his face, Emma knew she had never been more frightened in her life. It was eerie seeing an Aaron who wasn't Aaron—gutted out and hollow. Her stomach clenched again.

"You lying whore." With that, his open hand cracked across her mouth, and Emma's head swung around from the force.

"Buttwipe!" Leelee shot up from the floor and lunged at Aaron.

In her swimming vision, Emma watched Leelee make a single upward slice with her forearm, knocking the gun from Aaron's grip. The gun went sailing over the bed just as Leelee jumped Aaron, knocked him back on the mattress, and straddled him, hitting and punching wildly.

Emma was on her feet, ready to do whatever she could to beat Aaron to a pulp and get them out of there, when the door was bashed open and two men stumbled in. They both had guns.

"Hey—it's a party," said the uglier of the two.

Thomas raced down the lane, gravel and dust flying around the Audi like a swarm of hornets. He saw Emma's truck, and his heart soared—then sank. The driver's side door was flung open, and Beckett was standing in the driveway—in tears.

"Beck?" Thomas flew out of his car and ran to the old man. He grabbed him by the shoulders.

"They're gone. Something happened. I think he has them."

"Emma's gone? Leelee?"

"Aaron's got 'em."

"What do you mean he's—"

"Here." Beckett handed him a fine-grained black leather wallet. "Hairy had it in his teeth when I got back from the Super Fresh just a minute ago. The dog was going nuts—spinning and jumping and crying. I think Aaron has the girls."

"Did you look—?"

"House. Barn. Everywhere. They're gone."

Thomas looked down at the mishmash of tire prints in the gravel. Hell if he could tell if another car had been here. Then he saw the deep cuts in the stones, like somebody's feet had been dragged across the lane.

"I'm calling in." Thomas ran to the car, yelling over his shoulder. "How long ago, Beck? How long ago do you think?"

He shook his head. "I've been home no more than five minutes. That's all I can tell you."

Thomas dialed Reg and told her to get an APB on Aaron Kramer. He flipped open the wallet and started reading from the expired Maryland driver's license.

"White male, DOB 6–14–67, five-nine, one fifty-five. He's got brown eyes, brown hair. He's—"

Thomas stopped. He stared at the little picture at the top right corner of the license and turned it in the light. He imagined what that clean-cut man would look like in a scraggly beard and a pair of blue contact lenses.

"He's Larry. Oh, fuck."

"Who's Larry?"

Thomas dumped the contents of the wallet onto the front seat and started looking for something—anything—that might indicate where Aaron had taken them. He found two condoms, two obviously stolen credit cards, a few bucks, and a handwritten receipt for a motel room—paid up until tomorrow.

Thomas gave Reg the address to the King of Hearts Motor Court in Bowie, then gave her the physical descriptions of Leelee and Emma. "Bring in the STATE team," he said. "Get everyone in position for a possible hostage situation. I'm on my way."

"Done. Meet you there."

Beck was waiting on the other side of the car door, his face drawn in worry. Hairy was cradled in his arms.

"I swear to God I'll bring them home," Thomas said. "I'll call you as soon as I know anything."

"The hell you will!" Beckett ran around to the other side and jumped in shotgun. He tossed Hairy in the back. "We're all going. Now drive!"

Thomas was soon back on the road, blue light flashing, keeping the line open with Reg. The Special Tactical Assault Team Element was already on the way. Troopers from the Prince George's County barracks were on site, awaiting orders. The motel manager was being interviewed. The rest of the motel and all nearby buildings had been cleared.

"She's pregnant," Thomas said.

The old man stared at him with startled blue eyes, then looked him up one side and down the other. He broke out into a wide smile. "And?"

"And I'd like your permission to marry her, sir."

Beckett howled with laughter. "Son, my Emma's a grown woman with a mind of her own, in case you haven't noticed. Now, I'm not saying I don't appreciate the old-fashioned courtesy, but it's her permission you need, not mine."

"Yes, sir."

"Congratulations," Beck said. His chin quivered. "Now let's go get our girls."

Thomas pressed the gas, thanked God it was past evening rush, and let the whole mess whirl around in his head. The fear he felt was desperate, potent. And he realized that he'd only felt fear like this one other time in his life, when he was just a kid. When his mother had left.

And it occurred to him that he'd spent the rest of his life making sure he never set himself up to be this afraid again, because obviously, this kind of fear was the flip side of love. When you loved people they became your whole life. And losing them became the worst fate imaginable.

He saw their faces—Emma and Leelee and a baby that was probably no bigger than a pea but was already real to him, real to his heart.

He refused to lose them.

He'd just found them.

Thomas swallowed hard. "Hang on, Pops," he said, putting the pedal to the metal.

Emma and Leelee were nicely trussed up again, this time sitting in the corner, back to back, wrists linked. There was no way she was going to get out this time, Leelee realized.

The two goons scared her more than Aaron did. They'd obviously done this sort of thing before, whereas Aaron was an amateur. She should be glad to see Aaron shaking and crying as he sat tied on the bed, but she couldn't be glad about anything.

She had a feeling she and Emma were really going to die.

"If you'd just let me follow through with the plan . . ." Aaron tried once more.

The ugly guy laughed again.

Man, he was ugly.

He had hair like Squiggy from *Laverne & Shirley* reruns. Leelee didn't think actual people wore their hair like that, but obviously she'd been traveling in the wrong circles. He was dressed in a mighty attractive yellow polyester golf shirt and a pair of those stretch pants men can order from the back pages of *Parade* magazine. He had more tattoos than the girls at the tractor pull, but fewer teeth. And he smelled bad.

His skinny friend was obviously the assistant manager of their criminal enterprise. He did whatever the ugly one told him to do, including tying her and Emma together a moment ago.

The last few minutes had been just full of surprises, and by this point, Leelee had put the whole twisted story together. Aaron had owed Scott Slick lots of money and Slick was tired of dealing with him, so he sold Aaron's debt to Goons Incorporated here for pennies on the dollar, and they'd started harassing Aaron to pay up. Aaron was royally pissed, and followed Slick home one night and tried to convince him to give him one more chance to pay his debt. Slick said no-can-do. They argued. Aaron snapped, he said, grabbed a kitchen blender, and whacked Slick in the head with it.

He swore he hadn't meant to kill him.

So there the three men were now, arguing about who they should kill and how they were going to get their hands on money.

Leelee swallowed hard. Obviously, if the goons killed Aaron they wouldn't be getting any more money from him, right? So the Ugly One must be considering Aaron's plan to kill them. That had to be why the three men were now staring at Emma and her like they were juicy T-bones laid out on ruffles of Bibb lettuce.

At least she hoped that money was the only reason they stared.

Leelee started to shake. She shoved down the fear and started talking.

"Hey, did you guys know that Scott Slick was actually an alias for a guy named Simon Slickowski, who lived in a trailer park in Smyrna, Delaware, and was last year's World Canine Disco Dancing Champion?"

"What the fuck is that?" the Ugly One asked, frowning.

"Be quiet, Lee," Emma whispered through clenched teeth.

"It's where people wear funky costumes and dance around to disco music with their dogs—you know, Donna Summer, Rose Royce, Peaches and Herb."

"I've always loved Peaches and Herb," the assistant manager said, then began singing, " 'We're bumping booties, havin' us a ball . . . ' "

"This is messed up," the Ugly One said. "Everybody just shut up a minute while I think."

"And Slick has a bunch of money stashed up in Delaware," Leelee added. "We can take you to it."

The men began arguing again.

Emma twisted her fingers around to clutch at Leelee's hand.

"Lee! How in the world—? Were you listening in on a private conversation between Thomas and me? When?"

Leelee rolled her eyes. This was no time for another lecture from Emma. "I just overheard you one night."

Emma hissed and tightened her grip. "Well, just be quiet, would you?"

"I can't! I'm so scared!"

"It's going to be okay."

Leelee grunted. "How?"

"Thomas is coming for us," she whispered. "I can feel it."

Leelee rolled her eyes—their knight in shining Audi! God, how she wished it were true! Thomas was great, but he wasn't exactly a hero. She knew better than to believe in heroes.

"How much is up in Delaware?" the Ugly One asked.

"Over half a million," Leelee said.

"How in the hell did you know Slick anyway?"

Uh-oh. Maybe she should have kept her mouth shut.

"You're making all this up, aren't you, you little bitch?"

"No! I swear! It's true!"

The Ugly One took a step closer to them while looking over his shoulder at Aaron. "How much did you say the wife was worth, Kramer?"

"Quarter of a million." Aaron slumped further onto the bed.

"Okay. Everybody hold on a minute while I do the math."

Leelee couldn't help it. "Don't hurt yourself," she said.

Emma clamped down on her fingers.

The Ugly One bent down, touched Emma's hair, then Leelee's. He chuckled. "Whatever we do, I think we're going to keep the little one alive."

Emma whipped her head around and sank her teeth into the Ugly One's arm.

"Ow! Shit! Fuck! Hell!"

Things were really starting to disintegrate.

* * *

When they reached the scene, Thomas was told that sniper surveillance showed three men inside, one of them Aaron Kramer, and at least three weapons. The women were tied in the far southwest corner of the room, directly below the front window, Emma facing out. The hostage-takers seemed disorganized and the young girl had managed to keep them off balance by not shutting up.

"Thata girl, Lee," Beckett said.

The STATE team plan was simple: create a diversion and surprise them. Five men were poised at the motel room door, weapons at the ready. Two snipers were positioned in trees in the back. A remote-controlled explosive device—designed more for noise than destruction—was in place under the bathroom window.

Thomas and Regina were right behind the STATE team, tucked into Kevlar vests. The rest of Thomas's team waited in a staging area on the service road, along with five waiting ambulances and an assortment of state police and Prince George's County Sheriff's Department vehicles.

Thomas knew from experience that tactical maneuvers like these could be over in seconds—it was possible that within moments he'd have Emma in his arms. That is, if she'd come anywhere near him.

Snipers reported that Emma had just bitten one of the hostage-takers, and the instant of chaos that followed was all the STATE team needed.

As the hostage-taker dropped his weapon and ran screaming to the bathroom, a loud explosion rocked the room. STATE officers crashed in the door. Two officers immediately covered the women while the other three tackled and cuffed the hostage-takers. The takedown was over almost before it had begun.

The next few moments were a blur for Thomas—he

watched as Emma and Leelee were cut loose and hugged each other, crying. A STATE team member led them to sit on the edge of the bed and called for the EMTs.

They were alive. That's all that registered in his brain. They looked cut and bruised and beyond exhausted, but they were breathing.

He hadn't lost them. Now he prayed he hadn't lost them.

Emma slowly turned toward Thomas. His heart lurched. His eye squinted. And after a second that seemed to hold his entire world over his head, Emma offered him a soft smile.

"I knew you'd figure it out," she said, and held out her hand.

He got to her instantly, squatting down, his hands racing all over her body.

"Are you hurt? Where did they touch you?"

"I'm okay," she said, shaking her head.

Thomas reached over for Leelee. "Are you all right, Lee?"

She nodded, mute, her lips trembling. She had a shiner that was going to take up most of the left side of her face. Thomas took another look at Emma, and saw a swelling welt along her cheek and a split in her lower lip.

What he really wanted to do was kill Aaron with his bare hands.

What he did instead was open his arms, and the two women fell against him, sobbing with relief, shaking from the adrenaline crash, and all he could do was pull them tighter, kiss them both, tell them they would be all right— everything was going to be all right.

Then he allowed himself to believe it, too.

Thomas felt something worming its way between his feet, and Leelee pulled back enough that Hairy could jump into her arms. His little tongue licked her face and he yipped in joy, tail twirling like a propeller.

"Hairy!" Leelee screamed. "Our hero!"

Within a few moments, an EMT escorted Leelee to an ambulance and Thomas asked the crowd in the motel room for a few minutes of privacy. Once everyone left, he sat next to Emma and cupped her face in his hands.

"We need to get you checked out, too." He drank in the sight of that sweet freckled nose, those shell-shocked blue eyes, the face of the woman he loved.

She nodded. She sniffed. In a very small voice she said, "I'm glad you didn't give up on us."

Everything inside of Thomas clenched. "Forgive me, Emma. There's no excuse for the things I said to you. I went crazy. It's just . . . well . . . I'm not very used to believing in miracles, you know? It's kind of a challenge for me."

She smiled.

"I acted like a conflicted idiot."

"You did."

"But I'm a conflicted idiot who loves you with everything I am—an idiot who trusts you completely."

"I'm glad to hear that."

"And God, here's the deal, Emma—you can do whatever you want to me now—poison my cornflakes—"

She was already laughing.

"—put a bomb under the hood of my car, or ground glass in my popcorn, or booby-trap the basement steps, and baby, I'd never see it coming because I love you so much it's killing me."

Emma finished laughing and kissed his cheek. "Or, I could just put all that creative energy into loving you—did that ever occur to you, Thomas?"

He raised her scraped wrist to his lips and kissed tenderly. "It does now."

"I'm glad we've got that cleared up."

"I'm going to do my best, Emma." Thomas's voice went

rough and his gaze held hers. "I might screw up again, but I'll always do my very best for you and our family."

She looked into those tortured silver eyes and knew that was all she could ask. It was all she needed—all she'd ever needed.

"I don't think love is perfect, Rugby Boy." Emma pulled his big hand to her heart and held it there. "It's messy and confusing and complicated, but what else is there? What else is there besides love?"

She grinned, clutched his hand tighter. "I'll take my chances with you if you'll take yours with me."

He pulled her to him, and Emma felt herself relax, curve into his sturdy body, safe and complete.

"I want to love you every day for the rest of my life, Emma Jenkins."

She moved his hand to her belly and pressed it close. "I think we're free."

"Tommy?"

Regina Massey stood in the doorway, smiling. "I'm sorry, but we need to get back in here. We also need to get the doctor and her daughter to the hospital."

He walked Emma to a waiting ambulance, got her settled, and kissed her softly. "I'll be back in a minute. I've got a few loose ends to tie up."

Leelee sat on a stretcher, back straight, chin steady, holding a cold pack to the side of her face with one hand and clutching Hairy with the other. Two EMTs busied themselves around her in the ambulance bay.

She turned toward him, letting the cold pack fall away. She grinned.

"Hey, Thomas."

He smiled, propped a foot on the ambulance fender, and leaned toward her.

"I hear you gave the bad guys a hard time in there."

"Nerves. I talk a lot when I'm nervous."

"Thank you, Lee."

She turned away.

Thomas met the gaze of one of the EMTs, and they both hopped down from the vehicle to give him a moment alone with the girl. He nodded in gratitude.

Thomas cleared his throat. Emma had been right—Leelee was never an easy crowd to work. "Do you know what I'm thanking you for?"

That got her attention. She looked down at him warily. "Sure I do. Emma got out of there alive."

He shook his head. "That's not all."

Leelee tried hard to cloak her expression in her all-purpose bored look, but was failing miserably. Her shoulders were starting to shake and her fingers trembled as they stroked Hairy's skin.

"What, then?"

"Thank you for being the smartest and bravest kid I know. Thank you for loving Emma as much as I do."

"Sure." She shrugged.

"I have something I'd like to ask you."

Leelee sighed and rolled her eyes to the ambulance ceiling. "I know. You want to marry Emma. I know she's pregnant. Nice going, by the way. Ever hear of a condom? So whatever. Go ahead. I don't care."

Thomas chuckled. "That wasn't what I wanted to ask you."

Leelee gazed down at him, shocked by the tender look in his face, the affection she saw there. And it wasn't a creepy kind of affection at all—it was just nice. Just warm and nice, and it was the weirdest thing, but the hole inside her was being filled up—filled up with whatever it was she saw in this man's eyes.

"Do you think Emma can learn to share?"

"Share what?"

Thomas grinned, raised a hand and began to fiddle with

one of her errant blond curls. He let his fingers stray to her cheek. "You, Elizabeth. I was hoping Emma might be willing to share you. I was hoping you might be willing to become my daughter when Emma becomes my wife—kind of like a package deal."

There was nothing Leelee could say, because this was the single most wonderful moment of her life. Of all the men in the world who could have been her father, she'd wound up with Thomas.

She'd somehow ended up with the best.

"So what do you say, junior?"

She felt herself smile, despite her best efforts. "Sure. Whatever." Then she tossed Hairy to the stretcher and flung her arms around Thomas's neck.

Epilogue

You Make Me Feel Like Dancing

"So where are we eating?" Rollo asked.

"Bayside Stella's." Thomas ushered everyone out into the convention center parking lot to the three waiting cars, his arms laden with costumes.

"Yeah? Well, I sure hope you called ahead." Pam threw him a scowl as she herded Petey and Jack into their minivan. "We'll be waiting hours otherwise."

"I called ahead," Thomas answered patiently, then nodded toward Franco. "Outside table for ten with a high chair and the okay to bring two lapdogs."

"He thinks of everything," Franco laughed. "You'd have made a great wedding planner, Thomas."

"I think he should stick to coaching and teaching, don't you, honey?" Beckett squeezed Mrs. Quatrocci's hand.

"Absolutely," she said, smiling up at him.

Sigh.

What a motley crew we are. I can hardly remember the days when it was just Slick and me. It seems like another lifetime—I guess it was.

Uh-oh. Quiche Lorraine, that little minx, just winked at me again. Can't you see I'm exhausted, woman?

Females. What can you do?

"Dadda! See goggy!"

"Yes, T.J., I see the dog. It's Hairy."

"Goggy! My!"

Nope—not even Thomas Jenkins Tobin is going to ruin my good mood today. Because of all my victories, this one was the sweetest.

The instant we stepped into the competition ring and Leelee's eyes latched onto mine, I knew that Junior Free-style trophy was ours.

Sometimes, you just know *it's going to be good.*

"We'll see everyone at the restaurant!" Emma yelled, waving.

It was the finest performance of my career, no question. That instant of magic with the piano intro. Then: "At first I was afraid. I was petrified . . ."

Left paw out, around in a dramatic sweep to my side. Repeat on the right, while Leelee did the same with her hands.

Then the pound, the soul-rocking beat, and we were on our way—one, two, stop, turn. One, two, stop, turn. Fabulous!

"Come on, champ, get in the car." Thomas grinned down at the little dog, sitting on the asphalt, staring off as if deep in thought. Then Hairy looked up at him, and damned if he didn't smile.

Weave to the left. Weave to the right. Feel it. Move it. Work it. Be the song. Leelee's nose was high, her chin defiant—that girl is a born diva! And she looked smashing in the silver lamé jumpsuit and top hat . . .

"Hairy! Come on up, boy!" Leelee called from the back seat of the Montero.

Uh-oh. Looks like I'm going to have to sit between Bright Eyes and the Little Mutant. The thing is a brute. The other night it got hold of me and I thought for sure my neck was going to snap like a twig. Scary. But what can I do? It was already half again my size the day it was born. God only knows how much it weighs now, but it looks like a miniature Big Alpha running around the house, only with a lot less balance.

"Come on, ace. You're holding up the show."

I suppose I'll manage. The thing seems to make everybody smile, especially Soft Hands. Seems she's always smiling, she's so in love with Big Alpha. So happy with her kids and her farm and her work.

It was crazy for a while there—Big Alpha fainting when Soft Hands started to whelp, the bad man's trial, Leelee's adoption, TV Man and Big Alpha switching houses like they did. But things have settled down. And life is good.

Thomas's voice was loud. "Would you come *on*, Hairy?"

Yeah, yeah, keep your shorts on.

"Goggy! Goggy! See!"

"Watch out, honey. T.J.'s got Hairy by the throat again."

Thomas peeled the baby's fingers from the dog's neck and gave Leelee a kiss on the cheek. Then he got behind the wheel, next to his wife. It made him grin every time he thought about it—his family. His wife and two kids.

Not bad for a sterile guy.

As they drove to the restaurant, listening to the latest Backstreet Boys CD, Emma reached over and grabbed his hand. Thomas pulled it to his lips and kissed her knuckles, and realized he couldn't remember what he'd done before she became his companion and lover. His center.

"It's strange, isn't it?" Emma said.

"What is?"

"Life," she said with a sigh. "Life is just weird, you know?"

He pressed his lips against her hand again, hiding his chuckle. Yeah, he knew what she meant—they'd just spent six hours at the Annual World Canine Disco Dancing Championships, and that was as weird as it got. But not necessarily weird in a bad way—just odd. Different.

Ah hell, it'd been a blast.

"I think that as long as we're all on the ride together, life's just perfect, Emma."

"Excuse me while I hurl!" Leelee yelled from the back seat.

"Goggy!" T.J. shrieked, yanking on the white poof of hair on the dog's head.

Hairy sighed.

Then his nose twitched.

And he wondered just how much longer it would be before the thing was housebroken.

It was only nine, so if she were good, she'd use this time to do her Tae-Bo tape. No, wait—Charlotte had just read an article that said it was self-defeating to label yourself "good" or "bad" when the focus should be on the behavior itself. The article said that people make just two kinds of choices in life: harmful ones or helpful ones.

So after she checked on the kids, she headed downstairs and made the choice to find the box of Triscuits and the can of squirt cheese. Then made the choice to sit at the kitchen table and chow down.

"You only live once," she said to no one, popping another salty, crunchy, squishy, artificially colored tidbit in her mouth, thinking the whole time of the Chippendale dancer next door.

This was bad.

After a few more savory concoctions, Charlotte stuck the cracker box under her arm and tucked the squirt cheese in her shorts pocket and wandered out to the back patio. Though the days were growing longer, it was fully dark by now, and the neighborhood was quiet. She took a seat at the patio table and propped her feet on an empty chair.

Right after Kurt died, more than a few well-meaning

people asked if she planned to sell the house. The answer was no, not if she could help it.

She topped another cracker, a little shocked at how loud the aerosol sounded out here in the quiet.

She loved her home—the acre of yard that provided privacy and plenty of play room for the kids and Hoover, the mature shade trees, the roomy floorplan. She loved that her children felt like they belonged here. She loved that they felt close to Kurt. —

What she didn't love was the mortgage—$2,400 a month, every single month—even after refinancing.

She munched down hard on the Triscuit, wiping a few errant crumbs off her scout-leader shirt.

She'd told herself countless times that it could have been worse—Kurt could have died with no insurance instead of a modest amount. He could have died leaving a mountain of debt instead of a few conservative investments. It's just that no man thinks he's going to drop dead at age thirty-four. And no woman thinks she's going to walk into the family room to rouse her napping husband for dinner only to find him cold.

The bottom line was they weren't prepared for the wage-earner in their family to die. And Charlotte refused to go out and get a full-time nursing job with the kids this young. They needed her attention. They needed her time. They needed *her*—because she was all they had.

Multi-Tasker, Inc., was something she could do while the kids were in school. It was something she could juggle in the summer, and something she could set aside if one of them were sick. With the life insurance, it made them just enough money to squeak by.

She squirted out a big, sloppy pile of day-glow cheddar on a cracker and shoved the whole thing in her mouth.

She immediately stopped chewing and her ears pricked.

"Thud-a-ba, thud-a-ba, thud-a-ba, thud-a-ba . . ."

It sounded like muffled gunfire. She quickly swallowed the cracker and sat up straight, her ears straining to identify its source.

"Thud-a-ba, thud-a-ba, thud-a-ba, thud-a-ba . . ." Then she heard a loud, *"Uhmph!"*

Charlotte shot to her feet and stared up toward the children's bedroom windows. It wasn't coming from there.

"Thud-a-ba, thud-a-ba, thud-a-ba, thud-a-ba . . ."

Bonnie and Ned's house was quiet. And it wasn't coming from the Noonans' over the back fence because they were still in Florida and their security system could wake the dead.

"Thud-a-ba, thud-a-ba, thud-a-ba, thud-a-ba . . ."

Her head whipped around—it had to be the Chippendale guy!

Charlotte gathered her snacks and tiptoed around to the driveway, where she stood half-hunched in the darkness, listening.

"Uhmph! Uh! Mmmm, mmmm, uhmp!"

"Good Lord," Charlotte whispered to herself. Still hunched over, the Triscuits tucked close under her elbow, she glanced furtively up and down the street, making sure there were no cars or dog-walkers coming. She then slipped past the pine trees to the edge of her property, and sidled up to the privacy fence around the Connors' in-ground pool and patio.

The sound was definitely coming from behind the fence, but it wasn't the pool pump. It wasn't mechanical.

Charlotte pressed her face up to the fence boards, and though she tried several angles—twisted around until her neck hurt—she couldn't quite find a way to align her eyeball with the small vertical slits. She sure couldn't peek over the fence—it was nine feet tall! So all she saw was a sliver of light and indistinct movement.

*"Thud-a-ba,   thud-a-ba,   thud-a-ba,   thud-a-ba . . .
uhmph!"*

Someone was being murdered! That had to be it. She
suppressed her gasp and skittered away from the fence, running full speed to her own patio, then slid inside the back
door. Hoover lay in wait, hair on end, ready to pounce—
and his whole big body shuddered with relief that it was
only her.

"Good boy, Hoov."

Charlotte bolted the lock. She did the same to the laundry room door leading to the garage, the front door, and
the double doors that opened from the family room.

Then she took the stairs two at a time and, for lack of
any other source of reassurance, she spoke to Hoover.

"We may have a situation on our hands," she said.

The dog blinked and yawned, exposing a set of huge
white canine teeth. He waited briefly for some kind of command, then burped and went into Matt's room, where he
collapsed in a heap.

"You call yourself a watchdog," she muttered.

Then she saw them.

The spy binoculars sat precariously on the edge of
Matt's small desk, the lenses reflecting the hall light. She
grabbed them, slinked down the hallway to her bedroom,
and locked her door.

Now if this wasn't the lowest point in her life, she didn't
know what was. She was going to spy on her new neighbor!
And after the lecture she'd given Matt that very afternoon!

But that sound—it could be anything, right? And those
animal noises! If it wasn't murder, maybe he was injured.
What if her new neighbor were having some kind of spasm
or epileptic fit and swallowing his tongue?

She turned off all the lights in her room. She stood at
the window facing the drive, and tried to figure out how to
focus the binoculars. She certainly wouldn't be discovering

any new solar systems with these cheap plastic things, but she hoped they could at least put her mind to rest about the tongue-swallowing.

She aimed out the window, and in the light from the Connors' patio she guided the binoculars over the trees, located the fence, and tilted down until she could see the pool area.

A punching bag. The guy was pounding on a punching bag. That realization took about a nanosecond to register in her brain before the real important information came to the forefront: LoriSue, God bless her little slutty soul, had been absolutely correct. He was male stripper material, and he'd been nice enough to strip to a pair of athletic shorts on his very first night in the neighborhood.

Charlotte prevented herself from crumpling to the carpet by leaning against the window frame. The binoculars clicked against the glass.

This was so wrong. So illegal. So bad. And so incredibly *gratifying!*

She chuckled to herself and found a comfortable stance, immediately deciding that the term "gorgeous" didn't quite describe the man framed in the binocular lenses. In fact, she didn't think she knew a word for a man like him.

And he just kept punching, his back toward her, the little bag blurring and spinning from the impact of his boxing gloves. His long hair was wet with perspiration and black against the back of his neck. His cut shoulders, back, and arms rippled, glistening with sweat, an image made all the more surreal by the haze of moths drawn to the patio light.

"Moths to a flame," Charlotte said out loud.

She stared, stupefied, watching his feet dance and his thighs and calves bunch up and release, his tight backside bounce and jut, his lungs pump air in and out of his body.

And just then, a thick, slow-moving fog of déjà vu began to roll through her. It was like she'd once had a dream about this, or that her subconscious was whispering to her that this man reminded her of someone she once knew—or wait—maybe she'd once seen a movie where some pathetic, lonely widow stared at her attractive neighbor with her son's cereal-box binoculars!

She groaned, and was about to put an end to the whole sorry business when the man stopped. He pulled his hands out of the gloves, tossed them on the pool deck, then shook his sweaty hair. He reached around, grabbed a water bottle and playfully tossed it up over his head.

That's the moment he turned to face her, reaching up to snag the plastic bottle in mid-air. That's the moment she got her first clear view of his face.

Charlotte's legs didn't hold.